Return
to
Appleton

Return to Appleton

SYLVIA BAMBOLA

MOODY PUBLISHERS
CHICAGO

Also by Sylvia Bambola

Waters of Marah
Tears in a Bottle
Refiner's Fire
A Vessel of Honor

Published in association with the literary agency of Alive Communications, Inc., 7680 Goddard Street, Suite 200, Colorado Springs, CO 80920.

ISBN: 0-8024-7906-5
EAN/ISBN-13: 978-0-8024-7906-8

Library of Congress Cataloging-in-Publication Data

Bambola, Sylvia.
    Return to Appleton / by Sylvia Bambola.
        p. cm.
    ISBN 0-8024-7906-5
      1. Real estate development—Fiction. 2. Women detectives—Fiction.
    3. Grandmothers—Fiction. I. Title.

PS3552.A47326R48 2005
813'.6--dc22

2004022405

1 3 5 7 9 10 8 6 4 2

Printed in the United States of America

To Jack, in loving memory

Acknowledgments

ONCE AGAIN I WANT to mention the following books which I found of great use when researching ecoterrorism and various issues of environmentalism: *Eco-Scam* by Ronald Bailey, *The Skeptical Environmentalist* by Bjorn Lomborg, *Ecoterror: The Violent Agenda to Save Nature*, and *Undue Influence*, both by Ron Arnold.

A big "thank you" goes to Andy McGuire, fiction editor at Moody; Michele Straubel, my editor, who was ever so thorough and patient and kind; and my former agent, Andrea Christian, who truly has a servant's heart.

Another "thanks" to the terrific writers at ChiLibris who are never at a loss for words or advice or humor when needed. What a group! And what a blessing!

And last but not least, I'd like to acknowledge my wonderful family: my son, Cord, for his encouragement; my daughter, Gina, for helping me smooth out some of those rough edges and for her valuable input; and my husband, Vincent, for his patience, love, support, and for just being who he is.

How gracious and loving of God to give me such co-laborers!

HE WHICH HATH BEGUN A GOOD WORK IN YOU WILL PERFORM
IT UNTIL THE DAY OF JESUS CHRIST.

—◈ PHILIPPIANS 1:6 KJV ◈—

Chapter One

———

CUTTER PRESS DIDN'T BELIEVE in miracles. Or divine intervention. Or any of those easy, feel-good explanations people used to explain the unexplainable. Not after living under the pragmatic tutelage of Virginia Press these past twenty-nine years. But the woman sitting in front of him made him think that perhaps miracles happened after all—at least small ones.

He studied Gloria. She had never looked so good. And it wasn't just the way her hair hung like velvet across her cheek or the way her makeup made her face look so contoured and lovely. Rather, it was because of something in her eyes, some inner quietness and confidence that made them sparkle like the zircon earrings Virginia was so fond of.

He knew he was violating all rules of polite conduct, but he continued staring, in a perverse test to see how long her composure would last. To see which of them would break first. But she didn't fidget. And she didn't nibble her nails—a sight which always filled him with an urge to dunk Gloria's fingers in a bowl of his mother's Clorox-water, the concoction Virginia swore, if applied correctly, kept ants from nibbling the food in her kitchen.

And that was the miracle. Not only to see Gloria Bickford back in his office, but so relaxed, with her hands resting like doves on her lap, her ankles crossed, her feet tucked discreetly under the director's chair.

Then there was that smile. So sweet it made perspiration pool around his white starched collar and run down his back and chest like raindrops against a window. A smile like that could make a man say something foolish, and Cutter Press had spent the better part of his life trying not to say anything foolish to Gloria.

Tried and failed. A hundred times.

He broke eye contact first when he picked up a dart. The firm metal shaft, pointed at one end and fluted at the other, felt good between his fingers and gave him a feeling of control. He could direct it wherever he chose or hold it as long as he wished. Not being a dullard, he understood that it was just a silly diversion he used whenever he felt the need for one. Like now.

Be a man, Press, and look her in the face.

"I never expected to see you here. Never expected you to leave Mattson Development." He deliberately focused his eyes on her.

For the first time Gloria looked uncomfortable and shifted in her chair. "It was impossible to stay . . . after learning what was going on, after learning what . . . Tucker was doing. It's still hard to believe he deliberately tried to stop the development of your Lakes property."

Cutter grunted. "The environmentalists still have it all tied up. Don't know what it's going to take to get the EPA and the rest of them off our backs. My partners are fuming . . . but that's another matter." He fingered his dart. "Anyway . . . here you are back in Appleton. I think your mother was the only one who really believed you'd return. You surprised a lot of us."

"I surprised myself."

Cutter had heard through the grapevine that after Gloria left Tucker Mattson she took a job in an Eckerd City print shop. He wondered why she had left that job and come all the way back here to this dead-end town. He twirled the dart in his fingers. He couldn't imagine why she was still smiling like that. Didn't she understand that coming home was a form of failure? An admission that she couldn't cut it in the big city? Only . . . right now she looked like she could cut it anywhere.

"If you've come for your old job, it's filled." He was taken back when he heard light laughter. Strange how everything about her seemed to surprise him. He had spent years trying to figure her out, and just when he thought he had . . .

"I have a job at Appleton Printers. I've been there for over a week."

Cutter had heard that too, but hadn't believed it. *Not in that little mousehole of a business.* Even now, after Gloria's confirmation, it seemed implausible. Why would she want to work in a place like that when she could work at Medical Data? He tented his fingers and glared, as though daring her to explain. "Okay, if you don't need a job, why have you come?" Strange how disappointed he felt. Had he wanted to see her squirm? *Beg* even?

Gloria shook her head as though reading his thoughts, her shiny brown hair barely moving. Her hair was different from the last time he saw her in Eckerd. It was longer and fell over one eye, almost like that actress Veronica Lake. That hair had made Veronica a big star, and when she cut it, she cut herself out of a career. Strange how hair could do so much for a woman. Just looking at Gloria's hair now and what it did to her face made the perspiration soak his collar even more. "If you haven't come for a job, why have you come?" he repeated, hearing the snarl in his own voice and wondering why she irritated him.

"I've come to ask your forgiveness."

This was one surprise too many. Cutter hurled the dart at the dartboard—the only object hanging on the left wall of his office. As the tip sank into the bull's-eye, he felt his lip curl. He was wrong to want her to grovel, but this cool-calm-collected manner was intolerable, almost infuriating, as if she thought she were above it all . . . superior even. And yet . . . that gentleness, that composure . . . He searched her eyes. What was that look? Soft and kind and . . . He felt the need to turn away, and that annoyed him.

She had to be playing with him. What forgiveness could she possibly need? *He* was the one needing forgiveness. The memory of her last visit here still made him cringe. It had nearly rubbed his brain raw from the number of times he had relived it. He had been rough and arrogant—demanding she give an explanation for refusing his marriage proposal. A business deal, he called it. How could he have expected her to sell herself so cheaply?

No wonder she had left town.

"I wanted to see you in person, to tell you how sorry I was about the *Mattson Newsletter,* and to ask you to forgive my part in it." She pulled a handful of folded flyers from the pocket of her Windbreaker and put them on the desk. The Windbreaker looked new, stylish, not like one of those cheap folded-up plastic things she used to wear, the kind that came stuffed in a pouch. The rest of her clothes looked new too, and . . . stylish. And he couldn't help but notice how nicely she filled them out. Must have put on at least five pounds since he saw her last. And all in the right places. He watched that smile come over her face again when the pile of flyers teetered, then watched her push them closer to him. "Here are some of the *Conservation & Common Sense* flyers Harry Grizwald—my old boss at E-Z Printing—and I have done."

If she smiles that way one more time . . . He picked up a flyer, swiveled his chair to the side so she was no longer in his line of vision, and began reading.

"I know the flyers haven't undone all the harm those newsletters did to The Lakes, but they've helped. Harry says more and more people are calling him with their stories. And many are letting him print them too, hoping to expose the radical environmental movement. We're going to continue the flyers, for now anyway. Maybe in time it will force the EPA to back away, so you can build."

Cutter sat silently in his chair, wondering how he should react. Truth was, he no longer held those newsletters against her. It should be easy for him to just come out and say so. It would go a long way in making him look like a big man. But the words stuck to the back of his throat like wallpaper.

He watched Gloria rise to her feet. *Say it, man, say it.* When she extended her hand, Cutter smelled perfume and felt his irritation rise. What was that all about? She never wore perfume. Women wore perfume to attract men. And Gloria wasn't into that sort of thing. Or maybe she was.

Maybe he didn't know her at all.

"Well . . . I just wanted to tell you how sorry I was and to show you the flyers." Gloria took his hand and shook it. "And to show you that my remorse extended beyond words, that I was backing it with actions."

Cutter allowed Gloria to give his hand another shake before he pulled away, lamenting both that the moment to be magnanimous had passed and that Gloria's perfume continued to linger in his nostrils.

"I know it's a reach, but maybe we could try to be friends," Gloria said, still smiling.

Cutter thought he saw a pained expression on her face, as though she were choking over the words, as though someone—like her mother—had forced her to say them. And that possibility irritated him. "At this point, why bother?"

"Appleton's a small place. There's no need for it to be unpleasant every time we bump into each other."

Cutter twisted his heavy Appleton High ring around his finger, feeling the familiar lines of the beveled garnet. So that was it. It wasn't forgiveness she wanted. It was a truce. She was afraid he would make life unpleasant for her now that she was back.

Well . . . she could stop worrying. The last thing he wanted was to make her leave Appleton again.

⚘ ⚘

Gloria shut the door behind her as she exited Cutter's office, feeling like an ambassador of goodwill who had not managed to create any goodwill at all. She hadn't expected it to be so hard, this business of reconciliation. In Eckerd, when she was high on that mountaintop with her Jesus, the thought of coming back and putting things right with Cutter, her mother, and Tracy all seemed so simple. How different things looked from the trenches, where the mud could be ankle deep and coat everything, including your perspective. Here, from this observation post, Cutter was his usual obnoxious self, her mother was still impossible, and Tracy . . . Tracy didn't even return her phone calls.

Well, I tried. But even as Gloria walked away from Cutter's door, she knew her lame declaration wouldn't cut it. Jesus would expect more. He always expected more. That was one of the exasperating things about Him.

Cutter's secretary, Sadie Bellows, sat in the outer office, wrapped in a floral sarong that made Gloria think of the Caribbean, and frantically filed her nails. Shells, strung together, two inches long, dangled from her ears. Gloria ignored the frosty glare Sadie gave her as she passed.

She had come here for nothing.

It had taken her a full week to get up the nerve to face Cutter. Even as late as this morning, she had to gulp down two Alka-Seltzers to calm her stomach. And that bothered her because she had given Jesus her hurt, passed it to Him like you'd pass the potatoes at a family gathering. But obviously not all of it. There was still more—a deep layer that needed His healing touch. Okay, so be it. If Jesus had taught her anything, it was that He could be trusted—trusted with her life, and that included her past as well as her future. My goodness, she was back in Appleton, wasn't she? And that in itself testified to what Jesus could do.

❀ ❀

Geri Bickford tapped across the kitchen in her high-heeled slippers, ignoring the fact that they were shedding pink feathers all over her nice clean floor. Her eyes never left the phone cradled beside the gleaming chrome toaster oven. One call. Only one call in a week. You'd think a daughter would call her mother more than that . . . just to say hello. Just to make her mother feel loved and wanted and appreciated. And if for none of these reasons, then out of respect. Surely out of respect. But Gloria hadn't even told her she was coming back to Appleton. Just showed up one day, after she had already found a job and a place to live.

17

Typical.

Gloria had always been difficult. Even as a child. How many times did Geri have to force corrections in Gloria's life? Discourage her when she saw Gloria going the wrong way? Just like this whole Eckerd City thing. At least Gloria had finally come to her senses on that one and returned home where she belonged.

But not without a fight.

Gloria always fought her no matter what Geri tried to do. Look at the way Gloria fought her about her makeup and hair. All Geri ever wanted was to help Gloria improve. Give her daughter a heads-up. God knew Gloria needed all the help she could get with her looks. At least Gloria finally came around on that one too. She was looking a lot better these days. Everyone who saw Gloria complimented Geri on how good she looked. Still . . . if Gloria had come around sooner, life would have been easier for both of them.

Nothing changes.

Not the important things, anyway. Loneliness was still the only houseguest Geri Bickford entertained. She had wanted to spare Gloria that. But Gloria's stubbornness had ruined all of Geri's hard work. Had spoiled probably Gloria's only chance for marriage and security and . . .

But hadn't Geri herself been lonely even after she married Gavin? The *G&G* embroidered on their towels and pillowcases with white silky thread had looked so lovely. So had their wedding pictures, with their arms entwined. It was hard to tell where one left off and the other began.

Too bad that's as far as it went.

Sometimes Gloria didn't have a brain in her head. Couldn't she see what Geri was trying to do? Teach her? Help her over some of those rough spots? With Gloria's silly expectations, she was sure to be disappointed. And even though Gloria was finally using makeup and not frizzing her hair, and was even wearing more stylish clothes, did she think that was all there was to it? Geri had beauty titles to fill a wall, and tricks and tips that could make even Phyllis Diller look good before she had all that plastic surgery. Yes, if it were that easy, then Geri would never have been lonely.

Geri opened the refrigerator and stared vacantly at the container of nonfat yogurt. What was she doing? It wasn't food she wanted. With a snap of her wrist, she closed the refrigerator, then stormed over to the phone like it were an enemy. If Gloria didn't call by tonight, then she'd call her—not to try to talk her into anything. It was far too late for that. But just to guide her, direct her, help her in whatever way she could, to have some input in her life. It was a mother's responsibility to turn out a sensible child.

If only Gloria understood that you never got used to loneliness.

❧ ❧

Gloria pecked the keyboard with exaggerated force and watched the sluggish response on the monitor. "Wanda, you've really got to get new computers."

A thickset bleached-blonde straightened her bent body and moved one step from her inconspicuous place in the corner. "I guess working at that la-di-da city printer has given you airs. This computer's been doing the job just fine since—"

"Since my senior year at Appleton High! Honestly, Wanda, it's not even a Pentium, and nobody but nobody uses Windows 3.0 anymore."

Wanda Lugget patted down the sides of her short bouffant

hair, a style even older than her computers, then shoved aside a box of unopened toner with her foot. "Paul . . . Paul, get in here. The little city girl has a complaint."

A tall, thin man, with graying temples and a bald spot on top, entered from the back, wiping his hands on a small green towel. "Now what?" There was a smile on his face.

"She says we need new computers. Thinks we're the Rockefellers or something. First she wanted Quirk-whatchacallit; now it's computers." Gloria saw Wanda wink at her husband. "For over thirty years we've been using clip art, cutting boards, and trimmers. Seems that's not good enough anymore."

Gloria pressed one finger down on the letter *J* and pointed at the monitor with the other hand. "Look . . . look at that! It's slower than Miss Whittle."

Wanda laughed. Miss Whittle, the music teacher at Appleton High for the past twenty years, was notorious for moving like molasses uphill. When anyone in Appleton wanted to say something was slow, he would inevitably make the Miss Whittle comparison.

Gloria continued pressing her finger on the *J*, and only when she heard Wanda snort, "All right already, I *see* it," did she release the key. She loved working with the Luggets, even though Wanda could test the patience of Job with her shrill dispensing of orders and hyped-up nerves during a deadline. Once, Gloria had actually heard Wanda threaten to shred Paul's prized *Offset Lithographic Technology* book if he didn't stop dillydallying. Paul was a perfectionist and wasn't always a good counterbalance to Wanda's manic side.

But Gloria should be used to it. It was Wanda who had taken Gloria under her wing when she was a senior working on the yearbook and taught her about tints from the Murphy Color Wheel. The Luggets had been helping the Appleton High yearbook staff—gratis—for almost all of the thirty years they had owned the shop. Even back then, there were times when that woman could have benefited from a little Prozac, though Gloria always suspected Wanda's problem was hormonal.

"If you get the computers now, we'll have them in place before the Apple Festival." Gloria tilted back in her chair. It was one of Wanda's calmer days and safe to banter. "This year we could really knock their socks off."

"Well, listen to her, Paul. Now she wants to go knocking people's socks off."

"Time some people around here had theirs knocked off. Matter of fact, I was thinking that very thing yesterday. That's why I ordered two new HPs, along with two seventeen-inch flat-screen monitors. Think the little city girl can work now, Wanda?"

"She better. How else are we going to pay for all that stuff." Wanda winked again, just as her husband flipped the green towel over his shoulder and headed toward the pressroom.

"In that case, I'll call Charlie Axlerod at the Chamber of Commerce and see if he'd like to commission some posters for the Apple Festival." Gloria tried to look serious. "I'll tell him about our early-bird special."

"What early-bird special?"

"The one I thought we should run so we can get advance orders—at a five-percent discount. You know things are going to start getting crazy around here in a few weeks. I thought the special would help even the workload." *And keep Wanda calmer.*

"You learned a few things in that big city of yours, didn't you?" Wanda said, heading toward the box of toner.

"Just a few." The smile Gloria had been trying so hard to suppress finally broke through. She thought of Harry Grizwald's print shop and how it wasn't much bigger than this, and of Perth and how Gloria had left her so ready and eager to start Eckerd Community College. God had taken Gloria on an amazing journey last year, one that had changed her life. She wondered what He had in store for her now that she was back in Appleton.

⌁ ◉⌁

Gloria unlocked the door of the little apartment at the back of Sam Hidel's Grocery and watched Tiger, her new calico cat, the one Clive McGreedy had given her as a homecoming gift, scoot by her on the way out. She made no attempt to stop him. The fresh air would do him good, and he'd come back when he got hungry.

Gloria still couldn't believe she had a cat. Mother had never allowed pets. They were messy. They carried fleas—and who knew what else. It had taken a year in Eckerd for Gloria to get the courage to do something like this. Mother would be furious when she found out. She'd tell Gloria she didn't have a brain in her head. And when Tracy found out, she'd probably laugh and say Tiger wasn't a cat, but a declaration of independence. They'd both be wrong.

Gloria closed the door behind her, then flipped on the lights. She hadn't been able to get her old apartment back. The subletters had recently signed a new two-year lease. But she wasn't sorry. Though Sam Hidel's apartment wasn't as nice or as big, it was a lot cheaper, and that would help Gloria save for a car. It was one thing not having a car in the city, but here in Appleton, it was impossible.

Gloria thought of her old car, the one Grandma Quinn had named Silver Streak after the movie, the one Grandma had given her when she could no longer drive because of cataracts. It suddenly struck Gloria as odd that both Silver Streaks, her grandma's 1985 Buick Century and the train in the movie, had the same ending: they crashed.

She only wished hers would have crashed before she spent all that money on a new radiator. She had just had a fight with her mother and wanted to go somewhere quiet to clear her head. The next thing she knew she was on the Old Post Road, along the western perimeter of Clive McGreedy's farm. The road was slick with black ice, and she had been going too fast. It didn't take much to slide off the pavement and careen into Clive's rail fence. The crash splintered one of the rails, causing it to pierce the grillwork of the Buick like a lance, straight through her brand-new radiator.

Life was funny like that. You think you've fixed a thing, but it doesn't always stay fixed. Just like her relationship with her mother. If she had a car now, she'd drive over. God had softened her heart, had made her willing to forgive and forget that her mother had tried to force her to marry Cutter Press. Had made her willing to forgive and forget all the grief her mother had given her. Had made Gloria willing to love her mother even if her mother couldn't love her back, couldn't accept the fact Gloria wasn't the beauty she had hoped for. Jesus had shown her that her mother was a deeply unhappy woman. Although Gloria didn't understand why. Maybe, in time, Jesus would reveal that to her too.

"Oh, Lord, help me to be the daughter You want me to be," she whispered as she placed her black leather purse on the kitchen counter. Then, without changing or grabbing a snack, Gloria headed for the phone and punched in the familiar number.

"Hi, Mother—"

"So, your fingers aren't broken. I thought for sure they had to be since you haven't called in days."

Gloria rolled her eyes, stopped herself, then quickly asked God to fill her with His love. "How are you, Mother?"

"Well . . ."

⊸◖ ◗⊷

Gloria had just finished the dinner dishes and was about to hem the bottom of a pair of slacks her mother had bought for her over a year ago and only now fit, when the phone rang. Maybe it was Tracy returning her call. She had been trying to get in touch with her for days. She hadn't seen her friend since Tracy had left Eckerd City so suddenly. And that was months ago.

She picked up the phone. "Hello."

"Gloria!" Harry Grizwald's voice was raspy, out of breath, almost like he had a cold. It took her a second to realize he was just excited. She felt mildly disappointed that it wasn't Tracy. *When was that girl going to call?* "You won't believe this, but someone just phoned saying he has information about The Lakes . . . but for a price. Five thousand, to be exact. First, I thought he was a crackpot. 'Til now, people have been free with their information. But then he mentioned Eric Slone."

"Who's Eric Slone?" She pictured the curly white-haired Grizwald in his kitchen, wrapped in his Pillsbury Doughboy apron, and suddenly felt lonely.

"You're kidding, right? Eric Slone is to investments what Bill Gates is to computer software. Some say he's got the Midas touch. That when he invests in something, it produces. He's a bull even in a bear economy. A billionaire. For heaven's sake, Gloria, he was on the cover of last month's *Time.*"

"Sorry, never heard of him." She heard Harry sigh.

"Well, the problem is I don't have five thousand dollars.

Not to spare, anyway. Not since retirement is right around the corner and since Dorie and I might . . . well, we might make it a permanent thing."

"Harry! How wonderful." Gloria felt a tinge of jealousy slither through her genuine feelings of joy, and was disappointed in herself. That issue had been turned over to the Lord. No sense in yanking it back now or second-guessing Him. He would bring someone into her life, or not, as He chose. "Have you set a date?"

"No, we're just tossing the idea back and forth. Dorie hasn't said yes yet. Said she's been a spinster so long she's not sure she wants to start changing things now. But she doesn't know how stubborn I can be. Anyway . . . I wasn't even going to tell you— it's just too early—so let's get back on track here. About the five thousand—like I said, I don't have it to spare, but since this involves that friend of yours . . . what's-his-name . . ."

"Cutter Press?"

"Right. Maybe he'd be interested. You want to run it by him? See if he's willing to lay out that kind of cash? I wouldn't even bother with it except that if this guy's really telling the truth, if Eric Slone is involved, it would be worth knowing about. So . . . what do you think? You want to ask your friend?"

"Ah . . . okay . . . sure."

Great, now she had to go back to that hateful office.

❦ ❦

Chapter Two

CUTTER WATCHED GLORIA take the black director's chair in front of him. She certainly didn't look happy to be here, with her forehead crinkled and her mouth firm as a biscotti. And that troubled him because it reminded him of the countless other times he had caused her to look that way.

He had been surprised when Sadie told him Gloria wanted to come around noon. Obviously her lunch hour, obviously at her convenience. But she was full of surprises these days. He had spent a full half hour trying to guess the reason for the visit and came up empty.

What could she want?

It was hardly a social call. Her face told him that. She was pleasant enough, even forced a smile and inquired politely about the health of his mother, but Cutter knew that something outside Gloria's will had brought her here. He let her get comfortable. Let her fold her skirt under her like a prim schoolmarm and spread the front of it neatly over her knees. Then let her fold her hands on her lap. She carried no purse, and he wondered if she had walked the two miles from Appleton Printers. It wouldn't be out of character for her, even though it was unseasonably hot. He looked for signs of wilt but found none. Instead, she sat remarkably cool and calm, even with that crinkled forehead, looking lovely and stylish, and he suddenly felt the urge to pick up a dart.

No, he wouldn't hide behind a diversion.

He took the executive's chair behind the desk, the one made of cheap leather and with armrests so narrow you could never get comfortable. His mother had picked it out, along with the rest of the furniture, when she remodeled his office. Leave it to Virginia to find ways of cutting corners as painfully as possible.

"You told my secretary it was important?"

"Yes. Did you have a chance to read any of the flyers?"

"I read them all. And if you want a pat on the back, forget it. Although I admit they were informative. Okay. You got your pat." There was that smile again. And the light sound of laughter. The crinkled forehead had disappeared, for the moment at least.

"I'm glad you found them of some worth. Since we—Harry Grizwald and I—started doing them, it's amazing how many people have come forward."

"You told me all this yesterday." Cutter tapped his neat, square-cut nails on the desk. What did she really want? If only he could burrow inside her head like a termite and nibble away at that façade of hers, see what she was thinking. He had always believed he understood her. But she was so different now.

When the tapping started sounding to him like Morse code, and worse yet, an SOS, Cutter pulled his hands from the desktop and gripped the narrow armrests. He stared her down, mostly to make up for his display of nerves, and saw that although she smiled, her forehead was crinkled once more. He wished her discomfort would give him pleasure, but it didn't. It never had, though he had often been accused of the opposite.

"Yesterday, Harry got a call from a man who read one of the flyers." Her forehead smoothed a bit. "He claims he has information about The Lakes—says there's a connection between The Lakes and Eric Slone. But he wants five thousand for his trouble." She paused to clear her throat. "We . . . Harry and I . . . don't have that kind of money, so if it's something you'd like to know, you'll have to come up with it yourself."

Cutter tented his fingers and leaned back in his chair. Eric Slone was a rich, powerful man who owned dozens of companies and sat on the board of dozens more. He was hardly the type to be involved with the mess at The Lakes. No, Cutter's troubles came from the loony fringes of Terra Firma and the EPA. Gloria's proposition was almost an insult to his intelligence. Yet there she sat, hardly looking like she wanted to insult anyone.

"I have no intention of passing around my money like carrion to all the vultures your flyers attract," he finally said. "Tell your friend, no dice." *There she goes, smiling like I just told her she was the most beautiful woman in the world.*

As Gloria rose from her chair, his disappointment rose with her. "What? No argument? So you think it's a hoax too?" He was surprised when she shook her head. "Okay, why not?"

"Because Harry doesn't think so. And I trust his instincts."

"Yeah, with my five thousand."

<hr/>

You could have bowled Gloria over with a tennis ball when she saw Cutter come into Appleton Printers in his blue suit and white starched shirt. Gloria watched him size up the place and guessed by the look on his face what he was thinking—that she was a fool to prefer to work in this small, crowded store rather than in his big, spacious Medical Data.

"So this is where you work," he said as he reached her desk. The way he said it made Gloria wait for him to finish the sentence with *and there's no accounting for taste.*

When he said nothing, Gloria pointed to a wooden folding chair near some boxes along the wall. "Maybe you'd like to pull that over so you can sit." He was in her world now. Even if he looked down his nose at it, she'd be polite.

"No need." Cutter fingered his cuff link. "I'm not staying."

Gloria recognized the small oval gold-plated links clamping his sleeves. They were the pair her mother had forced her to give him for Christmas when she was thirteen. She couldn't believe he still had them. Or that he actually wore them.

"I just came to tell you to go ahead and make that appointment."

She didn't think anyone wore shirts with cuff links anymore. She certainly couldn't remember seeing Cutter wear one, not for years. She just couldn't get over seeing him with them now.

"Make that appointment," Cutter repeated. "But I want you to know I'm going ahead with this on your say-so. Based on your confidence in Harry Grizwald. And I guess I'm a little curious about Eric Slone's involvement."

"Five thousand dollars is more than a 'little curious.'"

"You trying to talk me out of it?"

"No. I'm trying to say that this man may think his information's worth five thousand, but you may not. If you go in with high expectations, you might be disappointed." Gloria cringed. She was starting to sound like her mother.

"Don't talk out of both sides of your mouth, Gloria. You

told me you had confidence in Harry's judgment. Now you're squirming. Why?"

Gloria's lips tightened. Cutter never made anything easy. "Just don't blame me if you're not satisfied, that's all."

"Oh, so that's it. Little Gloria doesn't like being on the hot seat."

Gloria felt her cheeks burn, felt that old hostility rise up like magma in Vesuvius. When was she going to stop letting him push her buttons? "I'll tell Harry to set up the appointment." She rose from her chair. "Now if that's all—"

"Naturally, I expect you to come. I don't know this Harry Grizwald from Adam, and—"

"That's out of the question."

"Why?"

"Because I think little Cutter is capable of doing this all by himself." Gloria could tell by the look on Cutter's face she had surprised him. And by the sick feeling deep inside her, Gloria could tell that Jesus hadn't appreciated her remark either. She felt ashamed for stooping to Cutter's level.

"I see. Tit for tat."

"Sorry, that was . . . unnecessary."

Cutter brushed her apology aside with a flip of his hand, more out of impatience than magnanimity, it seemed to Gloria. For an instant, the small oval cuff link caught the overhead light. "What if I asked nicely? Would you come?"

Gloria shook her head, looking at the shimmering link on his sleeve and feeling more annoyed by the minute. What was he trying to prove anyway? Wearing those cheap, silly things?

"Aren't you the one who appeared in my office yesterday asking forgiveness for your part in The Lakes' mess? And didn't you tell me—now, what were those words again?—oh, yes . . . that your 'remorse extended beyond words'? And the first time

I give you a chance to do a little extending, you refuse."

"You don't need me along. I'll make the arrangements with Harry, but that's it. And just for the record, Cutter, I don't appreciate being manipulated. Frankly, I'm tired of it. I've been manipulated all my life. By the best, remember?" Gloria watched Cutter's face cloud, watched him run a finger between his white starched collar and his neck, watched the oval cuff link glint in the light of the little side window, then nearly fell over when she saw his lips part into a smile.

"We've both been manipulated by the best." He stepped closer to the desk. "I suppose I should have asked you a little nicer. About coming with me, I mean. Okay, I'm asking."

"Why is it so important?"

"Because when I talk with this guy I want to know if I'm being conned. Harry might not give it to me straight, but he'll be straight with you."

"I can't afford to take time off from work."

"So set it up for the weekend. I'll drive, pay all expenses, even buy you lunch, dinner, whatever."

Again, Gloria shook her head.

"I don't want to say you owe me, because it wouldn't be true. But it would go a long way in making me believe your apology was sincere yesterday."

"I thought I already proved that with the flyers."

"Flyers are nice—so crisp and neat and impersonal. Just the way you like things, Gloria. But it's a little different, isn't it, when someone asks you to stick your neck out?"

❧ ❦

Gloria couldn't believe she was sitting in Cutter's black Saab heading for Eckerd City. She stared out the window at the rows and rows of maples and poplars lining the sides of I-80 and thought about how in a few weeks they would begin turning color. Things were always changing . . . turning. What was that song? About one season following the other? Life was whirling along, dipping and turning so fast—just like the Tornado, the ride the Chamber of Commerce put up annually at the picnic grounds during the Apple Festival. Only a year ago she had traveled this same route by bus, on the way to a new city and a new life. It was an experience she'd never forget.

But how unlike this trip it was. She had been full of excitement and, yes, trepidation. Full of the promise of starting over and all that entailed. This time, she was bored and angry. Bored because she couldn't find one thing of interest to talk to Cutter about, and angry at herself for allowing him to pressure her into coming.

He had gotten his way. *As usual.*

She glanced at him out of the corner of her eye. He wore jeans and a tan cardigan over a white polo. Wind, whipping through the open window, made his hair whirl around his head like angry wasps. For some reason he almost seemed handsome, and Gloria had to restrain herself from laughing at the thought. She just wasn't used to seeing him so casual. Or out of the office setting.

She shifted in her seat, trying to get comfortable. She avoided looking at the little laminated photo of a woman in a bikini dangling from Cutter's mirror. On the back was the Playboy logo. The woman was curvaceous and top-heavy, like all the Playboy pinups. In some ways the photo reminded her of Sadie Bellows. It swayed with the car, almost hypnotic in its movements, and as if by some strange power, kept drawing Gloria's eye to it.

It seemed rather infantile, hanging up a picture of a woman

you didn't even know just because she had a great shape and was sexy looking. But then, Gloria had never understood the male psyche.

Oh, why had she agreed to come?

They still had an hour to go. That was sixty minutes— 3,600 agonizingly long seconds. How would she fill them? Conversation? A glance at Cutter told her his mouth was shut tighter than a clam. If any pleasantries were going to be exchanged between them at all, she would have to initiate it.

With a sigh, she began talking about the first thing that popped into her mind—her and Harry's next issue of *C&C, Conservation & Common Sense.* And for the next thirty minutes, she rattled on about how wealthy foundations use the environmental movement for their own agenda.

From the look on his face, Gloria was sure Cutter would be fast asleep if he hadn't had to drive.

～❦ ❦～

Gloria was surprised Cutter was actually heading down the bumpy dirt road instead of parking his car along the highway and walking the rest of the way like she and Perth had done the first time they came to see The Lakes. The way the car bounced over the ruts, jerking and lurching along like a malfunctioning carnival ride, made Gloria's teeth ache. She couldn't imagine what it was doing to Cutter's shocks and undercarriage. When she saw Cutter's jaw tighten, she figured he was having second thoughts about the whole thing too.

"I suppose it's been a while since you've been here. I guess you've forgotten how awful the road is."

"You could have picked a better place to meet," he growled, ignoring her remark. As if it were her fault that Hugo Pratt, the former owner of The Lakes, had failed to maintain the dirt road before he died.

"I didn't pick it. The informant did. And Harry agreed. Besides, you asked for someplace private."

"Yeah . . . well . . ." The vein along Cutter's right temple zigzagged in a blue bulge. "Does this informant have a name?"

"He said to call him Santa Claus."

Cutter frowned. "Is that supposed to be funny?"

"Don't look at me. I didn't pick that either."

"How will we know him?"

Before Gloria could stop herself, she laughed. "You mean in case the place suddenly becomes overrun with people?" When she saw Cutter work his jaw, she stopped laughing. "He said he has a mole on his right cheek."

Cutter pulled the Saab off the road and parked under a clump of trees next to another car. Gloria recognized Harry Grizwald's vacant blue Plymouth. She scanned the area. It was hard to see between the thick clumps of oaks and evergreens, assorted pampas grasses and wildflowers, but finally she spotted him about eighty yards away, standing near the edge of the lake.

She got out of the car and shouted, then waved. Cutter got out too and scanned the area, obviously looking for Santa Claus.

"Where's the informant?" Cutter looked like he had swallowed a dozen limes.

"Maybe Harry knows something," she said, happy for an excuse to sprint away. Somewhere between their car and the lake bank, her friend met her with a big bear hug and a kiss on the cheek. "You're a welcome sight, let me tell you."

"Oh, it's *soooo* good to see you too," she said, pressing her cheek against Harry's soft, curly white beard and inhaling the familiar scent of Old Spice. The sight of him made the three miserable hours she had spent with Cutter suddenly worth it.

"So where's Santa Claus?" Cutter said, making no attempt to be cordial.

"He said he'd meet us here at noon," Harry answered.

Cutter checked his watch. "It's ten after."

Though Gloria felt it was a bit anticlimactic, she introduced the men to each other, then laced her arm through Harry's. "If we have to wait, let's at least enjoy ourselves and sit by the lake." The two walked toward the water's edge and didn't even stop when they heard Cutter's disagreeable voice say, "We didn't come here to enjoy ourselves."

When they reached a small clearing near the bank, Gloria flattened a section of tall rye grass with her foot and sat down. Harry followed suit. Then both of them watched Cutter trudge off in another direction without a word.

Gloria watched the sun skating across the lake like a shimmering fairy; watched oak leaves flutter in the breeze; watched the tall grasses, which looked more like sheaves of wheat, sway and bow to the sun; marveled at the colorful wildflowers covering much of the clearing like a tapestry. It suddenly seemed incredible that a person like Cutter, who lacked the capacity to enjoy such beauty, could own this place.

A gentle breeze fluttered around Gloria like a monarch butterfly. She breathed deeply of the fresh, sweet air, feeling at once the familiar invisible hand move her heart and remind her she was neither judge nor jury.

When was she ever going to be all that Jesus wanted her to be?

~◈ ◈~

An hour later, Santa Claus still hadn't shown up, and even Gloria was getting antsy. She had passed the time listening to

Harry talk about Perth's college ups and downs, all the papers she had due, her lack of a love life; and about Dorie's "babies," Mark and Cleo——her two Shih Tzus—and how Harry wasn't all that crazy about either one of them, but, if pressed, thought Cleo was okay and suspected that was because she was a female and females generally had better dispositions—and that supposition about females, according to Harry, cut across the full spectrum of the animal kingdom.

But now Gloria was finding it difficult to sit still. Cutter had returned from his wanderings long ago and sat alone, off to the side. Those times when Gloria ventured a glance his way, she saw his face streaked with impatience and ill will.

If Santa didn't show, Cutter would be impossible going home. She could just hear him now, telling her what a colossal waste of time it had been, and how next time a crackpot calls, she should leave him out of it. And the scowl on his face would punctuate the whole dissertation like a big black period.

Oh, it was going to be fun.

"You want to go?" she finally asked. When he nodded without a word, they all got up and walked silently back to their cars.

That's when Gloria noticed the flock of crows overhead. Noticed them dip and swoop down into the grass several yards to the right of the trees where their cars were parked.

"What's going on?" She pointed to the crows.

"Probably a dead animal," Harry said.

By the sheer number of crows flying back and forth, Gloria knew it had to be a large one. She didn't know why, but she felt a sudden urge to investigate. "Let's take a look."

Harry shook his head. "Nothing we can do now."

"I'm not interested in wasting any more time here," Cutter said, his voice heavy with irritation.

But Gloria was already sprinting in the direction of the

activity. The snapping of twigs told her Harry followed closely behind. When she glanced back, Cutter had already disappeared from her line of vision, but she pictured him scowling and standing with his arms stiffly at his side, like one of those old Civil War generals cast in bronze. He was sure to be put out by all this, but it didn't matter. She was a woman on a mission. And she couldn't explain it, either, this sudden need to see the spot for herself.

The closer to the flock of cawing birds, the thicker and more inhospitable the vegetation. Briarlike growth scratched and clawed Gloria's ankles, tearing at her socks and jeans and sinking sharp thorns into her flesh. She was about to tell Harry that she had changed her mind and that they should turn around when something in the underbrush caught her eye. She pushed through the thicket, ignoring the throbbing pain in her ankles. There it was. Only a few inches more—something shiny, reflecting the sun. She stooped to reach for it, then gasped and pulled away. A silver watch sparkled on the ground only inches from her foot.

Attached to a hand.

She heard Cutter call impatiently, heard Harry's labored breathing coming up behind her. But she couldn't move, couldn't answer. The hand was almost obscured by the underbrush and looked like one of those fake rubber things you find at a freaky curio shop. She was afraid to look further, afraid to follow with her eyes where the hand would lead. But she did, all the way up to the face—the face of a middle-aged man, poorly dressed, with a mole on his right cheek and one bullet hole in the middle of his forehead.

Oh, faithful Jesus.

"What is it? What do you see?" Harry shouted, struggling with the underbrush, trying to reach her.

Then she heard Cutter's voice and his footsteps breaking the vegetation behind her. "What's going on? What is it?" He passed Harry and reached her first.

Gloria pointed down at the body. "I think we've just found Santa Claus."

✶ ✶

Chapter Three

THE DEATH OF SANTA CLAUS still haunted Gloria. At night, whenever she closed her eyes, she saw his body lying faceup in the underbrush, covered with briars and blood. And this vision finally forced Gloria to acknowledge there was danger associated with the flyers in general and with investigating The Lakes in particular. Back in Eckerd, she had received a threatening phone call from someone who didn't like the flyers. Harry had received one too. But this was a far cry from a troublesome phone call.

Someone was dead.

She had spent a long time with Jesus explaining all this, then asked if He didn't think it was best for her to back off from this radical environmental stuff. He did not.

And there was the dilemma. She had lost her stomach for it. And she suspected, by the look on Harry's face after they'd spent the better part of Saturday with the EPD trying to explain Santa Claus, that he had as well.

So . . . now what?

It took Gloria almost three full days to decide that she'd

simply wait on the Lord, put the flyers on hold until she got some direction. No point in running ahead. That never worked anyway. And that face, that rubbery blank face in the underbrush, was a constant reminder of why her decision was a good one.

Gloria closed her Bible and listened to Tiger purr next to her ear, felt him rub his head against her shoulder trying to get her attention. She stroked the soft, velvety patch of his nose, then around his ears, and watched his paws curl as he closed his eyes in ecstasy. The calico fur felt coarse between her fingers, and she wondered if that was because he had spent the first ten months of his life in McGreedy's barn.

She glanced at the cat bed in the corner of the living room. A big green pillow bulged inside a rattan oval shell on the floor. Next to it were half a dozen cat toys. She couldn't believe she had had Tiger for less than two weeks. Already he was a big part of her life, providing companionship and love, and asking so little in return. He still liked going out, but most of his days were spent indoors, content with his new, soft life.

Soft life.

Was that what she was after? Having everything easy? To stay in the sheltered cocoon of her small world and not brave the dangers of the larger one?

No. If that were the case, then she never would have left Appleton. Or returned.

Oh, Jesus, I know You're able to keep me in the palm of Your hand. Safe. Secure. And You've removed my timid nature, made me strong—a lot stronger than I was before. You've done so much, only . . . can we slow it down a bit?

There was Santa Claus again. Looming large in her mind's eye.

She rose from the couch, suddenly detesting the thought of spending another night locked in her apartment in front of the

TV. She had to get over this. It had been a while since anything had frightened her. She hated to keep calling that guy at The Lakes, Santa Claus. Maybe if she knew his name, she could bury him, bury his memory once and for all.

"Enough of this, Gloria. You're going out, out, out." She headed for the tiny bedroom to freshen up. But where? Maybe she'd ride her old Schwinn—the one Sam Hidel sold her for ten dollars—to church. Hook up with the Wednesday night prayer group. On Sunday, Ivy Gordon had reminded her they were still meeting at the usual time and had asked her to join them. But Gloria had made some excuse about still settling in and being too busy. The truth was she didn't want to ride home in the dark.

And wasn't that silly? This was Appleton. Not Eckerd City. People could ride a bike alone at night. She'd wear her new jeans—the ones with straight legs so she didn't have to worry about her pants getting caught in the chain. The chain guard had fallen off days ago.

Okay, so jeans it was. Gloria stopped halfway to the bedroom. In Appleton, news traveled fast. It would be only a matter of time before her mother found out she had worn Levi's to church. That prospect, and her mother's subsequent reaction, was almost as scary as riding her bike in the dark. "Get over it, Gloria," she said, racing for the bedroom—if she didn't hurry, she'd be late. "Just get over it."

❧ ☙

Cutter Press stared at the notes in his hand and fumed. What was his mother up to now? If she thought these messages from her doctor were going to carry any weight with him . . . He crumpled the purple-lined notepapers, tossed them, and watched them bounce against the rim of the tall kitchen garbage pail and land on the floor. Then he stomped out, not bothering to pick them up.

Sadie Bellows had handed him two messages from Dr. Grant before he left the office. Both said "Please call." He had been down this road before. Had gotten numerous messages like this over the years from Dr. Grant. Every time his mother felt she was losing her grip over him or the business, she thought a trip to Dr. Grant's would solve it. The scare-everyone-into-submission ploy. Leave it to Virginia. Didn't she realize he had enough pressure? Especially now, after the death of that guy . . . Santa Claus. The police were still calling Cutter, asking questions. Didn't Virginia know when to back off? Why did she have to be so shameless in the lengths she'd go to manipulate others? The only person coming close to her tactics was Geri Bickford. Close. But not surpassing. Not even equal.

Still . . . the last time he saw Virginia she did seem listless, pale even. *Suppose something was really wrong this time?* Cutter stripped off his tie, flung it over one shoulder, then carefully removed the oval gold-plated cuff links. He stared at them for a moment, then cupped them in his hand. He unbuttoned his shirt as he walked through the posh, spacious house he was renting from a friend.

All right . . . he'd call Dr. Grant tomorrow . . . just to make sure. But if Virginia thought for one second that he was going to move back home, she was in for a rude awakening. Dr. Grant could call every day, three times a day, seven days a week for all the good it would do him . . . or Virginia.

~❧ ☙~

Gloria felt ashamed and wondered what Jesus was thinking. The prayer meeting had gone on a little longer than usual, on account of all the ladies making a fuss over her and telling her, each one in turn, how happy they were she was back. After that great reception, Gloria had suddenly felt a need to justify their validation that she was a person of worth, show them she was especially important to the prayer group. That's when she purposely let her Bible flip to one of the heavily highlighted pages, and instantly felt an immodest satisfaction that her page was more heavily marked than the one Ivy Gordon had opened.

Everything quickly went downhill after that. As each of the ladies took turns lifting up prayer requests, Gloria barely listened. Instead, she spent the time mentally composing a prayer in her head, playing with the words, arranging them just so, then rearranging them. She desperately wanted it to flow like theirs so they could see how much she had grown. When her turn came her prayer was flawless, like she had read it off a script, which she had. She could see that everyone was impressed. But inside, her spirit wept.

Spiritual pride. She had never felt it before. It was alien and dark and made her feel rotten inside. After the prayer meeting, she would have gladly pried open her chest, reached inside, and torn out the pride if she could. Ripped it out like the weed it was. She had left Appleton a spiritual baby and returned, it seemed, a spiritual baby.

How far she still had to go! A lifetime wasn't long enough for Jesus to accomplish His will in her. She had come back to Appleton for reconciliation, because she knew that's what He wanted. What made her think it would be a cakewalk?

With a heavy heart, she kissed and hugged everyone, then went outside into the darkness and headed toward her bike, wishing she had just stayed home and vegged out on the couch.

~✷ ✷~

Right from the start, Gloria knew someone was following her. First there was that long shadow near the rectory parking lot that moved in her direction as soon as she reached her bike. Then footsteps—heavy, clumping footsteps that could only belong to a man. And finally, running, when she mounted her bike and sped away.

Her heart pounded in her chest as her legs pedaled faster and faster. What if the guy had a car? She listened for the sound of an engine, for tires on the asphalt behind her, then whipped her head around to give her eyes a chance to detect what her ears couldn't.

But she saw only darkness. All the way home she continued listening, but heard only the screech of an owl, the slapping of wind against her body, and the *click click click* of her thin twenty-six-inch, hook-edge rim tires. And even when she ducked behind Sam Hidel's Grocery to her apartment, got off her bike, and raced to her door and opened it, she listened.

Quickly, she closed and locked the door. This was silly. No one was out there. She was letting her imagination run wild. Her breath came in short, spastic gasps as the face of Santa Claus suddenly flashed before her eyes. She had to get a grip. She had to forget about that poor dead man in the underbrush.

~⊛ ⊛~

Gloria sat in front of her new HP, her fingers flying over the keyboard as she worked on the posters commissioned by Charlie Axlerod on behalf of the Chamber of Commerce. She knew her early-bird special would get him. Some people said Charlie still had the first dollar he'd ever made. But that was just a spiteful remark from those of the tax-and-spend persuasion in town. Charlie was a generous man, but frugal as all get-out when it came to someone else's money.

She felt much better today. Last night, she had spent over an hour taking all those dark thoughts captive and making them obedient to Christ. Scripture told her she had not been given a spirit of fear but a sound mind, and it was time she started acting like it. When she finally went to bed, she slept like a log. And this morning when she woke up, the face she saw wasn't Santa Claus's but Grandma Quinn's. Tonight, after work, she was going to peddle the five miles to Grandma's house and stay as long as Grandma wanted her to, even if that meant she'd ride home in the dark.

⁓

Cutter Press held the phone tightly against his ear with one hand and twirled a dart in the other. With a graceless motion, he hurled the dart, missing the board altogether. "What do you mean there's something wrong with my mother?"

"She hasn't told you?"

"No, Dr. Grant, she expects you to do that, as usual. So tell me, what's wrong with her this time? A queasy stomach? Have I been a bad boy and given her indigestion again?"

"I think you should talk to her and ask—"

"I have no intention of talking to Virginia."

"She has forbidden me to say anything, so I must honor her wishes, but I strongly urge you to speak with her."

"I'll tell you what, Doctor, why don't I just run through a list of previously assumed illnesses and you can cough when I hit the right one. This way you can accomplish your objective without violating any doctor-patient confidentiality, and I can accomplish mine, which is ending this conversation as quickly as possible. So here goes: angina, diverticulitis, gallstones, kidney stones, hypertension, hypotension—"

When the phone went dead, Cutter placed it in its cradle. That should keep Doc Grant from bothering him for a couple of weeks. Still . . . there was something in the doctor's voice Cutter didn't like. Some strain, some tension.

Had Virginia really gone and gotten herself sick this time? Just to spite him?

~❦ ❦~

Geri Bickford let the door of Sam Hidel's Grocery bang shut behind her as she stepped onto the sidewalk. One of these days Sam was going to modernize and get himself one of those automatic doors that slid open when you got close to it. She nodded politely to Ivy Gordon as she passed, thinking how that woman kept looking younger and younger every time she saw her. But Ivy would never have Geri's looks, no matter how many plastic surgeries she had.

Geri was sure that's how Ivy was doing it—keeping that youthful look—with facelifts and tucks, even though everybody said no. Even Pearl Owens. And Pearl was always ready to spread the news when there was some. So maybe it wasn't true. Still . . . Geri threw back her shoulders, tilted her chin upward, and headed for her car. Ivy would never have much looks to speak of.

Three brown paper bags were strapped to Geri's carrier, and she wheeled them across the street to the parking lot, feeling more irritated with each step. She supposed she shouldn't think ill of Ivy—after all, Ivy was a good enough sort. Never went in for gossip. Not like some. Geri squeezed her shoulder blades together and tilted her chin higher. No, it wasn't Ivy's fault. Ivy had nothing to do with Geri's bad mood. Nothing at all.

But it did have everything to do with this Venus's-flytrap of a town—a town that ate its own inhabitants alive. More and more it felt like Appleton was closing in on her. It was getting so she didn't want to go anywhere. Not even to Sam's. The embarrassment was just too great. She might as well go around with a big fat *F* on her back—for *Failure*.

First, she had to endure the indignity of Gloria's renting that disgusting little apartment in back of Sam's. How Gloria could choose to live in a grungy little shack rather than in a nice, clean, spacious house was beyond her. Everybody had to be talking about it. A single daughter who preferred squalor to living with her mother cast doubts on that mother. It said something about Geri. At least, Geri was sure that's how the townspeople saw it.

And now, this new offense. Sam had some nerve discussing it right out in the open, right in front by the door so everyone could hear. Did she know that her mother had run up a rather large bill? Sam had asked, looking at her like she should just open her wallet and pay it right on the spot.

Of course she knew. Sam had told her about it last month, and the month before that. "And what was it for?" she had asked, already knowing the answer because he had also told her that two months running—flour, sugar, eggs, raisins, oatmeal, and the like. Her mother must be baking like a fiend. Anyone passing 52 Elm Street could smell there was something in her oven.

But who was eating all that stuff? Most of her mother's friends were in nursing homes or in assisted living. So why was her mother running up bills at the grocery and baking for an army?

Dementia. It was a sure sign of dementia. Her mother had been on the edge for years. That's why Geri had tried so hard to keep Hannah and Gloria separated. A mother had a right to protect her young. Not that Gloria appreciated being protected.

Geri pressed the automatic opener and popped the trunk of

her car, then placed her three packages neatly inside. This situation couldn't go on. Either she'd stop going to Sam Hidel's or her mother would. She couldn't have that crazy woman running around town embarrassing her.

Crazy? Well, maybe that too. All that baking. All that wild singing at the top of her lungs—so loud that people across the street could hear. Her downright refusal to wear that little Freedom FS hearing aid Geri had spent so much money on. Her illogical insistence on maintaining that huge two-story house. Oh yes, it was beyond dementia. Beyond the normal old-age foibles. It was . . . loony. Geri was surer of that now than ever before.

Her mother was crazy.

Maybe it was time Hannah Quinn joined her friends in that nursing home.

⌁ ⌁

Gloria stood in the front entrance of the aging Victorian getting the life squeezed out of her by a pair of chubby arms. A full, round face, framed by gray hair pulled into a bun, beamed, like Gloria's Eveready flashlight, with love. The aroma of freshly baked cookies wafted from the kitchen. And the familiar ticktock of Grandma Quinn's prized 1805 Whiteside clock drifted from the living room.

Gloria was home.

"My goodness, child, it's wonderful to see you. I heard you were in town. Been expecting you." Hannah Quinn released her granddaughter.

Gloria smiled as she noticed the little molded flesh-colored object that sat in the concha of Grandma Quinn's left ear. "You're wearing your hearing aid."

"Figured one of these days you'd take it in your head to come traipsing out here and say hello. I wanted to be ready."

Gloria let Grandma Quinn enfold her in her soft, fleshy arms again and cover her cheeks with kisses. Oh, how she had missed those hugs and kisses!

"Let's take a look at you," Grandma finally said, pushing Gloria from her and holding her at arm's length. When Grandma squinted and moved her head this way and that, Gloria wondered if her cataracts had gotten worse.

"My, how you've changed. You look . . . you look . . ." But Grandma Quinn didn't finish, as though wanting to keep her observation to herself, and just led Gloria down the narrow hallway toward the kitchen. The tired oak floor creaked beneath their feet and gave Gloria a sudden shudder of pleasure. Oh, how many times had she walked these boards!

They passed the living room, and Gloria was surprised to see it cluttered with old newspapers. On the couch lay a pile of clothes needing to be folded. The small TV in the corner and the coffee table in the center of the room were covered with so much dust it almost looked like mold had grown over them.

What happened? Grandma had always been as neat as a pin.

When they got to the kitchen, Gloria took the chair Grandma offered and sat quietly waiting while Grandma hunted for her glasses—which were nothing more than tinted glass that helped keep down the glare. But Grandma swore they made her see better.

Drawers banged shut, one after the other, as Grandma sifted through them. All the while, Gloria pretended not to notice. If Grandma was vain about anything, it was this. Grandma hated the hearing aid and the fact that she had subcapsular cataracts. She hated to admit that parts of her weren't working as well as they used to. Actually, weren't working nearly as well as they used to.

Gloria scanned the kitchen as the drawers continued to open and close. It felt so good to be here. It was the place she had missed most in all of Appleton. She loved the smell of freshly baked cookies, the warmth of the oven, the familiar red gingham covering the window and chair cushions. She didn't remember it being so messy, though. Or that big black smudge running the length of the wall behind the stove.

"What happened to the wall, Grandma?"

Grandma Quinn pulled a pair of wire-rimmed glasses from the drawer she had just ravaged and inspected them in the light. "Pfffff. I keep putting these silly things in the wrong place." With the corner of her apron she cleaned the lenses, then put them on.

"The wall, Grandma, what happened to it?"

"Oh, that's nothing." Grandma Quinn flicked her hand in the air. Then she walked over to the table where Gloria sat. "Well, goodness gracious, look at you. So . . . so . . . ." She turned partially to the side, lifted her apron, and used it to dab the perspiration from her forehead. Then she smoothed down her hair, tucking wisps of gray here and there into her bun. "And me, looking like something the cat dragged in."

"You look wonderful. Just wonderful. You can't imagine how much I've missed you. There were times in Eckerd when I wanted to give up and come home, I think just to see your face, and for one of *these.*" Gloria rose and walked over to the counter and grabbed an oatmeal cookie off one of the cooling racks. "I can't believe you're still making them. And so *many.*" Gloria's eyes scanned the countertop. There had to be at least five dozen cookies cooling.

Grandma gave her a gentle swat on the backside, then shooed her back to her seat. "Never you mind about the number. I have uses for them. Tell me how you've been. And tell me all about Eckerd City and why you came back. I especially want to know why you came back. Honestly, pumpkin, I never expected you to."

"Neither did I." Gloria bit into the cookie and tasted the raisins and oats and sugar and Grandma's secret ingredient, shredded coconut. Nobody made oatmeal cookies like Grandma. How many times had she sat in Grandma's kitchen and eaten so many of these her stomach ached? "I'll tell you all about it, *after* you tell me what you thought when you first saw me. Your very first impression, and be *honest.*"

"That's a queer thing to ask. Why do you?"

Gloria brushed crumbs from her mouth and shrugged. "I guess I want to know if you think I've changed."

"Gracious, child, you know you've changed. No need to ask. But . . . if you want to know what I was thinking, well . . . I was taken back by how much you suddenly reminded me of your mother."

❦

Gloria spent almost an hour telling Grandma Quinn about Eckerd City, Harry Grizwald, Miss Dobson, Perth. Then another twenty minutes filling in the blanks regarding Tracy and her brother, Tucker. Finally, she told her how she believed God had called her back to Appleton for reconciliation.

"That sounds like our Jesus, all right. Just the thing He'd ask someone to do. You think you're up to it?"

Gloria rose from her chair and headed for the counter to get another cookie. "Grandma, now look who's asking the odd question. Jesus loves these people. And He's put His love into my heart. He's made me love them too." And it was true. Jesus had done a miracle in her heart. It ached to make things right.

To see reconciliation become a reality. But she also wanted Cutter and Tracy and her mother to find Jesus for themselves. She loved her mother more than she had ever loved her before. That went for Tracy too. But Cutter . . . well, she loved him because Jesus loved him, but she certainly didn't like him.

"Jesus has made me love these people," Gloria repeated. "And I want to reach out to them with that love."

Grandma rose from her chair, wiped her hands on her apron, then walked slowly toward the counter. "Sometimes, child, love just isn't enough."

~❦ ❦~

Chapter Four

GLORIA FELT LIKE A CHILD, standing beside her old red Schwinn and staring up at the freshly painted white Cape Cod with its window boxes full of geraniums. The green shutters were freshly painted too, and sprouted alongside each window like eyelashes, making the windows seem to return the stare. Hydrangea bushes hugged both sides of the stoop, and in front of these, short perennials, packed closely together, weaved a colorful ribbon between the hydrangea and the rye lawn. Surrounding it all was a three-foot-high white picket fence that for years had been able to keep out unwanted visitors but never the rabbits.

She tried to draw encouragement from the gaily chirping robin in the nearby maple, but couldn't, and just stood there as if her feet were Krazy Glued to the sidewalk.

Finally, she stirred herself enough to kick the stand and rest her bike. How many times had she stood on this sidewalk in front of her house? Feeling like she did now? Not wanting to go in? She tapped the chrome handlebars. Why did the sight of this place still give her a sense of uneasiness, the kind one feels when going to the dentist after years of absence?

Because more likely than not, it would be painful.

She glanced up at the immense blue sky that went on forever, and at the white cotton-candy clouds that looked so close you were tempted to believe you could dive into them like a soft, comfy bed. She imagined the footstool of God being this beautiful and suddenly felt close to Jesus. This is why He had brought her all the way back from Eckerd. This is why He had poured all that love into her. There was no need to fear. He was with her. She felt renewed strength. Maybe today was the day she'd tell Mother about Jesus. Tell her why she came back from Eckerd. She didn't know what to say, exactly, but Jesus knew. He'd put the right words into her mouth.

~◉ ◉~

"Are you crazy?" Gloria shouted, her hand moving in an exasperated gesture and accidentally knocking over her mother's Spode bud vase. The vase spun around in a circle on the tabletop, spewing water everywhere. In seconds the vase had emptied, and water ran off the table edge onto the floor. A yellow rose, one Gloria knew came from her mother's prize rose garden in the back, lay sprawled like a beached goldfish with its petals helplessly flopped in all directions.

Now why had she said that?

She could have been more tactful. Prayed before she opened her mouth. Given Jesus a chance to calm her down. But when her mother said those words, those awful words "nursing home," Gloria forgot all about the love and patience of God.

Her mother darted to the sink, looking wounded, and grabbed a sponge and bucket from the louver cabinet.

"Let me do that." Gloria tried to take the sponge, but her

mother brushed her hand away, then frantically mopped up the water as if it were acid eating into her white-tiled tabletop and white-tiled floor.

Trust Mother to always clean up the least important mess first.

Gloria ran sweaty palms down her new cargo pants and walked over to the counter, giving her mother space. There was no use trying to stop her. Mother wouldn't rest until everything was perfect. Again.

"I'm sorry," Gloria said, feeling angry with herself for her outburst. "I know I shouldn't have gotten so excited, but I can't believe you're actually thinking of putting Grandma into a nursing home."

Geri Bickford lifted her head to scowl at Gloria. A little rivulet of water on the floor had begun streaming between Geri's shoes, and she bent to attack this new menace. "You haven't been around." Her mother's hand moved swiftly, mopping up the liquid with her sponge in remarkable time. "You haven't had to listen to the complaints, the whispers." She straightened, then carried the little red pail to the sink and emptied it.

"Is this about what people are saying? Or is it about Grandma?"

"You never did value a good name, a good reputation. You never seemed to care what people thought of you. A good reputation isn't something you can buy at Sam Hidel's, Gloria, or Kelly's. You've got to earn it. Even when you do, there's always someone trying to spoil it. Take it away. And once it's gone, once it's lost . . . well, it's lost."

"Mother, please, let's discuss one thing at a time. I want to know why you think Grandma should go into a nursing home."

Geri wiped her wet hands on a pink and green dish towel that matched her curtains. She had made those curtains herself.

Actually made them three times, ripping them apart and sewing them until she was satisfied. "Her mind is gone. I've been telling you for years that I had my doubts about your grandmother's mental state. Well . . . now all doubts are gone. She's finally crossed over into Neverland."

"I just saw Grandma a few days ago. She seemed fine to me."

Her mother gave her a pained look before picking up the bud vase to examine it for damage. "Your grandmother's been running up high bills at Sam's, buying unnecessary things, silly things, like sugar and flour and chocolate chips, and coconut flakes. She must be baking like a fiend. Making enough cookies for an army. One person can't eat that many sweets. So I have to assume that after she bakes them, they go in the trash."

Gloria's insides twisted as she pictured Grandma's five cooling racks loaded with oatmeal cookies. She pulled out a kitchen chair and sat down. No. One person couldn't eat all that.

"And she does this *every week*. Every week, back she goes to Sam's and charges more flour and sugar and . . . well, you see the problem, don't you? She's flipped. And I have to endure being flagged down by Sam Hidel and having him, in a very loud voice I might add, tell me how high my mother's bill is getting, and then I see the look in his eyes and everyone else's who's listening. And quite frankly, Gloria, I can't take that look."

"What look, Mother?" Gloria hoped she didn't sound irritated. She so wanted to make up for her previous outburst, but . . . this whole thing was crazy. *Put Grandma Quinn into a nursing home?*

Never.

Geri placed the vase in the center of the clean, dry table, apparently satisfied it had no chips or cracks, then took a seat opposite her daughter. "I know what Sam and the others are thinking when they look at me like that. They're thinking I'm not a good daughter. That I'm not doing my job by keeping that silly old woman from harming herself."

"Oh, for the love . . . Mother, how is Grandma harming herself?"

"By running up debt she can't possibly pay. And—I didn't want to tell you this, but since you're questioning my decision, I will—about six months ago, your grandmother almost burned down the house. If it had gone up in flames, she could have killed herself and others, and taken half the neighborhood out too."

"What happened?"

"She left a batch of cookies in the oven. Fell asleep on the couch while they were baking black as tar balls."

Gloria remembered the big, muddy-looking smudge behind Grandma's stove. No wonder Grandma didn't want to talk about it.

"If Ivy Gordon hadn't stopped by when she did, no telling how it would have ended. 'Course I wish it could have been someone other than that Holy Roller. She probably delights in lifting poor, crazy Hannah Quinn up in prayer every Wednesday night."

"Mother, that's unkind, calling Ivy a Holy Roller and making her sound like a . . . like a gossip. Ivy's a lovely lady. As a matter of fact, I went to her prayer group Wednesday, and she never even mentioned Grandma."

Geri twisted her face into a knot. "Yes, I heard about your Levi's. Disgusting, Gloria. Absolutely disgusting. You act like you were raised in McGreedy's barn. Honestly! You should have more respect than to wear jeans to church. What were you thinking? Sometimes, you don't have a brain in your head." Geri brought her hand up to her forehead, and with a discreet, dainty motion of her finger, wiped away the perspiration that had begun beading across her hairline. "And why you or anyone else would want to sit around for hours listening to other people's problems and then talking about them under the guise of 'prayer requests' is beyond me."

"Mother, it's not like that at all."

Geri dismissed Gloria's remark with a wave of her hand. "Forget it, Gloria. Let's not go there. It's still a sore spot. First Grandma gets religion and now you. Oh, I don't mind you going to church—that's a good thing—but the rest of it, all that Bible reading and praying . . . I wanted you to be strong, not go looking for a crutch to hold you up every time something bad happens. And it always does, Gloria. Sooner or later, something bad happens."

Gloria rubbed her throbbing temples. It had been a long time since she had had one of her headaches. "Mother, I think it's wrong of you to want to put Grandma into a nursing home just for the sake of appearances, just to stop people from talking, if they're even talking at all. But I'll admit the house is getting too big and . . . Grandma doesn't keep it up quite as nicely as she used to. But that doesn't mean she's ready for a nursing home. Just something smaller. Maybe we should look into that little retirement community off Route 485 and see how much their condos cost. It's only twenty minutes away and might be just the thing. Lots of Grandma's friends are already there, and—"

"Why can't you face the fact that your grandmother is incompetent and can no longer care for herself?"

"Because it's simply not true, Mother, and you know it."

Geri rose from her chair, clenching the pink and green dish towel in her hands. Red finger-sized streaks ran up her cheeks, making it look like she had just been slapped. "Did you come here to . . . to insult me? Is that it? I don't understand why you're so difficult, Gloria. Why you're so pigheaded and never listen to anyone. Why you take everyone's side but mine."

"And I don't understand why you *hate* Grandma."

"I . . . I don't hate her." Geri's face went from red to white. "I just . . . well, we just don't get along."

"You mean like you and me?"

Geri let the dish towel fall from her hands onto the table, then lowered herself onto the chair like an old woman. Her mouth sagged to one side like Ivy Gordon's did after her stroke two years ago, and for a second Gloria wondered if her mother wasn't having a stroke too. But when Geri picked up the dish towel and began rubbing it, with small circular motions, over the already clean table, Gloria knew she was all right. Only, for the first time in Gloria's memory, her mother didn't look glamorous. She just looked old and tired and sad.

"I suppose you're going to tell me that's all my fault, us not getting along." Geri's hand continued making those little circles. "I suppose you're going to tell me that I'm the one who's difficult."

How could her mother be so predictable? So blind? Gloria suddenly thought of Tucker and how she had secretly loved him, or thought she loved him, for years. Hadn't she, Gloria, been blind too? Unable to see the obvious? And what about not seeing how selfish she was in Eckerd when she wouldn't even give a hurting girl the time of day, until it was too late because the girl ended up committing suicide? When you got right down to it, the whole human race was blind as bats, with faulty sonar to boot, bumping along the walls of life.

Gloria touched her mother's hand. "No, Mother, I'm not going to say it's your fault. I just want to say maybe we should both try harder."

Geri dabbed her eyes with the dish towel, covering it with

black mascara. "You don't understand what it's like being a mother. How difficult it is. All the sacrifices, the heartache. If you did, you'd be more appreciative."

"That's why I came home, Mother." Gloria saw the startled look in her mother's eyes, then saw it replaced by that old stubborn glare.

"Well . . . that's something anyway."

"I came home because I love you and wanted you to know that." Should she finish it? Should she follow it with *and because Jesus loves you*? When she decided the answer was "yes" and said it, her mother left the table.

❦

"You're so pale, Virginia, you're starting to look like one of those Kabuki dancers." Cutter walked over to the heavily draped Palladian window and pulled open the velvet curtains. "What you need is some sunlight. Some fresh air."

Sun crept over the Berber carpet, the small brocade armchair that was as old as the Flood, the scrolled mahogany bedposts that were even older, the mauve and cream dust ruffle and floral comforter covering the queen-size bed, and finally over the pasty, wrinkled face of Virginia Press. When Cutter opened the window, she sank deeper against the five pillows bracing her and covered her face with one hand.

"Did you come to harass me? No loving, thoughtful son would let that howling wind buffet his mother's sick body. For heaven's sake, close that infernal window! And those drapes too."

"You can't hide out in here forever." Cutter poured himself a glass of cold water from the sweating silver pitcher on the nightstand. "It's time you joined the human race."

"Says who? And that's my water. Who invited you to come into my room and take over? Is nothing sacred? I'm a sick woman."

"Don't you want to know what your precious Medical Data is doing?"

Virginia dropped her hand and closed her eyes in an obvious attempt to shut out the slice of light cutting across the bridge of her nose, then brought her comforter up under her chin. "Go away."

"I thought you'd like to know that I was thinking of throwing out that disgusting office furniture you bought from the Salvation Army—"

"I *didn't* get it from the Salvation Army!"

"And when I say I'm throwing out the furniture, I'm talking about the furniture in all the offices, and replacing everything with Ethan Allen. I hear they have a new line . . . Hemingway, I believe. Very expensive. Very *comfortable.*"

"You're the son from hell."

"And you, Virginia, are a . . . phony."

Virginia opened her eyes and squinted at him. Her birdlike fingers curled around the edge of the comforter. "Why can't you call me 'mother,' like other children?"

"Why aren't you like other mothers?"

Virginia rolled onto her side, her bony fingers disappearing under the covers. "I'm taking a nap. You can go or stay. Suit yourself. Just spare me the sound of your voice."

"Seems I remember you doing this when I was in fourth grade and Sam Hidel called about the five candy bars I stole. Then again in seventh, when the principal called and told you I was the worst disciplinary problem he had seen in years. And what about the time I almost failed tenth-grade English? I believe you stayed in bed for five days then. 'Course there were other times, so many I can't even remember the reasons." *And now this, just because he'd refused to get married and had moved out.* "You need to get a new act, Virginia. Something more original. This gig has gotten stale."

"Your father would turn over in his grave if he could hear you now."

"You've never held out this long before. You want to tell me why?"

"I don't want to talk to you about this or anything else."

Cutter walked over to the bed and sat down. "But Dr. Grant thinks we should talk."

Virginia turned, but not enough for Cutter to read the expression on her face. "What did that big mouth say?"

"Nothing."

She rolled back onto her side. "Well, doesn't that tell you there's nothing *to* say?"

"Then why have you stayed in bed for nearly three weeks? Even for you, that's a record."

Virginia curled into a tighter ball under the covers. "Has anyone told you you're becoming more disagreeable every day? I'm only glad your father didn't live to see how you turned out."

This time the barb about his father hit the mark. "You'd make a great guppy, you know—they eat their young too."

Virginia twisted around, then with some effort pulled herself to a sitting position. "I don't know why you insist on being so disgusting."

"Maybe because you always insist on being so unkind. You just can't leave my father out of it, can you? Does it gall you so much that I loved him? That I miss him?"

Virginia's eyes became as hard as ball bearings. She rolled them across Cutter's face, as she had all his life, leaving invisible grooves. For a minute she looked as if she was going to say something.

When she didn't, Cutter rose from the bed. She looked so small and shriveled. He resisted the urge to press on the covers to determine how much was body and how much blanket. For an instant he pictured her melting away like the wicked witch in Oz and was only mildly startled to find no objection rising in his breast.

"I'm afraid you've cried wolf once too often, Virginia. My sympathies only stretch so far."

With a shrug that conveyed a resignation bordering on defeat, Virginia slid down under the covers until she was nearly flat. Then without a word, she turned back over on her side.

She did look frail. And her face, with all the new lines marking her forehead and cheeks like furrows in Clive McGreedy's freshly plowed fields, made her look five years older than she had before taking to her bed. *What if there really is something wrong?* Cutter watched the small mound move up and down as she inhaled and exhaled. After a while, he assumed she had drifted to sleep, and turned to go.

"Geri told me Gloria's back in town."

Cutter stopped. No . . . he wasn't going to go through that again. He wasn't going to allow his mother to manipulate and shove and push him—or Gloria—to the altar. Virginia could stay in bed till next Christmas for all he cared. He walked toward the door in silence.

"I'd like to see her. Will you tell her that? Will you tell her I want her to come visit me?"

"I doubt she'll come," Cutter said without turning. He hoped his voice sounded sufficiently gruff to discourage this new direction their conversation had taken. When he reached the heavy oak door, he took one last look at the wispy figure coiled beneath the comforter. "But I'll ask." His words surprised him, then made him fume. Conditioning was a powerful tool, and didn't she know it?

~♦ ◈~

Gloria pulled the long white shoelace across the floor of her living room, keeping one step ahead of Tiger as he pounced and jumped and slunk after it. From time to time she let him capture it, then laughed as she watched him roll entangled around on the floor. She couldn't believe how wonderful it was to have her own pet, or how attached she was to him already. And she supposed that in his own way, Tiger was attached to her too.

She stretched out on the rug to watch him, and that's when he pounced—on fingers, arms, legs, anything that moved, and Gloria squealed with laughter.

"A merry heart doeth good like a medicine." Yes, it did. And wasn't it working now? Already she felt the healing balm of joy flowing through her.

Mother had drained her, sucked her dry of all the love Jesus had put into Gloria. And the thing with Tracy was draining her too. Four calls, and Tracy hadn't returned one of them. What was that all about?

She rolled onto her side and lay quietly. Tiger stopped pouncing and curled up near Gloria's cheek. She propped up on one elbow and rubbed his ear, then watched him close his eyes and curl his paws. Funny how it wasn't just dogs that liked having their ears rubbed. They were content now, she and Tiger. In this insignificant little moment, she felt God's love return and fill her and realized that He must have filled a thousand such insignificant moments before, but she had never noticed. And

66

then she understood He had enough love to fill all the insignificant moments that were to come in her life.

Tomorrow, right after church, she'd go visit Tracy.

~❦ ❦~

Chapter Five

PEOPLE ARE STARTING *to talk about the way you're dressing, Gloria.*
That's what her mother told her last night over the phone, just
before Gloria went to bed. A year ago, that rebuke would have
made Gloria toss and turn all night. But she had slept like a
clam.

The wind caught Gloria's hair, whipping her face as she
pedaled down Main Street on her Schwinn. She released one
handlebar and swiped at her eyes, but it was futile. Another puff
of wind, and Gloria again squinted through a tangle of brown
strands. All this "talk" wasn't really talk at all; it was Mother
still annoyed over Gloria wearing jeans to the Wednesday night
prayer meeting. And this continual harping was meant to keep
Gloria from doing it again before there really was talk. Wait till
Mother found out she hadn't worn a dress this morning to Sunday service either. You couldn't wear a dress and ride a bike at
the same time. Mother should understand that.

Honestly. The things Mother worried about.

As Gloria's legs moved in rapid circular motions, she felt the rolled-up cuffs of her chocolate-brown slacks begin to slip. She'd have to be careful. If her cuffs caught in the chain, it would be good-bye, pants. She stopped by Cameras & More long enough to roll her pants to just below her knees, then headed for South Cranberry Street. A sudden gust of wind filled her beige blazer like a sail, popping loose one of the metal buttons and making it hit the pavement with a ping. Now her open blazer flapped in the wind like newly sprouted wings. What a sight she must be—with her hair swirling, her partially bare legs moving a mile a minute, and her blazer flailing around her. Wait till Mother heard about this.

Oh, faithful Jesus, I sure could use a car.

~❧ ☙~

The white colonial with brown, muddy-looking shutters appeared more tired than the last time Gloria saw it. It sagged with an air of resignation, like an old beauty queen who had seen better days and knew it. In its prime, before Tracy's parents split up, it was the envy of the neighborhood. The lawn had looked like a cropped and edged emerald carpet, the hedges were trimmed in pleasing shapes, the flowerbeds infused with a different assortment of colorful annuals every year—"just so no one gets bored looking at it," Tracy's mother would say. Now the lawn was brown and needed mowing, the hedges stuck out in all directions, and the flowerbeds held weeds and little else.

Gloria dismounted, flipped the metal kickstand, and parked her bike. When she got to the door and rang the bell, she was surprised to notice her hand trembling. *Why so nervous?* She and Tracy went way back. Tracy had been Gloria's best friend—and most of the time her only friend—all through grade school and high school and right up to last year.

But things were different now.

She heard movement behind the door, then the sound of footsteps, but the door didn't open. She wondered if the bell was working and pressed it again, this time listening for the familiar strains of the *1812 Overture*, which alerted the household to visitors.

Okay, the bell worked. So why wasn't anyone answering? Several minutes passed, and Gloria pressed the bell again. And again. And again. She hadn't worn slacks to church and pedaled all this way looking like a windswept waif to be discouraged now. She pressed firmly on the button and didn't release it until the door finally opened.

"For crying out loud! Can't you take a hint, Nic—Oh . . . hello, kiddo. I didn't know it was you. I thought it was . . . My goodness! What happened? You look like you've been run over by a Mack truck."

Tracy sounded as shrill as that irritating whistle her brother, Tucker, used to blow when they all played school together and he was the principal and forever sending Tracy to detention. Gloria threw her arms around her friend, surprised to feel the bones of her vertebrae beneath the baggy T-shirt. Tracy hadn't gained an ounce since she had left Eckerd. But that was another matter, something Gloria would place on the back burner. Right now she needed to work at repairing the jagged edges that had developed in their relationship. They hadn't seen each other since the night Tracy had sneaked out of Gloria's Eckerd apartment, leaving a note behind on the coffee table.

"It's wonderful to see you," Gloria said, giving Tracy a Grandma-Quinn-size hug.

Tracy returned the hug, only out of politeness it seemed, and she was the first to pull away. "You want to come in?" Her eyes scanned the street like she was looking for someone.

Gloria thought it strange that Tracy should have to ask. It was almost like Tracy was uncomfortable or, even worse, like she wanted to be rid of her. Was Tracy still embarrassed . . . or maybe angry about Gloria flushing her marijuana down the drain?

"How long have you been in town?"

"Almost three weeks." Gloria walked through the entrance while Tracy held the screen. "I called you four times," she said, unable to restrain herself even though she had promised herself she wouldn't bring up Tracy's unresponsiveness. She felt mildly irritated that Tracy hadn't mentioned it first. "How come you never called back?"

"I've been meaning to, but you know how it is . . . Things come up . . ." The screen snapped shut with a grinding metallic sound, and Gloria noticed it wasn't hanging properly. She saw Tracy's eyes follow hers to the hinges. One was badly bent. "Nick Cervantes got a little rambunctious. Almost tore the door right off."

"*Nick Cervantes?* I thought he was in jail."

"Nope. Got out almost a year ago."

"What's he doing tearing doors off your house?"

Tracy chewed the end of her ponytail and shrugged. "He comes over once in a while. And he didn't tear the door off. He just bent it a little."

An uneasy feeling enveloped Gloria, like a layer of her mother's greasy body oil, as she followed Tracy upstairs. "Since when have you two become friends?" Nick Cervantes had been sent to prison on drug charges.

"Gloria, what is this? You writing a novel or something? Can't a girl have some secrets?"

"*Please* don't tell me you're romantically involved with him." Tracy opened the closed door of her bedroom and flipped on the light, even though the room was bright enough from the light pouring through the triple Andersen windows. "I didn't get a chance to straighten today, so don't look, okay?" Tracy stepped over shoes and a crumpled pair of pj's before flopping on the bed. With a flip of her wrist she shoved the stack of magazines that covered her pillows onto the floor. "Sheesh. I can't believe I'm twenty-eight and living at home. Who would believe it? I mean, I figured I'd be settled on my own long before you, and here you are. I *hate* living at home. Mom's cool, but she's dating like crazy—right now it's some guy from New Canterbury with a crop of hair plugs around his temples. Reminds me of those scrawny azaleas Clive's wife put on both sides of the hen house one year. Remember? Anyway, can you believe it? My mother has more dates than I do. The woman is never home. Still . . . we manage to get on each other's nerves."

Tracy reached over and pulled open the nightstand drawer. "The other day we had a doozy of a fight. Mom thinks I'm a slob. Said so right to my face." Tracy sifted through the crammed drawer. "'Course she's right. But then she really frosted me when she said I didn't pull my weight around here. That I'd trip over the garbage before I'd pick it up and that I'd sooner buy new dishes than wash the old ones." Tracy yanked out a bottle of purple nail polish and gave it a good shake. "But yesterday, she topped it all. Actually blew a fuse because I didn't weed the stupid flowerbeds out front while she was off gallivanting with Mr. Hair Plugs." Tracy twisted open the top, pulled out the applicator, and began coloring her fingernails. "Can you imagine? *I'm* the one with the full-time job while she's happily living off her alimony checks and partying. And *I'm* supposed to weed the flowerbeds." Tracy shook her head. "I've really gotta get outta here—find another place to live."

"I hear you're working at Dooley & Dooley." Gloria sat

down on the desk chair, feeling vaguely sad for Tracy's mother and not knowing why.

"Yeah . . . it's just temporary, until I get something better. You should see the place. What a zoo! I never knew people needed a dentist so often. And what babies! Sometimes I have to be real nice and encouraging, even to the adults. You'd think they could handle a little thing like a root canal. It's not like they're getting their arm sawed off, for heaven's sake. The kids are the worst, though. Some of them cry and carry on like crazy in the waiting room, and the Dooleys expect me to quiet them down with lollipops and funny faces, as if I don't have enough to do managing the front desk and sending out all those statements, not to mention fighting with the insurance companies. And the pay is pathetic. It doesn't come close to Medical Data, but I burned that bridge, it seems . . . Anyway, no use rehashing ancient history—"

"I wish I could make it right. I'm sorry you lost your job because of me."

"Yeah . . . well, like I said, ancient history. But it's gonna take me longer, with this crummy salary, to pay off all those credit cards."

"How's it going?" Gloria glanced at the desk and saw a dozen credit card statements littering the top, then quickly looked away.

"At this rate I'll be thirty-eight before I get outta here. Unless of course I can find some man to marry and pay them for me."

"Speaking of which, how's Stue Irving?"

Tracy sluggishly painted her last nail, shoved the applicator back into the bottle and twisted it shut.

"The brilliant Stue Irving? Remember him?"

The bed creaked as Tracy put the bottle of polish on the

nightstand, then brought her feet—shoes and all—onto the mattress. "Rats. Now how am I gonna get these off?" She stared at her Nikes as if willing them to come off on their own. When nothing happened, she looked up. "Gloria, would you be a pal?"

Gloria rose from her chair, went over to the bed and unlaced Tracy's sneakers. Then she slipped them off Tracy's perfect size-six feet and watched her wiggle her stocking toes.

"I hate to be a bother, but mind getting the pillows for me too?"

Gloria fluffed two pillows and tucked them between Tracy and her brass headboard, positioning one slightly higher to support Tracy's neck. "Stue Irving? Remember?"

"Can you believe Jennifer Lopez and Ben Affleck split up, and now she's married to that singer already?" Tracy absently blew on her nails, then flapped her hands up and down like a bird ready to take flight. The movie magazines Tracy had thrown down were scattered across the floor by her bed. Gloria thought Tracy had stopped reading those years ago.

"What do Ben Affleck and Jennifer Lopez have to do with anything?"

"They seemed like the perfect couple. Didn't they? I kinda envied them all that romance and excitement."

"That's not real life, Tracy. It's just make-believe. Who knows what goes on after the cameras shut down? Most of those big stars are miserable. Their lives are a mess. They're hooked on drugs or alcohol and—"

"I don't know what I ever saw in Stue. He's only marginally good-looking, and sometimes when I catch his profile a certain way, especially right after one of Horace Beezley's haircuts where he buzzes the sides too short and leaves the back too long, he's almost homely. Besides that, Stue's got no sense of humor, and he's tighter than dry rawhide with his money . . .

"I guess if I had to describe Stue in one word it would be *dull*. Positively dull. Did you know you can tell what day of the week it is by his sandwich? Boar's Head bologna is Monday, chunk light tuna Tuesday, mushroom and pimiento meatloaf Wednesday, egg salad with onion and celery Thursday, and lettuce, tomato, and white American cheese Friday. Now, I ask you, is that the kind of man who could keep a girl's interest for long?" Tracy lightly touched her thumbnail to see if it was dry. It must have still been tacky because she started blowing and flapping all over again. "No. I need a man who's more exciting, willing to live on the edge, take some chances. Someone who keeps me guessing, who's full of surprises."

Gloria felt queasy. "I hope you're not talking about someone like Nick Cervantes."

"Suppose I am." Tracy fanned out her fingers in front of her and stared at them. "Just suppose I am."

"Oh, Tracy, you can't be serious! He's been in and out of jail since high school. He's not the kind of man you could settle down with."

"I see how it is. Your Christian faith, and all that talk about forgiveness, doesn't cover someone like Nicky. It only covers those who wear suits and have steady jobs and hang around the right people."

A year ago Gloria would have let Tracy intimidate her with that statement, would have let Tracy twist things around and make her feel foolish. Now, she rose to her feet, mainly for effect, or perhaps to gain some psychological advantage by achieving the greater height. "You know perfectly well what I mean. This has nothing to do with forgiveness, but everything to do with common sense. I know how you operate, Tracy. You like to play with guys, string them along, squeeze their last dollar from their wallets. But you'd be a fool to take on someone like Nick Cervantes. He's trouble. And he's dangerous. Why did he nearly rip the screen off its hinges? Did you have a fight? Did you do something he didn't like?"

For a moment, Tracy sat like a propped popsicle. Then she closed her eyes and began to laugh. "I really had you going, didn't I? You really fell for it, didn't you? Imagine me and Nicky Cervantes! What a laugh."

"So it was all a joke?"

"Of course, kiddo. Whaddaya think?"

Gloria thought Tracy was lying.

~~@ @~~

Gloria's ancient Schwinn sped down Baker Street, where the sidewalks were ample and she didn't have to concern herself with traffic. It was the longer route to her apartment, but since her mind was preoccupied, she figured it was best she take the safer course home. The air was heavy with the scent of dahlias from Pearl Owens's garden, and Gloria inhaled deeply, trying to take the scent with her. It reminded her of the sweet things in life, and right now she could use some reminding.

The wind had died down. It didn't whip Gloria unmercifully like it had on the way to Tracy's. It was barely strong enough to flutter the leaves on the maples lining the sidewalk. Her legs moved slowly, almost like she had weights tied to her ankles.

And to her heart.

Instead of drawing Tracy closer, her visit had made them seem farther apart than ever. And Tracy and Nick Cervantes? *Oh, my heavens.* If it was true, if it wasn't just Tracy's sick idea of a joke, then Tracy was heading for trouble. And she would need a friend.

A charley horse in Gloria's right calf had started making its presence known on Baker Street. By the time she got to the corner of Spoon Lake and Main, it was so painful she had to stop. She rested the Schwinn on its kickstand, then limped to the bench in front of Tad's Ice Cream Parlor, and sat down. Sam Hidel's Grocery and her apartment were less than a mile away, but she couldn't make it with this mother-of-all-cramps. She hunched over and massaged the back of her leg—kneading it like it was a lump of Grandma Quinn's garlic-bread dough. It took several minutes, but finally the muscle relaxed and Gloria settled back on the bench. She'd sit a few minutes, then pedal the rest of the way home.

From her vantage point, she watched traffic snail along Main Street as though the drivers had nowhere in particular to go and had come out just to see what the rest of the world was doing. Funny how Main Street seemed so provincial, so *small* after Eckerd, and yet . . . exactly the same. People married, raised families, and went to work just like in Eckerd. And there was plenty of sin and sadness here too. Sometimes, when she thought of it, her spirit would weep and she'd find herself praying, "Come quickly, Lord Jesus." But then she'd remember Mother and Tracy and Cutter. If Jesus came now, they would be lost forever.

When Cutter's black Saab suddenly roared up along the curb in front of her, she couldn't help but smile. Wasn't that just like Jesus? Prepping her heart. Making her think of Cutter's lost condition one minute, then sending him to her, like an airmail package, the next?

He popped out of the car as if his legs were pogo sticks, and Gloria listened to the *tap tap tap* of his brown Florsheim shoes as he approached the bench.

"I'm glad I bumped into you."

Gloria resisted the urge to laugh. She'd hardly call this a "bumping into." She made room on the bench so Cutter could sit, and when he did, she was startled to see a look of embarrassment on his face. It reminded her of the time she had caught him leaving an apple for Miss Summerworth, his fifth-grade teacher.

"Virginia's having one of her tantrums. Been in bed for over three weeks."

"Yes, I heard. Mother told me she wasn't feeling well. Said your mom had a series of tests. But I wasn't sure if there was really something wrong or . . ."

"Or if I had been a bad boy?"

Gloria laughed. "Well . . ."

"I guess I've been bad. I moved out, did you hear?"

Gloria nodded.

"Yeah . . . shortly after you left Appleton. That was one thing Virginia never expected. She figured I was too spoiled to manage on my own. Figured anyone who didn't know how to make his own bed or run a washing machine or boil an egg wasn't going to survive in the wilds."

Gloria felt a stirring in her heart—a potpourri of pity and compassion and kinship, as though she and Cutter belonged to a secret society of those who had suffered at the hands of their parents. "Mother never expected me to leave home either. And then when I left town, when I actually left Appleton, she was beside herself. I suppose she counted on my timidity to keep me here forever. And it almost did . . ." Gloria didn't know why she had said that and would have been sorry except for the smile that creased Cutter's face as he settled back on the bench.

"She spent the better part of your life trying to make you frightened of almost everything."

"I don't know if I'd go as far as—"

"She did, Gloria. Let's be honest. That was her way of trying to control you, just as Virginia's way of trying to control me is her sickbed. And for a while there I really thought your mother had finished you for good. But when you left Appleton, I knew you were going to be all right."

The two sat quietly side by side like AARP cardholders, not saying anything, just watching the Sunday traffic wind along Main Street, with Gloria thinking it strange that she didn't feel uncomfortable.

After a while, Cutter sat upright, then cleared his throat. "Virginia asked for you. Said she'd like you to come see her."

Gloria felt the old hostility return. "Cutter . . . I can't go through this again. All the pressure, all the—"

"I know. I know. I told her you wouldn't come. But I promised I'd ask. And I don't think it's about . . . I don't think Virginia will talk to you about us getting married."

They fell back into silence, each gazing into his own space. "I'll pray about it," Gloria found herself saying. "I won't promise anything other than I'll pray about it." And Cutter nodded as though what she said made perfect sense, even though Gloria knew he didn't believe in prayer or in her faithful Jesus.

⋙ ⋘

Why did she always come out looking like the villain? Like Joan Crawford instead of Doris Day? It just wasn't fair. But Geri Bickford had learned long ago that life wasn't fair. She carefully creamed off her makeup with a Swisspers pad, using an upward stroke across her cheeks. No use giving gravity any more assistance. Her skin had already begun to sag. Soon it would match her heart. That had been sagging for years.

Geri could still see that look in Gloria's eyes, like Geri had killed Bambi or something, when she suggested they put Grandma Quinn into a nursing home. She just couldn't catch a break, not even from her own daughter. Why couldn't Gloria understand?

Geri carefully screwed the top back onto the little green jar of cream and returned it to its place in the medicine cabinet beside the skin toner. She didn't know why she was getting ready for bed so early. It was barely dark. Maybe it was more about routine and occupying her time. Eating, dressing, cleaning the house, shopping, getting ready for bed, all testified that the old heart was still ticking and the lungs still inflating. Movement told you you were still alive.

Sometimes it was the only proof you had.

The *click click click* of her high-heeled slippers broke the crypt-like silence in the house as Geri made her way to the living-room window and carefully peered through the Venetian blinds. The street lamp caught the shiny reflectors on the pedals as a neighbor's child rode by on a bike. Parents nowadays let their kids stay out till all hours, then wondered why they turned into juvenile delinquents. *Like that Nick Cervantes.* He was probably prowling the streets right now peddling his drugs. Rumor had it that he and Tracy had been seeing a lot of each other ever since he'd gotten out of Dolby. *Tracy.* Geri always did think that girl was trouble—a bad seed—just like that girl in the movie *The Bad Seed,* only Tracy wasn't a blonde and she hadn't killed anyone, God forbid. But imagine, hanging around the likes of Nick Cervantes. Geri would rather see Gloria a spinster forever than take up with someone like that. Now this was one more thing for Geri to worry about. Tracy had always exerted a negative influence on Gloria. How in the world was she going to keep Gloria away from Tracy and that awful boy?

She spread the two slats farther apart and studied the now-quiet street before letting them snap back into place. Seems the whole world was going to hell in a handbasket. *Oh, Gloria, Gloria. Will you ever understand? I wanted to keep you safe and help you achieve some measure of happiness. And oh, how I wanted to save you from your own expectations. Nothing is ever the way you want it, Gloria. Nothing.*

Geri's heels tapped across the hardwood floor like a wood-pecker as she headed for the living room and her only nighttime companion, the little fifteen-inch Zenith. At least Gloria's expectations, like her looks, were meager. And at least Gloria didn't have to live up to the expectations of an entire town. Sometimes Geri wished she had never been a Miss America contestant. Appleton never forgave her for not going all the way and winning the title. At least that's how she saw it.

Whenever Geri got on that kick, Virginia told her it was utter nonsense and to stop being so self-absorbed—this from the queen of self-absorption. But brains, not beauty, had been Virginia's ally. How could Virginia possibly understand what kind of expectations a thing like beauty could generate? Besides, Geri had long suspected that Virginia held a secret contempt for the beautiful. People could say what they wanted, they could say they valued a keen mind, but when one of those so-called brilliant businessmen finally got around to dumping the little wife, it was never an ugly woman who became her successor.

Oh, Gloria! Gloria! How can I make you understand?

~⦿ ⦿~

All the way home Cutter whistled along with the music blaring from his car radio. He didn't know why he was so happy, why he felt as light as a marshmallow. He flipped off the radio. No use acting like an idiot. But there, in the silence, he felt his lips pucker and heard a poor rendition of Barry Manilow's "Looks Like We Made It" twittering from his mouth.

Don't be a fool, Press.

What was the big deal, anyway? He and Gloria had finally had a normal conversation. So what? But she had *actually* shared her thoughts with him, had *actually* let him into her very private space.

But it was only for a minute. Then she clammed up.

Cutter pulled his Saab into the driveway of his friend's sprawling Tudor and got out. The house was much too big—made him feel like the lone occupant of a hotel. But he wouldn't admit that to anyone, especially Virginia. The rent was cheap, and that was the main thing, since all his extra cash these days was going to pay legal fees. He and his two partners had finally retained a high-powered attorney to fight the EPA for the right to build on The Lakes, and that was costing plenty. Still, he'd be happy when the lease on the Tudor was up. Then he'd find some modest condo somewhere.

Actually, if the truth were known, it really wasn't the size of the house that bothered him. It was being alone. He wasn't used to it. Virginia had always crowded him. He unlocked the door, then flipped on the light.

His footsteps tapped out a ragged tune as he walked down the marble hallway into the kitchen. At the touch of his fingers the overhead high-hats went on, flooding the room with light.

What's the matter, Press? Trying to chase away the boogieman?

No. Boogiemen didn't frighten him. Only thin, shy girls who seemed to get prettier every day. *Knock it off, Press. You blew it. Gloria Bickford hates you. Has hated you since you both were kids. And you have only yourself to blame.*

The keys made a clinking sound as he tossed them on the counter. A few steps more and he was by the little built-in desk tucked between the kitchen and laundry room. He checked the answering machine. No messages.

Just look at the grief he'd given Gloria over Santa Claus, as if it were her fault he was dead. The fact that someone killed the guy before he could talk should have raised a red flag. Made Cutter take the whole thing seriously. On the other hand, characters like that had lots of enemies. Santa Claus could have been killed for any number of reasons. Still, he could have been kinder to Gloria about it. Why was he so obnoxious with her, anyway? Always giving her a hard time? He never seemed to say the right thing.

It was time to change. Time to stop being so all-infernal . . . rough? opinionated? obnoxious? unreasonable? Okay . . . okay, all of the above. It was time he stopped worrying about Gloria getting the upper hand. Gloria wasn't Virginia Press. She wouldn't try to manipulate him, control him. At least, he didn't think so.

He opened the bottom drawer of the desk and pulled out the phone book, then flipped to "Private Investigators." *See Detective Agencies.* A few seconds more and he found the right page. When Gil Crestmore's name was the only one that appeared, Cutter closed the book. What did he expect in a town the size of Appleton? Gil handled mostly domestic stuff: infidelity, locating deadbeat dads, and the like. He'd have to get a PI from somewhere else—Eckerd City, maybe—and have him check out this Santa Claus. Maybe have him check out Eric Slone too.

Then he'd have to apologize to Gloria and tell her he was taking all this a little more seriously.

~◆ ◆~

Chapter Six

GLORIA FLIPPED OPEN her bankbook and looked at the total. Almost $3,000. She couldn't believe she still had that much in her savings considering her recent relocation, which included furnishing Sam Hidel's apartment. And she'd need every penny. Already she had put feelers out around town regarding a good used car.

Only . . .

Grandma Quinn was running up high grocery bills, and Mother seemed bent on using that as an excuse for putting her into a nursing home. Gloria couldn't let that happen.

❧ ☙

Geri Bickford smiled at the overweight matron taking her through the winding halls of Clancy County Home for the Aged and tried to ignore the overpowering smell of urine and rubbing alcohol. Already she had seen the cafeteria and rec room, both of which would benefit from a gallon of Lysol and some paint. Now the matron was taking her to one of the women's wards, and Geri found herself slowing her pace. Groans and unintelligible words, mingled with muffled sobs, wafted through the halls, and suddenly Geri wasn't sure she was up to it. It was nothing like she'd expected. Where were the army of smiling, helpful nurses and aides? The carts full of candy and flowers and greeting cards? The clean, happy patients?

Down one end of the hall, Geri watched with a sick, fluttering stomach as an orderly the size of O.J. Simpson strapped an old, shriveled woman into a chair.

"We have to restrain some of our patients; otherwise they'd fall—just slip right out of their seats," the matron said as though sensing Geri's revulsion.

Years of practice enabled Geri to widen her smile as she saw the old woman, limp as spaghetti, offer no resistance. Geri had not stopped smiling since she'd entered Clancy County, and her cheeks ached. The endless cycle of beauty pageants had helped her develop that stock smile, the one she had been wearing for ages and ages—ever since she had returned home from the Miss America pageant a loser. But now, even her stock smile was hard to keep on. Maybe she was getting old. Maybe gravity was sagging more than her skin.

Her lips had never felt so heavy.

"We take pride in our patient care." The matron, dressed in a gray two-piece suit with a light-gray silk blouse and neat, short gray hair apparently thought Geri was enjoying the tour because she kept glancing over at her and smiling approvingly. "Safety is number one with us. You're lucky your mother lives in Clancy County. We're one of the best nursing homes around. Not like some of those other meat warehouses that pass themselves off as homes for the aged. But see for yourself." The matron swung her arm in a wide arc as if she were a tour guide for the Metropolitan Museum of Art showing Geri a series of Rembrandts. Geri peered through the open door of the ward, where twenty beds formed two rows and were filled with women in various stages of coherency. Only one bed was empty, and Geri guessed it belonged to the little shrunken woman strapped in the chair at the end of the hall. The smell in the room was overwhelming—a noxious mix of body odor and body waste and antiseptics and vomit.

Geri was sure she was going to vomit too and pushed past the matron.

"Your mother's fortunate we have a few vacancies in the next ward." The matron trotted behind her. "She won't have to sleep in the hall. But I suggest you get your application in quickly. Our beds fill up fast."

Geri clutched the packet of papers to her chest, forced that smile back on her face, then made her way to the lobby as fast as she could.

How was she ever going to convince Gloria to leave her grandmother in this place?

❧ ☙

"What do you mean, someone's trying to buy Clive McGreedy's farm?" Gloria swiveled in her chair so she could face Wanda, and what she saw told her this wasn't a joke.

"Yeah. Can you believe it? Now everyone's trying to figure out why. Guess they think it could make their property worth something too. Paul says he heard it was for a new 725,000-square-foot super-mall that's gonna have all kinds of shops and a huge movie complex, plus some restaurants. But Pearl Owens says someone told her it's for tollbooths and a new interstate. So looks like no one knows for sure what's going on."

"I can't believe it. Clive's farm . . . that's like saying we're selling Appleton High, or Town Hall, or—"

"Gloria, it's only a *farm.*"

"It's more than a farm. It's an important community institution, it's a . . . a memory maker."

"A what?"

Gloria shrugged. "I can't explain it. All I know is that Appleton wouldn't be the same without Clive's farm. He's not selling, is he?"

"Can't say." Wanda's huge hips rolled from side to side like an ocean liner in rough seas. She anchored beside Gloria's desk and patted her teased hair that didn't move an inch. "Hugh Bascome at the *Gazette* said it would be good for our town—bring some money in."

"How does he figure that?"

"Hugh's smart. Can sniff out the *whys* and *wherefores* of a thing. Guess that's what makes him a good newspaper man. Anyway, he said Clive's farm, the way it's situated on the Old Post Road, is pretty centrally located between the Four Towns." Wanda was referring to New Canterbury, Shepherd's Field, Dolby, and Appleton. "He said if you drew a circle around Clive's farm on a map, you'd see it's like the hub of a four-spoke wheel with the Four Towns radiating outward. It's the perfect place for a shopping mall. A central location like that could make it lucrative for some of those big chain stores."

"Yeah, and kill Main Street businesses."

Wanda placed both hands on the sides of her head and pushed up on her hair, making it rise and look like an inverted bird's nest. "Well, people *would* come from miles away. Hugh said he always thought Clive's farm would be a great place for commerce. Guess someone else thinks so too."

"Well, I for one hope it never happens. And for now, I'm happy it's all just speculation."

"Not all. The shopping center thing is speculation, and the interstate. But not the fact that Clive was offered good money for his land."

"Says who?"

"Says Clive. And he said it was so much money he'd be a fool not to think about it."

Gloria turned to her computer and tried to tune out Wanda's dissertation on how smart Hugh Bascome was and how he was never wrong. Instead, she began to think about what life would be like in Appleton without the McGreedy farm, and she decided she didn't think she'd like it.

❧ ❦

Cutter Press dialed the number he'd gotten from searching Google and felt stupid. Who hires a private detective off the Internet? He had never ordered anything off the Internet, not even that pair of Kenneth Coles he liked so much and could have gotten for half price. But he had been impressed with what he'd seen on the Web site. Looked like the agency covered everything from IT security to full-blown investigations and intelligence, with an emphasis on corporate whistle-blowing. If the agency did half of what it claimed, it might just be the perfect vehicle to uncover the identity of Santa Claus and any possible connection he might have had with Eric Slone.

"Hello?" A soft, almost girlish voice sputtered over the phone line, and Cutter was about to hang up when the voice followed with "Bryce Detective Agency." It had to be Bryce's secretary.

"Ah . . . is Mr. Bryce there?"

"Speaking."

No way. This feminine-sounding person couldn't possibly be a detective. This had to be a hoax. *Way to go, Press. Want to buy the Brooklyn Bridge? Off the Internet?*

"This is Sam Bryce," the voice said, sounding a bit impatient. "How can I help you?"

"I'm looking for a detective . . . a real detective . . ."

The soft voice chuckled. "I *am* a real detective, with a license and everything. It's posted on my Web site. You can check it out if you want."

"Sorry . . . I'm just a little uncomfortable . . . about using the Internet, I mean. And you don't exactly sound like a detective."

"Yeah, I get that a lot. I guess people are expecting Humphrey Bogart. Anyway, if you read my Web site, you'll see that I take on only a handful of cases a month, and I'm pretty booked. Besides, I don't do divorce or that kind of thing. So if your wife's cheating and you want a nice big photo to prove it in court, I'm not your guy."

"What do you do?" Cutter asked, even though he had read every word on that Web site and already knew.

"Fraud, mostly. But also bribery, extortion, industrial espionage, money laundering, stuff like that. I've got access to a load of databases and can find out how to get access to more if I need to. We're very high-tech here, Tallulah, Christine, and me."

"Tallulah?"

"My computer, and Christine is my wife."

It defied reason, but Cutter was beginning to take Sam Bryce more seriously. "Do you have much experience?"

Laughter wafted over the phone. "Been in the business fifteen years. Ever hear of the Knickerbocker case?"

"You mean the one about the guy who embezzled millions from his company?"

"That's right. That was us. We cracked the case wide-open."

Cutter whistled softly. Charles Knickerbocker, a purchasing agent for Xavier Corp., had funneled small amounts of money from hundreds of accounts into a dozen bogus companies—all his. The embezzlement had covered a period of ten years, at the end of which Knickerbocker had amassed 2.3 million dollars. The case caused a big stir because, unlike the arrogant and outlandish crooks in the Tyco and WorldCom scandals, Charles Knickerbocker had been a most patient and unobtrusive thief. Cutter vaguely remembered that the case had been cracked through a series of small, unrelated details that finally led to Knickerbocker's Swiss account. "Maybe you are the right guy after all."

"Like I said, I'm pretty booked, but tell me your problem, and if it interests me, maybe I'll stretch a bit and take you on."

For the next half hour, Cutter told Sam Bryce about Tucker Mattson, The Lakes, Spencer Jordon, the EPA, the newsletters, the picketers, and finally Santa Claus. When he was finished, there was a long silence.

"Well. Does the case interest you?"

"Yes, Mr. . . ."

"Cutter, Cutter Press."

"Yes, Mr. Press, it interests me very much."

⌘ ⌘

Gloria ignored the tinkling of the hanging overhead bell as she entered Sam Hidel's Grocery. It had been a long day, and before she headed for her apartment in the back, she needed to take care of some business.

Sam Hidel was behind the cash register, as usual, and Minnie, his wife, was on the floor stocking shelves and talking to the customers, making sure they found everything they needed. The store was nearly empty, with the dinner hour approaching, and Gloria was pleased when she saw that Sam was alone at the register. She headed straight for him.

"I've come about Grandma's account," Gloria said quietly, not wanting Pearl Owens, who was down aisle two by the Doritos, to overhear. Appleton's saying "Tella Pearl, tella world" wasn't without foundation. "I'd like to see how much she owes."

"Why? You planning to pay it?"

Gloria nodded.

"Well, now, I thought your mother would be taking care of that." Sam tilted his head backward as though waiting for an explanation. He looked disappointed when Gloria didn't give one.

"How much does she owe?" Gloria repeated.

"Well, now. Let's see. I got it right here." Sam pulled out a green metal box from under the counter and opened it. It was full of alphabetized index cards. He flipped to the Qs, then pulled out a card that had figures scrawled over the front and back. Sam squinted at the last notation. "$726.31." He smacked his lips. "Never should have let her run it up that high. Just didn't have the heart to turn her down."

Gloria pulled an Appleton Savings Bank envelope from her purse. It contained ten one-hundred-dollar bills, the money she had withdrawn from her savings during lunch. She opened the envelope, counted out eight bills, and placed them on the counter in front of Sam. "Please let me know every time she puts anything on account, and I'll give you the money."

"You mean you still want me to let her charge? Even all that flour and sugar and stuff?"

Gloria nodded.

"Well, now." Sam scratched the top of his head. "Guess you don't have the heart to turn her down either."

Cutter Press couldn't believe he was standing in front of Gloria's apartment and actually knocking on her door. Would she think he was a loser? Too late now. The lock snapped, then the door opened, and Gloria stood in front of him in her bare feet and sweats, looking so pretty he wanted to gulp but didn't. And that expression on her face . . . just like the time he'd trapped her in Clive McGreedy's barn—no, not quite—not as panic-stricken, but it was obvious she was more than surprised to see him.

"Ah . . . I was in the neighborhood . . . and there are a couple of things I wanted to tell you . . . Mind if I come in?" He was about to push past her, then held himself in check. No. He'd wait to be asked, and if she didn't invite him in, then he'd know she thought he really was a loser.

"Sure . . ." Gloria opened the door wider, surprise still on her face. "Come in. Excuse the mess. I just got home and—"

"Gloria, you don't need to apologize. Not to me." Cutter bit the inside of his lip as he walked past her. *What exactly was that supposed to mean?*

She pointed to a pale blue plaid couch with floral throw pillows. "Have a seat. I'll make us some coffee. I only have decaf . . . and it's instant. That okay?"

Cutter nodded and sat down, then watched her traipse off into the kitchen. He could hear her opening cabinets, then the sound of clanking pots and the subtler sound of mugs knocking together. He studied the apartment. It was a fraction of the size of his place, but even at a glance he preferred it over his, with its cozy stuffed couch and chair and small TV tucked in the corner. Plants and pictures filled the rest of the space.

Cutter had heard that Gloria had furnished her entire apartment from the thrift store on Brandise, but somehow she had managed to make the apartment look anything but bargain-basement. He had always thought her hardworking and resourceful, so he wasn't surprised. He tried to find the mess she spoke of and saw only a folded newspaper on the pine coffee table and a pair of sneakers near the stuffed chair. On the end table was an empty glass, a small plate, and a tuft of hair that must belong to the cat he had seen scoot under the couch when he came in. Hardly a mess. But he could see how, after living with compulsively neat Geri Bickford, Gloria would exaggerate this minor clutter.

Strange how he felt comfortable here. And not nearly as nervous as he thought he'd be.

"You still take cream and sugar?" Gloria said, poking her head out of the kitchen. Cutter nodded.

"I see you have a cat," he shouted, wanting to fill the silence. "Didn't see any broken legs, though." He was referring to Gloria's proclivity for taking in wounded animals. It was one of the many things he liked about her.

"No, Tiger's a fine, healthy cat." Gloria entered the room carrying a tray, then set it down on the coffee table. The sugar bowl and creamer and jar of instant coffee were full; the two mugs were empty. "But you didn't come about my cat." She stood looking down at him as though waiting for his explanation, but she didn't seem annoyed or in any hurry.

"I hired a private detective to check out our Santa Claus character," he said. "And if something turns up, maybe even Eric Slone."

"I thought you were through with all that. I thought you said he was just a crackpot and you didn't want to get involved."

"Well, maybe I was wrong."

"Cutter Press wrong?"

"Yeah, hard to believe." Cutter watched Gloria settle into

the recliner, watched her swing her bare feet under her and wiggle her bottom until she got comfortable, just like she used to do when she was a little girl. "Can't be right about everything." He was relieved when he heard that light, lilting laughter of hers. This was easier than he'd expected.

"So what will you do if your detective turns up something? Are you really prepared to take on Eric Slone?"

Now Cutter laughed. "One thing at a time, Gloria."

She shrugged, gave him a smile that made perspiration bead around his neck, then rose from her chair at the kettle's whistle and headed for the kitchen.

"You hear about Clive McGreedy?" he asked in a loud voice.

"Yes, the whole town's talking about it." Gloria reappeared, holding a steaming kettle in one hand. "I hate the thought of that old farm going. I would miss it, and Clive too, of course." She filled his mug, then hers.

"I didn't think you were that attached. I thought you hated the place since that's where I . . . embarrassed you."

Gloria placed the kettle on the tray, her mouth tightening. "We've never talked about that."

"No. You want to now?"

"I don't know. It was so long ago and . . ."

"For whatever it's worth, I know I acted like a jerk. And I was wrong. I embarrassed you and made you feel small." He could see he had touched a nerve. Red blotches marred her cheeks like rosacea.

"I don't think you understand just how . . . just how small you did make me feel. Kissing me like that in front of everyone as if it was a personal challenge to change the frog into a princess."

"Boys can be stupid, Gloria. And thoughtless." She sat down, but didn't look comfortable. "It wasn't my intention to hurt you." He heard her gasp.

"Then why, *for heaven's sake,* did you do it?"

"To show off. I was just showing off. I guess I wanted to impress—"

"Your devoted followers?"

"Yeah. And *you.*" Cutter could see he had said something very wrong. Maybe he was moving too fast. Trying to heal the relationship between them too quickly. Or maybe he was just a bonehead and Gloria was never going to come around. Would never forgive him for his past stupidity. "I wanted to impress you," he repeated against his will.

Gloria's eyes looked like Oreos, then lemon wedges as she squinted at him. "You think it impresses a girl when you insult her by calling her a frog?"

Cutter waved his hand impatiently in the air. "You really think I meant that?" He could see by the tears welling up in her eyes that she had. He really was a bonehead. Guys called each other names all the time. It had never occurred to him that a girl would be sensitive about a thing like that. He put his hand back on his lap and just stared at Gloria, at her lovely eyes and fine, strong chin that gave her face character, at her shiny hair that made her look so attractive it caused him to perspire, at her mouth that could form a sunny smile so wonderful it would make any man forget his worst day. "That was just talk, Gloria. I never, *never* thought you were a frog."

⁓◈⁓

It had been a long time since Gloria had wept on her pillow, but after Cutter Press left, she had herself a good cry. And then she felt better than she had felt since returning to Appleton.

⁓◈⁓

96

Chapter Seven

GLORIA FOLLOWED AGNES KELLER down a dingy hallway, then up the narrow stairs that creaked and groaned with age. All the visible curtains were drawn, and the lack of light and fresh air made the house look and smell like an old museum. She really didn't want to come, but Jesus had overruled her. On top of that, there was Cutter's offhanded apology, which, for some reason, made her feel obligated.

So here she was.

About to enter the den of the Dragon Lady.

Agnes ushered her into a large room, cavelike and dark with all that heavy furniture and no visible light, then closed the door. It took a while for Gloria's eyes to distinguish the shape on the bed as being that of Virginia Press.

"Come closer," said a thin, dry voice.

Gloria opened the door Agnes had just closed, and chided herself. Virginia Press was a sickly, diminutive woman. What did Gloria have to fear? Still, she crept only as far as the middle of the room, and stopped.

"Agnes told me you were coming. In forty years I've never heard Agnes tell a joke, so I knew it was true. I'm glad you're here."

Maybe it was Virginia's words or the sight of her, so small and pathetic, that dispelled the foreboding Gloria had, but something broke it, and she walked over to the bed. "Nothing's changed. This room is still how I remember it." She heard a soft chuckle that sounded almost like a cough.

"What were you? Ten, the last time?"

Gloria nodded. "Yes," she said when she realized that in the poor light, Virginia probably hadn't seen the nod.

"Cutter paid dearly for that. Putting you up to such a thing."

"I was as much to blame. He dared me, and I took him up on it. But I didn't have to." Gloria thought it strange that they should be having this conversation. Surely Virginia Press hadn't asked to see her just to rehash a past misadventure? Although, lately, the Presses seemed to be going in for that sort of thing.

"What was it again? You were to steal my perfume—"

"No," Gloria said, looking down on the frail woman. "I was merely to bring it to Cutter to prove I had gone to your room all by myself."

"And then you broke it. It took Agnes months to get that smell out of the hardwood floor and to glue that bottle together. She swore it shattered into a million pieces. It was very expensive crystal . . . a gift from Cutter's father. So I insisted. Of course, it was unusable after that . . . but I kept it just the same . . . don't know why exactly. I'm not really sentimental."

"It all seems so silly now. That stunt got me grounded for a month. But honestly, I never expected to see you coming up those stairs as I came down."

"Yes . . . I suppose for a child of ten it would be scary seeing the Dragon Lady heading her way."

"How did——?"

"I know that Cutter and his friends called me Dragon Lady?" Virginia rose on one spindly elbow. "Oh, child, there wasn't anything Cutter did or said that escaped me." She fell back against the great scrolled mahogany headboard that must have taken a skilled craftsman months to carve. Gloria found herself fluffing pillows and helping Virginia rise to a sitting position. "Cutter was always thinking up mean names for people. But you already know that, don't you?"

Gloria picked up the frosted pitcher from the nightstand and poured fresh ice water into Virginia's empty glass.

"I know how thoughtless he can be, but I suppose all the psychiatrists in the world would say that's my fault. And they would be right. I always had too many brains and not enough heart. I've always tried to roll and stretch Cutter, like dough, into a more acceptable shape. And I haven't been too gentle about it either. But you already know that too, don't you?"

Gloria handed Virginia the water and wondered what was going on, then realized Jesus already knew and, in due time, would let her in on it too.

"And now that shape is someone I don't like and someone who doesn't like me."

"Mrs. Press, I don't think——"

"You're going to have to start calling me Virginia, or we're not going to get very far."

"I . . . don't think I can. In the first place, I'm not used to it. And in the second place, Mother would have a fit if she found out. Then, for months, I'd have to listen to her go on about how important it is to respect your elders."

Virginia chuckled. "Yes, Geri was always one for appearances. But that needn't concern us. I really want you to call me Virginia. *Please.* Chalk it up to the foible of an old lady. Nobody needs to know. It'll be our little secret. What do you say?" She held out her hand as though asking Gloria to seal their secret pact with a shake.

Gloria took it, thinking how much like a dried leaf it felt and fearing it would crumble at the slightest pressure. So she just held it, as though it were something precious, all the while noting how thin Virginia's wrist and arm were. "Okay . . . Virginia."

The elderly woman smiled and seemed inordinately pleased. "I know you're wondering why I wanted to see you. It's about Cutter."

Gloria released Virginia's hand. "That's a dead horse. Let's not beat it anymore. Cutter and I are simply not going to get married. We have no interest in each other. As a matter of fact, we hardly get along. So no amount of coercion's going to work; it's just going to—" Gloria stopped when she heard a faint chuckle.

"No. I've already coerced myself out of a son . . . and a daughter-in-law. I don't want to force anything on anyone anymore."

"Then what do you want?"

"I want you to come and see me once in a while. Let me talk to you about Cutter and—"

"*Virginia.*"

"No, not about marrying him. Nothing like that."

"Okay, then why?"

"Because I want you to understand him. I want you to understand why he's the way he is, and maybe in the process understand me a little too."

"Virginia, I don't see what purpose that will serve. And to be honest, I have little interest in understanding why Cutter does anything."

"You've always had a kind heart. Oh, yes, I heard all about that bird you tried to save, and Clive McGreedy's kittens, and so many other things that made me know you. And in the coming months, Cutter's going to need a friend with a tender heart. One that can help him wade through all the issues he's got stacked up in his head like magazines." Virginia laughed. "He's got a thirty-year subscription to *Life* stored in that brain of his, all piled up and needing to be read." When her laughter turned into a cough, Virginia covered her mouth until it passed. "A lifetime subscription, Gloria," she finally said, "and he needs a friend to help him come to terms with those issues. You two have a lot more in common than you think. And I know my son well enough to say this—you are the best possible person for the job."

"I'm not a psychiatrist, Virginia. If Cutter needs therapy, you've got to get him professional help."

Virginia's frail-looking hand gripped Gloria's wrist like steel pincers. "He doesn't need a psychiatrist, child. He needs a *friend.* You may not believe this, but even though I don't like my son, I do love him. In my own way, I do love him. And I worry about him. I worry about him having no one when I'm gone. And quite honestly, I could use a friend myself. Because I don't mind telling you, I'm a little unnerved by all this. Geri won't be much help. She doesn't have the courage for it. But you—someone who can steal perfume out of the Dragon Lady's room—someone who can leave Appleton just like that—someone who can buck probably the two pushiest, meanest females in town, now that's someone I'd like to have in my corner."

"For heaven's sake, Virginia, what are you talking about?"

Virginia released Gloria and slumped back against her pillows. "I'm dying. Dr. Grant says I've got less than six months, more like three." She closed her eyes. Her eyelids looked purple in the dim light, and puffy, and when she opened them again, Gloria saw the fear. Suddenly, Virginia lunged, reclaiming Gloria's wrist. "But you must swear you won't tell Cutter. Not a word. Swear it!" And she wouldn't let go until Gloria nodded.

～❦ ❦～

"I want to thank you, Gloria, for visiting my mother."

"Who told you?"

"Agnes." Cutter changed the phone from his right to his left hand and wondered why Gloria sounded so strange. "She said you stayed for over an hour. That was kind."

"It doesn't take a lot of kindness to visit someone you've known all your life."

"Yeah . . . well . . . I know my mother can strain the limits of human endurance after five minutes. So, thanks. What did the Dragon Lady want, anyway?"

"Haven't you gotten over calling people names?"

"Sorry . . . didn't think it would upset you. I meant it more as a joke, really. Anyway . . . what did my mother have to say?"

"Maybe you should go visit her and find out for yourself."

Cutter couldn't put his finger on it, but there was definitely something wrong. "Yeah . . . well . . . I just wanted to say thanks and to tell you that Clive McGreedy just put his car up for sale. Only seven years old. And you know how he takes care of things. You can eat off the floor of his barn. I imagine that car engine won't be much different. How about I drive you over and we take a look? You did me a favor. Now I owe you one."

"For heaven's sake, Cutter, you don't owe me anything!"

Boy, was she touchy. And here he was thinking he was making some progress, getting on friendlier ground. "Look, you're the one who's been going all around town asking if anyone has a good used car for sale. I was just trying to be neighborly. You want to see the car or not?"

There was a long silence, then, "How much?"

"Thirty-five hundred. But I bet you could get Clive to come down a bit. He's always liked you." Another long silence.

"I don't think so," Gloria finally said. "It's a bit too pricy."

"I thought you were looking for something around three thousand." Cutter twisted his Appleton High ring around his finger and wondered why women were so confounded unpredictable. "Isn't that what you've been saying? At least, that's the price Pearl Owens has been broadcasting." He heard Gloria sigh.

"I'm going to have to pass. But thank you, Cutter. That was very nice of you."

The peevishness had finally gone from her voice. At least that was something. "Well, okay. If you don't want to look at it." He twisted his ring again. "What's your bottom line, anyway? In case I come across another good buy?"

"Actually, I'm going to have to put this whole car business on hold for a while. But Cutter . . . thanks. I mean that." Her voice had lost its edge and was sweet, almost as sweet as one of Clive McGreedy's apples. "I really appreciate the call."

Absently he traced figure eights on the kitchen counter with his finger. "Sure . . . anytime." Why couldn't a woman be more like a man? Solid and sure? Say what she means?

"And Cutter . . . please go see your mother."

There went Gloria's voice again, changing like the weather, suddenly stormy and cold. "Why? You trying to tell me something's wrong?"

"I'm not trying to tell you anything. I'm just saying your mother would welcome a visit. She . . . misses you."

After Cutter hung up, he paced the floors of the big, lonely Tudor replaying the entire conversation. Twenty minutes later, he still couldn't make sense of it and turned on the TV.

Gloria Bickford could still rattle him like no one else.

~꽃 꽃~

Gloria sat on the couch with Tiger sprawled across her lap. She listened to him purr and tried to get her mind off Cutter, but it wouldn't budge. She shouldn't have been so curt. It wasn't his fault she had made that unreasonable promise to Virginia. How could she have let Virginia talk her into something so wrong? A son had a right to know when his mother was dying.

Gloria let her hand slide to the side, then felt Tiger nudge it with his head. "Where is your pride?" she whispered, smiling at his shameless effort to get attention. She resumed the gentle scratching behind his ears and thanked God for giving her such a pleasant companion. Then she began thinking about Cutter again.

She had been almost rude. And here he was trying so hard to be nice . . . so . . . what was the word Cutter used? Neighborly. Yes, so neighborly. And she had been so miserable.

Oh, why did she make that promise to Virginia?

~꽃 꽃~

Geri Bickford pulled her gold Volvo to a stop in front of 52 Elm Street, then turned off the engine, and just sat for a long time, staring out the window. What was she going to do? Sit here all day? Suppose someone spotted her and came over to ask what she was doing? She twisted the rhinestone tennis bracelet around her wrist, then drilled the steering wheel with her fire-engine-red nails.

When she spotted Ivy Gordon's car in her rearview mirror,

Geri sucked in her breath and held it, as if the slightest exhale was capable of alerting the world to her presence. But Ivy passed without noticing her and drove down the street out of sight. Geri scanned the neighborhood and was relieved to see it deserted. That's all she needed, some busybody grilling her.

Sunshine streaming through the passenger windows made the interior of the car swelter. No way could she stay like this much longer. Either she'd have to open a window or open the door and get out.

Instead of doing either, she pulled down the visor and checked her hair in the mirror. Now why was she doing that? Her mother never noticed her hair anyway. Or her makeup or what she wore. It never seemed to matter to Hannah *what* Geri looked like. At least Geri had put more effort in with Gloria. She had tried for years to help her daughter improve herself. Surely, that was to her credit. Nobody could say she hadn't tried. Not that Gloria appreciated it.

Gloria.

How was she going to tell Gloria about Clancy County Home for the Aged? Maybe it would be best to first get Grandma Quinn to agree to move there before bringing it up with Gloria again. But Geri had spent half the night trying to come up with a convincing argument, and she couldn't think of one single thing that would carry any weight with her mother.

Geri fiddled with her bracelet, running her fingers, over and over again, across the zircons and then the gold-plated clasp. Even from where she sat, she saw that green paint was peeling off her mother's front door; saw that the front step was listing to the right; saw the crop of weeds overrunning the small flowerbed to the left. *The neighbors must really love this. They must talk about this eyesore of a house. About crazy Hannah Quinn who sings gospel hymns at the top of her lungs while baking like a fiend. About the possibility of crazy Hannah really setting fire to her house next time and, inadvertently, to the whole neighborhood as well.*

No. Geri couldn't allow this to go on. She'd have to march right in there and explain things to her mother. Lay it all on the line. Tell her what people around town were saying. Point out the pathetic state of her house. Confront her about those ridiculous grocery bills. Tell her that she was going to a nursing home and that was that.

Geri gave her bracelet a final twist, but instead of opening the door and heading for the listing step and peeling door, she turned the key in the ignition and drove away.

~◐ ◑~

"Well, the madness has started." Gloria handed Wanda a pile of new print orders and watched her blow wisps of bleached-blonde hair from her forehead. "Charlie Axlerod wants flyers listing all the contests the Chamber of Commerce will be sponsoring. Tad Bicks wants raffle tickets for his 'Ice-Cream Extravaganza' sweepstakes. And Sam Hidel wants a bulletin of specials he'll be running the whole two weeks of the Apple Festival. And that's just the beginning."

Wanda flipped through the rest of the POs in her hand and grinned. "Yeah. Don't you love it?"

Gloria's eyebrows arched. Maybe she'd love it more if Wanda didn't get so crazy. But Gloria knew that by the middle of the Apple Festival both she and Paul would be tempted to put tranquilizers into Wanda's daily SlimFast. "Well . . . *love* might be too strong a word."

"Okay, how about the word *appreciate*? Because it's going to be all this Apple Festival work that pays for that new computer you're so fond of."

Gloria eyed her Pentium 4 HP and her seventeen-inch SyncMaster flatscreen monitor and smiled. "*Appreciate* is a good word."

"I thought so." Wanda's big hips bounced from side to side as she moved around Gloria's desk, going nowhere in particular. "But we've gotten a lot more orders than last year, and for the life of me I can't figure out why."

"Maybe because word's gotten out that you have an innovative genius on staff."

"Think so?" There was a mischievous look in Wanda's hazel eyes.

"Could be."

"Then you're taking responsibility?"

"Responsibility? You mean credit, don't you?"

"No. I mean responsibility. And since you obviously are, I think it only right you also take responsibility to correct the situation."

"What are you talking about?"

"Overtime. It looks like you'll have to work lots of overtime."

Gloria leaned back in her chair and smiled. "Sure, Wanda. I *love* overtime. I've got some extra expenses, and at time and a half I should clear them up in a jiffy."

Wanda's face reddened right up to her bleached roots. "Now . . . who said anything about time and a half?"

"Paul." Now Wanda looked positively purple.

"Paul! Paul! Get in here!" Presently, the tall, lanky man appeared with a green towel slung over one shoulder. "Did you promise this upstart time and a half for OT?"

"Wanda, you know people around town swear that both you and Charlie Axlerod have the first dollar you ever made. You don't wanna go playing into that misconception by taking advantage of your help."

"*Taking advantage?* Pfffff." Wanda dismissed her husband with a wave of her hand, then turned and winked at Gloria. "Before you know it, the upstart's going to own the place."

～❦ ❦～

Gloria unlocked her bike chain and shoved it in her backpack. The lock was something new. Something she'd stop using once the Apple Festival was over. But the festival wasn't even here, and already strange faces were crowding the shops and streets. She had stayed late trying to fill some of the POs she had given Wanda earlier and could see, by the last dying glow of the sun, that she had stayed longer than she'd intended. Not that she was afraid of pedaling home in the dark. She had gotten over Santa Claus a while ago and no longer felt skittish at night. But now it was too late to go to Grandma's. The trip took at least thirty minutes by bike, and that meant another thirty minutes home, and she was just too tired. *She could sure use a car.*

But that dream was on hold. Sam Hidel had just given her another one of Grandma's bills. Seventy-five dollars. It seemed like every time Gloria had extra money, something came up. At this rate she'd be eighty by the time she got her car.

She kicked the stand up and was about to mount when she saw a man standing in the shadow of the building. A second look to see if she recognized him told her he was a stranger, an out-of-towner—probably here for the festival. But why was he hanging around this end of town? The shops were closed. The movie theater, Tad's Ice Cream Parlor, and the arcade all were at the other end of town.

No, she wasn't going down that road again. Letting every

fluttering leaf and scampering squirrel make her jump. She had buried Santa Claus once and for all. Quickly, Gloria got on her bike and pedaled away. Not ever bothering to look back.

❦ ❧

When Gloria came out of Appleton Printers the next night and saw the same man lingering in the shadows, she wasn't as calm about it. And when she pulled away on her bike, she looked back for one brief second.

❦ ❧

Chapter Eight

IT WAS SATURDAY, and Gloria sat in Grandma Quinn's kitchen watching her mix oatmeal cookie dough in her beat-up metal bowl. Already the batch in the oven was causing Gloria's mouth to water. And the smell . . . Back in Eckerd, Gloria had dreamed of her grandma's kitchen and these smells. There was something about the aroma of cookies that made Gloria feel that all was right with the world, even when she knew it wasn't. Like now.

Grandma said she was baking them just for Gloria, but Gloria wasn't so sure. Just this morning Sam Hidel told Gloria that Grandma Quinn had been in twice that week, emptying his shelves of flour and sugar and other baking goods. The expense was getting enormous. And that wasn't counting the cab fare every time Grandma came to Main Street.

Mother hadn't mentioned putting Grandma into a nursing home again, but it was only a matter of time. And what was Mother going to say when she found out Gloria was paying Sam Hidel's bill? She'd probably blow her stack.

Well, let her.

Still.

Gloria should try to put a stop to it. She should try to persuade Grandma to go shopping only once a week, and when her baking supplies ran out . . . well . . . they just ran out, that's all. But the happy look on Grandma's face as she scooped rounded spoonfuls of batter and dropped them onto the lightly greased baking sheet cracked Gloria's resolve.

She sipped the green tea Grandma had made her and tried to regroup. Maybe taking another route was best. She thought for a moment, then hit on an idea. "Grandma, you think you're on your feet too much?" Gloria was glad Grandma was actually wearing her hearing aid so she didn't have to shout. "I mean, with all the baking you're doing these days."

"Geraldine been complaining?"

"Nooo . . . well . . . she *is* concerned."

"She thinks I'm off my rocker. Go ahead, Gloria, and tell it like it is. I know what's been going through that brain of hers. She thinks I've lost it. But you don't, do you, pumpkin? Oh, mind you, I'm not as sharp as I used to be, but Grandma's still got her marbles. At least most of them."

"I know that, Grandma. Only . . . only, I wish Mother understood. She's—"

"Thinking of putting me away. That's it, now, isn't it?"

"Oh, Grandma, it won't happen, so don't worry."

"But she's thinking about it all the same. Geraldine's thinking about it, isn't she?" Grandma put down the wooden spoon, wiped her hands on her red-checked apron that was made from the same bolt of fabric she had used for the curtains and chair cushions, and turned to face Gloria. "It doesn't shock me, and it doesn't hurt me either, so don't you fret. It's what I would expect from Geraldine. She's got no reserves to draw on. Not like you and me. She's got no Jesus to go to with her troubles, and believe me, Geraldine's had plenty of troubles. So we have to be patient with her. We have to excuse some of her ways."

Gloria tried to swallow her anger by taking another sip of tea, but the indignation stuck in her throat like one of Tiger's hairballs. "I don't see how you can be so forgiving. I think it's downright disgusting that Mother could even think of doing such a thing. I mean, look at you, Grandma. You're no more ready for a nursing home than I am."

"Resentment's still got a hold of you, pumpkin." Grandma Quinn walked over to the table and sat down on one of the red-checked cushions. It was the only fabric Gloria had ever seen in Grandma's kitchen. Years and years ago, Grandma Quinn had bought an entire bolt of the stuff, and she always redid the cushions and curtains and aprons with it whenever they got worn. "Oh, you've made some progress, but it's still got its teeth in you, and you've gotta shake yourself free. Anger's a funny thing, pumpkin —either you are going to master it or it's gonna master you."

"I try to understand Mother, and I try to be patient. But sometimes it's hard."

Grandma's soft, chubby hands smothered Gloria's with warmth. "You gotta know this . . . Geraldine was always beautiful. Even when she was a baby, people would stop and stare. I tried to downplay it. Not fuss too much with her hair or clothes, so she'd blend in more with the other kids. But by the time she was ten, there was nothing I could do to hide her looks. And by then, Geraldine had discovered she was beautiful too. I remember it like it was yesterday. I caught her staring at herself in one of those pink plastic long-handled mirrors she used to keep on her dresser. She knew I was there, but she never took her eyes off the mirror. And then she said, 'Mama, did you know I'm the best-looking girl in my school?'" Grandma Quinn rose and walked to the oven and opened it.

"Well, what did you say?"

"Nothing." Grandma pulled out a sheet of hot oatmeal cookies and put it on top of the stove. "I just went to the bathroom and had me a good cry."

"But *why*, Grandma?"

"Because I knew right then and there that Geraldine Quinn was destined for heartache."

Gloria shook her head. "I'm sorry, Grandma, but it's hard for me to feel sad for someone so beautiful, so popular. Someone who had it all."

"*Had it all?* Oh, pumpkin, you got it so wrong. Geraldine had nothing. Nothing at all."

Gloria felt her chest constrict. Felt her anger creep across her face like red fingers. What Grandma was saying made no sense. It made absolutely no sense. Maybe Mother was right. Maybe Grandma was losing it. And Gloria couldn't bear the thought of that. She quickly rose to her feet and grabbed one more oatmeal cookie, then kissed her grandmother on the cheek. "Gotta go," she said, then raced out the door.

❧ ❧

The phone was ringing as Gloria opened her apartment door. She hurried to get it, stepping over cat toys littering the carpet, and almost stepped on Tiger himself as he darted for her legs in his customary greeting.

Her hand pulled the phone from its cradle just before the answering machine got it, and she managed a breathy "Hello."

"Hey, kiddo."

"Tracy?" Tiger circled Gloria's legs, rubbing against her ankles.

"The one and only."

How should she react? After her visit to Tracy's house, she had called her friend three times and left messages. This was Tracy's first call back. "Well, how are you?" Gloria opted for cordiality.

"I got your messages, and I've been meaning to call. But you know how it is. Not enough hours in a day."

"Aha."

"I feel bad calling you now. For a favor, I mean, instead of just for the heck of it. It took me a while to get up the nerve 'cause I didn't want you to think I was using you or anything. Then I said to myself, 'Tracy, she's still your friend. Maybe not your best friend anymore, but she's still your friend.' So I called. And I was right . . . wasn't I? I mean, we *are* still friends, aren't we?"

"Of course we are." Gloria felt uneasy. "What's the matter?"

"You know that crummy job I told you about? The one that paid next to nothing? Well, I don't have it anymore."

"*What?*"

"Yeah. The Dooleys fired me last week."

"Oh, I'm so sorry, Tracy. What happened?"

"Dr. Dooley—that's Dr. Stacy Dooley, the witch—told me I had an attitude problem. Just because I came in late a few times, she got all bent out of shape and started raising her voice and making it sound like I was some kind of incompetent jerk. I tried to tell her I was sorry—that I'd watch the time from now on—but she just went on and on like a stuck CD. Well, a person can only take so much, and I finally lost it and told her that for what she and her husband were paying me, she was lucky I came in at all. That's when she told me, 'Then don't.' I said, 'Don't what?' And she said, 'Don't bother coming in anymore.' Can you beat that? I was so mad I wanted to spit."

"What are you going to do now?"

"I have a few things lined up. Something should open up in about three weeks. Only problem is, I can't last that long. I've made financial commitments. And some of those buzzards are threatening legal action if I don't come through. I figured a thousand would do it. Tide me over till things open up. I'll pay you back. Every penny. I promise. What do you say?"

"*A thousand dollars?*" The prospect of a car was fading into oblivion.

"Right, but it'll only be for a little while."

"Okay . . . sure." What else could Gloria say? Tracy had been there for her a thousand times. She just couldn't step away now when it was her turn to be on the giving end.

"Thanks, kiddo. I knew you'd come through."

"So what sort of things do you have on the back burner?"

"Well . . . Nicky has this cousin over in Shepherd's Field who's looking for someone to tend bar three nights plus weekends."

"Nicky, as in Cervantes?"

"Well, who else, silly? He said I'd make a fortune with all the tips."

"But *tending bar?*" Gloria thought of the time she went to The Tomb with Tucker in Eckerd City—with its loud music and pungent smells—and couldn't imagine anyone wanting to work in a bar. "You always hated being around guys when they got drunk. You said they . . . they got offensive."

Tracy laughed. "Well, kiddo, if a girl has any kind of decent face or figure at all, then guys *are* gonna get offensive, drunk or sober."

Gloria thought about Jenny Hobart in Eckerd and all the problems she'd had because she was so beautiful. "Well . . . I suppose. But you don't know the first thing about tending bar. Besides, don't you need some sort of license?"

"See . . . there you go, Gloria, looking at all the negatives instead of being happy for me. But you don't need to worry. It just so happens that Nicky's cousin knows the owner of a bartending school where I can get my license quick. And Nicky's cousin said his friend would be willing to wait for payment, with some interest, of course, till I started work."

"I don't know, Tracy; it all sounds so iffy and vague. Why don't you just go back to telemarketing? You're really good at it. The best I know. How can you give that up?"

Tracy snorted with laughter. "What's to give up? My last telemarketing job gave me up, remember? Even though I brought in more sales than anyone. I ran circles around those other marketers, Gloria, and what do I have to show for it? Nothing. No appreciation, no pat on the back, no job. Now, I'm finished with all that. I'm tired of knocking my brains out to fill someone else's pocket. I'm going for the easy money. If I can mix a few drinks and smile real big and have someone pay me for the privilege, then I'm doing it. I've got to find some way to pay off my bills. And I'm *not* going to live at home forever."

"I don't know, Tracy. I just wish you'd think about it some more, or at least—"

"Don't worry, kiddo. I know what I'm doing. Hey, did I tell you? Mom heard from Tucker the other day."

"How is he?" No point in continuing the argument. When Tracy locked her mind onto something, there was nothing Gloria or anyone else could do to unfasten it.

"He's still not talking to me, but he seems to be doing okay—at least, that's what he told Mom. Should I ask her to send your regards?"

"He's not talking to me either."

"I *know* that. But if you still have a thing for him, maybe Mom can put in a good word."

"No. That's all over." Gloria felt profoundly grateful that her brush with foolishness was history.

"Okay, kiddo, okay. If you say so." But Tracy didn't sound convinced. "So when can I have the thousand?"

Gloria glanced at the kitchen clock. If she hurried, she could just make the bank before it closed at noon. Otherwise she'd have to wait and pull out the money Monday. "I'll head for the bank now," she said. "Meet me there."

"Thanks, Gloria. You're terrific. A real friend. You don't know how much this will help me."

Gloria said goodbye, then hung up, questioning if this loan was really the right way to help her friend at all.

❧ ☙

Cutter Press meandered down the aisles of Sam Hidel's Grocery, filling his basket with whatever caught his fancy. There was nothing he really needed. He was on a fool's expedition, hoping to encounter Gloria. He knew he had only to go to her apartment in the back and knock on the door because he'd seen her red Schwinn leaning against a tree by her driveway when he drove past. But he wanted a less direct approach. A chance meeting, then some polite conversation, and maybe an invitation to coffee. He knew he was being an idiot and forgetting his cardinal rule of always trying to keep Gloria off balance. But so far that had gotten him nowhere. And he had already decided to change tactics. But this was unfamiliar territory, and he wasn't sure just how he should go about implementing that change.

He was reaching for a jar of Prego when he spotted Pearl Owens at the end of the aisle and quickly did an about-face with his cart, nearly running over Wanda Lugget's foot. After a brief apology, he rounded the corner, safely out of view. Pearl was always looking for someone's ear to bend with the latest gossip, and he didn't want it to be his. He hadn't gotten far when he heard Pearl's voice drift over the top of the aisle.

"Good to see you, Wanda. How's business?"

"Couldn't be better."

"And Gloria? How's she working out?"

At the sound of Gloria's name, Cutter pulled his cart to a stop.

"A real asset. We've got new business pouring in from all over, thanks to her."

"You must be paying her well."

"Why do you say that?" Cutter thought Wanda sounded defensive.

"Well, haven't you heard? She's paying Hannah's grocery bills. Saw her myself. Just peeled off eight one-hundred-dollar bills, like it was Monopoly money, right in front of Sam's register. 'Course, I find it unconscionable of Geri to allow her daughter to assume such a responsibility. But you know how Geri feels about Hannah, and maybe . . ."

Cutter stopped listening and pushed his cart as far away from Pearl Owens as possible. So that's why Gloria suddenly couldn't afford a car. Well . . . maybe this was a way he could get her attention. But he'd have to be careful and do it right. If he overplayed his hand, everything could backfire.

~•● ◑~

Gloria stepped through the doors of the Appleton Savings Bank and onto the sidewalk. A stream of people passed by. Those she knew called her name and waved hello; those she didn't passed without a word. Gloria peered through the crowd and spotted Tracy, directly in front of her, leaning against the hood of an old, beat-up green Ford. Nick Cervantes sat behind the wheel with his head resting against the seat, his eyes closed.

"Hey, kiddo. What great timing. We just got here."

Gloria walked over to Tracy with the bulging envelope in her hand and tried to ignore the queasy feeling in her stomach. "I didn't know he was coming."

Tracy shrugged and glanced back at Nick. So did Gloria. Nick now sat upright as if he had actually smelled the money in Gloria's hand, and the smell had revived him. One eye was swollen and bluish—Gloria assumed as the result of a fight. Unwashed hair hung over his forehead and around his ears. His cheeks and chin were black with stubble. There was no way around it—Nick Cervantes needed a good bath and shave.

Tracy didn't look much better. Her clothes were crumpled as if she had slept in them, or maybe they had been sitting in the dryer too long. Her red hair looked as greasy as Nick's and was pulled back in a ponytail, except for some renegade wisps around both ears and at the nape of her neck. She wore no makeup, and that, plus the messy hair, made her look haggard. The only things that seemed out of place were her Reeboks. They looked new.

"I didn't expect him to be here," Gloria repeated.

"Does it matter?" Tracy took the envelope from Gloria's outstretched hand.

"I worry . . . that's all."

Unexpectedly, Tracy reached over and gave Gloria a hug. "Don't, kiddo. Everything's going to be all right. I just know it." Then, after a quick kiss on Gloria's cheek, Tracy jumped into the old Ford and gave Nick's shoulder a nudge, and away they went.

Gloria watched the car until it turned down a side street and disappeared. Then she headed for the bicycle rack and her Schwinn, and when she did, she saw that someone else was watching too. Only, he was watching *her*—the same man she had seen twice before near the print shop.

She tried not to show her nervousness, but her fingers fumbled awkwardly with the bike chain, and it seemed to take forever to get it off. She tossed the chain and lock into her basket, then mounted her bike, but not before deliberately looking the man in the face. "Nice day," she said. But the man just stood there glaring, and all Gloria could do was pedal away.

Was it just coincidence?

~◈ ◈~

"Hi, Harry. Just have a quick question." Perspiration beaded Gloria's forehead—as much from the brisk ride from the bank to her apartment as from her nagging uneasiness—and the phone felt slippery in her sweaty palm.

"Well, hey there, stranger."

"I need to know if you ever printed those flyers. The ones we wrote just before we found Santa Claus."

"Well, actually I did. Wasn't sure if I was going to, not after that nasty business, but I finally decided we shouldn't let the flyer go to waste. Been getting a lot of calls, too, on that new 800 number I set up. Almost all of them are about that piece on nonprofit groups making big profits on real estate sales to the Forest Service. But why are you asking?"

"Because . . . well . . . I think someone's following me."

Chapter Nine

VIRGINIA DIDN'T LOOK THAT GOOD—actually worse than last time—all drawn and shriveled like dehydrated fruit. Gloria pushed the door open all the way, noting it didn't make a sound as it moved on its hinges, then stepped into Virginia's bedroom. The whole house, and in particular this bedroom, had taken on a stillness as though holding its breath, waiting for death to arrive. Agnes Keller hadn't even taken Gloria up, just pointed to the tired, creaking staircase and said, "She's expecting you." But how could one so frail have any interest in entertaining visitors? Maybe Gloria would come back another time. Before she could take a single step backward, she heard a dry, crusty voice.

"Well, don't just stand way over there. Come in."

Gloria lingered by the door. "You sure you're up to it?"

A laugh that sounded more like a cough parted the stale air. "People have been underestimating me all my life. I'm tougher than I look."

"If you were, then you'd tell Cutter the truth."

The covers rustled as Virginia rose, her thin, clawlike hand feeling for the pillows behind her. "Come prop me up." There was the barest hint of a smile on her face.

Gloria walked over, fluffed the five massive pillows, and positioned them in a way she thought most comfortable. "He's your son, Virginia. He has a right to know. You need to tell him the truth."

"Cutter doesn't want to know the truth."

"You said you were worried about him. That after you're gone he's going to need to deal with some issues. But you're not helping any. And you could. You could make what happens later easier, by letting him make his peace with you."

Virginia arched her graying eyebrows and peered at Gloria with small, dark, almost-black eyes that reminded Gloria of a crow's. "What makes you think he'd want to make peace?"

"I have no idea what Cutter would or wouldn't want, but that's not the point. The point is, you must give him that chance."

Virginia's bony hand pointed to a sweating pitcher on the nightstand. "I'll take some of that."

"My, but you're good at giving orders." Gloria poured ice water into a glass. "Are you as good at taking them? Now, that's the question."

"You never fooled me with that timid, cellophane-wrapped Emily Post facade. I always knew you had grit, Gloria. Didn't I tell you? But I wasn't expecting you to get so sassy with me. I'm not sure I like it."

"You opened the box and asked me to step in. Remember? Call me Virginia, you said, and we'll play by different rules."

Virginia chuckled. "A good invitation, I believed. Still do."

"But the rules are about to change."

"They can't, since *I* make them."

"Not anymore." Gloria picked up Virginia's thin, veiny hand

and pressed it between her fingers. "And that's what you've got to realize. God is calling the shots now."

"Then I don't want to play."

"Soon you won't be able to. It's the last inning, and you're up at bat. Don't you want to see if you can hit a home run?"

Virginia's blackish eyes misted, but she remained silent.

"Forgiveness, Virginia. Give Cutter your forgiveness, just like Jesus wants to give you His."

"Oh, forgiveness, forgiveness. Pffffff. It's just a word. What does it mean? I *forgive* you, Cutter, for not loving me? I *forgive* you, Cutter, for making me miserable most of the time? I *forgive* you, Cutter, for doing everything in your power to embarrass and frustrate me? I *forgive* you, Cutter, for wasting our lives together? Is that what you want me to say, Gloria?"

"Yes, something like that."

"Will it bring back the wasted years? Will it give me a son who is capable of honoring his mother? Oh, yes, Gloria, I do know some Scripture, and I know a child is supposed to honor his mother and father. Will your word—*forgiveness*—give me all that?"

"It won't change the past, but it can give you peace, now, in the present." Gloria felt Virginia's hand tighten around her fingers.

"I won't promise anything except that I'll think about it. I suppose it's not fair to leave everything in a mess and expect you to clean it all up after I'm gone." Virginia cocked her head and peered at Gloria. "But you're a mean one, Gloria Bickford, to show no pity for a dying old woman, to push me hard like that." She let her hand slip from Gloria's. "I'll think about it. I surely will do that. For now, maybe you'll be nice to me and sit awhile? Tell me some of the town news?"

Gloria smiled at the elderly woman with her matted hair and liver spots and cabbage-vein hands and wondered how this small, frail-looking woman had ever been capable of terrorizing her and Cutter all their lives. "Here's a shocker," she said, sitting down on the edge of the bed. "Someone wants to buy Clive's farm. I hear he was offered . . ."

⁓◉ ◉⁓

Geri Bickford sat across from Gloria, feeling strangely uncomfortable. She picked at her burgundy-blush nails like a nervous schoolgirl. "When you called and asked me to lunch, I never expected it to be La Fontaine. Just look at these prices!"

Gloria laughed. "I haven't seen you in a while and wanted this to be a treat." She brushed her ponytail away from her neck as though it were irritating her skin.

It was certainly irritating Geri the way Gloria kept fooling with her ridiculous hair. What made her decide to change it, anyway? And just when she was actually starting to look some-what attractive. Didn't Gloria know ponytails went out in the sixties?

And what was with Gloria's outfit?—a dungaree skirt and white short-sleeve cotton sweater. Geri didn't much care for that either. Far too casual for La Fontaine. Luckily, Geri had picked her good linen slacks and English blazer to wear instead of that polyester outfit she had originally taken out of the closet. *But Gloria should have warned her they were coming here.*

"Honestly, Gloria, sometimes you don't have a brain in your head. You don't have this kind of money. And why make us drive all the way to New Canterbury? We could just as easily have gone to Marty Grossman's old diner—what's its new name? So taste-less, Marty must be livid. But that's what he gets for selling it to an outsider. What's that name, now? Eats and . . . ?"

"Eats Galore."

"That's it." Geri shook herself as though she'd heard a fingernail running down a blackboard. "Terribly tacky. Anyway . . . we could have gone there or to Tad's. Tad makes a nice sandwich, and I hear he's running a bunch of specials. I rather like his tuna melt, even though he gets a little carried away with the cheese and I usually end up taking most of it off—not terribly good for the waistline. But La Fontaine. What were you thinking?"

"I was thinking I wanted to make our time together special."

"Well . . . that's nice . . . I guess. But next time let's go to Tad's."

"Okay, okay." Gloria laughed. "Next time we'll go to Tad's."

Geri flipped the menu open and tried to concentrate. "I wonder if they have any Sunday specials. They must. People love to go out to eat after church. Though I never went in for that myself. Always thought Sunday was best spent at home, with family." She glanced at Gloria's face, which was all politeness and smiles, but there, tucked behind her eyelashes, was a blank look, and the corner of Gloria's mouth twisted as she stifled a yawn. Geri had seen it for years: Gloria's mastery at looking like she was paying attention when she wasn't. Geri didn't want to admit it, but she had looked forward to their lunch together, had so wanted it to be pleasant. Maybe if she talked about something Gloria liked. Maybe that would break this uneasy feeling. "So, how was church this morning?"

"I don't know. I didn't go."

"Does that mean you have to go to confession?" She waited for the exasperated sigh, but heard none.

"You know they don't hear confessions at Full Gospel. And even if they did, the answer is no. 'The Sabbath was made for man, not man for the Sabbath.'"

"Don't waste your breath quoting Scripture to me, Gloria. I'm never going to be one of you." When Gloria just sat sweetly, staring at her menu, Geri became agitated. "Okay, so where *did* you go?"

"To visit Virginia."

"You mean Mrs. Press, don't you? Really, Gloria. It seems like you've forgotten all your manners."

"Virginia asked me to call her Virginia, so I am. By the way, when did you see her last?"

"About a week ago."

It was clever of Gloria to change the subject, but since it concerned Virginia, Geri allowed it, especially since she had been worrying about Virginia lately and had no one else to talk to about it.

"I'm worried about her, Gloria. She doesn't look at all well. And Virginia's never taken to her bed this long. Sometimes . . . well, sometimes I think Virginia does it—feels sick, I mean—when she's irritated with Cutter. His moving out really put her over the edge. But that was a while ago, and I expected her to be over it by now." Geri felt a moment of panic. Maybe she shouldn't have revealed Virginia's tactics to Gloria; after all, there were some things children shouldn't know about their mothers, or about someone else's mother, either. She studied Gloria's face, and when she failed to see shock or horror or disgust, she cleared her throat.

"Anyway . . . I never expected Virginia to stay in her room this long. I know Dr. Grant has run all kinds of tests. He checked everything imaginable when you were in Eckerd, remember when I told you?" Geri waited for Gloria to nod before continuing. "That's when she took to her bed the first time over Cutter leaving home. But that lasted only two weeks. Virginia claims Dr. Grant found nothing, either in those tests he did last year or now. But . . . I'm starting to worry."

"Why don't you try to see her as much as possible? That might lift Virginia's spirits."

Geri couldn't get over how Gloria was calling Mrs. Press Virginia. She would have made more of a fuss if Gloria hadn't said it was Virginia's idea. Though Geri could hardly imagine such a thing. The whole situation irritated her.

She scanned the menu, trying to take her mind off Gloria's impertinence. "Oh, for Pete's sake . . . this menu's in French. *Pôchouse?* Now, what's that? Where are the sandwiches? The tuna? Or chicken salad? Or turkey club?"

Her irritation was mounting by the minute, and when the waitress came to take their order, she couldn't keep from snapping at her like a crusty old turtle. "How am I supposed to know what I want? It's impossible to read this without a translator! Would you *kindly* tell me what this is? *Croque-madame à cheval?*"

The waitress told her it was a hot ham-and-cheese sandwich with a fried egg on top, and Geri was certain she heard disdain in her voice.

"Well, why doesn't it just say so?" Geri didn't see the look of embarrassment that usually clouded Gloria's face whenever she behaved this way. What was making her daughter act so strangely? "Okay. Just give me that *croque* thing," she muttered, then listened to Gloria calmly rattle off her order.

If Gloria wanted to act so calm about everything, so above it all, then maybe this was a good time to bring up Clancy County Home for the Aged. "I've come across a nice nursing home," she said after the waitress left.

Suddenly, Gloria didn't look so above it all. Her face contorted with a frown, and her eyes flashed something her mother could identify only as determination. "Mother, we're not going to put Grandma into—"

"If we act quickly, we can get one of the few beds that are left." Well . . . she could be determined too.

"I won't do it, Mother. I just won't do it."

"It's not up to you, Gloria. And I don't need your permission. But it would make the whole process easier if you were more supportive."

"I'm sorry, Mother. I can't help you. I *won't* help you. Not in this. Grandma doesn't need a nursing home. There are other alternatives we could look into."

"Like what?"

"Like that retirement community I already told you about, right off Route 485. A lot of Grandma's friends already live there, and they like it too. We could look for a small condo. I understand they take care of everything: the lawn, the shrubs, and even snow removal in the winter."

Geri twisted the expensive white linen napkin on her lap like a rope. "You honestly believe your grandmother is capable of living by herself?"

"Yes."

Geri didn't think Gloria looked convinced. "I see." The napkin twisted tighter. "And you won't even come with me to check out Clancy County?"

"No."

Geri squared her shoulders. Slowly, patiently, she smoothed out the twisted napkin with her fingers, removed it from her lap and carefully folded it, then placed it alongside her empty plate. "Then I don't think we have anything more to discuss." She rose to her feet.

"Mother, what are you doing?"

"I'm leaving."

"Mother, don't be like that. Please sit down, and let's discuss this like adults."

"I've already said everything I'm going to say. It's obvious you have only disdain for my opinion on this matter, and quite frankly I don't care for yours, either."

"But your lunch, Mother . . . you haven't eaten. At least stay and eat your lunch."

"You eat it. I've lost my appetite." Geri pushed her heavy high backed chair out of the way, then gave her daughter one last disapproving look. "And for your information, I don't like your hair all pulled back into a ponytail like that. And your outfit could have been more thought-out—less thrown together. But what I really, really dislike is the idea of you calling Mrs. Press Virginia." She spun around and walked out of the fancyschmantzy restaurant she didn't think Gloria could afford and headed for her car in the parking lot. And all the way home, she chastised herself worse than she had ever chastised Gloria. Why couldn't she handle things better with Gloria? Why were they always at odds? And why did she always seem to come out looking like the bad guy?

It wasn't until Geri spotted her white picket fence and pulled into the drive that she realized she had left Gloria stranded at La Fontaine without a car. Well . . . let her find a ride home. But even as Geri had that thought, she was backing out of the driveway. It took her forty minutes to drive back to New Canterbury, another five to park her gold Volvo and walk to the restaurant, and another forty-five minutes to reverse the whole process when she found out Gloria had already left in a Four-Towns taxi.

❧ ❧

"Sorry to call on a Sunday, but it's been 24/7 around here." Cutter sat on the expensive black leather sofa in his rental home listening to the excited voice of Sam Bryce spiral through the phone.

"Took on just a few too many cases this month. But yours is the most interesting, I must admit. Anyway, got a match on your Santa Claus. The name's Wendell Holt, but he goes by the name of Benny. Don't ask me why. No jail time, but he's had a few brushes with the law. Picked up once on bribery charges, but the case never went to trial, and the charges were dropped. And he was picked up once for possession of marijuana, but the police lost the evidence and had to let him go. Hardly a Dillenger wannabe."

"I thought you said this case was interesting." Cutter felt annoyed for allowing himself to go down another blind alley.

"It gets better. You know what Benny did for a living? He was a professional agitator. One of those guys who comes into an area and starts making noise about some issue or other and then continues to ratchet up the rhetoric until he's got everyone in a frenzy."

"So he's a picketer?"

"A *paid* picketer. There's a difference."

"Who was he working for?"

"So far I can only trace him back to Terra Firma, but I'm sure he's worked for other groups. I'll keep digging. Unless, of course, this is enough for you."

Cutter rose from the couch and paced across his friend's expensive Oriental rug. "No. Keep at it."

"Fine. You know where to send the check."

Cutter powered off the phone and placed it on its cradle, feeling more hopeful than he had in a long time. Maybe this wasn't a dead end, after all. Maybe Sam Bryce would dig up some information that could help Cutter get The Lakes out from under the thumb of the environmentalists, and then he and his partners could finally, finally build.

⚜

Cutter was a full fifteen minutes early for his appointment with Clive McGreedy. Off to the side, near the barn, Cutter saw the '97 blue Ford Escort with the handwritten For Sale sign propped on the windshield right under one of the wiper blades. He got out of his car and sauntered over.

There was a walnut-size dent on the left bumper, but the rest of the body was perfect. He peered into the window and saw the spotless interior, the pristine gray dashboard and gray fabric-covered seats. He was pleased to see that the cruise controls were mounted on the steering wheel, along with the airbag. The radio was stock, though—AM/FM and cassette deck, not like his aftermarket radio and monitor connected to a PS/2 for DVDs. The econobox-type rubber shift boot was stock too, but he was sure Gloria wouldn't care either way. Finally, he checked the tires. All new. The car was a bargain at thirty-five hundred. Clive could get four thousand for it, easily. But Cutter would try to drive the price down, for Gloria's sake, because this car was perfect for her. She was sure to love it.

Once he got her to take it, that is.

⚜

Cutter thought of turning back a dozen times. And even when he headed down the alley beside Sam Hidel's Grocery and stopped next to the old red Schwinn, he was still thinking that it wasn't too late to change his mind. He didn't have to see his steering wheel to know it was covered with sweat.

133

This was just plain crazy. Whatever had made him do it?

It had seemed like such a good idea at the time. A great way to get Gloria to notice him. Now he saw it as a great way to get her good and mad. Even so, he turned off the ignition and got out. He had come this far. Might as well see it through, even if it made him look like a fool.

He walked slowly to the door, half fearing Gloria wasn't home, half fearing she was. Then he tapped lightly on the door. When it opened, all he could do was stand silently, like an errant student before the principal.

"Cutter? What . . . brings you here?"

"I have a surprise." He leaned against the door frame, as much for support as to assume a casual air he didn't feel. "But you've got to promise you won't get mad."

"I can't do that. I've seen your surprises before—the worms in the cupcakes you baked for my tenth birthday; the skates you let me borrow, but not before you loosened the wheels; the—"

"Okay, okay. I was a miserable kid. But it's not that kind of surprise. I promise." Cutter watched Gloria shrug, watched her ponytail swing behind her, and thought how he liked her hair this way. How attractive she looked.

"Okay, you've got my interest. Come in." She smiled a big, sunny smile that made Cutter's neck bead with perspiration. "I'll get us something to drink. Coke, coffee, tea? What?"

"Coke is good." Cutter followed Gloria into the small living room and sat when she gestured with her hand.

"And how about something to eat? I have a leftover ham-and-cheese sandwich I'm looking to unload . . . a La Fontaine original. Mother and I went there for lunch today, and she left early."

Cutter was surprised to see a twinkle in her eye. "Oh, one of those lunches. Sure . . . bring it on. I'll take it off your hands." Cutter was beginning to feel more relaxed. Maybe this wouldn't be so hard after all.

"So what's the surprise?" Gloria asked, when she returned with a tray. "And, so help me, you're going to wear this sandwich if it's anything stupid."

Cutter chuckled, thinking how much Gloria had changed, and yet how much she was still the same spunky kid he had grown up with until her mother had crushed her. "You know my eye still hurts where you punched it."

Gloria placed the tray on the coffee table. From it, she took a tall glass of water. The sandwich and Coke remained for Cutter. To his surprise, she sat on the couch next to him instead of choosing the overstuffed chair.

"You gave me my first black eye, my very first. I thought it would be one of the other guys; you know, Tommy Mulligan, Tony Bonjorno, one of them. It was hard to live down. I really got razzed . . . getting punched like that by a *girl*. Sort of hurt the old ego."

"Well, that was an awful crack you made about my legs. Telling me they were the best legs you'd ever seen on a frog. I suppose I overreacted. I shouldn't have punched you like that. Is it too late to say I'm sorry?"

Cutter picked up the sandwich and grinned. "No need. I didn't say I didn't deserve the punch. I just didn't expect it. But that was one of the things I always liked about you, Gloria. Your spunk."

"Really?" Gloria seemed genuinely surprised.

The sandwich looked good, and Cutter took a man-sized bite. "It really bothered me when you stopped fighting back," he said, when his mouth was no longer full. "When you let your mother, me, all of us, get to you." Her sweet, stunned face made his heart thump.

"You were such a . . . such a . . ."

"Bully? Yeah, I was. And obnoxious. And *stupid.* I actually believed I was doing you a favor—actually thought if I teased you enough, you'd fight back. I thought I could keep you from losing your grit. But I only made things worse. Like I said, I was stupid."

"That's the second time this week a Press told me I had grit." Gloria put her glass on the tray. "I only wish you had talked to me like this years ago. It might have made life more pleasant for both of us."

Taking another bite of the sandwich gave Cutter time to decide what to say. Bluster and pressure and manipulation hadn't worked with Gloria. Maybe the truth would. "I always wished we had been better friends. Hindsight tells me I made that impossible. And for what it's worth, I'm sorry. It would have been nice having a friend who understood . . . about my mother."

Gloria nodded. "Yes . . ."

"We both had nightmare mothers who kept the pressure on so tight, it's a wonder we didn't break. And I guess we coped in our own ways too."

Gloria tilted her head as though thinking. Then peace drifted over her face like a shaft of sunlight drifting over a long-neglected corner of a garden. "You know, I never thought about that before. But you're right. We *did* cope in different ways. I wonder why I never saw it. I mean, it's really so simple and basic, and doesn't take a psychology major to understand that you coped one way, I another. I became introverted. You became . . ."

"Obnoxious?" He studied Gloria's face to see if she would confirm his last word with a smirk, but her expression was so sweet, so full of compassion, it made him want to cry. "I don't know why I'm saying all this now. Maybe so you don't try to sock me again when I show you the surprise."

"I'm sorry, Cutter. Really sorry."

"For what? Socking me?"

"For all the years I've misjudged you, held you in—"

"Contempt?"

Gloria laughed. "Well . . . not in the highest esteem. And I was wrong."

"Does that mean you think we can be friends now?"

"We can try."

Cutter put the fragment of sandwich remaining in his hand back on the plate and rose to his feet. Then he dug into his pants pocket and pulled out a key and a folded sheet of paper. "With that in mind, I brought you this."

"What is it?"

"Clive's old car and a payment schedule of two hundred dollars a month, based on a thousand-dollar deposit."

"What?"

"I know why you don't have the money to buy it outright. Pearl Owens has got that bit of news plastered all over town. And I don't expect you to let any false pride get in the way either. I just expect you to take it and say thank you." Cutter saw red streaks run up Gloria's cheeks and held his breath. It could go either way. But if she was half the woman he thought she was, it would end okay.

"How did you get Clive to agree to stretch out the payments?" she asked. Cutter thought it was from between clenched teeth.

"I didn't. I bought the car. You're making the payments to me."

"What?"

"Clive's car is a bargain, Gloria. It's a perfect size for you, four-door, only seven years old, only fifty thousand miles, in mint condition. Another week and it would've been gone. So I saw you could use a little help here and stepped in, just like a friend would."

"Are you *utterly* out of your mind? Do you think I can let you do this? You have more gall than—I mean, the nerve of—" Gloria stopped, looked at Cutter for a long time, then burst out laughing. "I must be out of *my* mind. Turning down a deal like this."

"You mean you'll take it?"

Gloria nodded. Cutter could see she was having trouble containing herself and looked almost as if she was going to jump up and down. "Can I see it?" she asked, joy lighting her eyes like sparklers.

"Sure, it's in your driveway. I thought we could—" Gloria was already out the door and all over the Escort, checking the tires, running her hands along the gleaming blue exterior, sitting behind the steering wheel, fingering the seat fabric, opening the glove compartment, then opening the trunk, the hood, checking the oil . . .

"Well, what do you think?" Cutter said when Gloria had stopped swarming over the car.

"It's wonderful! Absolutely wonderful! Thank you. Thank you so much!" Then she did something unexpected. She threw her arms around him and gave him a big hug. And as Cutter stood awkwardly, returning her hug, he thought that she was every bit the woman he'd thought she was, and more.

So much more.

~❦ ❦~

Chapter Ten

———

GLORIA HEADED FOR 52 Elm Street, taking the long way just so she could enjoy driving her new car. She went south on Main passing Baker, then Union, then the three-story brick building of Appleton High. Two teenage boys dribbled a basketball in the dusky parking lot. A handful of others hovered under a light near a parked car. Sweaty T-shirts clung to their young, muscular shoulders. Looked like Gloria wasn't the only one working late—practice must have gone on longer than usual. But aside from the boys, the whole area, including the street and sidewalk, was deserted.

She slowed the car over the tracks grooving Railroad Avenue and laughed to herself when she caught sight of Eats Galore. Maybe she should have gotten a bite there instead of going all the way back to her apartment after work. Well, next time.

The car continued sailing down Main as if it were riding the wind instead of an old paved road that already had a few pot-holes even before the official pothole season had begun. When her tires found one of them and bounced in and out almost effortlessly, she smiled. Her Bluebird had taken it like a champ. She called her '97 Escort "Bluebird" because of its color and because of the way it seemed to fly over the roadway. It was a blessing she still found hard to believe, made harder by the fact that her faithful Jesus had used Cutter Press in its dispensing. But maybe it wasn't so strange after all. Jesus was in the renovation business—renovating and restoring relationships. And if any relationship needed restoring, it was hers and Cutter's.

Only—sometimes . . . when Cutter looked at her a certain way . . . almost like the way she imagined he looked at Sadie Bellows when they were alone . . . she got nervous, and all sorts of thoughts flooded her mind. *Get real, Gloria. And get a grip on that imagination of yours.* Only suppose . . . suppose it wasn't her imagination. Suppose he wanted to be more than friends. She wouldn't like that. She was barely used to Cutter as a friend. *A friend.* Now, wasn't that a laugh? Jesus sure had a sense of humor. Obviously, He wasn't just shooting for reconciliation, but a friendship too.

Funny thing was, she didn't mind a bit. But friendship was as far as she was willing to go.

When Gloria crossed Candlewick Road, she slowed down. Elm was coming up. A few more yards and she made the left by Comics & Cards. She had been taking this route for years and could do it with her eyes closed. Several miles later, she felt disappointed when she found herself in front of the tired old Victorian. Not only was her ride in Bluebird over, but she could no longer put off the inevitable.

She parked by the curb and sat a moment. The long day at Appleton Printers had knocked her out. With her working OT every night, there was no way she could have seen Grandma Quinn this week if she had had to go by bike. And she needed to see her. Ever since her lunch with Mother, she'd known she'd have to see Grandma and lay it on the line.

What else could she do?

She glanced at her Timex. Eight thirty. No use procrastinating. With a flip of her wrist, she opened the door and got out. The streetlight illuminated the cracked walkway and sagging stoop far more than Gloria wished and reminded her of the importance of her mission. Her trek over the uneven concrete seemed to take forever, though it was only a few yards, and Gloria found herself feeling not only sorry for herself that this task had fallen on her shoulders but also nervous about being the messenger. Grandma would be hurt—that was a given. It was just a matter of degree. This whole thing was distasteful. Only problem was, the alternative was even worse.

Before Gloria reached the sagging steps, she smelled the aroma of fresh-baked cookies and groaned. *Oh, Grandma.*

She didn't bother knocking. If Grandma wasn't wearing her Freedom FS, she wouldn't hear it anyway. Instead, Gloria searched her key chain until she found the old, discolored Baldwin and inserted it into the lock. But after turning the key the only way it would go, Gloria discovered she had locked the door rather than unlocked it, which meant the door had been unsecured all along. *Oh, Grandma.*

She opened the door and stepped into the hall, letting the screen bang shut behind her. At once the warmth of the house engulfed her almost as if it were Grandma's invisible arms waiting to hug all who entered. Then the sweet vapor of freshly baked cookies again filled her nostrils. Normally, a smell like that would make Gloria's mouth water. Today it made her angry. *Why was Grandma baking at this hour?*

"Grandma! Grandma!" she shouted all the way to the kitchen, not wanting to take Grandma too much by surprise and frighten her. No response. At the kitchen entrance, Gloria stopped and watched Grandma take a batch of cookies from the oven and place the pan on top of the stove. Then, with a spatula, Grandma began transferring cookies to the only empty rack out of the half-dozen cooling racks scattered all over the counter. Gloria bit her lip. *Oh, Grandma.*

Then she walked to the center of the kitchen. "Grandma!" she shouted once more at the top of her lungs and watched her grandmother jerk her shoulders in fright.

"Land sakes, child. You gave me a start." Grandma placed the spatula on the hot baking sheet, then with surprising agility and speed was beside Gloria, hugging her, squeezing her face as if it were a peach she was testing for ripeness, and finally paving both cheeks with kisses.

When they separated, Gloria pointed to her ear, and Grandma Quinn nodded with a frown. "Okay, child," she said, retrieving her hearing aid from a small side drawer. "Okay."

"Grandma, you've *got* to start wearing that thing all the time. It's really important. Promise me you'll do it," Gloria said as soon as her grandmother installed the hearing aid. *"Promise me."*

Grandma Quinn nodded.

"Suppose I was a burglar? I could have rolled up with a U-Haul and emptied your entire house before you would have been the wiser."

"That's just plain silly. What do I have that's worth stealing?"

"That's not the point, Grandma. Did you know your door was unlocked, and I screamed your name a dozen times before you heard me? You know you should keep your door bolted this time of year—so close to the Apple Festival. The town's already swarming with strangers. Just the other day, Pearl Owens said a couple of people she never saw before came right into her yard and helped themselves to a dozen dahlias."

"Oh, that gossip. You can never take anything she says seriously." Grandma patted Gloria's cheeks like she used to when Gloria was little, then walked to the stove. "What's really troubling you, child? You're huffing and puffing like a steam engine." Gloria followed her.

"Those, for one." She pointed to the handful of cookies still on the baking sheet. "You've got to stop charging your baking goods at Sam's, and you've got to stop baking all this stuff. People are talking, saying you're not right . . . in the head."

"Pffffff. Let 'em say what they want."

Gloria took the spatula from her hand. "I can't, Grandma. Because it's causing problems."

Grandma Quinn's eyes narrowed like coin slots in a machine. "You just sit down over there and let me get you some cookies and milk. Then you tell me all about it."

"No cookies, Grandma."

"Oh, my. This must be serious."

Gloria nodded and put the spatula down on the counter, then guided Grandma to one of the red-checked-cushioned chairs. She took the seat beside her.

"Okay, pumpkin, what's this all about?"

"Mother wants to put you into a nursing home." Gloria avoided her grandmother's eyes.

"Oh, I *already* know that."

"No! No . . . you don't. She's picked one out. Clancy County Home for the Aged. She must have gotten the paperwork because she knows just how many empty beds they have. And . . . I don't think there's a thing I can do to stop her, unless *you* stop doing these things . . . these things that make her think you're not right." Gloria suddenly felt her grandmother's soft, warm hands on hers.

"Hush, child. Stop your fretting and just listen to me. There are things going on here you don't understand. This goes deeper than my baking cookies or running up a bill at Sam's. This goes all the way to when Geraldine was young. She never could stand to have people talk about her, to think ill of her. She always had to be the star. And for a while there, she even believed her own press. Believed she was perfect like all those beauty pageants make you feel. But she learned soon enough she wasn't perfect. She was taken down a peg, more than a peg, and hard too. And not only by this town, but by your father."

"Grandma, what are you talking about?"

"Your mother bought into this town's expectations of her, and when she didn't come through, when she didn't deliver the Miss America title, she couldn't forgive herself. And your daddy? Well . . . he broke your mother's heart."

Gloria was on unfamiliar ground and found it frightening, as though she had just jetted into the stratosphere on a space shuttle. "I don't understand, Grandma. What does this have to do with Mother wanting to put you into a nursing home?"

"Everything, pumpkin. Absolutely everything."

～❦ ❦～

Gloria tossed and turned in bed, drifting in and out of sleep. Finally, around three in the morning, she flicked on her nightstand light and sat up. Grandma's remark about her father still had Gloria upset. Why hadn't she questioned Grandma further instead of running out like a child? She hadn't even shown Grandma her new car. Oh, why had she acted like such a baby? What was she so afraid of?

Gloria reached over and picked up her Bible. She supposed she could justify her behavior by blaming her grandmother. Grandma certainly hadn't helped her case. Talking crazy. Acting crazy. How did Grandma expect Gloria to help her? There was only so much Gloria could do against Mother's determination. Surely, Grandma had to know that.

Slowly, Gloria ran her hand over the leather cover of the Bible. This past year she had turned to it often. It had given her comfort, direction, assurance. Gloria's insides churned.

It had also given her truth.

She let her fingers rest on the raised patch of leather that was sewn to the cover and contained her name inscribed in gold letters. Grandma had given her this Bible as a gift. Absently, Gloria traced her name with her finger. Truth. Did she want that now? Yes. Always. But . . . what Grandma said about her father couldn't be true. That was inconsistent with the man she had known. And if it wasn't true, then that meant Grandma was in worse shape than Gloria knew. That meant Mother may be right about wanting to put Grandma into a nursing home.

But what if it was true?

Gloria opened her King James and began reading Proverbs twenty-three. She stopped when she got to verse twenty-three. She read the verse again, then again, and finally out loud. "Buy the truth, and sell it not; also wisdom, and instruction, and understanding."

"Oh, Jesus," she whispered, "sometimes Your ways are so hard."

⋙ ⋘

Cutter listened to Sadie's high-pitched voice telling him, over the intercom, that a Sam Bryce was on line two. He quickly picked up the phone and punched the flashing number.

"Sam. What've you got?"

The soft voice chuckled. "Was that your secretary?"

"Yeah."

"She must be a real looker."

"Why do you say that?"

"Because no one would put up with a voice like that if she wasn't."

Cutter scribbled curlicues across the legal pad he used for notes. "She has other assets."

"Of course she does."

"So what do you have?" Cutter said curtly, feeling his cheeks burn.

"Last night Tallulah—that's my computer—came across something very interesting: a group photo of Slone Foundation employees. And would you believe, Benny was right there in the second row listed as Benjamin W. Holt."

"You sure it's the same guy?"

"Positive. I enlarged the photo, then compared it to another picture I obtained from a different source."

"So you're saying there's a connection to Eric Slone?"

"Not necessarily. This only proves there's a connection to the Slone Foundation. And so far, my research shows that Eric Slone has little involvement in it."

"Okay. So then who runs the show?"

"Eric Slone's daughter, Erica. And you wanna know her pet project? The environment. And heading that list is *land preservation*—as in buying private land and selling it to the federal government."

Cutter remembered the article Gloria had written for the last issue of *C&C*, the one about nonprofit groups buying up land that bordered national parks or reserves, then selling it to the government for a profit. "Did they make a profit?"

"Don't know. Have to see if I can get ahold of some of their financial statements."

"How do you plan to do that?"

"A lot of this is a matter of public record. The rest—you don't want to know."

~⊛ ⊛~

All morning Gloria had listened to Wanda nitpick her husband, had watched Wanda's big hips bounce around the shop like a pinball machine, had felt Wanda's tension like a jolt of electricity every time Wanda passed her desk.

"Will you calm down?" Gloria finally said, unable to stand it any longer.

"It's Tuesday!" Wanda huffed. "We have only the rest of the week to get these orders out. Come Monday, everyone will want their stuff for the Apple Festival. Either that or our heads!"

"I'll stay every night if I have to. Stop worrying."

Wanda blew strands of bleached-blonde hair off her forehead. "It's not you I'm worried about. It's Mr. I-Gotta-Have-It-Perfect in there." Wanda pointed to the back, where Gloria could hear the sound of a press running. "He did Sam Hidel's flyer twice. Twice! Because he didn't like the way some of the pictures bled into the margins."

Gloria pushed back from her desk and laughed. "Paul has a spirit of excellence. You should be proud of that."

"Well, he can have that 'spirit of excellence' thing in February or March when our workload is way down. But not now. Not at our absolutely busiest time of the year!"

Wanda walked to her desk and began sifting through the top drawer. Gloria knew she was searching for her pack of spearmint gum. In the last week, Wanda had taken to chewing gum like mad. Gloria thought it beat Prozac.

"Look, when I'm all caught up, I can help collate, staple, trim, bind, whatever you need."

Wanda worked her face into a smile. "You're a good kid, Gloria. A hard worker. I wouldn't be surprised if you ended up owning this place someday." Then the smile slid off her face like melting ice cream. "Now, if you could only put a burr under you-know-who's saddle or make the presses run faster or—" Suddenly, Wanda spun around. "What's the use? Some things a person's got to do herself." Then she bounced toward the back room.

❧ ☙

"How's the car running?"

Gloria was surprised to hear Cutter's full voice boom over the phone. "Great."

"I was wondering if you'd like to take a drive to Spoon Lake after work. Do a little night fishing."

Gloria laughed. "I haven't done that in years. And it would be tempting, except we're swamped and I need to work OT. The Apple Festival has got us backlogged."

"Sounds like a lot of stress over there."

"You don't know the half of it." Gloria tried to ignore the angry voices coming from the press room where Wanda was still laying into Paul.

"All the more reason to go. There's nothing like fishing to relax you."

"By the time I get home and change and . . ."

"That's why it's called *night fishing*, Gloria. You can do it anytime of the night. How long you plan on staying at the shop?"

"Maybe till eight."

"Then I'll pick you up at nine. I'll bring dinner and the fishing poles. Your job is to get the bait."

"But I'll have to dig for it. In the *dirt!*"

"Exactly."

Gloria saw Wanda storm in from the back room and head for her desk, then start rummaging for her spearmint. "Okay, you're on." She hung up the phone, smiling. Obviously, her fears about Cutter were unfounded. There was no way he looked at her in any way but a friend. He'd never ask Sadie Bellows to dig for night crawlers.

~❦ ❦~

Cutter sat in one of the two folding chairs he had brought, his pole dangling over the bank. Two small Coleman lanterns on the ground—one by his chair, the other by Gloria's—bathed the bank in soft light. He hadn't felt this relaxed in a very long time. He glanced to the side and watched, by moonlight, as Gloria struggled with her line. Somehow, she had managed to get it tangled into a ball. Well, he'd let her struggle a while longer before he offered his help.

He nudged the brown paper bag at his foot with the tip of his shoe. It was more than half full of night crawlers and must have taken Gloria the better part of an hour to get. She was still digging when he came to pick her up. He couldn't help but smile as he thought of it. And the smile stayed with him as he watched her let out her line, then work the giant knot, then let out her line some more. Maybe he wouldn't offer his help at all. Maybe he'd wait until she asked for it. That thought made him smile all the more. She'd probably never ask. Not him. At least not yet. Perhaps someday. Some wounds took more time than others to heal. He was just beginning to understand that.

But it was nice being here with her. Like this. In the quiet evening. Listening to the crickets and watching the moonlight play with her hair. The last time he was here with her, it was so different. He and his friends had come upon her and Tracy swimming in the lake. It was the summer between their junior and senior years of high school—an age one would think too old for practical jokes. He cringed now when he thought of it. He and his friends had chased Gloria and Tracy to Clive's old smokehouse about a half mile away, locked them in . . . and left them there for three hours. In the light of maturity, it seemed so cruel—two girls, alone and wet, in that dark, bug-infested, dilapidated smokehouse. They had to have been scared and terribly uncomfortable. For the life of him, Cutter couldn't understand how he had thought a thing like that could be funny.

"You know that detective I hired?" he asked, hardly wanting to break the silence, or the spell this simple scene had cast on him, but suddenly fearing that Gloria would remember the smokehouse too. Gloria nodded, still struggling with the line. "Well, I heard from him again today. There's definitely a connection of some kind between Benny Holt and Slone, or rather the Slone Foundation."

"Oh?"

Even by moonlight, Cutter saw the worried look on Gloria's face. He quickly told her what Sam Bryce had found out. "I wanted to tell you I was wrong. I shouldn't have been so hardheaded about that whole meeting with Benny at The Lakes. I can be such a bonehead sometimes. Anyway, I just wanted to tell you, thanks. I know you and Harry Grizwald were only trying to help."

Gloria put down her pole, tangle and all. "Harry printed that last batch of flyers. I didn't think he would, but he did. Do you remember what I told you they were about?"

Cutter nodded. "Kind of coincidental, you writing about

how these nonprofit groups are making millions, and now this thing with Benny."

"I don't believe in coincidence."

"What do you mean?"

"I mean, I think I'm being followed."

❧ ☙

The next day, Wanda was in a fouler mood than ever, so when Gloria heard the cheerful voice of Harry Grizwald booming over the phone, she was grateful for the interruption.

"Congratulate me, Gloria! I finally did it. I finally got Dorie to say she'll marry me."

Gloria let out a loud whoop, then covered her mouth and scrunched lower in her chair when Wanda gave her a dirty look. "I never doubted for a second you'd win her over."

"I don't know. Dorie can be pretty stubborn. It wasn't an easy sell."

"What finally convinced her?"

"I think it was my cooking."

"No, I'm serious, Harry."

"So am I."

Oh, how she missed Harry and Dorie and Perth. It had been a while since she had seen them.

"Why don't you come up this weekend? We're all getting Gloria withdrawal," Harry said, as if reading her thoughts.

Gloria watched Wanda tie string tightly around a box of Sam Hidel's flyers as though wishing it were her husband's throat. "I'd like nothing better. But I can't this weekend. We're swamped here, getting ready for the Apple Festival."

"Then how about next weekend?"

A quick mental run-through of her schedule told Gloria she was free. "That would be perfect."

"You could hop the early bus and—"

"I have a car now, Harry."

"Well, well, well. Now aren't we the up-and-coming yuppie? Okay, so hop in your car, and we'll see you and your new car next weekend. Got any other surprises? Anything else going on in that life of yours?"

"It will keep till I see you." She didn't have the heart to spoil Harry's happy announcement by telling him about Sam Bryce or Benny Holt, or about the man who was still following her—who, in fact, had stood right outside the print shop door this morning and glared at her as she passed.

~❦ ❦~

Chapter Eleven

THE TRAFFIC WAS CRAZY—congesting normally quiet road-ways all over Appleton and leaving a lot of townspeople feeling frazzled. But not Gloria. The congestion was child's play compared to working with Wanda these past few weeks. This morning, Wanda had already chewed through two packs of spearmint, and Gloria dreaded seeing what she was going to be like by quitting time.

A second pass in front of Tad's Ice Cream Parlor convinced Gloria there were no empty parking spots to be had anywhere. She pictured herself driving around endlessly in a circle like a moving figure in a cuckoo clock.

Wanda would sure love that.

During her third pass, Gloria spotted a car fifty feet in front of her, pulling out of a space. She managed to slip into it just before an SUV did and felt only mildly guilty at her lack of graciousness. This was too much like jousting with cars. She couldn't imagine having to fight for a parking space every day like they did in Eckerd City. It would hardly be worth owning a car then. Gloria turned off Bluebird, scooped up Tad's flyers and his rush order of sweepstakes tickets, and got out.

The sidewalks were as jammed as the roads, with people everywhere. But that was to be expected. This was the end of town where most of the tourists congregated—though the rest of Appleton managed to get in on some of the action too, because a portion of the visitors inevitably wandered past Brandise and Larkspur and Baker Streets. Some even went as far as the elementary school and beyond that to Railroad Avenue. It was strange seeing them by the Wilson Brothers Funeral Home or the Western Union office or Carpet King—peering into windows or sitting on benches or standing in groups on the corners.

The tourists were as welcome as refreshing rain to most of the locals. Charlie Axlerod called them manna from heaven. Some, though, like Gloria's mother, called them a giant bother. But bother or not, the tourists were needed. Many merchants claimed that if they didn't score big financially during the Apple Festival, they wouldn't make their year.

Gloria squeezed past a family of four devouring triple-scoop cones just outside Tad's, the bundled boxes of flyers and tickets feeling heavy in her arms. She was glad Tad's promotion was going so well that he needed this second printing. Tad's place always got a lot of traffic and was one of the favorites with tourists during the Festival. Even in the fall, ice cream was a big seller.

Inside, people were jammed like pickles in a jar, making it difficult for Gloria to get to the counter. "Here's your stuff," she said to Tad when she'd finally pushed through. She almost choked when she saw that he was busy building one of his Banana Big Boats, called Triple B by the locals. It was a treat for two that held six scoops of ice cream, two different toppings, at least two tablespoons of nuts, a mound of whipped cream and a maraschino cherry, all on a bed of cut bananas. In Gloria's senior year, Tracy had dared her to eat one all by herself. And she did. But not without having to end her victory by going home and crawling into bed with a stomachache.

Ever since that dare, Gloria had not been able to look at a Triple B without wanting to gag. "Where should I put these?"

Tad squirted a mound of whipped cream over his creation. "Just stick them in the back."

Gloria slipped into the back room just as Tad placed a dripping red cherry on top of the whipped cream. She passed the batch freezers and one old Taylor soft-serve machine. Tad's newer soft-serve—his prized Taylor 772—and his Taylor 444 shake machine were in front, behind the counter. She found a cleared space on one of the tables and emptied her arms.

"I thought Wanda was gonna deliver them," Tad said when she returned.

"She was. That was before she started breathing like a goldfish because Paul hadn't started Pearl Owens's Fall Clearance Sale flyer. When Wanda actually turned orange—I'm not kidding you, bright orange—I offered to drop off your stuff."

Tad laughed as he handed the customer his change. "Yeah, I heard she's been pretty stressed. Guess we all have. I don't know why she and Paul just don't sell the place and retire. 'Course, I can't imagine anyone around here wanting to buy it."

Gloria shrugged, then waved good-bye, all the while thinking that she knew just the person who did, and marveled that the knowledge hadn't taken her by surprise.

~♦ ◈~

When Gloria returned to the print shop, she noticed a man dressed in a black leather outfit and heavy black leather boots sitting on a Harley-Davidson Fat Boy. The crowds here were not as thick as those near Tad's, but there were enough people around that she normally wouldn't notice someone unless he stood out. Black leather stood out in Appleton. So did motorcycles with chrome trim and gleaming pipes and custom wheels and fourteen-karat gold "Born to ride" emblems that caught the sun.

The man's face was turned to the side as he fiddled with something on the handlebars. Gloria had the vague notion she knew him, and she walked close to the curb hoping to get a better view. When a child's cry made him turn his head, she understood why he seemed so familiar. It was the same man she had seen lurking in the shadows so many times this past week and a half. When he saw Gloria, he cranked up the Harley and sped away.

Maybe it was time to report this to the sheriff.

⌇⋙ ⊙⋘⌇

Gloria watched J.P. Gordon, Ivy Gordon's husband and sheriff of Appleton, frown, then shake his head. "I always get nervous this time of year with all the strangers milling around, but so far I've only had to worry about shoplifting, traffic accidents, littering, maybe some vandalism. Never expected we'd get ourselves a stalker."

"I'm not saying he's stalking me."

"Then what are you saying?"

"I'm saying he's . . . *following* me."

J.P. raked stubby fingers through his salt-and-pepper crew cut. He was an ex-military man who still kept his hair short, his body trim, and his life disciplined. "Seems like stalking and following are about the same thing. But I won't split hairs. You know this guy from anywhere?"

Gloria shook her head.

"Any idea why he's following you?"

Gloria looked at J.P.'s kind face. She had known him all her life. What's more, she trusted J.P. He was a deacon at her church, and he walked the talk, just like his wife, Ivy. But for some reason she didn't want to tell him about Santa Claus or the Slone Foundation or the *C&C* flyers. She didn't know why, exactly. Maybe because, even to her, it all sounded too fantastic, too ridiculous to have anything to do with Gloria Bickford from Appleton.

"Any idea what he's after?" J.P. repeated.

"Two weeks ago I never knew he existed," Gloria returned truthfully, but feeling like she had deceived her old friend.

⁓⊛ ⊛⁓

It was almost dark when Gloria got home, so at first she didn't notice that her front door was open, just a crack. But when she went to insert her key and the door swung away, she knew that someone had been there. She called out in a shaky voice, then realized that if anyone was inside, he certainly wouldn't advertise the fact. She reached in with her hand and flicked on the light, then slowly pushed the door open all the way.

Her tiny apartment was quiet. Nothing looked like it had been disturbed, at least not the parts she could see from the door—her living room and half of the kitchen. Even so, she was hesitant to go inside. There was still the bedroom and bathroom. Someone could be hiding.

"If anyone's here, you better come out," she yelled, then realized that was foolish too. Did she really want to come face-to-face with an intruder? Maybe she'd go around to the front and get Sam Hidel. There was safety in numbers.

She was about to do just that, then stopped. If nothing was disturbed and nothing was taken, then the natural assumption would be that she'd just forgotten to lock her door and it had blown open. If she got Sam involved and the gossip wheel got hold of it, the whole town would get the idea that Gloria was not only forgetful about things like locking her door during Apple Festival season, but had an overactive imagination to boot.

Better keep this to herself.

She stepped into the living room, listening for sound. Nothing. Then she crept to the bedroom and flipped on the light. All was as she'd left it this morning. Then she checked the bathroom. Nothing wrong there either. She sighed with relief and was glad she hadn't involved Sam. That piece of news would have spread around quick enough and reached her mother in no time. Then she'd have had to listen to stories of all the people who had gotten murdered in their beds over the last fifty years within a radius of five thousand miles.

Mother could be relentless.

Gloria went to the front door, closed and locked it. That guy in the black leather must have rattled her more than she'd realized. She headed for the kitchen, thinking she'd eat a sandwich, then take a long, hot bath to relax. With a flip of her hand, she turned on the overhead fluorescent, then walked to the pantry and opened it. First, she'd feed Tiger. With a start, she realized he had not met her at the door with his usual greeting. In fact, she hadn't seen him anywhere in the house. He'd probably slipped past her and out the door without her noticing. She hadn't exactly been thinking straight when she first got home. He'd be back when he got hungry. She headed for the corner where she kept his bowl. She'd wash it and have it ready.

When she bent over to pick it up, something behind the

nearby garbage pail caught her eye. A paper of some kind, and some fluff . . . orange and brown and . . . *Tiger*? Her heart thumped as she yanked the tall pail away from the wall, revealing her cat, motionless and stiff as a flagpole, a blank three-by-five card tied around his neck. Her hand trembled as she tried feeling for any signs of life—a breath, a heartbeat, a movement—but found none. She reached for the card. A hole was poked through one of the corners. White string threaded through the hole was tied around Tiger's neck. Slowly she turned the card over and was startled to see big, sloppy red lettering.

"STOP SNOOPING OR ELSE."

⚓ ⚓

Gloria watched Sheriff J.P. Gordon push his gun to the side so it wouldn't catch in the bend of his thigh as he took the empty space next to her on the couch. Even so, he didn't seem comfortable and stretched out his right leg to reposition his weapon. As he did, Deputy Charlie Watts walked past, carrying something in a black plastic garbage bag, and Gloria knew it was Tiger.

"You ready to tell me what's going on here?" J.P. said.

Gloria nodded, swallowing the walnut-size lump in her throat and fighting back tears. She let her head fall back against the sofa and closed her eyes. "But you might not believe it."

⚓ ⚓

Cutter lay prone on the posh leather couch, dangling his legs off the end and watching the Giants make the winning touchdown in the final five seconds of the game. He couldn't think of a better way to spend the evening, except maybe to go fishing.

With Gloria.

Ever since that night they'd gone to Spoon Lake, he had tried to think of some excuse to visit her or ask her out but hadn't come up with a single thing. *You don't need an excuse, Press. Just do it.*

It wasn't that easy. He was walking a fine line here. He'd have to take it slow, give himself time to build her trust.

Oh, you just don't want her to think you're an idiot.

But he *was* an idiot. Had been one for years. Why else would he have come back to Appleton? He had returned on a fool's errand, but now . . . now maybe it wasn't so foolish. For the first time he had begun to hope, had actually begun to see the faintest possibility that Gloria's heart could change toward him.

He heard the sound of a doorbell and thought it was the commercial. When he heard it again and then again, he quickly rose from the couch and answered it.

"Gloria!" Cutter felt his cheeks burn, as though she had been standing there reading all his thoughts. But her face told him that something far more troubling than his thoughts was on her mind. He invited her in, then directed her to the living room.

"Sit down," he said, pointing to his favorite spot. Then he turned off the TV. "You look like you could use a drink. A strong one. What can I make you?"

Gloria shook her head. "Nothing. I don't want anything except to talk."

"Okay . . . sure." He hadn't seen her this upset in a long time. "Go ahead. Tell me what's on your mind." He eased himself onto the couch next to her.

"I want you to call off the investigation. I want you to tell Sam Bryce to forget about it."

Cutter pushed forward, leaned his elbows on his thighs, then tented his fingers. "Why do you want to quit, Gloria? Tell me what's happened."

"I was right about someone following me." She quickly told him about the man in black leather, about her open apartment, her cat, and the note.

Cutter sighed. "I'm sorry about your cat. But for too many years you've let people bully you, Gloria. You can't let that happen now. You've got to stand. Don't let whoever is trying to intimidate you succeed."

Gloria shook her head. "At Mattson Development I saw firsthand what these people can do. And from the people I've talked to since Harry and I started putting out those flyers, I've seen and heard even more. Lives have been destroyed, homes and families damaged. I know The Lakes is valuable real estate, but you've got to find another way to develop—"

"The Lakes? You think that's the reason I don't want to call off Sam?"

"You stand to lose a lot of money. And I know you feel responsibility to your partners, but—"

"I guess you haven't changed as much as I thought." Cutter rose to his feet. "You still can't see beyond your nose."

"What's that supposed to mean?"

"It means that you don't know anything, Gloria. It means that you're *clueless.*"

"If it's not The Lakes you're thinking about, what then?"

"I told you."

"You didn't tell me anything." Gloria grabbed Cutter's hand and pulled herself up, obviously tired of having a conversation that required her to crane her neck. She stood so close he could see the tiny scar on her chin, the one he had given her when they'd had that mudball fight years ago and he had cut her with a small piece of glass he didn't know was mixed in with the mud. She tried to let go of his hand, but he wouldn't release her. "I don't know how to make it any clearer other than to say that I was only thinking of you."

Gloria nodded, but Cutter could tell by the look on her face she didn't believe him. "I want you to stand firm on this because . . . I love you. Is that clear enough?"

He had never seen a look like the one he now saw on Gloria's face. It was a mix of utter shock, fear, and . . . something else he couldn't quite identify. Disgust? He didn't think he'd ever forget it as long as he lived. He watched her go without saying a word.

You really are an idiot, Press.

❧ ❧

Gloria sped along I-80, her radio blaring, and knew she should slow down but didn't. She was glad it was Saturday and she could finally leave Appleton. Ever since finding Tiger in the kitchen with that note tied around his neck, and ever since her visit to Cutter's, all she'd wanted to do was get out of town. She knew it was akin to running from her problems, but she didn't care.

She pressed her foot on the gas and watched the turning leaves on the trees along the side of the road become a blur of red and yellow and brown. *Faster. Faster.* Her foot pressed harder. With every passing second, she was leaving her concerns farther and farther behind: the stalker . . . Tiger . . . Cutter.

For days they had all filled her mind until she was tired of thinking about them. Would she get a restraining order if she saw the man in leather again? Would she continue publishing her flyer with Harry? And Cutter . . . what about him?

Gloria eased her foot off the gas and felt the Escort slow. Why was she thinking about them again? Why was she letting them drag her back to Appleton instead of taking flight to Eckerd? Maybe because when she had prayed about the whole thing, all Jesus had said was "Trust Me."

She really disliked when He said things like that. She'd rather He spelled a situation out or put it on a flowchart so she could see how it was all going to wind up. But "trust Me" was hard.

Well, stop trying to figure it out, Gloria, and just do what He said.

When she got right down to it, why was it so hard to trust Jesus, anyway? Hadn't He shown her in Eckerd that He could be trusted? Yes. Over and over again. Only . . . her experience had also shown her that He didn't always work out things quite as she'd like. Now, take Cutter for instance. Wouldn't it be just like Jesus to have her end up with *him?* Gloria couldn't even get her mind around that idea.

So—it wasn't a matter of trust, then. It was a matter of getting her own way. She still wanted that—her own way. And she hadn't realized just how much that tendency continued to control her. When she felt her heart sink, felt her stomach churn, she turned off the radio and let the silence fill the car.

"Jesus," she finally said in a near-whisper, "I love You so much; I can't bear the thought of being out of Your will. If that means my will must be altered, then do it. Have Your way in me. Only . . . Cutter's not exactly the man of my dreams. I hope he's not the one You've chosen for me, and if he is, could You think about it some more? Maybe reconsider? Nevertheless, not my will, but Yours be done."

Gloria felt like a pressed sandwich by the time Harry Grizwald, Dorie Dobson, and Perth finished squeezing and kissing her. Then Dorie took Gloria's parka, and the air exploded with words as everyone started talking at once.

"Wait a minute! Wait a minute! Let's give the girl a chance to catch her breath," Harry said, taking Gloria by the arm and escorting her from the foyer of his apartment to the dining room. "Come sit here." He directed her to a captain's chair at the head of the table. "This way we can get a good look at you while giving you the third degree."

When Gloria sat down, Perth quickly sat next to her. "I missed you," she mouthed.

"Me too," Gloria said out loud. "I've missed you all."

"I figured we'd have an early dinner." Harry smiled sheepishly before bustling to the kitchen.

"Harry, for heaven's sake, it's only eleven o'clock!" Gloria said, laughing.

"I know," he shouted back, "but there's nothing like a nice meal to give us all a chance to catch up." Harry entered, carrying a steaming dish between two raggedy oven mitts. "Now, don't anyone burn yourself." He set it on a trivet in front of Gloria. "It's the hors d'oeuvres. My clam dip specialty. You spread it over the crackers." He pointed to the small basket of Triscuits in front of Perth.

Dorie took one and plunged it into the dip. "He's been cooking all week. Made enough food for an army. Tell Gloria what else you've got in that kitchen of yours."

"She'll find out soon enough."

When he headed back to the kitchen, Dorie leaned over. "He's got a pot of Bolognese sauce in there big enough to choke a horse, and he's cooking up a pound of linguine to go with it. Then he's got a half dozen Cornish game hens—with mushroom stuffing—a Waldorf salad, julienne carrots, and butternut squash. For dessert he made a double chocolate-chip cake. I've never known anyone who could cook like that man. Told him flat out that was the main reason I was marrying him." Dorie fussed with her white lace collar. "Of course, it isn't true, but I think he believed it. He actually said it was truer than I wanted to think, but he didn't care." Gloria smiled, remembering Dorie's former diet of TV dinners. "He said if that's what it took to get me, then it was fine with him. Now, what kind of man is that? Willing to settle for a woman who's only interested in her stomach?"

Gloria laughed. It felt so good to be among her friends again. She looked over at Perth, who had filled out a bit and no longer looked so gangly. "So, how's school?"

"I have to study *sooooo* hard, and I take more notes than anyone in class, but . . . so far I've been acing my tests."

"I knew you'd do well." Gloria's heart swelled with pride. "Didn't I tell you?"

Perth nodded. She looked so sweet with her long brown hair combed back and held by an emerald green scrunchie that matched the edging on her white shirt. The top two buttons were open, and Gloria could see the small rosebud tattoo under Perth's left collarbone, a reminder of how far she'd come.

"And your love life? Are you still seeing—"

"Spike number two?"

"Wasn't Spike the guy who ate live bait? I thought you were seeing another guy, Jud . . . now, what was his last name?"

"It's not worth remembering. Turns out he wasn't much better than Spike. And since I'm not having any luck in that department, I've decided to forget romance for now and concentrate on my studies. Which is just as well, since I need so much extra time to do what others seem to breeze through."

Gloria picked up a Triscuit and scooped out some of Harry's clam dip, all the while thinking how grown-up Perth seemed. Such a far cry from the skinny little girl with the toe rings who'd stolen groceries from the West Meadow Market. She popped the cracker into her mouth, feeling a fullness of soul and a contentment she'd hardly thought possible.

It was so good to be back.

~❦ ❦~

Gloria moved in a kind of sleepy slow motion—the kind that comes after a good meal and too much of it.

"Harry, you outdid yourself!" she said, carrying her plate full of picked-clean bones, then stacking Harry's on top. Dorie and Perth had already cleared their dishes. "I mean, you *really* outdid yourself."

"Why go to a restaurant when you can come to Harry's?" Dorie said with a wink. And Gloria thought, why indeed?

She piled her plates on top of the others on the kitchen counter, then began scraping them, one by one. The afternoon had been perfect. And she still had the evening and part of the next day before she had to go home. She couldn't believe how relaxed she felt and wondered if Cornish game hens, like turkey, contained tryptophan. Although she had had plenty of carbs too—and some scientists were now claiming carbs were responsible for making people so sleepy after a big meal, not tryptophan. But Gloria's money was still on the game hens.

Maybe she'd squeeze in a nap. A power nap of thirty minutes would go a long way. It would surely make her evening with Perth more enjoyable. Harry had already announced that he and

Dorie were going to a movie. Gloria guessed it was to give the girls time to talk. She looked forward to some alone time with Perth. Though they weren't related, Gloria considered Perth as dear as a younger sister.

Yes, either a nap or a walk. One or the other, because she needed to wake up. "I'm really sleepy," she said, stacking the scraped dishes into the sink.

"Me too," said Perth.

"Now, isn't that just the way of things," Dorie said. "Young people today don't have the stamina we did." She pointed to Harry, who stood leaning quietly in the corner with a grin on his face. "Harry here has been standing behind that stove for days, and he's not a bit tired. Are you, Harry?"

Harry stifled a yawn and pushed himself off the wall. "Not a bit, Dorie. Strong and vigorous as a bull, if you wanna know the truth."

"No need to talk about bulls, Harry. I'm making a point here. And the point being that young people today are lacking something. That's why the drugstores and whatnot are selling so many supplements. Can't keep them on their shelves. Everyone's on a supplement, don't you know. You girls take vitamins?"

Both Gloria and Perth shook their heads.

"Well, isn't that just the way of things? You best be looking into some supplementation before you waste away. For now, anyway, just get out of the kitchen and go for a walk. Get yourselves some exercise. That's what keeps me going. I take my little Cleo and Mark Anthony for a walk three, maybe four, times a day. Over a mile each time." Dorie had taken the plate Gloria was holding and began pushing her toward the door of the kitchen. "Go on. You and Perth get out and stretch your legs. Harry and I will finish the rest of these. Right, Harry?"

Gloria saw the grin on Harry's face slide off like melting

wax and stifled a laugh. "I can't do that, Dorie. Harry did all the cooking. It's only fair that Perth and I clean up." Over Dorie's shoulder, Gloria saw Perth nod in agreement. But Dorie only pushed harder, until Gloria found herself out of the kitchen and standing beside the dining-room table.

"Okay, Dorie. We'll go. But why don't you and Harry just leave the dishes, and Perth and I will do them when we get back?"

Harry gave Gloria a grateful smile. "Well, if you insist, Gloria, okay."

"Nonsense." Dorie pushed harder, bringing Gloria almost to the front door. "You're the guest of honor. You shouldn't be doing anything. Now, off with you."

The last thing Gloria saw before she and Perth grabbed their jackets and left the apartment was Harry strapping on his white Pillsbury Doughboy–looking apron and appearing very unhappy about the prospect of washing the mountain of dishes with Dorie. The thing Dorie Dobson had yet to learn about her intended was that while Harry loved cooking, he hated the cleanup.

--❧ ❧--

When Gloria walked arm in arm with Perth out the entrance of E-Z Printing and onto Pratt Parkway, the first thing she saw was a Harley Fat Boy parked by the curb, and her heart did a flip. *Don't get carried away, Gloria. You're in Eckerd City now. No one's tailing you.* But when she suddenly saw a man dressed all in black leather, she pulled Perth to a stop, then yanked her backward through the door. Even before the man turned and she saw his face, she knew it was the same person who had been following her all over Appleton.

"What's wrong?" Perth said, her eyes wide with concern. "You look . . . like you've seen a ghost."

Gloria slammed the print shop door, stopped only long enough to flip the dead bolt, then yanked Perth toward the stairs leading to Harry's third-floor apartment.

"What's going on?" Perth sounded frightened.

"I'll tell you when we get to Harry's. He needs to hear this too." Gloria took the stairs two at a time, pulling Perth behind her, all the while knowing she was just about to spoil their perfect weekend.

~❦ ❦~

Chapter Twelve

─────────

GLORIA SAT ON THE EDGE of the queen-size bed, holding Virginia's hand and praying silently. The woman lying propped on five pillows looked as fragile as the white filament of a dandelion, like the ones Gloria used to blow when she was a child and scatter on the wind.

Where would the wind take Virginia Press when it was time?

Dust to dust.

She hoped it would be into Jesus' arms, but so far Virginia had resisted all talk of heaven or Gloria's wonderful Lord. And time was running out. Even her untrained eyes could see that.

"You're certainly quiet today." Virginia's voice sounded gravelly. "Must have a lot on your mind."

Gloria shifted her weight. She didn't think she could cram another thing into her head. It was already filled with thoughts of the stalker and Cutter and Harry and Dorie and Perth. And now Virginia.

Dust to dust.

"So what's the town saying about me?"

"The usual. That you're angry with Cutter."

To Gloria's surprise, the frail woman chuckled. "And Cutter? What does he say?"

"The same."

"You sure don't beat around the bush, do you?"

"There isn't time." That one got Virginia. Gloria could feel the tension in the older woman's hand.

"You're rather surly."

"I suppose I am."

"You want to tell me why?"

Gloria caressed Virginia's hand in hers. It felt like a dry leather purse, the kind her mother used to use for loose change. "I've been coming here twice a week for the past several weeks, and I just realized I don't want to come anymore, and I've been trying to figure out a way to tell you." She heard Virginia gasp, felt the bony hand tighten around her own.

"Now, why would you say such a hateful thing to a dying old woman?"

"I didn't say it to be hateful. I'm sorry if that's how it sounded, but honestly, Virginia, you've got to stop using the fact that you're dying to manipulate everyone."

"There's a point you're trying to make, I suppose." Virginia's birdlike chest, with its protruding collarbones and shrunken breasts, heaved in a sigh. "So hurry up and make it. Don't stumble around like a mouse in a maze. I get enough of that from Agnes and Cutter. Well . . . I did from Cutter when he was a boy. Now I can't get one civil word out of his mouth." Virginia sank deeper into her pillows as though insulating herself. "So what's your point?"

"The fact is, Virginia, you won't accept reality."

"You've tried to introduce different rules. And I told you I won't play by them, or anyone else's for that matter. I told you *I* make the rules."

Gloria pressed Virginia's thin, dry hand to her lips when she saw the fear in her sharp eyes. "Then you're going to have to play by yourself."

"What's gotten you so mad? I don't understand—"

"I'm not mad. I just . . . can't bear to see you like this. You want to pretend that everything revolves around you, that you're still in control. And I can't help you live that lie." Gloria released Virginia's hand and filled her empty glass with ice water from the pitcher on the nightstand. She handed the glass to Virginia. "You were never in control anyway. Not really. But you never figured that one out."

"Can't you just let me pretend? Can't you just indulge a dying old lady?" Virginia's eyes misted as she waved away the glass.

Gloria shook her head and put down the water.

"Why not?"

"Because I care about you." She ran the fingers of one hand gently across the side of Virginia's cheek, across the liver spots that dotted her face like mud splatters. "Because I can't sit here and watch you die and not share my Jesus with you."

"You're . . . the only one who comes to see me." Virginia's lips quivered. "Even your mother doesn't come anymore, just calls on the phone. I think deep down she knows what's happening here and is afraid. I guess death frightens everyone." She suddenly grabbed Gloria's hand, her sharp, bony fingers looking like the talons of an eagle clutching its prey. "You *must* keep coming. You can't stop. You just couldn't be that heartless."

Gloria tried to pull away and was surprised by the strength of Virginia's grip. For a moment it almost resembled a tug of war. "This will be my last time," Gloria said, when Virginia finally let go.

"All right. All right, I'm *scared*. I admit it. You satisfied? Is that what you want to hear? I'm scared . . . and I don't want to die alone. Maybe it pleases you to see the old Dragon Lady reduced to this. You might even think I deserve what I got. That I deserve to die alone. And maybe I do. But I'm fool enough not to want to, and I'm fool enough to be scared by it all. But I'm not fool enough to believe that fairy tale about how there's a big God up there in the sky who loves me."

"What are you worrying about, Virginia? That someone will think you're soft because you believe in something bigger than yourself?" Gloria bent down and kissed the older woman on the forehead.

"You . . . leaving already?"

Gloria nodded.

"Will I see you Wednesday?"

Gloria's feet felt like lead as she walked toward the door. She squared her shoulders.

"Wednesday . . . will I see you Wednesday?"

"See, that's the trouble with you, Virginia." Gloria paused by the doorway. "You just don't listen. I told you I won't be here Wednesday. This is good-bye."

"Wait! Just wait a minute. If I . . . let you bring your Bible, if I let you talk about your Jesus . . . *then* will you come?"

Gloria felt a slow, deliberate smile spread over her face like a sunrise. "I'll see you Wednesday," she said without turning, then walked out the door.

◆ ◆

Cutter sat on the darkened stoop of Gloria's apartment, watching the blue Ford Escort pull onto the gravel. The headlights blinked off, and he watched by moonlight as the car door opened and Gloria's shapely figure stepped slowly out onto the driveway. When he rose to his feet, he saw her step back against the car and realized he must have frightened her, coming out of the shadows like that.

"It's just me," he said quickly. "It's Cutter." He wondered whom she'd rather see right now, the stalker or him, and decided it might be a close call. This was the first time they'd met since his rather awkward declaration of love. He thought it strange that he didn't feel embarrassed or uptight. But he could see, by the stiff way she walked up the driveway, that she did.

So let her.

"Cutter . . . what are you doing here?"

"We need to talk." He heard her groan. When she stopped in front of him and just stood there, he reached over and opened the screen door. "I'd like to come in."

"I don't know . . . it's late, and—"

He pulled the keys from her hand and unlocked the door. With his free hand, he reached in and flicked on the light. Then he walked through the door, closing the screen and leaving Gloria outside. A few minutes later he heard the door slam, and smothered a grin. She must be mad as a hornet.

"It's late, and I'm tired and hungry, and— Hold on, now. Just what do you think you're doing?"

Cutter had opened the refrigerator door and was pulling everything edible he could find out of it. He stopped when she positioned her body between him and the counter. The look on her face was steely. "You said you were hungry," he said sheepishly. "I thought I'd fix you something." His eyes rested on a plate of leftover meatloaf that he had already put on the counter. With one final lunge, he grabbed the whole wheat and the small jar of mayo, then closed the refrigerator. Without a word, he squeezed by her rigid body and began making two meatloaf sandwiches.

"I can't eat two," Gloria finally said, over his shoulder.

"The second one's for me. I figured you'd be more relaxed if I ate with you."

"This is silly. Why don't you just tell me what's on your mind and be done with it?"

He took her by the arm, then gently pushed her down onto one of the kitchen chairs. "A serious discussion should not be attempted on an empty stomach." He noticed that at the word *serious* Gloria tensed. "Don't worry. I'm not going to tell you again that I love you. But I'm not going to apologize for falling in love with you, either. You'll have to work through it, just as I will. And anytime you want to talk about it, you can." He thought he saw Gloria grit her teeth.

"I *don't* want to talk about it. But you sure did make things more awkward, and just when we were . . ."

"We were what?" Cutter rummaged through the cabinets until he found where she kept the plates. "Becoming friends?" He placed each cut sandwich on a plate, then grabbed some napkins, carried everything to the table, and sat down. "We *were* becoming friends, right?"

Gloria nodded.

"Good. It's a start. The rest . . . well, we'll get over that. You and me. Then it'll be more comfortable. Though I'm not the least bit uncomfortable." He took a big bite of his sandwich, then jumped up and poured them both a glass of milk. "But I can see that you are. Uncomfortable, I mean."

"No, I'm not. I'm fine with it. It just took me by surprise, that's all. But I'm fine with it."

Cutter placed the milk glasses on the table and sat back down. "You're uncomfortable."

"No, I'm . . . uncomfortable."

They both laughed.

"Okay. Now that we've cleared the air, there is something I need to talk to you about." Cutter shoved the last of his sandwich into his mouth, then washed it down with a big gulp of milk, all the while watching Gloria and feeling pleased that she wasn't looking at him with that pained expression anymore. "Did you see Virginia tonight?" He could see he had taken her by surprise. And he could see something else. The pained look was back.

"Yes," she said, taking the first bite of her sandwich.

Then, without knowing why, Cutter reached over and covered Gloria's hands, sandwich and all. "Virginia would never stay away from her precious Medical Data this long, not even to punish me, unless something was wrong. And I need to know what it is."

"Then why don't you ask *her*?"

"Because I'd rather ask you."

"Well, don't!" Gloria turned away.

"Why not?" He grabbed her chin and gently turned her face toward his, forcing her to look at him. "Gloria, I'm asking you, what's wrong with my mother?"

"I . . . promised I wouldn't tell."

"Then there *is* something wrong." He released her chin.

"Oh, Cutter, you know in your heart there is. Otherwise we wouldn't be having this conversation."

"Okay, how sick is she?" When Gloria absently poked her sandwich, his neck muscles tightened. It had been haunting him all week—this thought that something was wrong. But he had managed to push it out of his mind by making light of it. By telling himself Virginia was too ornery to die. Too cheap to go off to the netherworld and leave him a multimillion-dollar business. *A business she couldn't control.*

Cutter leaned over as far as he could. It was important he catch every detail of Gloria's expression when he asked the next question, because her face would tell him what he needed to know. "Is Virginia dying?"

Gloria's lips pinched, and there was a catch in her throat as she tried to swallow. Her eyes wandered past him, refusing to look his way, and her tense shoulders arched backward as though trying to ease the strain.

Without another word, Cutter rose from his chair and walked out the door.

It took only a second for Gloria to realize she couldn't let Cutter walk out alone. Not with the knowledge he was taking with him. She grabbed her keys, locked the door—and she wouldn't have bothered to do that except she remembered the stalker—then ran down the gravel driveway. She saw Cutter walk under the streetlight, toward his Saab parked in front of Sam Hidel's deserted store. She was able to reach him before he unlocked the car.

"Let's walk," she said, pulling on his arm and leading him back to the sidewalk. He offered little resistance, as though he were sleepwalking. Without a word, she slipped her arm through his and first led, then walked quietly beside him.

They crossed Millhouse Street, then passed Kelly's Hardware, Dooley & Dooley—the husband-and-wife dental practice —then Regis Clock Company. They crossed over Larkspur, where a row of old Victorians stood guard over a lovely brass street lamp that was different from all the rest. It wasn't until they were in front of Atlantic Electric that Cutter broke the silence.

"I don't know why I should be surprised. Why I should expect Virginia to end her life any differently than she lived it. But I am. I guess I thought that when it came right down to it, when the end came, Virginia would finally show some motherly instincts. Would at least let her son know she was dying. Would at least not make me learn it through a third party. Does the whole town know? Does everyone know but me?"

Gloria let her arm drop, then slipped her hand into his. "I think only Dr. Grant and Agnes know." She felt his hand tighten around hers and marveled how different his hands were from Virginia's. Cutter's were big and bulky, with knuckles the size of lug nuts. Virginia's were small, birdlike, and veiny. Yet of the two, Virginia had always wielded the heavier blow. "I don't think she knew how to tell you."

"She didn't want to tell me. Even to the end, she wanted to punish and humiliate me."

"She's frightened, Cutter."

Cutter snorted with caustic laughter. "The only thing the great Virginia Press is afraid of is losing control."

Gloria thought of Virginia's agonizing resistance earlier, and now of Cutter's open honesty. Virginia seemed so afraid to let down her guard and reveal her vulnerability, while Cutter seemed willing enough to reveal his. At least, this new Cutter was. "Maybe in some ways you're stronger than your mother. Bear that in mind when you deal with her."

"What do you mean?"

"I mean, if you want to make peace, then it'll be up to you." Now she felt Cutter's resistance. It was as powerful and piercing as an electric shock. "Go see her, Cutter, before it's too late."

"Well, well, well. Now, isn't this a pretty sight."

Gloria turned toward the sound of the voice and saw Tracy standing near the corner of Main and Brandise, only feet away from the entrance to Hoolahan's Pub. The way she staggered suggested she had just come from the bar.

"Oh . . . hi, Tracy." Gloria followed Tracy's gaze to the hand that was entwined with Cutter's and self-consciously let go.

"You sure are full of surprises." Tracy sauntered closer in her tight miniskirt that was only inches shy of being pornographic. "Never expected to see you two an item."

"We're not—" Gloria stopped. There was no way to explain this without embarrassing Cutter. "You're a bit of a surprise yourself." Gloria tried not to gawk at Tracy's outfit. It was worse than anything Sadie Bellows would wear. If Gloria didn't know better, she'd have taken Tracy for one of the hookers she'd seen in Eckerd City. "I didn't expect to see you in town. I thought you'd be working."

Tracy flipped a mass of red hair over her shoulder. "My night off."

"Aha. Well . . . how's everything?" Gloria noticed that Cutter had inched away and was already in front of Cameras & More, which butted the left side of Hoolahan's.

"The tips are good, but the pay's lousy. And you wouldn't believe the jerks that come into the place. Some of the customers figure since I'm behind the bar they have a captive audience and can tell me their life story. Like I'm supposed to care? Then if I *am* polite and try to listen, they think I might be interested in other things too." Tracy had difficulty standing straight.

Gloria glanced to the side and saw that Cutter was moving farther and farther away. "Maybe we could meet for lunch one day this week and catch up?"

"Well . . . I don't know. Things are a little tight with those credit card bills, and—"

"It's my treat. C'mon, Tracy. What do you say?"

Tracy shrugged. "I guess it could work out." Then she tossed her head, making her red hair fly in all directions, and laughed as she caught sight of Nick Cervantes exiting Hoolahan's.

"There you are, Babe," Nick said, coming up behind Tracy and putting his arms around her slim waist. He eyed Gloria with suspicion. "What's the frog doing here?"

Tracy slumped against Nick's lean chest as he kissed her neck. "I don't have a clue." She narrowed her eyes, then said to Gloria in a near-whisper, "I can't believe you're going out with the Monkey. You sure turned out to be a surprise."

Gloria thought she could say the same as she studied Tracy reeling unsteadily on her feet, her hair disheveled, her skirt so tight it left no room for mystery, her spandex top looking like a Band-Aid across her chest and barely covering her breasts, and Nick Cervantes, the drug dealer, pawing at her. But she didn't. She only wished she could take Tracy in her arms and tell her how much Jesus loved her.

❦ ❦

"Hey! Wait up." Gloria trotted along the sidewalk past Cameras & More, past Pearl Owens's Today's Woman clothing store and the Bake Shoppe, until finally she caught up with Cutter in front of Rosie's Beauty Parlor. He had stopped and turned at the sound of her voice and was waiting, a glum expression on his face.

"I suppose you're going to blame me for that, now." His voice was surly.

"Blame you for what?"

"I haven't seen Tracy since . . ."

"Since you fired her?"

"I heard she wasn't doing well, but I never expected to see her like that."

"You could have been kinder. You could have kept her on. She *was* your top telemarketer."

"I knew you were going to blame me."

"I'm not blaming you." Cutter seemed to relax and threaded his arm through hers. The act was so natural it took Gloria a second to notice. "Only . . . sometimes I don't understand you."

"A man in love tends to do stupid things."

"I thought we weren't going to talk about that anymore."

"You brought it up."

"I didn't—"

"You wanna know why I came back to Appleton after NYU? Why I came back to work at a job I hated, to a town I wanted to get as far away from as possible, to a mother who still can make my insides twist and turn? It was because of you, Gloria. Only because of you."

"Cutter, *please* . . ."

"I just want to set the record straight. I just want you to understand why I took what Tracy did so hard. After coming back and putting up with all this stuff in Appleton, biding my time, waiting patiently, Tracy turns around and *gets you out of town.* I was beyond frustrated."

Gloria wished she hadn't allowed Cutter to hold her by the arm. She felt the need to put some distance between them but didn't know how without being rude. His arm was too tightly entwined with hers. But the memory of his proposal—the humiliation of it—was still too vivid. That day in his office, over a year ago, he had treated her like a hired servant. Had humiliated and embarrassed her. And now . . . his words didn't line up. Did he really expect her to believe he had made that proposal out of love? And yet, somehow . . . it was even more difficult to believe that Cutter was lying now. "You said your proposal was a business deal."

"Well, what did you expect? I knew you hated me. If I just came out and said I loved you, you would have laughed in my face. But I was getting desperate, tired of waiting. It seemed like we were never going to get anywhere. When my mother insisted I get married, I saw my chance."

"But all those women you brought to her? Sadie Bellows and the rest . . ."

Cutter laughed. "I knew Virginia would never accept them. And I didn't want her to. It was always you, Gloria. I've loved you since before I kissed you in Clive McGreedy's barn. Only you could never see it."

"But you were always so . . . mean."

"Don't you know that young boys tease girls they like? Or pull their pigtails or pelt them with mud balls?"

"Or call them *frog?*"

Cutter stopped, bringing Gloria to a stop also. "You could never see beyond your nose, Gloria. You could never see anyone for what he really was." In the lamplight Gloria saw an expression on Cutter's face so tender it embarrassed her, and she looked away.

"C'mon." Cutter tugged on Gloria's arm. "It's getting late. I'll walk you back." They turned around on the sidewalk and headed for Sam Hidel's. "Thanks for coming after me. Hearing about Virginia was . . . well, it was like when you punched me in the eye that time. I should have seen it coming but didn't, and boy, did it hurt."

Gloria slipped her hand into his. "I know. I'm sorry."

"For what? Punching me in the eye?"

"No. For Virginia."

Cutter gave her hand a squeeze; then they walked quietly for some time.

"I saw Harry Grizwald last weekend and told him about the

stalker and Tiger and the note." She deliberately avoided telling Cutter that the stalker had followed her to Eckerd. "Both he and I agree we want to continue the flyers." They passed Hoolahan's, with no sign of Tracy or Nick Cervantes. "I have some stuff for another article and plan to work it up this week."

"Really?" Gloria could feel rather than see Cutter's smile. "I'm glad. But now I owe you one."

"No, you don't. What about you getting Clive's car for me? Then setting up such easy payments, even Tracy could make them?"

"That doesn't count."

"Why not?"

"Because it didn't take courage. Just money. Your decision to continue with the flyers took courage. So I owe you."

"I see. You want to do something for me that takes courage?"

"I guess. If you put it that way."

"Okay, then make peace with Virginia."

Chapter Thirteen

"ARE YOU AND CUTTER BACK together again?" Geri Bickford asked, directing her voice toward the small slotted speaker of her phone. It left her hands free, and she sat on the cushioned wooden stool in her kitchen giving herself a manicure. It had been a long time since she'd felt like doing her nails. But she couldn't believe how elated she was—like someone had just told her she was on her way to the Miss America pageant all over again. Maybe Gloria was developing some sense after all. "So, are you and Cutter back together again?" she repeated.

"We were never together."

Gloria's reply made Geri smear Cranberry Wine all over her thumb. "What do you mean? Someone saw the two of you walking down Main Street, holding hands." She heard Gloria make a peevish noise that sounded like *tsssss*. Why did she act like that? Like it wasn't important? And why couldn't this rumor about Gloria and Cutter be true? It would be nice seeing her daughter set up in a home with a husband. Especially a husband as well off as Cutter Press. Then maybe, just maybe, Geri could stop worrying. "The whole town's talking about it. Pearl Owens said the buzz is just everywhere." Again the peevish sound. "Now, why are you getting annoyed?"

"Because I hate it when people jump to conclusions. Someone saw Cutter and me—"

"Then you *were* with Cutter last night?"

"Yes, and—"

"And the two of you were holding hands?"

"Yes, but—"

"If you two were out on a date and holding hands, then for heaven's sake, why are you trying to deny it?"

"We weren't out on a date, Mother."

"Well, call it what you want," Geri returned, refusing to let her daughter's sullen manner get the best of her. "But I'm glad you've started seeing each other again." The next thing Geri heard was the sound of a click coming through the speaker, and she knew that Gloria had hung up. Now, what had she said that was so wrong? Couldn't a mother ask a simple question anymore? She didn't think she'd ever understand that daughter of hers.

~❦ ❦~

Just as Gloria hung up, she saw Wanda bounce toward her, her teased, bleached hair looking like a squirrel's nest. Without a word, Gloria pulled the top page off her pile, the one Wanda had asked her about at least five times since she came in that morning. It was a PO from Charlie Axlerod.

"It says here he won't be coming in for the proof till noon," Gloria said, hoping to head Wanda off at the pass. But it didn't work.

"It also says it's an *emergency*—a high-priority job." Wanda planted her chubby hands on her hips, looking all too much like a female wrestler. "You got it ready?"

Gloria shook her head, thinking Wanda looked mad enough to pin her on the floor in a scissor lock. She wished Charlie Axlerod, in this, the final week of the Apple Festival, hadn't come up with this brilliant idea, or at least what he thought was a brilliant idea. He had decided he wanted the town of Appleton drawn as a game board, and every time a tourist shopped in a store and bought something, he moved along the board, as it were, and collected a token—a red paper circle with the name of that store neatly printed in the center. The person with the most red circles won a free night, plus dinner and breakfast the next morning, at Charlie's Bed-and-Breakfast. He had already gotten his secretary to cut out a zillion red construction-paper circles and pass them along to all the store owners. Now it remained for Gloria to create the game board listing all the stores, and for Paul Lugget to print it up.

"I'll have it ready by noon," Gloria said, hoping she sounded firm enough to end the discussion. Wanda took several rapid breaths, as though hyperventilating. Gloria felt sorry for the interruptions this morning. First there was the call to Tracy setting up a lunch date for today, then her mother's call.

"I *really* wanted to see it before Charlie came in," Wanda said, tearing the foil off a piece of spearmint, then wadding the gum into a ball and shoving it into her mouth.

"Okay, okay. I'll have it ready by eleven forty-five."

Wanda tossed the foil into Gloria's garbage pail, her jaw muscles working. "I'm beginning to hate this job. Everyone wants their stuff *yesterday*." Gloria heard the gum snap between Wanda's teeth. "And forget the help—sassy upstarts who think they know it all and spend too much time on the phone. I swear, one of these days I'm just gonna up and sell this place. You just see if I don't."

Gloria watched Wanda disappear into the press room, probably to give Paul an earful. Then she turned to her computer and pounded the keyboard. She had only one hour to get Charlie Axlerod's brainstorm on paper. Then she had to pick Tracy up for lunch and didn't want to be late. It had been hard enough getting Tracy to agree to go. And ever since bumping into her by Hoolahan's, Gloria had known it was more important than ever to reestablish their friendship.

~♦ ♦~

Cutter was about to tell Sadie Bellows to just leave the folders on his desk and he'd file them himself, but she was already bent over the bottom drawer of the file cabinet. With a quick ticking of a violet fingernail, she flipped through the files until she found the proper place, then jammed in the folder. Then she slammed the drawer so hard his dartboard fell off the wall and nearly landed on her head.

"You all right?" he said, rising from his chair but not moving from the spot. He didn't want to get too close. All morning she had banged drawers, rustled papers, and stomped around in her lavender spikes. Now, as she turned to him, he could see he had said the wrong thing.

"No, I'm *not* all right."

Cutter held his breath.

"The whole place is talking about it. You could at least have had the decency to tell me. Though I can hardly believe you'd give that little twerp a second glance." Sadie's heels tapped loudly across the tile floor, giving Cutter the impression she wished it were his head. "How do you think that makes me feel? You and that twerp?"

He thought about it a minute and realized he was clueless. He had no idea what Sadie's thoughts were about anything. They had never spent much time in conversation. But it surprised him a little to think she might be hurt.

"How long has this been going on, anyway?"

Cutter looked at Sadie and frowned. Her demanding attitude annoyed him. He picked up a dart and fought the urge to tell her so. He supposed he should make some concession to a woman he had slept with. But he'd always found it strange that once he had gone that final step, a woman always made certain assumptions—the most erroneous one being that he cared for her.

"Well, how long?" Sadie tapped her left foot impatiently.

"I hardly think I have to explain anything to you." The look on Sadie's face told Cutter he had devastated her.

"Well . . . I assumed . . . that is . . . I thought we had something special. That you cared."

What he knew about women could fit into a shot glass.

"Does this mean we're through?"

Cutter looked into his secretary's bewildered eyes. "Sadie, it means whatever you want it to mean." He might as well have taken his letter opener and plunged it into her carotid artery.

"You . . . you never walked down Main Street holding *my* hand. And it would have been nice. If you had. Just once."

Cutter watched her walk to the door, her hips moving in that melodic way that could drive a man crazy.

"Consider this my two weeks' notice."

Now he was really stunned. He watched her close the office door without a word. What had she expected? A trip to the altar? A house outside town? She was a diversion. It had never occurred to him that she felt differently, or if it had, he'd pushed it out of his mind. And it had never occurred to him that he could hurt her deeply.

When it comes to women, Press, you're a real dunce.

No wonder Gloria hated him. Well, not hate. Not anymore. She was softening on that score. She had been kind to him last night. Kinder than he deserved. But that was because she was kind. While he was a downright brute.

Just ask Sadie.

Well, what could anyone expect? With a mother like Virginia Press? What kind of role model was she anyway? How could a man learn anything good from a woman like that?

C'mon, Press, you going to blame Virginia for everything?

"You bet I am."

❧ ☙

Gloria pushed impatiently on the doorbell and listened to parts of the *1812 Overture* for the sixth time. She had been leaning on the bell for five minutes. She was sure Tracy was inside, from the noises coming from the small opening in the upstairs window. Finally, Gloria backed away from the door, then down the two steps of the front stoop and almost halfway into the yard. From this vantage point, she could clearly see the open window with the navy Ralph Lauren curtains fluttering ever so slightly on the sides.

"Tracy!" No answer. "Tracy!" Gloria picked up a small pebble and tossed it like she used to do when she was younger. The pebble missed the window and landed in the gutter along the roof line. She looked around for another one. They were easy enough to find amid the dying sod interspersed with large patches of dirt. She chose a small stone close to her foot and dug it out with her fingers. Then she brushed it off and hurled it at the window. It made a loud clinking noise when it connected, and Gloria feared she had broken the glass. She squinted up through the sun and was relieved to see that the window was still intact. "Tracy!" Now why would Tracy ask to meet here, then not answer the door? "Tracy!"

"All right! I'm coming!" A pair of hands raised the window; then a tangle of red hair appeared.

"We had a lunch date, remember?"

"Yeah . . . right . . . sorry . . . I was just lying down."

"What's the matter? You're not sick, are you?"

"No . . . just tired. This night job's killing me. By the time I get home and change and . . . oh, whatever . . . Be down in a sec."

Gloria walked back to the front door and waited. When it finally opened, she was startled by what the daylight revealed. Dark circles cupped Tracy's eyes like athlete's grease, and her skin had the look of jaundice. It was obvious she was neither eating nor sleeping well. And there was something else. She looked like she had aged five years.

"Why don't you just quit that job?" Gloria said, entering the foyer.

"Because it pays the bills."

"There are better jobs, especially with your background." Gloria followed Tracy to the kitchen. Dishes cluttered the sink, and a crusted pan, which someone had obviously used to make an omelet earlier, was on the stove. "You can do better than bartending."

Tracy opened the refrigerator and pulled out a container of orange juice. "I always thought I was going places. You know? I thought someday I'd be in charge of Medical Data's telemarketing department."

Gloria stuffed down the nagging reminder that *she* was the reason Tracy had lost her job. The thing about guilt was that once it grabbed hold, it took something a lot bigger to make it let go. "I hear there's a Chase Bank opening in New Canterbury. Maybe you could get a job there?"

"Doing what?"

"Telemarketing. Calling people to see if they'd like to open an account." Gloria shrugged. "Oh, I don't know. I guess I'm just talking out of my hat." She watched Tracy gulp down an eight-ounce glass of juice. "But I do know this: you can do better than bartending."

Tracy dropped the plastic glass into the sink. "Mind if we skip lunch? I'm just not up to it. I'm not even hungry. I thought I'd feel better by now, but my head's still splitting from a hangover."

"See, that's another thing. If you were in telemarketing, you wouldn't come home from work with a hangover."

"You're such a simpleton, Gloria." Tracy stepped over one of her sneakers, then kicked the other one out of the way. "You make everything sound easy."

As Gloria followed Tracy to the living room, she noticed that her friend's gray sweats hardly concealed how thin she was. "Why don't we go job hunting?" Gloria sat on the ottoman while Tracy plopped on the nearby couch. "We'll collect all the Four-Towns newspapers and start looking. There's got to be something in there for you."

Tracy's left arm dangled off the side of the couch, forcing her hand to rest on the woefully outdated and worn brown shag carpet. "I don't know . . . Nicky's working on something for us. He's been thinking of leaving this crummy town and getting a brand-new start. Says he has a cousin in Vegas who can get me a job too."

"*Vegas?*"

"Did you think I wanted to stay in this jerk town the rest of my life? And when I go, it'll be for good. I'm not coming back."

Gloria knew that was a rebuke. Tracy never had understood why Gloria had returned to Appleton. And there was no point in trying to explain it. "Nick Cervantes isn't the kind of guy I'd go pinning my future on. I mean, what job could his cousin get you? Cocktail waitress?"

"Oh, excuse me!" Tracy lunged upright, her expression fierce, the one that years ago had earned her the nickname Fire and Ice. "Just because Nicky isn't rich like that monkey of yours doesn't mean you have the right to look down your nose."

"I'm not looking down my nose. I just don't want you to sell yourself so cheaply—"

"*Sell* myself? Oh, look who's talking. The girl who couldn't stand Cutter Press is suddenly making nice with him? What's that all about, huh? A million bucks, maybe? Did it finally occur to you that you could be rich? That you wouldn't have to worry anymore about paying rent for a crummy apartment? I mean, you think there's anyone left in Appleton that doesn't know Cutter bought you Clive's car? Now who's selling herself?"

"It's not like that at all."

"Oh, *puh-leeze.*"

"No, I mean it. You've got it all wrong. The night you saw us, I . . . we . . . Cutter and I were discussing his mother. You know she hasn't been feeling well, and I was . . . concerned."

"That old windbag? Everyone knows her shenanigans. Virginia Press is gonna outlive us all. You wait and see. Besides, you needed to *hold hands* while discussing her?"

Gloria started to open her mouth, then stopped. No explanation was possible without violating her promise. "It's not what you think" was all she could say.

"Yeah . . . well, maybe the job in Vegas is not what you think, either."

Gloria sighed. There had to be some way to keep Tracy from getting any more involved with Nick Cervantes. She'd have to think of something, and fast.

~◦ ◦~

By the time Charlie Axlerod came into the print shop and made some last-minute changes to his board game, and by the time Gloria incorporated those changes and then drove the final proof down to the Chamber of Commerce at the other end of Main Street, it was pushing three o'clock. Paul was supposed to have started printing the game almost two hours ago.

Wanda was a bundle of nerves. Even chewing three packs of spearmint hadn't helped. But her misplaced anxiety had found an easy target, and she'd yelled at Paul a good ten minutes over his failure to order a new plate cylinder for the Ryobi. "Now you tell me?" she had screamed. "This is the busiest time of year! What if that old thing doesn't hold until the Apple Festival is over! What will happen to our business?"

Wanda had yelled so loud, Gloria had worried she would blow an artery. These days Wanda was strung tighter than Grandma Quinn's clothesline. Another week and the Apple Festival would be over. Both she and Paul were counting the days.

Gloria stepped out of the Chamber of Commerce building carrying the proof with Charlie Axlerod's signature, wondering if she should just call the okay in to Wanda or drive back. The streets were clogged with tourists, and by the time she got out of her parking spot, which was around the corner, and made her way down Main, a good twenty minutes could pass. The picture of Wanda's red-apple face, wormed by bulging veins, made Gloria decide to call it in.

She was about to go back into the Chamber building and ask Charlie if she could use his phone when someone grabbed the proof from her hand. She looked around in surprise. The sidewalk was thick with people. A group of senior citizens were crowding past her. Behind them were a man and woman pushing twins. In front of her was a cluster of young Asians, speaking what sounded like Japanese and licking ice-cream cones from Tad's.

She saw a man dash across the street, then stop on the sidewalk and face her. He was dressed in black leather, and one gloved hand waved a paper in the air. There was a smile on his face. It took only a second for Gloria to recognize him. Some foolish impulse made her walk over. As she did, he tossed the paper into the garbage can by the curb and waited.

"Who are you?" she said when she reached him. "What do you want?" She had never been this close to him before. He looked younger than she'd originally thought, with freckles and the beginnings of a sandy beard. His shoulder-length light-brown hair was pulled back into a ponytail. He wore a small silver nose ring through the skin that separated his right and left nostrils. It reminded her of a picture of a bull she had seen in a magazine.

"What do you want?" she repeated.

"Ever see the movie *Chinatown*?"

Gloria remained mute, not moving a muscle.

The young man leaned closer. "Guess not." He smiled, showing two chipped teeth. "Well, there was this nosy detective that wouldn't mind his business, and somebody had to teach him a lesson. You know what happened?" He opened his leather jacket and pulled something from an inner pocket—something metallic, black, and deeply grooved. He held it in his hand until a group of people passed. Then, using his shoulder and arm as a shield against unwanted onlookers, he pressed the spring latch to flip out a long, double-sided blade. "He got one of these stuck up his nose, and it didn't feel good."

Gloria gasped and backed away, bumping into the garbage can. She could feel her heart pound in her throat. *If only J.P. were close by.*

"You got a detective snooping where he's not supposed to. You call him off, or you'll both get this." The man in leather flicked his wrist, moving the switchblade in a quick slashing motion before it disappeared again into his jacket. "You've been warned, lady. Now I'm not responsible for what happens if you don't listen." Then he walked away.

Gloria felt blood rush to her head, heard the sound of her heart roaring in her ears like surf, as she stepped off the curb and raced for the Chamber of Commerce to use Charlie Axlerod's phone—not to call Wanda, but to call Sheriff J.P. Gordon.

~⚘ ⚘~

Gloria was exhausted. She had spent the last two hours giving J.P. a blow-by-blow description of the man in leather, as well as repeating his every word. Forty-five times. J.P. had issued an APB and had ordered his deputy to fish out Charlie Axlerod's board game from the garbage can and dust it for prints, in spite of the fact that Gloria had told him the man wore gloves. Both efforts, so far, had produced nothing.

Then she'd had to go back to the print shop with the crumpled game and a lame excuse about why she was so late, then listen to Wanda have a hissy fit. Now, instead of heading for home like she wanted, Gloria was heading for Grandma Quinn's. She dreaded her visit because it would be confrontational, but Sam Hidel had called just before her Chamber of Commerce excursion, and his call left her no choice. Her anger still simmered below the surface.

Why was Mother so difficult?

She just had to put this issue to bed, once and for all. Especially in light of this new, dangerous situation. She needed her mind free, her head clear. She just couldn't concentrate on Grandma, Mother, Tracy, Virginia Press, Cutter, and this stalker all at the same time.

Oh, Jesus, I know I'm not alone in this, but right now I sure do feel like it.

Gloria walked into the kitchen just as Grandma Quinn pulled a tray of cookies from the oven and listened to her singing "How Great Thou Art" at the top of her lungs. She waited until Grandma had the tray safely positioned on the stovetop before declaring herself. "Hey, Grandma!"

Hannah Quinn spun around like a dervish. For her size and age, she still moved well. "Oh . . . hello there, pumpkin."

Well, at least Grandma was wearing her hearing aid like she'd promised. Gloria took a seat at the kitchen table and resisted the urge to mention anything about Grandma's door being unlocked. Right now she had bigger fish to fry.

"You're just in time to sample my new cookies. I call them 'chocola.' It's a chocolate chip recipe mixed with granola cereal. I was getting tired of baking the same thing. Thought I'd try something new." Grandma used a spatula to put one of the hot cookies on a small plate and brought it over to the table. Then she went to the refrigerator, hauled out a gallon of whole milk, and poured Gloria a glass.

"It's a wonder I was never fat, with all the cookies and milk you shoved down me."

Grandma laughed and pulled out one of the other kitchen chairs and sat down. "So what's the trouble?"

Gloria's heart sank. Had someone told Grandma about the incident with the stalker? She didn't want her to worry. But since she and J.P. had agreed to keep a lid on this whole stalking thing for the sake of the Apple Festival, she couldn't imagine how anyone would know. "Who said there was trouble?"

"Your face did. Now, c'mon, pumpkin, what's going on?"

Gloria felt relieved. If Grandma knew anything about today's incident on Main Street, she would have said so.

"Tell Grandma what's wrong."

Gloria looked at her grandmother's kind face and wished she didn't have to go through with this. But there was no point in stalling. "Sam Hidel called this afternoon. He's cutting you off—no more charging your groceries."

"Now, why would he go and do a thing like that?"

"Because Mother . . ." Gloria stopped. Grandma was a proud woman in her own way, and Gloria didn't want her to know she had been paying her grocery bills. This afternoon, Sam had called and told Gloria that Geri Bickford had found out about their arrangement—and said if he didn't close Grandma Quinn's account, she'd make such a ruckus they'd hear it all the way to Eckerd City. "Because Mother made him," Gloria said, simply.

Grandma sucked her cheeks inward, then let out a sigh. "Oh, that Geraldine. Honestly. You'd think she'd have better things to do with her time."

"Can you manage without it? I mean, can you afford to buy your groceries out of pocket?"

"Of course I can. It's the baking goods that are the problem. Seems I need more and more every week."

Gloria shook her head. "Grandma, you're just going to have to stop doing all this baking."

"In a pig's eye!"

"Then cut it in half. Just bake every other day."

"That won't work either." Grandma pinched her lips together, indicating that in her mind, the matter was settled.

"You've got to be reasonable." Gloria pushed her plate away. "You've got to understand that Sam Hidel has cut you off. Without credit, how are you going to continue all this?" Gloria's head jerked in the direction of the cookie tray on the stove.

"I'll manage."

"You're usually not so stubborn unless you think it's important. So why are you making such a fuss about wanting to bake cookies every day?"

"I don't bake *every* day. Don't need to. Just when . . ."

"Just when what?"

"Just when there's a birthday at the elementary school."

"You bake every time there's a birthday?"

"No. Just when it's for one of the kids who wouldn't be bringing in any cookies from home. And there's plenty that fall in that category, believe me. Mostly migrant kids, but there's others too, like little Bessie Johnson, whose daddy's been laid up for six weeks with a broken leg. When there's no money coming in, things like birthdays and cookies just go by the wayside. Still, how do you think these little ones feel, seeing all the other kids bringing in cupcakes and whatnot when it's their birthday? Not good, I can tell you. But the teachers give me the names of the kids they think might not have any goodies on their special day, and I make sure I bake up a nice batch of something for them."

"How is it that nobody's heard about this? In Appleton people know when you pick your teeth, for goodness' sake!"

Grandma Quinn smiled. "Oh, that was part of the deal. I swore all the teachers to secrecy. No need for everyone to know the kids whose parents can't afford to even send in some cookies. That could embarrass the little ones, their parents too. And all the teachers agreed. When they need cookies, they call me in advance and come the night before, sometimes that morning, to pick them up. Then they hand them out, with nobody the wiser. And privately, the teachers tell the birthday child that someone made the cookies special just for him, and that does it. Sometimes the teachers tell me the kids cry with gratitude. Can you imagine crying over a few cookies? Tells you how important it is to those little ones. Now, I ask you, how can I give that up? How can I stop my baking?"

Gloria leaned over and kissed her grandmother on the forehead. "You can't, Grandma; you can't." Somehow she'd find a way to give Grandma the extra money she needed.

"I knew you'd understand," Grandma patted her chubby hands together as though ridding them of excess flour, or maybe as a sign that the matter was settled to both their satisfactions. "Now, we'll just have to explain all this to Geraldine."

"I don't know, Grandma . . ." Somehow, Gloria couldn't picture her mother understanding any of this.

"Your mother's not as unreasonable as you think. Sure, she can be like one of those whales I've seen on the Discovery channel—blowing up a tall spout around her, making a big splash, looming in your face when she should be invisible. But pumpkin, she loves you, and when all is said and done, she loves me too."

Gloria broke off a piece of cookie and popped it into her

mouth. It was delicious—so crunchy and chocolatey—but she was too disturbed by what Grandma had just said to tell her so. "I'd like to believe that, Grandma, but most of the time I think Mother is just disappointed in me. And sometimes . . . sometimes I don't think she loves me at all. And look how mean she's been to you all these years."

Grandma Quinn rose from her chair and walked to the stove. With stooped shoulders she began transferring the remaining cookies on the baking sheet to a wire cooling rack. Then suddenly, she put the spatula down and turned. "I'm gonna tell you something I shoulda told you years ago." Grandma walked across the linoleum as though it were a crate of eggs, then began wiping her hands hard on the apron tied around her waist like she was trying to remove a stain.

The action troubled Gloria.

"I'm gonna tell you the truth about Geraldine. I already told you when she was young and realized how beautiful she was, that knowledge turned her head clear around. Made her start thinking wrong. Wrong thinking gets you every time. Makes you go in directions you shouldn't. The idea came to her, sudden-like. She just woke up one morning with the notion she was gonna be Miss America someday. After a while, she had everyone else believing it too. She won Miss Apple Festival hands down. I should have stopped her then and there because I knew Geraldine didn't have the strength of character to handle any measure of success, but I didn't. I let her go on and enter every beauty contest in the state."

Grandma Quinn stood rubbing her hands so hard, Pontius Pilate fashion, Gloria thought she would make them bleed. "Truth was, I was proud. Proud that I had such a pretty daughter. It sort of gave me some measure of importance, in a roundabout way. 'Course, that was before I got to know Jesus. He would have set me straight on that one, for sure. Anyway, beautiful women attract all sorts of men."

Gloria thought of Jenny Hobart and how her looks had brought Jenny such problems in Eckerd City.

"And when beautiful women are silly and vain, well . . . you can see how they would fall prey to silly and vain men as well."

Gloria stiffened. "You're . . . not talking about Dad, are you?" She wondered if her voice sounded as pleading to Grandma's ears as to hers.

"Actually, pumpkin, I am. Now don't you go looking at me like I just drowned a whole litter of kittens. You hear me out. What you and your daddy had was one thing. He loved you; that's for sure. No one can say differently. But what he and your mother had was another matter entirely."

Gloria remembered all the times she and her father had played catch in the backyard, their fishing and biking trips, the countless times he'd bring her small surprises from the bakery. But she had no memory of her mother and father doing these things. She only remembered how Mother was always nagging him about one thing or another. Gloria had resented her mother for that. Perhaps resented her even now. But here Grandma was saying that something had been wrong with Dad. *How could that be?* She stuffed the rest of the cookie down her throat, trying to work up the courage to ask.

But Grandma didn't wait. "No use trying to make a girl knock her father off the pedestal she's put him on. That's like asking a person to perform surgery on his own heart. But you gotta get over this notion that your mother just popped out of a pod somewhere, fully grown, fully disagreeable. Things happen that can sour people, sour them like a vat of pickles. And without Jesus, people sour easily. Those people need extra kindness. Maybe some extra understanding."

"What . . . happened?" Gloria forced herself to say.

"Your father was a womanizer. All shapes, all sizes, all colors, all ages. Except not too young. Especially after you were born. Maybe the thought of someone, someday, doing to his daughter what he was doing to someone else's kept him from the young ones."

"I don't believe it! I would have heard about it. It would have been the gossip of Appleton."

"It was, before you were born. But things died down. That's because your father stopped having his flings with the locals. He'd go out of town for weeks at a time. 'Business trips' he'd call them, but Geraldine knew what he was up to. Land sakes, women called the house all the time looking for your daddy. I don't think a man could do a woman more hurt than to cheat on her. It nearly destroyed Geraldine. Took the heart right out of her."

"Why did she stay with him?"

"Ahhh . . ." Grandma Quinn began rubbing her hands again, and Gloria had to stop herself from jumping up and physically restraining her. "That's where I come in." Slowly, she eased herself onto a chair. "Sin's a terrible thing. Sometimes you commit it without understanding why. And sometimes it can be so subtle, like the ticking of the clock on a mantel; you hardly know it's there. And it seems so right. Sin can be just like that, pumpkin. Subtle and seemingly good. But Jesus always exposes the fake things."

Gloria looked into her grandmother's troubled eyes and saw sadness there. "Even when we're forgiven, even when it's been put under the blood, the residue of sin can be painful." Grandma reached across the table and covered Gloria's hand. "I remember the day like it was yesterday. It was raining, and your mother came dripping wet to the door with you, just a baby, in her arms. 'I've got to leave him,' she said. 'He's killing me.' That's when she asked me if she could move in with me and your grandpa. She didn't think she could support the two of you all on her own. 'What can an ex-beauty queen do for a living?' she said. She was still beautiful, but she was right. Her former victories hadn't produced a single cosmetic contract or any other work. And she only had a high school education, so what could she do? Work at Tad's Ice Cream Parlor? Or Pearl Owens's clothing store? Yes. But she wouldn't make enough to have her own place.

"Know what I told her? I told her to go back to her husband where she belonged. In those days, women didn't leave their husbands like they do today. They stuck it out, made it work. So I sent her back to the man who kept breaking her heart, thinking I had done right, that I had kept a family together. But when I came to Jesus, He showed me a thing or two. He showed me I was more concerned about the *disgrace* of a divorce than about fixing a marriage. He showed me I didn't want to have a divorcée for a daughter. I didn't want to put up with the wagging tongues and all the uproar it would cause. Now, don't get me wrong. God hates divorce. Says so right in His Word. But I was sending that child back into a situation she wasn't equipped to deal with. I was sending a vain, silly child into a relationship with another vain, silly child. I didn't offer the healing balm of Gilead, because I had none. What she needed was Jesus, and because I didn't know Him and she didn't know Him, she went back empty-handed and unable to cope with the years of unfaithfulness that followed. I often wonder if taking her in would have changed your daddy. Maybe if he had seen the consequences of his sin, had faced the prospect of losing his family, maybe he would have changed.

"But there's no denying it—in the end your daddy was an

unhappy man. Once I actually had a chance to share Jesus with him, and he cried. Maybe he was like that prodigal, and he finally saw himself in a pigsty of his own making. I can't say, 'cause he never came out and said anything, just cried . . . like a baby. That was right before he got cancer. He never seemed to have any fight left in him after that."

Gloria closed her eyes as she remembered the days of watching her father slip away in the hospital. Even the doctors had remarked that they had never seen anyone with his type of cancer go quite so quickly.

"Oh, Grandma," Gloria whispered. "Why do some people have to ruin themselves before they come to Jesus?"

⌐✦ ✦⌐

Chapter Fourteen

USING HER KEY, Gloria let herself into the tidy house with the white picket fence, then walked down the hall toward the kitchen. When she noticed she was on tiptoe, she quickly flattened her feet. Old habits died hard. Mother never liked dirty footprints on her clean tiles, and Gloria had become accustomed to walking cautiously over them.

She studied the kitchen. Spotless as usual. Nothing out of place. Except . . . a piece of paper lay on the gleaming white tile countertop. Mother never left anything out. Unless it was important and needed her attention. Gloria walked over and saw it was an application to the Clancy County Home for the Aged.

All filled out and signed.

Her stomach turned. Surely Mother couldn't sign Grandma into a nursing home without Grandma's consent. *Could she?* It was hard to imagine.

"Mother!" Gloria shouted, even though she knew her mother despised shouting in the house. Where was her mother, anyway?

The house was quiet. Gloria had called from Grandma Quinn's to say she was coming. "Mother!"

"Must you yell?"

Gloria turned toward the voice and saw her mother standing behind her. She must have come from upstairs. She stood regal and perfect in her coordinated brown linen slacks and long-sleeved autumn-colored silk blouse. On her feet she wore cocoa-colored Jil Sander pumps. Mother prided herself in dressing appropriately for each season, and that meant no white shoes or white handbags before Easter or after Labor Day.

Her hair was swept back in lovely waves and cupped her face, then ended at the nape of her neck in a brown net vaguely reminiscent of the '40s. She wore a smile like a badge of courage, and Gloria knew it was forced. But the eyes were the giveaway, all puffy and red despite the perfect application of foundation and shadow cream and probably a drop or two of Visine.

Mother had been crying.

"When you called, you said you had something to discuss." Her mother sounded defensive. She glanced at the white paper on the counter, then at Gloria, and visibly braced herself.

"Sam Hidel phoned this afternoon and told me what you said."

"Well . . . you can hardly imagine my shock when I found out you were paying Grandma's grocery bills!" Geri Bickford looked like a gladiator waiting for the first blow. To her credit, she turned fully toward Gloria. "I can't have that, Gloria! I won't have it!"

"I know. And I'm sorry, Mother. I should have consulted you. I should have discussed it with you first. I was wrong. I embarrassed you, and I'm sorry. Truly sorry."

Geri stepped backward. Obviously, the blow had not been the kind she'd expected. "You . . . you can't imagine the vicious talk that goes on. I've heard it all my life. One misstep, and there go the gossipmongers. Some people just live to spread dirt about others. They thrive on it."

"I know. It was a thoughtless thing to do."

"I've tried to do right, Gloria. I've tried to live a respectable life, bring you up properly. But when you do things like this, don't you understand you open me up to ridicule? You can't imagine what people are saying, but I can. They're saying that I don't care about my own mother, that she's got to rely on you because she can't rely on me."

Salty tears stung Gloria's eyes as she crossed the distance between them and slowly put her arms around her mother. "I know, Mom. I know. It's all right. Everything's going to be all right."

✥ ❦

As Gloria gave the final twist to the toothpaste cap and placed the tube back in the medicine cabinet, the phone rang. *At this hour?* Her toothbrush dangled between her teeth. Nobody called this late except her mother. She remembered her mother's face after Gloria had hugged her. It was sweet and vulnerable and . . . pained. Should she answer the phone? She thought for a second, then bent over the sink near the running faucet, withdrew her toothbrush, sucked in a handful of water and swished.

Then she raced to the phone and managed to pick it up before the answering machine did. "Hello?"

"Gloria, I just wanted to say . . . that is . . . I wanted to talk to you about Grandma."

"Okay, Mom, what is it?"

"I was thinking . . . well . . . I was thinking that maybe I should drive over to that retirement community you mentioned a while back and check it out. Maybe there's something suitable, something that's just right for Grandma. It can't hurt to look . . . I mean, before I send the paperwork to the Clancy County Home. You know, just in case. What do you think?"

Gloria's heart soared. "I think it's a great idea."

"Would you . . . that is, do you think you'd like to come?"

"Sure. Of course."

"How about Saturday?"

"Saturday's perfect." Gloria bit the inside of her mouth to keep from shouting "hooray" into the phone. "And Mom, I found out why Grandma's been buying all those baking supplies." Gloria quickly told her mother what Grandma Quinn had shared. There was a long silence on the other end of the phone. "Mom?" No answer. It took Gloria several seconds to realize that the reason her mother didn't answer was because she was crying.

~❦ ❦~

Cutter fumbled around in his desk drawer, trying to find where he had put that report on the Four-Towns General Hospital. They were the first ones using Medical Data's new ER Writer, the software that enabled doctors to record exams, diagnoses, and treatments, then instantly integrate the information into the hospital's Digital VAX multidepartment patient record. He was about to call Sadie Bellows but thought better of it. These days, he was keeping his distance. The way she stomped around the office and banged drawers and was generally disagreeable made Cutter sorry she still had another week left. Next Friday, Sadie would empty her desk. He had already put an ad in all the Four-Towns papers for a replacement and received twenty résumés. This afternoon he would be conducting the first interview.

He cursed under his breath as he thumbed through files, then gave up and closed the drawer. Next he rifled through a half dozen folders scattered across his desk. He finally found the report in the last folder, marked "The Lakes." How had it gotten there? Was Sadie deliberately misfiling? He was still considering the question when the buzzer on his intercom went off and Sadie told him he had a call on line one. "Sam Bryce," she said, her voice as flat as a dead man's EKG.

Cutter rose and walked to his door, then flipped the lock. That was another thing Sadie had started doing: barging in for no reason. Just to annoy him.

"Yes, Sam," Cutter finally said.

"I've got more information. It took a lot of digging into town and city records, but I've finally come up with something I think you could use."

Cutter grabbed a legal pad from his drawer, then picked up a pen. "Okay, shoot."

"Well, if you look at a map of the Too-Tall Mountain area and draw a wide horseshoe around it, something interesting happens. What you've done is highlight most of the property that's changed hands in the past two years. With the exception of The Lakes and a tract of land known as The Estates, the rest of the horseshoe has changed from private hands to government hands, via an intermediary."

"Could you say that in English?"

"Someone has been buying up all the property around Too-Tall—and we're talking timberland, pastures, farms—and selling it to the government. For a huge profit, I might add. Care to speculate who that someone is?"

"Eric Slone?"

"Close. *Erica* Slone, his daughter. And that's not all. When I dug deeper, I found that most of the sales were more like hostile takeovers. The owners didn't really want to sell but were forced to."

"What do you mean?"

"Well, what happens is that environmental protests, if they're loud enough and big enough, can generate government actions. For instance, that big fuss the environmentalists made over the large tract of land west of Too-Tall killed a huge timber sale to the Forest Service and all near-future contracts. The loss of the sale and contracts, the endless appeals and lawsuits, forced the owners to sell the land or go belly-up. Same thing with some of the ranchers. They were denied grazing rights and then ended up in a costly appeals whirlpool. Some of the other properties were wrangled from their owners through the Clean Air Act or the Endangered Species Act. One tract of land was actually lost because of the spotted owl restrictions, and only later was it proved, after the land was sold, that no spotted owls even lived there!"

"So you're saying that the Slone Foundation funded these protests, then went behind them and bought up the land, then sold the land to the government for profit?"

"Give the man a gold star." A soft laugh sputtered over the phone. "When I did more checking, I found similar things going on with other foundations. It seems private land around a national park or preserve is looked at with a covetous eye because it'll be sure to turn a profit."

"And if the owner doesn't want to sell, these foundations use the environmentalists to get it for them?"

"A little oversimplified, but yes, that's about the gist of it."

"And what do the environmentalists get out of it?"

"Most of them probably don't really know what's going on. All they know is that some foundation is interested in the same things they are. And if the foundation calls the shots and basically tells them what to protest, so what? They're still saving the earth and all that."

"Now who's sounding simplistic?"

Sam laughed again. "Anyway, it's safe to say that's what's going on with that Lakes property of yours. The horseshoe's not complete without your property and that piece north of you, The Estates. I didn't bother checking, but I bet they're having the same trouble you are."

Cutter thought of Tucker Mattson and his collusion with the agent from the Environmental Protection Agency. From what his partners in Eckerd City were telling Cutter, The Estates was having its share of trouble, but not from environmentalists. It was obvious, to anyone who cared to notice, that Tucker Mattson had cut a deal.

After he hung up, the first person he thought of was Gloria. He'd have to let her know.

◆

Gloria could hardly believe her ears. "Sell? You plan to sell this place? You're kidding, right?"

Wanda's chubby fingers tugged at her hair. "When you took so long coming back from Charlie's yesterday, I swear I thought I was going to have a stroke, right there by the copy machine. 'How are we gonna get this job printed in time if that girl's sashaying all over town?' I said to Paul. 'Course, when I found out you were with J.P. trying to give him a description of some troublemaker, I calmed down, but only a bit."

J.P. and Gloria had agreed to stay quiet about what had happened for another week, just until the Apple Festival was over. Their official story was that Gloria had spotted a suspicious character J.P. was looking for, and she needed to give him details.

It seemed to satisfy.

The Apple Festival always brought suspicious characters. Last year it was a pickpocket by the name of Sammie Post who apparently worked three states. The year before, it was the streaker who'd tried to run naked behind the float carrying Miss Apple Festival. Every year, there was someone. But Gloria never remembered anyone as dangerous as the stalker.

"So here I was on the verge of a stroke, when Paul says, 'Wanda, you're getting too old to percolate like our old coffee pot. And I'm getting too old to have all that heat and steam spill over me. It's not good for your blood pressure or mine. It's time we retired.'"

"I . . . don't know what to say."

"Neither did I. But when I finally got my wits back, I asked Paul who in the world would buy this place. It's old, needs a ton of TLC. And besides, I said, there's a brand-new printer just down the road a piece in Shepherd's Field. Well, he popped back just as fast as you please and said he knew the perfect buyer. 'Okay, Mr. Know-It-All,' I said. 'Name him.' And he said, 'Gloria.' Now, don't that beat all? Thinking a sassy little wannabe city girl could run this place all by herself?" Wanda patted down her over-bleached hair, which had turned almost orange around her ears. "So, what do you say? You wanna buy the place?"

Gloria's heart thumped. Of course she did. But how? She had no money, and she couldn't operate the presses. Hiring a pressman would be costly, plus there was the expense of running the business, not to mention paying off the bank loan she'd have to get. No, it was all pie-in-the-sky. "I'd love to, Wanda, but I can't afford it."

"You don't even know how much we're asking."

Gloria shrugged. "Okay, how much?"

The big blonde giggled. "To tell you the truth, Paul and I never got that far. All we know is that we wanna sell."

"I think you should buy it, Gloria."

Both Gloria and Wanda turned at the sound of the deep male voice and saw Cutter Press leaning against the wall behind them, his arms folded across his brown pinstriped suit. He must have been standing there for some time because it was evident he had heard most, if not all, of their conversation.

"I think it's a good investment for you," he added.

Gloria raised her eyebrows. This whole thing bordered on the ridiculous. "Come up with a price, Wanda, and I'll think about it." She didn't know any other way to end the conversation.

Wanda grinned, showing off huge white teeth that Gloria imagined were recently bleached, like her hair, then trotted toward the pressroom, straight to Paul.

"You should always view your options, Gloria," Cutter said when Wanda was no longer within earshot. "Never turn anything down prematurely, especially something you really, really want."

"How do you know I *really, really* want this place?"

Cutter gave her an exasperated look. "You think I expected you to stuff folders forever? I was just waiting to see some initiative."

All those years working at Medical Data, Gloria had believed Cutter viewed her as only a file clerk. Now it appeared she had been wrong, just like she had been wrong about so many things.

"Looks like I surprised you on that one. You've got your mouth open."

Gloria quickly closed it.

"We can talk about it over lunch. I've come to take you out."
Cutter chuckled. "You've got your mouth open again."

"Did anyone ever tell you that you are incredibly pushy?"

Cutter leaned over her desk, bringing his face within inches
of hers. It reminded her of the time in McGreedy's barn when
he'd kissed her on a dare. She felt herself cringe. "You can
always say no to my invitation. But then you won't find out what
Sam Bryce just told me about the Slone Foundation."

At the mention of the detective's name, Gloria rose to her feet.
"I'm going to lunch, Wanda," she yelled. "Be back in an hour."

⚜ ⚜

Cutter watched Gloria nibble on her BLT, then take a swig
of milk. He smiled when he saw a white mustache cover Gloria's upper lip, but apparently she knew it was there and wiped
it with her napkin.

"Seriously, I'd like you to think about Wanda's offer. If it's
a good deal and you want to go for it, I'd be willing to kick in
some money, become a silent partner. I'm looking to diversify.
I could use a half interest in something that's making money
these days."

"How do you know it'll make money?"

Cutter put down his hamburger and wiped his fingers.
"You're a hard worker, and everyone in town is pleased with the
new stuff you've designed. Wanda's creations were getting stilted,
boring. You've got flair, Gloria. Couple that with hard work, and
you'll make out fine. Take my word for it; I don't invest in anything unless I believe it's a moneymaker." Gloria smiled, and
Cutter felt sweat bead around his collar.

"That's really kind, but I'd have to think about it."

"Why?" He thought Gloria looked uncomfortable.

"Because people are already talking about us. Rumors are flying all around Appleton, and—"

"Yeah. I've heard them too. But Gloria, if you let these rumors stop you from taking advantage of a great opportunity, then you don't deserve to have the shop."

Gloria's face pruned. "Let's not talk about it now. Let's wait until Wanda gets back to me with some figures. Besides, we're here to talk about Sam Bryce. What did he find out?"

Cutter bit into his hamburger as he watched Gloria eat. He liked the polite way she ate, how she took a small bite, chewed it thoroughly, then drank from her glass, then brought the napkin to her mouth. He guessed he liked nearly everything about her. Always had. He wondered why he had wasted so many years trying to prove that he preferred women like Sadie Bellows, and suddenly he realized it was so Gloria wouldn't know how he really felt and get the upper hand. Was Virginia going to be the barometer by which he would forever gauge all women?

He washed down the last of his hamburger with a mouthful of Coke, then told Gloria what Sam Bryce had discovered.

"Well?" he said, when she just sat quietly, saying nothing. "What do you think about that?"

"It makes things clearer." Quickly, she told him about the latest incident with the stalker, how he had pulled a knife and threatened to hurt her if she didn't call off Sam.

Cutter hit the table with his fist. "Why didn't you tell me? If we're going to run this road together, then we can't have secrets; we can't hold anything back. We need to weigh the risks with the rewards. I think we both know now that this thing could get seriously out of hand. The Slone Foundation's not a penny-ante outfit. They have deep pockets and can buy all the help they need. That runs the whole gamut, Gloria, from thugs to lawyers. With one hand they can have someone knife you;

with the other, file a lawsuit. The thing that really bugs me is, why are they going after you instead of me?"

"I've wondered that myself." She smiled sheepishly. "Not that I want them to come after you, of course, but . . . why me? I don't know. Maybe they're trying to intimidate me because I'm the one doing the flyers. And because I am doing the flyers, they may believe I'm the one who hired Sam. They probably don't see you as a threat because they've already tied your hands legally. Stopped you from building on The Lakes."

"Well . . . maybe. I guess the real question is, what do you want to do now?"

"I want to do another flyer. Sam's information is a perfect follow-up to our last one. Instead of generalizations about how and why big foundations influence the environmental movement, we could give them specifics. Name names. A lot of people have lost their land around Too-Tall Mountain. I think we owe it to them to share what we know."

Now that the stalker had pulled a knife on Gloria, Cutter was sorry he had convinced her to continue the fight. He should have let her get out when she'd wanted to. If anything happened to her—

"All right," he said, because he knew he had to. "But any more encounters of the third kind, any more visits by our weird and dangerous friend, you let me know. Understand?"

"I don't get you." Gloria narrowed her eyes. "You're the one who said I shouldn't quit. So what's the problem?"

"The problem is I love you."

"Pfffffff." Gloria flipped her hand like she was swatting a gnat. "That's the reason you gave so I *wouldn't* quit. You're not making sense."

"Sure I am." Cutter watched Gloria fold her napkin neatly

alongside her plate, as though she were at a ladies' luncheon. "I'm making perfect sense."

"Well, I don't want to talk about it," Gloria said, placing her hands on her lap.

"I didn't expect you would. Before we go, anything else you *do* want to talk about?"

"Yes. Tracy Mattson. I'd like you to give her a job." Gloria giggled softly. "Now look who's got his mouth open."

—◆ ◆—

Gloria entered the bedroom, walked noiselessly across the beige Saxony carpet, then put the book she had tucked under her arm down on the nightstand and began smoothing the bedding. Virginia Press remained motionless. "Stop fussing, Agnes. Can't you see I'm trying to sleep?"

Gloria continued tucking the paisley sheets around the four-poster bed.

"I said, stop it." Virginia glanced over her shoulder and spotted Gloria. "Oh, it's you."

"Yes, and aren't you ashamed? Acting like a disagreeable, spoiled child."

"I am a disagreeable, spoiled child," Virginia said, showing discolored teeth that were badly packed with plaque. She tried to sit up. When she couldn't, Gloria gently pulled her up, then fluffed pillows and placed them behind and around her. Hemmed in by the oversized bedding, Virginia looked small and crumpled, like one of Gloria's old dolls that Grandma Quinn still kept in the attic, only with greasy hair that separated into clumpy strands.

When Gloria pulled the covers away from Virginia's chin, the odor that wafted up from the bedding said that Virginia was badly in need of a bath.

Had Virginia forsaken all personal hygiene?

"What's this?" Virginia said when she spotted the book Gloria had placed on the nightstand.

"A Bible. And don't give me that look. You and I made a deal, remember?"

Virginia shrugged. "I don't remember saying you could bring a Bible."

"You certainly did. And you know it." Gloria sat on the bed, disturbed by the little space Virginia's body took up—it seemed like less and less space each time Gloria came. She picked up the Bible, opened it to Luke 15:4 and began reading. "'Suppose one of you has a hundred sheep and loses one of them. Does he not leave the ninety-nine in the open country and go after the lost sheep until he finds it? And when he finds it, he joyfully puts it on his shoulders and goes home. Then he calls his friends and neighbors together and says, "Rejoice with me; I have found my lost sheep." I tell you that in the same way there will be more rejoicing in heaven over one sinner who repents than over ninety-nine righteous persons who do not need to repent.'"

"Of course, you're trying to tell me I'm that lost sheep."

"I'm trying to tell you how Jesus feels about you. How much He longs for you. How much He wants to pick you up and carry you on His shoulders. Carry you home."

Virginia's crowlike eyes narrowed. "You've got a mean streak in you, Gloria. You're bound and determined to see me crumble."

"Would that be so terrible?"

"I . . . don't know."

Gloria took Virginia's hand and quietly held it for a long time. When she saw that the older woman was struggling to stay awake, she closed the Bible and put it back on the nightstand.

"I'm leaving this here. It's yours. But I expect you to read the entire gospel of Luke before I come back."

"Humph. I suppose you'll ask me a hundred questions, just to make sure I did."

"You can take it to the bank." Gloria bent closer and kissed Virginia's cheek; then she exited the room as quietly as she had come in.

꠸꠸ ꠸꠸

After returning home from Virginia's, Gloria worked on the *C&C* flyer for several hours, incorporating all the details Cutter had faxed earlier to Appleton Printers. She had already notified Harry about her plans, and he had been excited. "We're close to breaking the back of this thing. I can feel it," he had said. And Gloria felt that way too. It was only after she had proofed her article for the last time and faxed it to Harry on her little Sharp UX 300 that she felt a deep sense of dread.

꠸꠸ ꠸꠸

Gloria listened to Wanda whistle a nameless tune and watched her bustle around the shop. Since announcing her retirement, Wanda had been more relaxed. Even so, saying Wanda was relaxed was like saying someone's favorite hockey team wasn't as violent as it used to be because after their last game, even though several players were bleeding, nobody needed stitches. But the change in Wanda, albeit slight, did make for a more relaxed atmosphere at the shop.

"Can't believe this is the last day of the Apple Festival." Gloria stretched out in her chair and stared at her computer. This was the first time in weeks she had nothing to do.

"Thank God. Now things can get back to normal around here." Wanda was a stickler for routine.

"All the work orders are filled. I've got time on my hands." Gloria rose from her desk and walked over to the disheveled shelves that marked the boundary of Wanda's work space. "Want me to do anything? Maybe straighten these up?"

"Sure, knock yourself out. Might as well get familiar with the rest of the business. Since it's gonna be yours."

"Wanda, don't start. I haven't committed to anything. I'm still thinking it over."

"Eighty thousand's a bargain, considering you get the building too."

Gloria pulled old manuals off the shelves and noticed some were for equipment they no longer had. "Don't you ever throw anything out?"

"Nope, and don't go changing the subject. You've gotta make a decision. The price is good, and if you want, Paul and I will even become salaried employees for six months or a year if you think that's better, just to give you a chance to get your feet wet. I know the place needs a facelift, but other than the Ryobi, the equipment's in good shape. And other than the inventory being a mite low, I don't see where the place needs any big cash infusion." Wanda batted the Xerox machine with a rag—her version of dusting—and sent a zillion dust mites into the air. "You've already looked at the books and see we make a good living. This place would be perfect for you. So what's the problem? It's either yes or no. We've given you the first shot. But Paul and I aren't gonna wait forever."

Gloria nodded. She couldn't remember a time she'd wanted something so much. The desire had been growing like bacteria in a Petri dish ever since Wanda had told her she planned to sell. Gloria had been praying about it every minute, and it seemed like her prayers had only intensified that desire. She'd even talked to Mr. Hotchkins, the manager of the Appleton Savings. He said he saw no problem with giving her the size loan she was asking for if she'd put down a 20 percent deposit. Twenty percent of eighty thousand was sixteen thousand. It might as well be sixteen million.

There was only one way she could do it. And that was to take Cutter up on his offer. He had already said he'd go in with her, become a silent partner. She'd be free to run the shop any way she wanted, without interference from him. Only trouble was, she couldn't get past the fact that he'd be part owner. How in the world could she ever go into partnership with Cutter Press?

Surely God wouldn't use Cutter as an instrument of blessing, again. *Would He?*

"Can you give me just one more week to think about it?" Gloria said, throwing the manual of the 1976 Heidelberg Kord into the garbage and wondering how one more week could possibly make any difference.

Chapter Fifteen

SATURDAY CAME FASTER than Geri Bickford wanted. She had promised Gloria she'd take a look at condos, and she'd make good on the promise. That wasn't the problem. The problem was facing Gloria. Geri still felt embarrassed that she had jumped to such wrong conclusions about her mother. Why didn't her mother tell her she was baking cookies for migrant kids?

And hadn't Gloria been so sweet about the whole thing? Even calling her "Mom." Gloria hadn't called her anything but "Mother" in years. Still, why had Geri been so silly about everything? Crying on the phone like that? Would Gloria mention it? No. Probably not. But now, just thinking about the way Gloria had hugged her, had said in that low, sweet voice, "Everything's going to be all right," made Geri want to cry all over again. Since Gloria was a baby, all Geri had ever wanted was to be a good mother and have a happy home.

Well, that goes to show you how foolish desires can be. Still . . . Geri could see that maybe some of the blame rightfully rested on her own shoulders. Maybe her unhappy marriage had made her put too much pressure on Gloria. Maybe she had expected too much.

Expectations again. See. That's what she had been trying to get Gloria to understand about marriage, about life in general. Expectations got you every time. The higher they were, the greater the disappointment. Maybe Gloria was beginning to understand that too. After all, she had started seeing Cutter again. That was a beginning. Maybe Gloria finally understood that love wasn't everything. You could live without it. Hadn't Geri lived without it for years and years and years?

But that hug.

And that sweet voice.

And that word, Mom.

There was love in them. All these years Geri had believed Gloria only loved Gavin. That miserable two-timer had never had trouble getting women to love him. Still, it hurt having Gloria be one of them. Especially since Gavin had been away so much, having one fling after the other—leaving Gloria without a father's love and instruction for days, sometimes weeks, at a time—while Geri remained behind, raising Gloria single-handedly and trying to make a decent home.

She thought about the last time she and Gloria were together, and how she'd walked out of La Fontaine in a huff. She would have to stop doing things like that. If she wanted their relationship to grow, then she'd have to make some alterations in her behavior. And she did want it to grow. Very badly. Just seeing that love in Gloria's eyes . . . well, it made Geri realize that it was worth any effort to see it there again, and to keep seeing it. Maybe there was still time to get some measure of love. Some small measure of love.

"Oh, stop being an old fool, Geri, and just forget it," she

mumbled, watching through the window as Gloria's car pulled into the driveway and feeling excited and hopeful in spite of herself.

꙰ ꙰

Gloria stood on the concrete sidewalk studying the Villas—connecting condos of gray-painted clapboards with slanting black-shingled roofs, quaintly clustered with plenty of common ground that held benches where folks could sit and visit. Mauve shutters hugged every window, and black wrought-iron window boxes, full of white and yellow mums, hung below the two large front bays of each unit. Through one of the windows, Gloria could see a spacious living room. Through the other, a galley kitchen. Though each lawn was miniscule—extending only ten feet from the house, front and back—the assortment of densely packed shrubbery beneath the bays and around the walkways gave a lush feel.

"Oh, I love it!" Gloria said, beaming at her mother.

"How can you say that? You haven't seen inside."

Gloria ignored her mother's cautious note and grabbed her by the wrist. "Okay, so let's go in."

Until now, the sales rep, a tall, beautifully dressed woman who looked to be in her sixties, had stood quietly off to the side. But at Gloria's words, she stepped forward and pulled out a ring of keys. "I'd be happy to show it."

Gloria and her mother waited quietly while the woman unlocked the door of unit 318, then stepped aside.

That's all the coaxing Gloria needed. She pulled her mother through the entrance and into that large living room she had seen from the window. "Look at the size of this! Plenty of room for Grandma's couch and recliner. And over there, she could put that hutch she loves so much, and over there her lovely White-side clock."

Even her mother's stony silence couldn't dampen Gloria's spirits as she pulled her into the spacious bedroom, with a walk-in closet and private bath, directly to the left of the living room. "Isn't this great?" Gloria said, examining the beige Corian sink and Kohler tub, the three-inch wood molding around the doors. When she'd exhausted all there was to see, Gloria led her mother back to the living room, bore right, then headed straight into a small breakfast nook. The nook opened into a galley kitchen loaded with appliances and a sleek, speckled cream Corian countertop.

Every room in the condo was bright and airy, with either a large window or, as was the case in the living room and break-fast nook, a window and an eight-foot sliding glass door that opened onto a small screened-in porch, which in turn over-looked a man-made lake.

"Can't you picture Grandma sitting out there with a cup of tea?" Gloria pointed to the porch. "Not bothered by mosqui-toes or flies or those awful giant water bugs. Isn't this just per-fect?" Gloria finally let go of her mother's wrist and tried to read her face. A page of misgivings.

"You say the lawn is totally cared for in the summer, and in winter someone comes and removes any snow on the sidewalks and driveways?" Geri Bickford had turned and was now address-ing the saleswoman.

"Yes, that's correct. For a small maintenance fee."

"How small?" Geri asked.

"A hundred dollars a month."

Gloria gave a little hop. "This is *too* perfect. The inside is small enough for Grandma to maintain, yet large enough so she can keep her favorite things. The whole outside will be taken care of for her, and with what that beautiful old Victorian of hers will fetch on the market, there'll be money enough to buy the condo outright, with some to spare. Grandma won't have any more money worries. What do you say, Mom?"

"I say you'd better ask Grandma and see what she says."

Gloria let out a whoop that she was sure could be heard in Appleton twenty miles away, but she didn't care. Her mother, in so many words, was telling Gloria that she would let the matter of the nursing home drop. Without caring that the saleswoman was in the same room, Gloria threw her arms around her mother and hugged her. "Oh, thank you, Mom. Thank you so much."

Now, all Gloria had to do was convince Grandma Quinn.

❧ ☙

Cutter Press had driven to Sam Hidel's in hope of seeing Gloria's blue Escort parked on the gravel driveway in back. His plan was to pop in for a surprise visit under the guise of telling her his decision concerning Tracy. It was Saturday morning, and he knew Gloria usually cleaned on Saturday mornings. He supposed a surprise visit was not in the best of taste. After all, he could just as easily call and tell her everything over the phone. But coming in person guaranteed that Gloria would see him. And that was the point.

All the parking spots in front of Sam's were taken, so Cutter slowed his Saab and inched past the gravel driveway, craning his neck to see if her car was there.

Empty. The driveway was empty.

Maybe he'd come by later.

You really are pathetic, Press. Why don't you just write idiot *across your forehead?*

Try as she might, Gloria couldn't get her mother to come to Grandma Quinn's with her to discuss the condo. She said things would go smoother without her.

Someday those two were going to make up. And Gloria hoped it would be soon. Grandma wasn't getting any younger.

Now, as Gloria watched Grandma rub her hutch down with a lemon-oil-soaked rag, she didn't know exactly where to start. She suspected the truth was the best place. "I just got back from seeing a condo at Willow Bend."

"Oh?"

"You know, the place where Minnie Olson and Olivia Grant live?"

"Aha."

"Have you been there lately?"

"No. Not since I gave you the Silver Streak."

"Well . . . when you went, did you like it?"

"It was nice enough. The apartments are a bit small, though." Gloria knew Grandma meant the condos. "But that was a while ago. Now . . . small doesn't seem like such a bad thing. Getting harder and harder to keep up a big house. Upstairs and down." Grandma rested her hand on the carved edge of the hutch. "But it's good exercise, I suppose. A body needs to keep fit."

Gloria felt disappointed with her grandmother's answer. "But you must miss Minnie and Olivia." She hoped throwing Grandma's two best friends into the mix would tip things more in her favor.

"No. They come regularly to the house for a visit. 'Course, with Minnie's cataracts, I don't know how much longer that'll last."

"Minnie's got cataracts and she's *driving*?" Gloria shuddered at the thought.

"Just the beginnings. Not full-blown. She can see well enough."

"What happens when she can't? See. I mean . . . Olivia doesn't drive. And you don't have a car." Nor would it be likely that anyone would allow Grandma to have one.

Grandma tossed her rag onto the dining-room table, walked over to the brown corduroy couch covered with cream lace doilies, and sat down. Gloria sat on the beige recliner nearby. "What's this all about, pumpkin? You've been fidgety since you got here. Why don't you just come out with it?"

"I don't know how you do it, but you always seem to know when I have something to say and I'm not saying it." Gloria rested her hands on her lap. "Okay, here goes. Mom isn't—"

"Mom?" There was a knowing smile on Grandma's face.

Gloria chose to ignore it. "Mom's not going to pursue the nursing home thing. Not after seeing that condo this morning. Oh, Grandma, it's perfect. It's so beautiful, inside and out. And you'd never have to worry about your lawn or painting the outside or any of that hard work. And there's a clubhouse and lots and lots of activities. You'd be with your friends, plus you'd make new ones. This house—," Gloria stopped and made a sweeping motion with her arm—, "this house is just too big, too much work. You said so yourself. Don't you think it's time for a change?"

The look on Grandma's face was not the one of happy anticipation that Gloria had been looking for.

"I don't know, Gloria. I was never one for something new. I got memories here. My roots are here. A home's a personal thing. It's not something you can up and leave, just like that. And Willow Bend's so far away. From you, from Appleton."

"It's only twenty miles."

"It's not like being right here in town. Besides, who'll bake for the kids?"

"We can work something out. Maybe get some of the class mothers to help out. The point is, Grandma, you can't hang on to this place forever. It's starting to deteriorate. The paint's peeling outside. The lawn's dying. You've got a shutter that's hanging by a thread. You've got to sell this place before it goes completely downhill. You've got to sell while you can still get a good price."

"I don't 'got to' do anything."

Gloria threw up her arms in frustration. "Okay. Okay. But would you at least do one thing?"

"What's that?"

"Pray about it." Gloria held her breath until her grandmother nodded. Now it was up to her faithful Jesus.

~✦ ✦~

Cutter picked up the phone and dialed the familiar number. After it rang several times, the answering machine came on and he hung up. This was the third time he'd called since coming back from Sam Hidel's. He couldn't imagine where Gloria was. Not that she owed him an explanation. But that last incident with the stalker had gotten him nervous, and he always felt more comfortable when he knew her whereabouts. At least now that the Apple Festival was over, it would be easier to spot a suspicious stranger. That was a comfort, albeit a small one.

Maybe he'd just hop in his car and take a ride back over to Sam's. And if Gloria wasn't home, he'd just wait for her in the driveway. *And then she'd really think he was an idiot.*

"Don't do it, Press," he mumbled as he picked up his car

keys from the marble dish on the foyer table and walked out the door.

⌇

When Gloria pulled onto the gravel driveway and saw Cutter's Saab, she groaned. Not that she still found him distasteful or that she loathed his company, but rather, going out early with her mother to Willow Bend, then to her grandmother's, had left her behind the eight ball in the cleaning department. Her place was a mess, and she had planned on spending most of the afternoon cleaning, then catching up on some paperwork. Now this interruption would cut into her limited time. On top of that, she didn't want Cutter to see how disorderly the apartment was, though the idea of caring what he thought suddenly seemed amusing.

But strangely enough, she did care.

When she opened the car door, she was surprised to see he looked nervous. This was not the Cutter she knew. Was he afraid she'd be rude? Or order him off the property? She waved, then closed the car door and headed for the stoop. "What brings you to the neighborhood?" she asked, purposely keeping her voice free of irritation. Though she didn't relish a visit from Cutter right now, she had no desire to embarrass him.

"I've been thinking about what you asked me regarding Tracy. And, okay, I'm willing to take her back."

Gloria burst out laughing and saw it surprised Cutter. "It's just the way you said it." She tried hard not to start laughing all over again. "Like she was an old girlfriend you had dumped." Gloria stood in a stiff, upright position, with one arm extended, aping Cutter's stance. "'I'm willing to take her back.'"

She ignored the dirty look he gave her and let him hold the

233

screen while she unlocked the bulky maple door. "But I'm happy to hear it. I'm happy you're willing to give Tracy another chance." Gloria led Cutter into the kitchen and gestured for him to take a chair, which he did, then put the kettle on the stove. "Tea or instant coffee?"

Cutter shook his head.

"What?"

"Let's go for a ride. It's too beautiful to sit in a tiny apartment. Ah . . . sorry, I didn't mean it the way it sounded. Your apartment's nice. I just thought we could—"

"Okay." She turned off the stove and removed the kettle. Cutter looked relieved. "How about we drive to Spoon Lake—to the old fishing hole?" Cutter's expression told Gloria she had picked the right spot. She opened the refrigerator. "Maybe I should make us some sandwiches. You know how hungry that place gets you." She was startled when she felt Cutter's large hand on hers, the one that was holding the edge of the refrigerator door. Slowly the pressure of his hand forced the door closed.

"I'll run into Sam's and have him make us something. You can change if you want. You're kind of dressed up."

Gloria had made a special effort to dress nicely for her trip to Willow Bend, mostly to please her mother. But Cutter was right, her black linen slacks and gray cardigan were far too dressy for the fishing hole. "Okay. How about we meet outside? Your car or mine?"

"Mine." The way Cutter said it didn't leave any room for argument.

This was more like the Cutter she was used to—far too pushy for her taste.

❦ ❦

It was a perfect Indian summer day. The cloudless sky was the color of Grandma Quinn's favorite blue dress, the dress she claimed made her feel twenty years younger every time she wore it. And though the air was cool and crisp, the overhead sun coated everything with a happy glow that was so contagious you couldn't help feeling happy yourself.

Gloria rode with the window down and let the wind claw her hair into a tangle. She felt relaxed in her gray sweats, and her fluttering hair gave her a sense of adventure—and a slight feeling of rebellion too, probably because she was going to while away the afternoon instead of doing the sensible, needful thing of cleaning her apartment.

Sitting beside her, Cutter drove without a word. The sandwiches from Sam Hidel's lay between them.

As they turned down the Old Post Road and headed in the direction of Clive McGreedy's farm, Gloria was reminded of Cutter's many recent kindnesses: the car he bought for her and was letting her pay off in small installments, his offer to go into the printing business as a silent partner just so she could afford to buy Wanda and Paul's shop, and today, his offer to let Tracy come back to work at Medical Data. She wasn't sure if it was the warmth of the sun or the warmth of his kindness that made her suddenly feel so warm toward him, but she did.

"Thanks for your willingness to take Tracy back. I really appreciate it. Sometimes you can be so nice."

"Sometimes?"

Gloria laughed. "Yes, sometimes. Of course, I don't know if I can really chalk this one up to kindness, since you've always had a crush on Tracy."

Cutter's eyebrows made Vs over his dark russet eyes, and his lips tightened as thought he was suppressing a laugh. "Whatever makes you say that?"

"The valentine—that big box of Whitman's you left on Tracy's porch when we were in eighth grade. Tracy must have gotten half a dozen boxes that year. "

"The valentine . . ." Cutter's face turned red. "Tracy thought that was for her?"

"Well, naturally. What else could she think?"

"But her name wasn't on the note."

"What note? There wasn't any note. I was there when she found it. And the only reason we even knew it was from you was because Tracy's mother saw you leave it."

"There *was* a note. I left it on top of the box . . . Guess the wind got it. That's what I get for not using tape."

"Well, if it wasn't for Tracy, who was it for?" Gloria leaned her back against the car door, facing Cutter.

"It was for *you*, Gloria." Cutter looked at her as if she had just arrived from Mars. "Who do you think?" He pulled the car to a stop, nose pointing toward Spoon Lake, which stretched out in front of them for over two miles and got its name from its elongated shape. They were only a mile from Clive's farm and only a quarter of a mile from the old smokehouse. Cutter gathered the sandwiches and two bottles of soda, gave Gloria another strange look, and got out.

Gloria lagged behind. She was still thinking about what Cutter had said. In all her life she had never gotten a valentine from a boy, but now Cutter was telling her she had. And from someone she had loathed and despised as a child. It seemed she had never really known him at all. It also seemed both silly and sad.

She watched Cutter pick a spot near the lake, shaded by a giant maple, and sit down. She took her time following, feeling upset and suddenly uncomfortable in his presence.

Why, for heaven's sake? The man's already told you he loves you.

She had never known what to make of his declaration. There was a part of her that had dismissed it as more of Cutter's mockery, his joking at her expense. And as long as that part held, she was free to dismiss his feelings completely. At least on that level, the love level. Now, suddenly, it came to her as clearly as the sun skipping across the water: *This was no joke.* Cutter had meant what he said.

She eased herself down beside him, then picked up the wrapped tuna sandwich he had left on the grass for her, and removed the paper. "Well . . . thanks for the valentine. It was good. Tracy and I shared the whole box—she ate the top layer and I ate the bottom—so I did get some of it."

"I suppose it was best you didn't know."

"Why?"

"Would you have eaten it if you had?"

"Probably not." They both laughed. "So . . . what other things did you do that I don't know about?"

Cutter removed the wrapper from his ham-and-cheese and rolled the paper into a ball. "That time my friends and I locked you and Tracy in the old smokehouse—well, I left my friends and doubled back so I could make sure you got out all right."

"We were in that dark, dirty smokehouse for three hours! It took us all that time to dig out the back."

"I know."

"I was terrified it was going to collapse on us."

"So was I."

Gloria eyed the dark, broad man who suddenly seemed like a stranger. She really didn't know him at all. "What else?" she said, fiddling with her sandwich wrapper. "What else don't I know about you?"

"That bird of yours, with the broken wing that everyone thought I killed? I didn't. Agnes Keller did. Oh, not on purpose.

She found the box in the laundry room where I had put it and was afraid the bird would get out and upset Virginia, so she poked holes in the box for air and put a bath towel over the top. I don't know how it happened, but the towel fell into the box and smothered the bird. I felt terrible. Really terrible. After all, I did steal it. And I was afraid of facing you and telling you what really happened."

"Afraid? Of *me.* Cutter, you were never afraid of anyone."

Cutter looked out over the blue, glistening water. The sun slicing through the overhead branches made his hair shimmer like a shampoo commercial. "I was afraid of you. Still am."

Gloria couldn't believe her ears. "But why, for heaven's sake?"

"I guess a guy's always a little afraid of a girl he loves but who doesn't love him."

Gloria stretched her legs out on the dry grass. "Anything else?"

"Remember when I took you to the senior prom and—"

"You didn't take me, Cutter; you were coerced by your mother, who was pressured by mine."

Cutter laughed as he twisted his Appleton High ring around his finger. "No. Virginia didn't need any pressuring. She's always liked you. Anyway . . . I had planned on giving you my high school ring that night, only—"

"Impossible! You acted like a beast! You left me sitting in a chair against the wall like some discarded coat and proceeded to dance with every girl in the room."

"I was trying to make you jealous."

"You are, without doubt, the most annoying, irrational, inscrutable man I've ever known, and—"

"I guess that's why you walked out on me that night, left me flat."

"And . . . you know absolutely zero about women."

Cutter raked one hand through the grass. "Obviously."

"But you have a decent side too. Do you want to tell Tracy about the job at Medical Data, or should I?"

"You can."

The two sat in silence for a long time, until Cutter's voice broke it. "The whole town's talking about Wanda and Paul selling their place. And everyone knows they've asked you to buy it. What are you going to do?"

"Mr. Hotchkins says I need a minimum of sixteen thousand. And I don't have it."

"You know where you can get it."

"I know."

"And you'd rather miss out on an opportunity that you'd love rather than ask me?"

"Yes." Until this moment, Gloria had still been struggling with the issue.

"Why?"

"Because, under the circumstances, I'd feel like I was taking advantage of you."

"See. That's where you and I are different. If the roles were reversed, I'd take your money in a heartbeat."

Gloria brushed sandwich crumbs from her sweatshirt. "That's exactly why the roles *aren't* reversed."

~♦ ♦~

Gloria raced up the dilapidated steps and noticed, as she banged loudly on the paint-peeling door, that the old screen Nick Cervantes had nearly ripped off its hinges had been replaced. *Oh, Tracy, please be home.* Gloria could hardly wait to tell her the good news. Hopefully, Tracy hadn't left for O'Riley's

Pub. Gloria had raced here right after Cutter had dropped her off. If she was in time, Tracy could give her notice tonight and be done with that bartending job.

Gloria tired of banging on the door and rang the bell. Just as the familiar strain of the *1812 Overture* was about to play for the third time, the door suddenly flew open, and Tracy stood in front of her. She wore black skin-tight pants, a white long-sleeve cotton shirt and a black vest that was only partially buttoned.

"Oh . . . hey, Gloria. I was just on my way to work. Like my outfit? Gary has us dress up on Saturday nights. Says it makes the place more sophisticated. Brings in a better class of clientele." She bent closer. "Just a bunch of hooey. The same crowd comes every Saturday, and after a few drinks they don't care what you're wearing. Gary's thinking of hiring some dancers to dance on top of the bar. Thinks it'll beef up business. But I don't think it'll do much, unless they're strippers, and Gary says he doesn't want to get into that. Still, he asked me if I'd be interested. Dancing, I mean. Isn't that a hoot?"

Gloria tried not to frown. "I've got great news. Cutter will give you your old job back."

Tracy stepped out onto the stoop, making it too crowded and forcing Gloria to reposition herself on the lower step. "You asked the Monkey to hire me?"

Gloria didn't answer.

"Are you out of your mind?" Tracy continued, as if Gloria had responded in the affirmative. "You think I'd work for him again? The creep. No way. He had his chance. And he blew it. I've got my pride, Gloria. Even if you don't."

"But . . . surely you don't want to work at O'Riley's for the rest of your life?"

"Of course not. Another month and I'm outta here.

Already told Gary. That's when this new casino opens in Vegas, and they're hiring like crazy. Me and Nicky already landed jobs there. Good jobs too, with good pay."

For a moment Gloria was speechless. *Oh, God, it can't be true.*

"Nicky's gonna do valet parking."

"What about his probation?"

Tracy flipped her long red hair over her shoulder and jutted her chin. "His probation is over in two months. I'll go first, then he'll meet me. His cousin's already found us a place to stay, and—"

"And what will your job be?"

"Well . . . cocktail waitress . . . but that's only temporary, until they see what I can do, until they see my potential and place me in the right spot."

"Which is?"

"I don't know . . . yet." Tracy walked back into the house, letting the new screen door bang shut between them. Through the mesh, Gloria saw worry lines crease Tracy's forehead. "There's always something opening up for a bright, enterprising person. I'm not going to be a cocktail waitress forever."

"But if you stay here, in two years you could be running telemarketing."

"Maybe, if that's what I wanted."

"It used to be."

"Yeah, and you used to hate Cutter Press. Things change, kiddo. Don't they?"

~❦ ❦~

Chapter Sixteen

"WHAT DO YOU MEAN, you don't want to buy the place?"

Gloria watched Wanda shove the box of electrostatic solution across the floor with her foot until it whacked against the wall and stopped. There was something in Wanda's action that made Gloria wonder if Wanda didn't wish the box were Gloria's head—as in the proverbial knocking sense into it.

"How could you not want to buy it? This place is perfect for you. Paul and I weren't much older than you when we started this business. It's been good to us, and it'll be good to you too."

"No use, Wanda. I can't come up with the sixteen thousand Mr. Hotchkins says I need."

"That old fuddy-duddy? About time he retired too and let someone with more imagination take over. Today's bankers are always coming up with new ways to give you money—balloon loans, bridge financing, debentures—unless, of course, they're from the Stone Age, like Hotchkins."

"Wanda, really. He was very kind, and he spent a lot of time trying to make the numbers add up, but they don't, so that's that."

"So *that's that*? No way. No, sir. You're not giving up so easily. You go back to the drawing board and think some more. And then you come back with the right answer. I'll give you another week. Paul and I can wait one more week."

"Wanda—"

"One more week!" Wanda gave the electrostatic solution box another kick, making Gloria cringe and return to her keyboard.

◆◆ ◆◆

Gloria climbed one step at a time, stopping periodically as if at a rest station. The creaking stairs of the old Victorian seemed longer tonight, and more than once, she wished she could turn around. But how could she disappoint Virginia? It was Tuesday night. She was expected. Work exhaustion had little meaning to a dying woman, and Gloria wouldn't use it as an excuse.

The last two steps felt like mountains, and she stopped one more time, at the landing. The pause and the height gave Gloria a sense of the house, and for the first time it occurred to her that a house, like a person, had its own personality. This one was gloomy, depressing. It was the house where Cutter had grown up, a house of hushed voices and dark-paneled walls and dark, velvet-covered windows that kept out the fresh air and seemed to stifle the very oxygen in your lungs, making you want to gasp.

Suffocating darkness. Such suffocating darkness.

She suddenly felt kinder toward Cutter. Some of this darkness and suffocation had naturally rubbed off on him. How could a child grow up happy in a place like this?

"Hi, Virginia," Gloria said, even before entering the room. She needed to hear a voice, even if it was her own. Through the partially opened door, she saw a shriveled form reading in bed and recognized the deep-cranberry-colored book as the NIV she had given Virginia. Her heart skipped with delight. It was the only delight she had felt since entering the house. She paused one final time and prayed silently for God to open Virginia's heart, then slowly pushed the door. Virginia looked up, then without a word, returned to her book.

"I'm glad to see you're reading Luke. How far did you get?"

"Clear through the whole twenty-four chapters." Virginia's smug look told Gloria she was proud of her accomplishment and expected to be praised.

"Teachers must have loved you," Gloria said when she reached the bedside. Again the feeling of delight. Virginia's hair glistened from a recent shampoo. And even from a standing position, Gloria could smell the unmistakable fragrance of Amarige. Something had invigorated Virginia, rekindled her desire to perform the simple tasks of washing hair and body. Maybe it was Luke.

Gloria peered down at the open Bible perched on Virginia's lap and saw it was turned to the parable of the rich fool. "So, what do you think?"

Virginia shook her head. "I don't know . . . Some of it's a little unsettling. Like this story." She poked the open page with her finger. "This farmer worked hard and reaped a bumper crop and needed bigger barns to store it. So he goes ahead and builds himself some. Now, what's wrong with that? It sounds reasonable enough. Yet God is ticked off and calls him a fool and tells him he's going to die that very night. I don't get it, Gloria. What did God want him to do? Be a bum? Lie around and do nothing? Why should God be mad because this guy worked hard all his life and got rich in the process?"

Gloria brushed a stray wisp of gray hair from Virginia's

forehead and wondered if faith, perhaps as fragile as the filament of Virginia's hair, was about to take root in the aging
heart. She sat down on the bed. "It's not about working hard
and getting rich. It's about greed and chasing after all the wrong
things. Look farther down and read what it says."

"'This is how it will be with anyone who stores up things
for himself but is not rich toward God.'" Virginia scrunched her
face—driving the crow's feet around her eyes deeper, until they
looked like rows of scars. "I . . . I always tried to work hard, set
a good example for my son. Doesn't that count?"

"I'm convinced that most of the things we do in life are
wood, hay, and stubble—all useless—and will be burned when
tried by our King and Judge, because our reference point is
wrong." Gloria watched Virginia clench her fists. "Most of the
time we're following our own agenda, doing what's right in our
own eyes instead of consulting God and seeing what He would
have us do."

"So . . . you're saying I'm a failure; is that it?" Virginia's head
dropped back against the pillows, her mouth an angry line.
"You're saying my life has been meaningless. Just so much . . .
what did you call it? Stubble? Wood, hay?"

"I'm saying you need to come to Jesus. You need to put your
treasure where it really counts."

"Before . . . it's too late?" Virginia's eyes suddenly looked like
the large black buttons on Gloria's trench coat.

"Yes," Gloria answered. "Before it's too late."

⚬◆⚬

For the next hour, Gloria told Virginia about her experi-
ences in Eckerd City and what Jesus had done for her in over-
coming her fears. She skirted the issue of Tucker and Tracy, and

when relaying that part of the story she referred to them as "my friends." Whether Virginia guessed their identity, Gloria could only speculate. But the dying woman listened avidly to the whole narration, and at the end she cried.

"I've never been afraid of anything," Virginia said, dabbing her runny nose with a tissue. "Until now." She crinkled the tissue into a ball. "I don't want to die. I don't expect I'm all that different from anyone else. No one wants to die. But I don't know if I'm more afraid of death or . . . facing God."

"Then you do believe in God?"

"Of course I do!" Virginia snapped, her eyes angry and flashing, yet fear-filled too. "A smart girl like you should have known that. It's just been more convenient to say I didn't, that's all. But now . . . oh, Gloria . . . what am I going to say to Him? When I see Him." Virginia balled her hands. "What am I going to say?"

"You're going to remind Him that Jesus paid for your sins, and that because they and you are all under the blood, you're now the righteousness of Christ and totally acceptable."

Virginia looked grief-stricken. "But I'm *not* acceptable."

"Of course you're not, but you could be." Gloria told her about the Fall and Jesus and why He had to come to restore sinful man. And when Virginia sobbed through the sinner's prayer, Gloria thought—no, she was *sure*—she heard the angels rejoicing in heaven.

❦

Gloria pulled a pile of envelopes from the black mailbox attached to the siding near her entrance, unlocked the front door—though the Apple Festival was over, she still locked her door because of the stalker—flicked on the lights, then bolted the door behind her. She went straight to the bedroom and tossed her purse onto the bed. Then she kicked off her shoes. She was beat. Virginia had drained the last ounce of her energy. First, she'd take a shower, then have some tea and toast. She wasn't hungry for much else. And it would be early to bed.

She flipped through the mail and stopped when she recognized Harry Grizwald's handwriting. Quickly she ripped open the four-by-nine envelope and pulled out the latest *C&C* flyer. Harry had outdone himself. The flyer was still only one page, front and back, and folded in thirds, but it was a high-end-looking three-color job on coated matte stock with the *C&C* logo swirling green and gold across the top. She scanned her article on the Slone Foundation and smiled. This should raise eyebrows. She'd show it to Cutter as soon as she got the chance, and when she did, she'd talk to him again about Virginia. If only he understood that time was running out. Reconciliation with his mother couldn't wait much longer.

⌒◉ ◉⌒

Gloria was glad for an excuse to get out of the shop. All morning, Wanda had pestered her about buying the business. "Don't let this opportunity go by . . . Don't be afraid—take the plunge . . . You have to take chances in life . . . You'll always regret it if you don't." And on it went. Why couldn't Wanda understand that Gloria simply couldn't get the necessary deposit?

Liar.

Okay. She *could* get it. But the thought of getting it from Cutter left her cold. Gloria had a nagging feeling that maybe it was her pride that couldn't handle asking Cutter for the money. All right, suppose she did ask. He'd say yes. Then what? People would start talking all over again. And how many times could she allow Cutter to come to her financial rescue before it became indecent? She still owed him for the car. To ask for more money would be taking advantage. You just couldn't keep asking a man who claimed he loved you for favors.

He loves you.

Cutter Press loves you.

The knowledge didn't seem as bizarre as it once had. Still, it was ironic that the only man in the world to have ever loved Gloria was the very one she had despised for years. Maybe it wasn't ironic. Maybe it was just comical and sad. Here she was, looking for love—she'd even, last year, traveled nearly two hundred miles to find it—and it was right under her nose. Only, she didn't want it.

I know there's a lesson in this somewhere, Jesus, but for the life of me, I can't figure it out.

She clutched Tad's menus under her arm, the ones with the new ice-cream flavors and new prices, and walked briskly down the sidewalk. She had purposely parked in the public lot down the block, rather than along the curb closer to the store, because she wanted to enjoy the beautiful day—low sixties, sunny, not a cloud in the sky, and the air so crisp you could almost hear it snap. Winter was just around the corner.

She inhaled the fresh air. This was her favorite time of year. She greeted by name those she knew as she passed. To others she gave a polite smile. Last year, while she was living in Eckerd, Appleton had been invaded by a horde of city people relocating to the country. It seemed word had gotten out about this beautiful little town. And more and more people were discovering it every day. Gloria was still finding it hard to get used to so many new faces that actually belonged here.

She passed the Bread and Pastry Shop and Rosie's Beauty Parlor, then stopped in front of Tad's—a corner store facing

Main Street, with a side entrance on Spoon Lake Road. Angry shouts, coming from around the corner, propelled Gloria past Tad's front entrance and around to the side. J.P.'s car was parked near the curb, hood facing away from Main, red strobe light whirling. The car directly in front of J.P.'s had run up on the sidewalk—at least, the two tires on the passenger side had. For a second, Gloria held her breath, thinking it was the stalker, then remembered that the stalker rode a Harley.

"Let go of me! I didn't do anything." The voice sounded distorted, like someone was trying to gargle with mouthwash and talk at the same time. But it was also . . . familiar.

Gloria exhaled. *Tracy?* No. It couldn't be. She jogged toward J.P.'s car and saw him standing over her friend, one large hand holding her, bent like a hinge, across the white hood of the other car. Tracy looked wild and dangerous—like a panther on a leash—and Gloria expected, any minute, to see her leap into the air, right over the car, her, everything, and sprint away.

"Hands behind your back."

J.P.'s tone frightened Gloria. It smacked of boot camp and brass buttons and twenty years of National Guard. It was the tone J.P. used for the more serious occasions. This was no minor traffic violation.

Gloria had to restrain herself from crying out when J.P. pulled a pair of cuffs from his belt and snapped them around Tracy's wrists. What was he doing? What was happening? This had to be a mistake.

"You creep! You lousy creep!" Tracy's voice shrilled.

"What's wrong, J.P.?" Gloria inched closer to Tracy's white Nissan.

"Gloria!" Tracy shrieked when she saw her. "Tell this baboon it's all a mistake. I didn't do anything!" Tracy suddenly lunged backward as though trying to bolt, forcing J.P. to pull down hard on the cuffs. "Ouch! Stop that! You're hurting me."

"Then stay quiet," J.P. said, his voice sharper than ever. Gloria caught his eyes as he looked up. "DWI," he said, as though answering her unspoken question. He pulled Tracy backward by her arms. "She almost ran someone over on the sidewalk."

Gloria glanced behind her and for the first time noticed Agnes Keller trembling against the side of Tad's store, a container of strawberry ice cream melting in her hands.

"Don't listen to him, Gloria," Tracy blurted. "It wasn't like that at all. He's just filling his coat . . . his quote . . . his . . . he just needs to hand out more tickets, 'cause . . . because . . . he . . . has to."

Gloria took a step in Tracy's direction but stopped when J.P.'s eyes flashed a warning. She watched, without a word, as J.P. led Tracy to his car and opened the door. She stood helpless as he pushed on Tracy's head so she would clear the opening, then tucked her in the backseat. The way he slammed the door gave Gloria the feeling that more than a car door was slamming in Tracy's life. When J.P. drove away, his strobe light still flashing, Gloria's heart sank. Things like this happened to other people, not someone she knew. It all seemed so unreal. She heard a sniffle and turned to see Agnes still cringing against the side of Tad's store. With a heavy heart, Gloria walked toward the shaking woman to see how she could help.

~◆ ◆~

By the time Gloria returned to the print shop, Pearl Owens had already called and told Wanda about Tracy's arrest.

"Where's that girl headed? That's what I wanna know." Wanda hovered around Gloria's desk, making loud snapping

251

noises with her spearmint. She was down to only a pack a day now. "Ever since she got back from Eckerd, she's been in one fix or another. Losing her job, hanging around that bad boy, Nick Cervantes. Told Paul months ago to look out. Told him Tracy was heading for trouble. Told him she was heading down the Alps without skis."

Wanda suddenly bent over Gloria's garbage pail. "Hey, what's all this?" She pulled out half a dozen discarded papers from the pail and held them clenched between chubby fingers. "You throwing away our inventory? How are you going to make a living from this place if you're this wasteful?"

"Wanda—"

"Anyway. I'm glad you're not hanging around Tracy like you used to." Wanda shoved the papers back into the garbage. "I swear, you used to be that girl's shadow. You two were insepa-rable. I called you the Bobbsey Twins. Just ask Paul if I didn't."

Gloria shut down her computer.

"What are you doing?" Wanda put a beefy fist on her hip. "It's not quitting time."

"I'm taking a few hours off. Charge it to my personal time." Gloria rose to her feet. "I just realized I have something to do."

"Now, what's so all-fired important that you gotta leave in the middle of the day?"

"Wanda, it's four o'clock." Gloria ground her teeth, hoping her shortage of patience was only temporary. "I just realized I should be with Tracy. Maybe there's something I can do to help."

"I knew you were going to say that! I just knew it." Wanda popped her gum. "Well, all right. You go ahead. But Gloria, honey, there's not a thing you can do for someone who doesn't want help. But I suspect you'll have to learn that on your own."

Gloria knew J.P. wasn't happy about her being there. His mouth sagged at one end and his eyebrows pinched together over the bridge of his nose. His fingers tapped the desktop like her old pair of ProMark drumsticks, and for a long while, he wouldn't even look at her. She sat quietly in front of him, hoping his mood would improve, and when it didn't, she finally reached over and tugged at his arm.

"C'mon, J.P., let me see her. Just for a minute."

"I already told you no. She's drying out. Drunk as a skunk. Blood alcohol's gotta be point-zero-eight or more, but we'll see what the lab says. You want to help that girl, you start praying, and praying hard. She nearly *killed* Agnes. Agnes wanted to file charges. Said she had been assaulted with a deadly weapon. I told her to go home and forget it. But Gloria, now I think I made a mistake. Maybe I should have let this be taken to the next level. Tracy's heading down the wrong lane."

This was the second time today someone had said that about Tracy. And it only confirmed what Gloria already knew. She *had* been praying. But it didn't seem to have made any difference. "What's going to happen now?"

J.P. fiddled with his notebook. "Well, at least she submitted to a BAC test. If she hadn't, I would have revoked her license for six months. It's her first offense, so that's a plus. But it's still a *criminal* offense, and she'll need a lawyer. If she's convicted, she could do jail time, get fined, or have to do community service. She could also lose her license. But she'll have to go before a district court judge and have her case disposed of there. If the lab results come back the way I think they will, she'll be convicted for sure. 'Course, Tracy can take it to the next level if she wants and appeal to a superior court. But it won't do her any good. Any way you look at it, your friend's in trouble."

Gloria sat staring at J.P., wondering how Tracy had come to this.

                           ⟡ ⟡

Cutter slipped a navy sweatshirt over his head, then pulled on navy sweatpants. He had not lingered at the office like he sometimes did but came right home so he could fit in his jog before Gloria stopped by. This was new, a two-mile jog around the posh neighborhood, something he'd started a little over two weeks ago, around the time he'd realized he was in desperate need of some discipline—a realization brought on by Sadie's resignation.

Discipline.

That good-old *D*-word, which he'd had, up until now, little use for. But hadn't his lack of discipline, his lack of self-control, gotten him into all sorts of trouble? He laced his Nikes and thought of Gloria.

He was glad she felt comfortable enough to stop by his house, even if it was just to show him the latest flyer. If he'd used more self-control when he was younger and not been so impulsive, maybe Gloria would feel even more kindly toward him today. Even now, his lack of self-control threatened to ruin everything. *How many more times are you going to tell Gloria you love her? Man, you just can't keep your mouth shut.*

But that was all going to change. He was going to become the model of discipline, even if it killed him. And . . . he was going to avoid temptation. He laughed when he thought of Mabel Anderson, Sadie's replacement, with her wrinkled face and short, square body. The woman had to be pushing sixty. Certainly no problem with temptation there. He had purposely picked Mabel because of her age and looks, although she did come with a good résumé and was proving to be a very capable assistant. Still, he was relieved he didn't have to see a curvaceous body sashaying in and out of his office every day. Until now, he hadn't realized what a strain it was having someone like Sadie around all the time, with all the sexual tension and innuendos.

He grabbed a bottle of Poland Spring from the refrigerator and downed half of it. Yeah, discipline, that's what he needed. He'd sweat this impulsiveness, this weakness, right out of him. He'd show Gloria he was a man of character. He put the bottle back into the fridge, then half-walked, half-jogged to the front door and yanked it open. He stepped back in surprise when he saw Sadie Bellows standing in front of him, her hand raised as if ready to ring the bell. She wore a black halter top and black pants that were so tight Cutter was sure they had to be made of spandex. Over that, she wore a little black cotton jacket. Her head was a mass of blonde hair—blown out in long, soft waves around her head.

Temptation with a capital T.

"I'm glad I caught you home. Mind if I come in?"

"Ah . . . I was just on my way out."

Sadie pushed past him, brushing her body against his. "I just came to pick up my stuff. It won't take long."

"What stuff?" Reluctantly, Cutter closed the door and directed her toward the den.

"My black lace nightie and my best compact." Without waiting to be invited, Sadie made herself comfortable on the brown Italian-leather couch. She kicked off her high-heeled slingbacks and curled up. "I could use a drink. I'm dry as toast. A beer, maybe, if you have one."

Cutter grunted and headed toward the kitchen, resenting Sadie's intrusion. But he'd be polite. It was the least he could do. He hadn't exactly treated her well. He rummaged through the refrigerator until he found a Corona, opened it, and without pouring it into a glass, carried it to the den. After the beer, Sadie would have to collect her things and get out. He wanted her long gone before Gloria got here.

"I see you still stock my favorite," Sadie said, obvious pleasure scrolled across her face.

Cutter didn't bother telling her it was a leftover from their last dinner together at the house. He took a seat in one of the leather chairs facing her and waited.

"I hear you have a real dog working for you. They say she's a cross between the Hunchback of Notre Dame and Cloris Leachman when she does her Nazi Fraulein thing."

Cutter gave her a dirty look.

"I'm only telling you what I heard."

"Mabel's a good assistant. I'm happy with her."

Sadie gulped her beer like a truck driver, draining a quarter of the bottle, then put it on the coffee table. "We didn't part on the best of terms. I guess that's my fault as much as yours." She rose to her feet and walked over to Cutter. Then she eased herself down on his lap, pinning him in the chair, and put her face close to his. "I'd like to make it up to you."

"Sadie, it's no use." Cutter pushed against her arms, trying to get up. "It's over."

"Don't you remember how good it was with us?" She brushed her lips against his.

"Sadie, stop." Cutter reached up and pushed hard against her shoulders, making Sadie almost fall backward.

But she recovered gracefully and scrambled to her feet, then looked down at him with a sad smile. "Just thought I'd give it one last shot."

Cutter glanced at his watch. Gloria would be here in twenty minutes. If Sadie didn't get out soon . . . "Just get your things, Sadie, and go. Let's make it a clean break."

"A *clean* break? You think it's that easy? You think it's easy piecing what's left of my heart back together? No, that's not clean. It's messy. And it's painful."

Cutter checked his Seiko again and felt he was watching the ticking of a time bomb. He rose to his feet and walked toward the bedroom. "Where did you leave your stuff?" He would gather her things up and bring them and Sadie to the front door, and out. He rummaged through his closet but found nothing. "Where are they?" he yelled between clenched teeth, fuming that Sadie hadn't joined in the search. When he turned, he found her behind him, her eyes awash with tears.

"You know the thing that bothers me most? It's that you never gave me any warning. One day we were an item; the next day we're . . . nothing? How can that be? You think that's fair? You think that's right?"

Cutter brushed past her and began pacing the room, his eyes scanning the corners, beneath the bed, around the sides of the furniture, under the curtain. He could almost hear the minutes ticking away. Her stuff had to be somewhere. He opened his dresser drawers, rummaged through them, even tossed some of his clothes on the bed in frustration and haste. "Where are those blasted things? Come on, Sadie, help me out here."

"Help *you* out? Is that all you think about? Yourself? What about me? What about helping me out? What about trying to help me understand what happened between us?"

Cutter was getting more frantic by the minute. He could see that Sadie wasn't interested in a quick exit. He had to get her out of here. He ran his fingers through the thick curls of his hair. He was beginning to believe there was no nightgown or compact—that Sadie had just made the story up as a pathetic excuse to come over.

"Are you going to answer me? Are you going to say anything?"

Sadie had followed him to his dresser and stood there, wiping her wet cheeks with the palms of her hands.

He turned and glared at her. He had no time for this. Couldn't she get it through her head that it was over? And why the big fuss, anyway? Their relationship had never been much. He had never made any promises, never made any declarations of love. But this wasn't the time to remind her of those facts, not with the second hand of his Seiko pulsing in overdrive. If Gloria showed up now, it would really clinch the whole mess. She'd never believe Sadie had come uninvited, not since the whole town knew why Sadie had quit Medical Data.

"Can't you at least answer?" Sadie's voice had risen several octaves, and there was an angry edge to it.

Cutter knew the signs and groaned inwardly. Sadie had a spiteful side when aroused, and she was working herself up for an explosion. That's all he needed. All-out verbal warfare. *Think, Press, think.* If he didn't get her out of the house in the next few minutes, their voices were going to disturb the peace of the neighborhood. He caught sight of his wallet lying on the dresser and quickly picked it up. Without a word, he opened it and pulled out a hundred-dollar bill, then handed it to Sadie. "I don't think your stuff is here. But if I find it, I'll get it to you. In the meantime, buy yourself a new compact and nightgown."

He'd never forget the look on Sadie's face—a cross between pain and utter contempt. She glanced at the bill in Cutter's hand, then, without taking it, turned and walked out. He heard the *tap tap tap* of her slingbacks all the way to the front door, then the sound of the door opening, followed by a loud bang as it closed.

❧ ❧

Gloria had stopped briefly at her apartment to pick up the flyer and change into casual clothes, then got two ham sandwiches from Sam Hidel's—one for her and one for Cutter. It was the least she could do after inviting herself. She didn't feel like staying home. That whole thing with Tracy had gotten her down. And J.P. hadn't exactly been a ray of sunshine with his "wrong lane" remark.

But it was the look in J.P.'s eyes that really got her. She had seen it before—when J.P. had stood up in church and asked for prayer for Willis Hargrove after Willis's last arrest. Everyone knew why Willis had been arrested. It was common knowledge that he beat his wife. But when J.P. stood in front of the congregation that Sunday, it was as though he had known—after Trudy Hargrove dropped the charges like she always did and J.P. was forced to let Willis go home—that this time would be the end of the Hargroves. Less than twenty-four hours later, Willis had shot and killed his wife and three children, then himself.

People in town said J.P. always knew when a person was ready to cross the "Maginot Line"—J.P.'s name for the invisible line that, once crossed, would ruin a life. Had he seen this in Tracy? Were her toes brushing the threshold of disaster? If so, how could Gloria stop her? The Medical Data job had to be the key. Maybe she could talk Cutter into urging Tracy to return to her old job. If *he* spoke to Tracy, that could make the difference. Somehow, she and Cutter had to keep Tracy from going to Vegas.

Funny how Gloria had thought of Cutter. How she wanted to see him and talk to him about Tracy. It was odd, but she felt a friendship for him she had never felt before. Their lives held so many common threads. Virginia and her mother, grade school, high school, Medical Data. She supposed it was only natural that they had finally become friends. Though she laughed at the word "natural." When she thought about it, there wasn't anything natural about it at all. Only Jesus could manage something like this.

So . . . here she was on the way to Cutter's, uninvited. That word stuck in her craw. Mostly because her mother's admonition kept whirling around in her head: *"No one likes uninvited guests, Gloria."* Well, maybe that was true most of the time, but Cutter had seemed all right about it when she'd called. Besides, he never even bothered calling before he came to see her, not that that gave her the right to violate proper etiquette. She laughed at herself for worrying. In some ways she was more like her mother than she cared to admit. *Get over it, Gloria. Just get over it.*

The blue Escort flew over the familiar roadway, whizzing past Spoon Lake Road, heading north. At any rate, the flyer would please Cutter. She'd show him that first. Then she'd tell him about Tracy and enlist his aid.

The Tudor, set back on a brick driveway nearly twenty feet, had grounds that were well lit, so it wasn't difficult for Gloria to spot Cutter in the doorway before she pulled up. He had mentioned he was going jogging. He must have just gotten home, so the timing was perfect.

She parked, gathered the sandwiches and flyer, then got out. Her sneakers made no sound as she walked up the drive, then up the paved sidewalk. She slowed when she got near enough to see Cutter's face. He wasn't a happy camper. His eyes were slits, and his lips were pinched together like two dried apricots. Maybe this hadn't been a good idea. Maybe her mother knew what she was talking about after all. And so did Emily Post. Self-invitations were not the fun, spontaneous thing they were cracked up to be.

Let that be a lesson, Gloria.

Still, Cutter could have been more honest and told her it

wasn't a good time. She slipped one of the sandwiches into her coat pocket. "Did you have a nice jog?" she said, coming up to the door. The light by the entrance erased any doubt that Cutter was agitated.

"Didn't have time for one."

There was no mistaking the icy tone of his voice. He opened the door wider, as if gesturing for Gloria to come in, but she shook her head. Instead, she stood her ground and just handed him the sandwich and flyer. "I really don't have time for a visit," she said. "But I thought you'd like a bite to eat while you read the flyer. Maybe you can call me later and tell me what you think." She backed away, gave a silly little wave, and sprinted to the car. *No one likes uninvited guests, Gloria.* The next minute, Gloria and Bluebird were whizzing over the red brick driveway in a hasty departure.

※　※

Cutter held the sandwich and flyer in his hand as he watched Gloria pull away, then cursed under his breath. So she did see Sadie's car leaving the house. He had been afraid of that. And just as he'd feared, she had misunderstood. What must she think? What could she think? If Sadie had just ruined his chances with Gloria, he'd—

He went back into the house, slamming the door behind him and feeling frantic. What could he tell her? Would she believe anything he said? *Calm down, Press. Just use your head for once.* This was not the time to show weakness. Women loved lap-dogs, but not men who acted like one. Besides, there was a slight possibility that Gloria hadn't passed Sadie's car. They could have missed each other by seconds. Or maybe she'd seen the car and didn't know it was Sadie's. He thumped around the apartment, wandering aimlessly from room to room. *Get real, Press.* Everyone in town knew Sadie drove a red Camry. She was notorious for speeding. More than one shop owner had reported her. And J.P. had already pulled her over three times—given her two warnings and one ticket. *Gloria had to know.* Why else would she have acted like that? Like she couldn't get away fast enough? Okay, so Gloria knew Sadie was here. So what? Everyone knew he and Sadie were . . . Yes, everyone knew.

He'd have to straighten this out. He couldn't let it go the way it was. He found himself standing in front of his dresser running a comb through his hair. *Don't you have any pride? You're sprucing up to go to a woman's house and grovel, and she doesn't even care.* He tossed the comb onto the bamboo tray that cradled a host of other personal items. When he did, he caught sight of the small gold-plated cuff links. He stood there a moment, staring at them. Sure, he and Gloria were better friends now than before—but that wasn't saying much since they were never friends before—and it didn't mean she cared about him—not the way he cared about her. What's more, she'd probably never feel that way about him. *Face it, Press—you're banging your head against a brick wall. What's more, you're acting like Sadie Bellows.*

Slowly, he reached over and picked up the cuff links, jiggled them in his hand a minute, then shoved them into the pocket of his sweats.

~◈ ◈~

Even before Cutter came to the door, Gloria knew he was there because she had seen the lights of his Saab as he pulled onto the gravel drive. She stood by the open door of her apartment as he walked up the stoop. By the porch light, she saw that beads of perspiration dotted his forehead and that his hands were jammed into his pockets like they used to be when a teacher marched him to the principal's office. Something was wrong. She immediately thought of Virginia.

"Everything okay?" She moved so he could pass and go into the apartment first. When he didn't answer, she closed the door behind her. He looked strange. His face was all pulled into a knot. What could be so important that he'd come to her house only minutes after she'd left his?

Cutter sat on the couch without being invited. Something was wrong, but since he seemed reluctant to say what it was, maybe she'd fill him in on Tracy. She didn't know what else to talk about, how else to satiate the empty silence. Maybe by the time she finished, he'd tell her what was on his mind. Gloria sat down beside him and quickly ran though Tracy's DWI incident and her plans to go to Vegas.

"So what I'm hoping you'll do is call Tracy, talk to her. Ask her to come back to Medical Data. *Urge* her to come back."

"It's not going to make any difference, Gloria. Nothing I say to Tracy will make any difference. But if it's that important to you, okay, I'll talk to her."

"It is that important." He really was kind. "I'm worried about her." Now, if he'd only tell her why he was so troubled. Maybe she could repay his kindness by helping him. Perspiration mustached Cutter's lip. Perhaps he was just hot in his sweats—though that was hard to imagine, since the temperature had dipped into the low fifties. Maybe he needed something cold to drink. "How about a soda?" She was already on her feet and heading for the kitchen. She filled two glasses with ice, then poured Coke from a plastic bottle. The foam was still fizzing when she carried them to the living room. She handed one to Cutter and watched him gulp it down, then place the empty glass on the coffee table.

"When you came . . . when you stopped by with the flyer, did you know that Sadie had just left?"

"No." It was true. Gloria had been in a kind of fog, reviewing what she was going to tell Cutter about Tracy.

"You didn't pass her car on the way?"

Gloria shook her head, wondering what in the world Sadie had to do with anything.

"You sure? I mean, you do know her car, right?"

Gloria laughed. "Everyone knows Sadie's red Camry. Now, what's this all about?"

"I just didn't want you to get the wrong impression, that's all. I just wanted to set the record straight." Cutter face was twisted.

Gloria folded her hands on her lap. "For heaven's sake, Cutter, what are you talking about?"

"I'm talking about Sadie and me. It's over. That's why she quit Medical Data. She just came to pick up some of her things."

Everyone around town already knew why Sadie quit. Cutter wasn't telling Gloria anything new. "You don't owe me an explanation," she said, confused by this rehashing of old news and feeling irritation rub like sandpaper. What kind of things could Sadie have left at Cutter's? She suddenly felt uncomfortable as her imagination sketched a steamy picture of tossed undergarments and negligees. And she felt resentful too, though she couldn't imagine why. Well . . . what difference did it make? So what if Sadie was there? Who cared what *things* she had left behind? "No explanation necessary," she repeated, though part of her suddenly wanted an explanation, actually wanted one very much.

"That's what I told myself on the way here—no need to explain to Gloria. I actually turned around by Hoolahan's and headed home. Got as far as Tad's, then turned around again." He shoved his hand into his left pants pocket and pulled out something that jingled in his palm. He held it in a clenched fist, and even when he rested that hand on his lap, his fingers remained coiled. "I can't change what I was. And sometimes I don't even know who I am or what I'm going to be. But I do know this, Gloria. I love you. And I know something else too. This is going to be the last time I tell you, at least until . . ." He opened his hand, exposing a pair of cheap gold-plated cuff links. Then, carefully, as though they were priceless heirlooms, he placed them in her hand. "You gave these to me for Christmas when you were thirteen."

Gloria crinkled her forehead. "My mother forced me to."

"I know. But all these years, I've sort of pretended you gave them to me because you wanted to, because they were a gift of the heart." There was something sad in Cutter's face as he placed his empty hand back on his lap. "Tonight, when Sadie came over, I was frantic because I was afraid you'd come and see her and misunderstand. Then it finally hit me, *really* hit me that you probably didn't even care. That it made no difference what woman I had there." Cutter picked up his glass. The soda was finished, but some of the ice had melted, and about an inch of liquid filled the bottom. He drained it. "Do you realize that all these years I've never stopped wearing my high school ring? I suppose you've never even wondered why. It's kinda silly, actually —I've worn it because I still believed I'd give it to you one day." Cutter put his empty glass on the table and rose to his feet. "But it's time to grow up. No more pretending." He pointed to the cuff links in Gloria's hand. "These don't have any meaning."

Gloria stared at the small ovals, feeling hurt and insulted by his rudeness. Maybe her gift didn't mean anything, but why bring it here? Why not just toss the cuff links, quietly, in the garbage pail at his house? "What . . . do you want me to do with them?"

"Put them away somewhere, and give them back to me when they mean something to you."

"Cutter . . . I can't promise that will ever happen."

"I know." Cutter walked to the door. "And I can't promise I'll still be around if it does."

For a full hour after Cutter left, Gloria sat clutching the cuff links, trying to stop the anger from stomping around her insides like a bull. The longer she sat, the angrier she became. He still had more gall than anyone she knew. Why should she care what woman was in his house? It was of no importance. Did he think that giving her these cuff links would change that? Was he trying to manipulate her again?

No. He had seemed sincere enough. But his nerve galled her. And for some reason, so did his honesty. *"I can't promise I'll still be around . . ."* Did anyone ask him to be? Who did he think he was, anyway? God's gift? Finally, in disgust she tossed the cuff links onto the coffee table.

Her father had been a womanizer too.

⁓❦ ❦⁓

Chapter Seventeen

GLORIA TRIED TO CONCENTRATE on designing Charlie Axlerod's new business card—he had several for the several hats he wore around town. This one advertised *Charles P. Axlerod, Attorney at Law.*

But Wanda was making it difficult. She hovered by Gloria's desk like a condor. "Poor Agnes Keller. She's still shook up about yesterday. As if her nerves aren't already shot. I mean, working for Virginia Press can't be easy. And now that Virginia's on a rampage, well, I tell you, it must be all Agnes can do to keep her sanity."

Gloria swiveled her chair to face Wanda. "Virginia's hardly on a rampage. The woman's sick."

"C'mon, Gloria. There's not a person in town that's not wise to Virginia's tricks. But no matter how long she stays in bed, she'll never get Cutter to move back home."

At the mention of Cutter's name, Gloria cleared her throat.

"No. Cutter's left for good. And there's nothing Virginia can do about it."

Gloria frowned and returned to her keyboard. Secrets tended to be a burden. Especially this one. She wondered how Wanda and the rest of Appleton would feel after Virginia was gone.

"Cutter's out from under Virginia's thumb now, and he's gonna stay out. Been carousing a lot, I hear. Especially with Sadie Bellows. Seems like an on-again, off-again kind of romance. Someone saw her car in Cutter's driveway last night. Guess they're back together. Guess her quitting Medical Data made Cutter take notice."

Gloria misspelled *Axlerod*, deleted it, then misspelled it again.

"Can't say I like his taste in women, but who am I? Wouldn't it just frost Virginia if Cutter ended up with Sadie? Sadie's shrewd. Been around the block a few times. Knows how to handle a man. Sadie Bellows and Cutter Press. Now wouldn't that be a hoot?"

Gloria struck the keyboard so hard she broke a nail.

"Of course, there was that rumor about you and Cutter too. Never took it seriously, though. But some did. I told Pearl Owens you weren't Cutter's type. That he'd never be interested in a quiet, well-mannered girl like you. Cutter's always had his wild side. I remember a time when Paul and I thought Cutter and Tracy—now, there's a wild child—anyway, I . . . we thought the two of them might get together. Gloria? Where . . . are you going?"

"To lunch." Gloria had already slung her purse strap over her shoulder and was heading for the door.

"But it's only ten thirty!"

Gloria didn't answer and continued walking, wondering why she was fuming. So Wanda didn't think she was Cutter's type? Wouldn't Wanda split her sides with laughter if she knew that Cutter was in love—not with Sadie Bellows but with quiet, well-mannered Gloria Bickford? Well . . . used to be in love, anyway. Maybe still was, if she could believe what he said. But that little cuff-link drama last night was more or less the final act. Which was fine . . . a relief, actually. But for the life of her, Gloria couldn't figure out why she still felt so . . . so out of sorts about it.

She walked down Main Street toward the small diner on the corner of Phyllis Drive, only a block from the print shop. It was all so silly. Why should she care if it was over between her and Cutter? It never was anything to begin with. Besides, Cutter couldn't possibly be the one God had picked for her. Cutter didn't know the Lord. And one thing Gloria knew—it would not please her faithful Jesus if she became unequally yoked. Still . . . it had felt good being loved by someone, even someone like Cutter Press.

"Hey! Just the person I was coming to see."

Gloria turned toward the voice and saw Tracy across the street in front of Dr. Grant's office, waving. Gloria waited by Harvey's Bait & Tackle until Tracy walked over. "I can't believe you're out of—"

"Yeah, well . . . whatever." Tracy tossed her long red hair. "'Course, they socked me with a $350 fine. Boy, those creeps are always looking for ways to squeeze money outta you."

"Tracy, you got off easy. J.P. could have held you for fifteen days. Don't you realize he gave you a break and that you—"

"He's a moron. You should have heard him preaching. Told me to think about what I was doing, that I was squandering my life. As if he really *knew* me. As if he *knew* my ambitions, my goals. Gimme a break. So I had one too many. You know how many people in any given day have one too many? What's he gonna do, go around arresting everyone who has a beer?"

"Tracy, you almost ran over Agnes Keller!"

"Oh c'mon. That old biddy has no life except cleaning up after Virginia Press. The slightest thing rattles her, makes her blow it up like the Goodyear Blimp. I didn't even come close to her, and she makes this big stink. But what can you expect from someone whose big hoo-ha every week is getting a pint of ice cream from Tad's?"

"There was a witness. Mr. Hotchkins, the bank manager, saw the whole thing. He said you missed Agnes by *inches.*"

"Yeah, well . . . whatever." Tracy picked at her polish-peeling thumbnail. "That's not what I wanted to see you about. That fine really put a crimp in my wallet. And just now I had to shell out more money to Grant. He refused to renew my birth control pills unless I had an exam, and that snooty nurse of his made me pay cash, up front, just as soon as she learned I didn't have any medical insurance. Boy, everyone's always looking to squeeze a dollar out of your pocket."

Tracy ran her thumbnail against the edge of her front tooth. "I could sure use a loan. Just until I get back on my feet. All these expenses tapped me out. And I really need to scrape some money together for Vegas. I can't go with nothing. It's a long drive. There's the gas, the hotels, food—"

"I don't have any extra cash." Gloria recognized Tracy's smirk as the look she made when she didn't believe something. But it was true. The down payment on Bluebird and the double payments she was making to Cutter each month left her little to spare. But even if she had the money, she wouldn't loan it to Tracy. There was no way she was going to help Tracy get to Vegas. Besides, there was still the matter of the last thousand dollars Tracy had borrowed and never paid back.

"I don't have any extra money," Gloria repeated. "And anyway, how can you go to Vegas with that DWI hanging over your head? J.P. said you'd need a lawyer, and—"

"Don't worry about it." Tracy's face hardened like baked clay, making it look like a mask. "And forget I asked for the money, okay?" Hurt tiptoed across Tracy's eyes, then disappeared as though behind a curtain. "Just forget I asked."

For a moment Gloria did mental gymnastics trying to figure out a way to come up with some money. But the moment passed, and she let Tracy walk away.

⌘

Gloria sat in the little diner a block from Appleton Printers trying to force down her tuna sandwich. It was too early for lunch, and she was already full of thoughts of Tracy and Cutter. She forced the sandwich down in tiny bites, swallowing them almost whole, as if she were a squirrel storing nuts against future hunger. By three o'clock her blood sugar would be low if she didn't eat now, and she couldn't bear the thought of asking Wanda for another break.

This was only her second time here—the first being when she dropped off menus with the new name, Eats Galore. The diner had recently changed hands. She didn't know the new proprietor well but had found him to be a jolly, pleasant sort of fellow. Now he stood over her, watching her take every bite, his face beaming as though he alone were responsible for the quality of the tuna and the bread and the mayo and everything else that was in it.

Gloria took a final bite, then pushed the rest away. Half a sandwich remained. "Could you wrap this? I'll take it with me," Gloria said, not wanting to leave the sandwich behind for fear of insulting Mr. Allonzo.

"What a skimpy appetite! Like a bird, you eat." There was kindness in his heavily accented voice.

"I'm really not that hungry, Mr. Allonzo."

"Giorgio. You call me Giorgio. And I'm-a glad you come today. You save me a trip to your shop. I gotta this note for you. I was-a supposed to give it to you last week, but my dishwasher, he don't come in, and then one of the waitresses, she goes home early with a toothache, and then the stove, she catcha fire. *Mama mia*, one thing after the other. Nobody told me the restaurant business was so . . . *pazzo* . . . how you say? Crazy. Not like the vegetable stand. I think maybe a vegetable stand is not so bad. Maybe I go back to that one day. But not here. The winters, they are too cold. Maybe I go where the winters are not so cold."

Gloria smiled politely. "You mentioned a note?"

"Oh yes. I forget already. You believe that? I just tell you about the note, and then I forget." Giorgio slapped the palm of his hand against his forehead. "I think maybe I forget my own name one of these days." He walked to the counter where the cash register sat and ducked behind it. Gloria watched his short, plump body bend and disappear, then reappear. He returned, carrying a white envelope in his hand.

"Here she is," Giorgio said, placing the envelope on the table beside her tuna sandwich.

Gloria picked it up—a simple three-by-six "peel and seal" envelope with no markings—and wondered who would send correspondence through an intermediary. Her curiosity made her open it even though Giorgio hovered over the table. The paper looked like standard typing paper, ripped in half and folded in threes. Carefully, Gloria unfolded it.

THIS IS YOUR LAST CHANCE. IF YOU DON'T STOP MEDDLING, I WON'T BE RESPONSIBLE FOR WHAT HAPPENS NEXT.

She rammed the note back into the envelope, ignoring that it was more balled than folded. "Who gave you this?" Her voice quivered, but Giorgio didn't seem to notice.

"A young man. I never see him before. He has-a coffee, then hands me the note, and says give this to the young woman in the print shop. I tell him, you go give the pretty lady the note yourself. It's better for a young man to be brave in matters of love. But he says no and hands me ten dollars. I don't want the money, I say, but he walks out leaving it on the counter, and I never see him again."

"Can you describe him?"

"He's tall, brownish-blond hair which he pull in a *cavallino-coda*, a *cavallino-coda*, how you say? . . . a ponytail . . . yes, a ponytail. And a nose ring. *Mama mia*—a nose ring like my uncle Enzo put in his bull's nose back in Palermo. He's maybe thirty. Maybe thirty-five. But you joke? Yes? My Carmella says women always know who is interested in them. But maybe she make it up. She does that. Sometimes Carmella pulls out sayings like they are ancient proverbs, but I know she has pulled them only from her own head."

Gloria gripped the note and rose from her seat. How had the stalker slipped into town without J.P. or Charlie Watts knowing it? And was he still here? When she stepped out of the booth, Giorgio caught her by the elbow. "You wait. I wrap the sandwich for you."

Gloria shook her head. There was no time to lose. First she needed to let J.P. know about this; then she'd call Harry Grizwald and tell him to be careful.

⚓ ⚓

After Gloria showed J.P. the note and repeated what Giorgio had told her, J.P. made Gloria give Deputy Charlie Watts her house key, then ordered Charlie to do a room-by-room search to make certain her apartment was secure.

"Starting tonight, we're keeping you under surveillance."

In spite of herself, Gloria laughed and tilted back in her chair. "Now, how are you going to manage that? There's only you and Charlie to take care of this whole town."

"I'm thinking of pulling Jack Springer out of retirement. He's been hanging around a lot lately, just looking for something to do. He couldn't wait to retire, and now that he has, I think he's bored silly. I'll put him on special assignment, and that will kill two birds."

Gloria wrinkled her forehead. "Did you have to say it like that?"

"Sorry." J.P. pulled his holstered Glock out of the top drawer of the desk. Slowly he removed the gun and pressed the magazine catch at the rear of the trigger guard. His thumb maintained pressure on the spring while he removed the magazine, then checked the number of rounds. He seemed satisfied because he quickly slipped it back in place.

The only time he and Charlie Watts carried a weapon was during the Apple Festival. But it looked like the stalker was changing that.

Gloria couldn't help feeling guilty as she watched J.P. rise to his feet and strap on the gun. Jesus had brought her back to Appleton for reconciliation. And she, it seemed, had brought the stalker.

She just hoped nobody would get hurt.

~♦ ◊~

"Well, well. Here she is, Paul." Wanda's large body stood in the aisle between Gloria's desk and the pile of boxes containing supplies that had come in yesterday and had yet to be opened. "Seems she thinks she already owns the place and can take two-hour lunches whenever she pleases."

Gloria squeezed past her, speed-talking until she finished explaining the situation, beginning with her first encounter with the stalker, then Giorgio handing her the note at Eats Galore, and then J.P. strapping on his gun and pulling Jack Springer out of retirement. She didn't bother waiting for Wanda's response but went to her desk and punched numbers on her phone.

Again, she spoke rapidly, without emotion, like a broadcaster relating a newsworthy story. Only at the end did her voice break. "You be careful, Harry." She swallowed hard. "And tell Perth too." So far the stalker hadn't shown any interest in Harry, but that could change. "Don't take any chances. You hear?" Only after she got his promise did she hang up.

She heard a garbled sound behind her and turned. Wanda hadn't moved an inch but stood as though rooted, cupping one chubby hand over her mouth like she was going to be sick.

"I'm sorry, I didn't mean to upset you."

When Wanda pulled her hand from her mouth, Gloria thought she looked gray. "Appleton's never seen the likes of this. The only thing worse was the time Willis killed his wife and kids. But this . . ." Wanda finally uprooted and walked to Gloria's desk, her large moon-face oozing motherly concern. "I just don't understand. How could someone you don't even know want to hurt you?"

Gloria shrugged. "J.P. and Charlie, and now Jack Springer, are all going to look out—"

"I don't know what we'd do if anything happened to you."

Wanda rubbed her chubby hands together. "I just don't know what we'd do."

Gloria was stunned by the emotion in Wanda's voice. "Well—"

"I mean, you do know that Paul and I love you, even though you're still a bit of an uppity wannabe city girl?" With that, Wanda turned her big frame and headed for the back room.

"I love you too, Wanda," Gloria whispered under her breath.

～❦ ❦～

"You need to come now. She's asking for you, and Dr. Grant says there's not much time."

Gloria held the phone to her ear, letting Agnes Keller's words sink in. When they did, her stomach heaved. She sat down in a nearby chair and felt perspiration from her hand coat the phone. "Is Cutter there?"

"No. I called and told him what Doc Grant said, and he just brushed me off. Said something like, if Virginia wasn't interested in him when she was lucid, she certainly wouldn't miss him now that she wasn't. I think there're only three people in the world Virginia cares about, and that's you and Cutter and your mom. Your mom's already on her way. It would be terrible if Cutter wasn't here when . . . Maybe you could get him to come?"

"I'll try, Agnes." Gloria moved quickly around her apartment, gathering up a sweater, purse, and keys. "But I can't promise anything." After Gloria hung up, she slipped the sweater over her head, ran a comb through her hair, then with purse and keys in hand, ran out the door, not even bothering to lock it behind her. She backed out of the driveway a little too fast and almost hit Jack Springer's parked car that was partially hidden by two huge rhododendrons. She gave him a barely discernable nod, then slipped her car into Drive and sped away.

When no one answered the bell, Gloria pounded the door. The beat of her heart felt like a clock: *ticktock, ticktock, ticktock. Please, Lord, keep Virginia alive until Cutter gets there.* From somewhere inside, she heard Cutter's deep voice. "Calm down! I'm coming!" When the door opened, she saw an angry face that yielded to surprise, then pleasure.

"Gloria . . . nice to see you. Come in."

"Get your coat."

"What?"

"Get your coat. We're going to your house."

Cutter's eyebrows knotted. The look of pleasure had vanished. "I guess Agnes called you too."

"Yes. And there's no time to lose."

Cutter stepped back. "I'm not interested in seeing my mother's little drama."

"Even if it's her last?"

"Especially if it's her last."

Gloria grabbed Cutter's arm and pulled him out the door. "This is it. Your final opportunity to make peace with Virginia, to say good-bye."

"Maybe it doesn't matter anymore."

"If you don't go now, you'll regret it the rest of your life." He resisted her pull, and Gloria was forced to stop. He had her by sixty pounds, maybe more. It would be impossible to drag him all the way to Virginia's. She released him and walked to her car, wondering if he'd follow. When she heard the front door close, her heart sank, only to become buoyant moments later when she heard the sound of sneakers slapping against the pavers.

They climbed into the car and buckled up, neither one of them speaking. Then Gloria started her Escort. *Okay. She'd get him there, but would they be in time?*

"Ever since I found out Virginia was dying I've tried to keep from thinking about it," Cutter said as Gloria pulled out of his driveway. His voice was low, even, like the sound of distant waves breaking over a reef, and gave Gloria the impression he was talking more to himself than to her. "How do you handle a lifetime of regrets? A lifetime of disappointment? I'm losing my mother, and I don't know if that's a tragedy or a comedy. I mean . . . how could you lose something you never had?"

"I know, Cutter." Gloria's heart ached.

"You want to hear the real kicker? I still want a mother. I'm almost thirty years old, for crying out loud, and I still want a mother. Doesn't that make you want to split your sides with laughter?"

No. It made her want to cry. But Gloria said nothing.

Doc Grant's car was in the driveway when Gloria pulled up to the old Victorian, and so was her mother's gold Volvo. The door was unlocked, and Gloria and Cutter let themselves in without any announcement. The stillness in the house was almost eerie and the air so oppressive Gloria wanted to shout, "Someone please open a window!"

She saw Cutter gnaw his lip, and reached for his hand. He allowed her fingers to lace with his but didn't look at her. Perspiration from his hand coated her palm as they put their feet on the first step of the old, creaking staircase. His head was

278

bent as though intent on watching his shoes. Gloria wondered if this was what a man going to the gallows would look like. She didn't rush him but let him take his time, go at his own pace, which was slow and deliberate. She found herself counting the stairs as they went, just to calm her nerves.

At the landing they heard voices—Gloria recognized one of them as her mother's and was hopeful. Virginia must still be alive. Maybe there was time for Cutter to make his peace.

The door was closed, and Cutter stood before it like a sleepwalker, not moving a muscle. When Gloria realized he was going to stand like that forever, she released his hand and turned the knob. A slight push and the door opened. Agnes Keller, Dr. Grant, and Geri Bickford stood around the bedside. Agnes was crying.

"I brought you some chicken with barley soup. It's downstairs in the refrigerator," Geri said. "Hannah's recipe. You've been trying to pry that recipe out of me for years. You always said it was the only thing I could cook. Anyway, I've decided to give it to you. Just as soon as you're up and about."

Agnes blew her nose on a white cotton hankie while Dr. Grant shuffled his feet, a stethoscope dangling from his neck like an obscenely large necklace. When the door of the bedroom swung back and hit Gloria's sneaker, Geri turned. She motioned with her hand for them to come in but said nothing.

Cutter stood like a wax figure. Perspiration discolored his blue cobble crew around the armpits and down the middle of his back, making him look like he was melting. Gloria nudged him. When he didn't respond, she grabbed his arm and pulled him along until they reached the bed. Dr. Grant and Agnes separated to make room for them. Geri Bickford held her ground. Somebody coughed. Someone else pushed against the bed, making it creak.

Then everyone focused on Virginia. The dying woman was propped on all sides by her customary five pillows. Her eyes were closed, her skin the color of a candlewick, her breathing barely detectable, but . . . there was a big smile on her face. Even in the best of times, Virginia Press rarely smiled. Gloria thought she had imagined it and looked again at the sagging jowls, the dry, partially cracked lips that curled upward like a tomato wedge. There was no mistaking it.

Virginia Press was smiling.

Dr. Grant put a hand on Cutter's shoulder and whispered something in his ear. Cutter hesitated, then bent over the bed, touched his fingers to his mother's cheek, then slowly sank down onto the bed beside her.

"We should leave them alone," Gloria said.

Agnes and Dr. Grant nodded and moved away. Geri stood in place, rigid and unyielding as a sentry at Buckingham Palace. "I'm . . . afraid to leave," she said when Gloria touched her arm.

"Cutter needs some time alone."

Geri's head swiveled backward as Gloria led her to the door. It was almost as if she dared not take her eyes off Virginia for fear of something happening. "I can't believe this, Gloria," Geri whispered. "I can't believe I'm losing the best friend I've ever had."

When they stepped into the hall, Gloria closed the door, and the three of them—she, her mother, and Agnes—held each other and cried. Dr. Grant stood off to the side, fingering his stethoscope and looking pained.

Five minutes later, Cutter emerged—his eyes moist as melon balls, his mouth twisted. "She's gone," he said, without a hint of emotion, as though implying his mother had gone out to the supermarket or to get her hair done at Rosie's.

"I'm sorry." Gloria reached for him, but he blew past her

and down the stairs, taking them two at a time. She didn't follow.

"I want to see her one more time," Geri said, streaks of black mascara paving her cheeks. She followed Dr. Grant into the bedroom. Then Agnes mumbled something about making everyone tea and disappeared downstairs. Now, standing alone on the landing, Gloria suddenly realized her primary feeling wasn't one of sadness, though it too shared a chamber of her heart. No. What she felt was immense relief.

Thank you, Jesus, for saving Virginia in time.

~⦿ ⦿~

Cutter Press sat by the old willow in the far corner of his backyard, shivering. He should have grabbed that coat Gloria had told him to get before dragging him to see Virginia. But maybe it wouldn't have helped. He wasn't sure if he shivered from the cold or from seeing Virginia go like that. Even now, the whole thing seemed more like an old Charlie Chaplin movie—a black-and-white, sad comedy. Only, he couldn't rewind this one and play it again.

Here one day, gone the next. Wasn't that the saying? Strange, but he'd never believed it applied to Virginia. She was the invincible *Merrimack*, complete with armor plating. She was going to live forever. Her "sickbed" had only been a tool of manipulation. Everyone knew that. *So what happened?*

Cutter wrapped his arms around his chest, feeling his anger mount. How many times had Virginia driven him to this tree? He could barely see it in the darkness, but every inch was familiar. It bore the marks of his past, traced his history through mirrored scars: the hollow just above his wrist was carved out after Sam Hidel caught him stealing those five Snickers, the nub to the right was the remains of the limb he broke when climbing it after he almost failed tenth-grade English. And the deeply grooved *CP* in front of him was carved after his principal had called Virginia, telling her Cutter was the worst disciplinary problem he had seen in years. After the call, Virginia had threatened to send Cutter to military school down south. He had carved his initials because he wanted to leave some proof that he belonged here. But these were only three out of a dozen or more marks, all etching a trail of pain.

This old tree held more secrets than the archives of the *National Enquirer.* And even now, even at the end, Virginia was able to send him here one last time. He didn't think he'd ever forget that look on her face when she opened her eyes and saw him. Even now it made him shudder. He had never seen her eyes like that—liquid and soft, oozing motherly love. He cursed her under his breath. And why had she done that—taken his hand in hers and pressed her fingers into his palm? It used up every ounce of strength she had.

And her words . . . They were the worst of it. He'd never forgive her for saying them. Even now they rolled around in his head like steel balls in a pinball machine. It would take more than a six-pack of Heineken to stop the rolling. And he hated her for that. He couldn't remember ever hating her more.

Why couldn't she just pass into the netherworld without waking up? Why did she have to look at him like that and tell him she was *sorry*? Tell him she *loved* him? Why now, after all these years? He was so furious he could hardly think straight. It was just like Virginia to spend the last five minutes of her life acting like a real mother, just so Cutter could spend the rest of his realizing how much he would miss. Realizing how much he had been cheated.

Cutter bent closer to the tree, until his chest touched and he could fold his arms around it, just like he had done so many times before. And after cursing his mother one last time, he bowed his head and wept.

✌ ❦

The funeral was simple—a reading of the Twenty-third Psalm by Charlie Axlerod at the gravesite, then finger sandwiches by Agnes Keller at the house. When the sandwiches disappeared, Agnes set out the ton of casseroles brought as offerings by sympathetic guests. Half the town showed up. And for over three hours Geri Bickford cooed, to anyone who would listen, which was basically only Agnes, about how much the town loved Virginia, and wasn't this a nice tribute to a great lady?

Gloria's opinion ran contrary. In her mind, the guests fell into one of three categories: obligated business associates, the curious who saw an opportunity to see the inside of the grand mansion normally closed to the public, and true mourners. Of the scores of people who filed through the house, only a handful fell into the last group.

Cutter put in an appearance at the gravesite and then again at the house. He shook hands and accepted condolences like an ambassador in a reception line—polite, dignified, and a bit standoffish. Then he disappeared for the rest of that day and three days more. No one in town saw him again until the reading of Virginia's will.

✌ ❦

Gloria's hand trembled as it picked up the phone and dialed the familiar number. She let the phone ring and ring and ring until finally the answering machine came on and Cutter's deep voice spewed out a short, crisp message. She hung up without a word.

Where was he? She'd been calling for two days. She had even driven past his house after she got it into her head that he had drunk himself into a stupor and lay passed out in his own vomit. But when she'd pulled up to the Tudor, there was no sign of Cutter's black Saab anywhere.

Maybe he had gone out of town to really tie one on. Cutter could always drink with the best of them, but he had never been one to crawl into a bottle, to go on an all-out binge. But there was always a first time. Gloria knew Virginia's death had left a big hole—bigger than Cutter was prepared for, bigger even than he would ever admit.

She felt her heart twist and turn as she pictured him somewhere in a bar full of strangers. One shouldn't be with strangers at a time like this. Then her heart plummeted to her toes as she pictured him and his Saab in a ditch along a deserted road. If only she knew he was safe, then she wouldn't worry so much.

Her hand reached for the phone, and before she could stop herself, she hit redial.

～◆ ◆～

Gloria sat in an olive brocade Queen Anne chair next to her mother. Alongside her mother sat Agnes, then Dr. Grant, then Cutter, all in a semicircle facing the ornately carved antique cherry desk. Behind the desk sat Charlie Axlerod, attorney-at-law. In addition to his Chamber of Commerce duties and his bed-and-breakfast—which was mostly operated by his wife and a staff of two—he also had a thriving law practice that ran the gamut of divorce, real estate, tax advocacy, and wills, a combination that could only be possible in a town the size of Appleton. He had handled both Virginia's personal and business matters.

"I, Virginia Bernadette Press, do hereby make, publish, and declare this to be my Last Will and Testament and do hereby revoke any and all other Wills and codicils heretofore made by me. I nominate and appoint Charles P. Axlerod as Executor of this . . ."

Gloria's mind wandered as Charlie read the endless legalese of Virginia's will, and she found herself leaning forward in her chair so she could get a glimpse of Cutter. She felt a strange, quiet pleasure in seeing him sitting safely in his straight-backed chair. And immense relief. Like everyone else in Appleton, she had not seen him for days. His neatly combed hair and heavily starched khakis and shirt didn't fool her. Those plum-colored circles under his eyes told Gloria she had been right about him going on a binge. Obviously, it had been a rough few days. She wanted to go up to him, to ask him if he was all right and to tell him she had been worried, but mostly to smile into his dark-brown eyes and let him know that she was there for him. Instead, she sent up prayers on his behalf and was still praying when she heard her mother gasp.

"Twenty thousand! Did you hear that, Gloria? Virginia, God rest her soul, left you twenty thousand dollars!"

"Why?" she said, when her mother's words penetrated.

"Gloria, *really.* That's hardly a grateful attitude. Obviously, Virginia thought highly of you."

Gloria shook her head. "I don't understand." She leaned over in order to see Cutter. "Is this all right with you?"

Cutter's eyelids drooped with fatigue. "I'm happy for you, Gloria. I'm glad she did it." Though his voice and face were somber, Gloria knew he meant it.

"*Really,* Gloria," her mother huffed. "Surely when you got

Charlie's invitation to the reading you knew you had to be mentioned? What did you expect her to leave you?"

"The crystal perfume bottle I tried to steal on a dare." She was rewarded by Cutter's laugh.

"I don't see what's so funny," her mother protested. "You were kind to Virginia in her final weeks. She just wanted to repay you."

And that was how all the gossip started.

~⁘ ⁘~

"The town's simply buzzing with the news," Wanda said when Gloria showed up for work the next day. "Now that you're a woman of means, maybe you'll change your mind about buying the place."

Gloria had already thought of that. So had several other people. Most people were happy for her. But there were some, like Pearl Owens, who mingled their congratulations with a snide, "Guess there's no faster way to make a dollar than by caring for a *rich* dying woman." The fact that Virginia had been so generous was what got most folks. Everyone knew how tight-fisted she'd been with money.

But Virginia had been generous with them all. To Geri she'd left her jewelry—worth untold thousands—to Agnes a 401k worth one hundred thousand, to Dr. Grant the deed to his office that she had held, marked "paid in full," to Cutter everything else.

Overnight, Cutter was worth millions.

"No excuses left now, Little Miss Moneybags," Wanda snorted. "So I'd appreciate it if you'd let me know ASAP. I think Paul and I have been patient enough. I don't think you should expect us to dangle on that string any longer."

Gloria felt as though a hummingbird were beating against the inside of her chest. She had spent half the night thinking about this very thing. She hoped she didn't appear overly excited. "Yes, you've been patient enough, Wanda. And yes, I've decided to buy the shop."

Wanda's shriek brought Paul running from the back. "What's going on?" he said, breathlessly, and stopped when he saw the two women hugging.

"Say hello to the new owner of Appleton Printers," Wanda returned, beaming.

～ ～

Cutter stood in front of the refrigerator studying the assorted casseroles and wondering what he should have for lunch. He had not gone to work today. Nor was he likely to go tomorrow. He suspected it would be a few more days before he'd be ready to do that.

He stared at the collection of covered dishes cramming the refrigerator shelves. There was a large tuna casserole from Molly Brennan. A green bean casserole from Sandy Stewart. A baked bean and frankfurter casserole from Polly Ann Sharp. A pan of baked macaroni from Connie DeAlberto. A lamb casserole from Virginia Connors, beef stew from Elvira Howell. And chicken and rice from Linda Peterson. All of the eligible and most desperate women in Appleton. Other eligibles had baked cakes or cookies, except for Sadie Bellows and Gloria. Sadie sent a sympathy card with a picture tucked inside of her in nothing but her birthday suit. A note scribbled on the back of the picture said, "I can help you forget—for a hundred dollars." And Gloria had sent one of those religious cards with the Twenty-third Psalm on the front and something about how God was with him in his time of sorrow. He would have liked it better if Gloria had sent a picture of herself tucked inside . . . with or without clothes. At least it would have been more personal.

He pulled out the chicken and rice, then closed the fridge with his foot. Dishes clanked as he retrieved a microwavable bowl from the cabinet. Then he scooped out a large spoonful of casserole and dumped it into the bowl. He shoved the bowl into the microwave, pressed the Express-2 button, and wondered, as he watched the bowl whirl around on a glass plate, if his brains were not getting nuked along with the food. He stepped to the side and thought about the rest of the casseroles in the refrigerator. One man couldn't eat all that in a month.

What did these Lilliputian women think? They were feeding Gulliver?

You should be grateful, Press, for their kindness. But even as he pulled the steaming chicken and rice from the microwave, he couldn't muster up any appropriate feelings of gratitude. That's because he suspected the casseroles were more of a means to get to his wallet than any genuine expression of sympathy. *A way to a man's heart was through his stomach.* And rich stomachs were always more highly prized. Well, they could have saved themselves the trouble. He wasn't interested in any of them. No sincerity, and much too obvious.

Only Sadie and Gloria were true to character. Sadie couldn't cook a casserole to save her life, but she knew how to get a man's attention. Always had, and wasn't shy about it either. She also knew how to drive home a point. Obviously she hadn't forgotten that tacky hundred-dollar-bill incident. And Gloria . . . still distant. He had expected more from her though. He had hoped for better. She could have suggested they go to the fishing hole. He would have liked that. *That* would have meant something to him.

C'mon, Press, be fair. You only got back to Appleton this morning.

Fair? Why should he be fair? Was it fair that Virginia had acted more like the Wicked Witch of the West than a mother? Was it fair that it took a deathbed to stir up enough emotion in her to tell him she loved him? Was it fair that he had heard her say those words only once in twenty-nine years? What was so hard about telling someone you loved him, for crying out loud?

Fair? Pfffffffff. Forget fair. Gloria should have called.

꧁ ꧂

Gloria fumbled over the keyboard, trying to reshape the Bezier path by moving a handle of its bounding box. She hit F10, the shortcut to Item>Edit>Shape. The flyer should have been finished an hour ago, but nothing she did seemed to produce the desired results. Maybe it was because her mind wasn't on it, but rather in a wind tunnel somewhere being blown here, there, and everywhere. What was wrong with her? Her mood was so foul it made her dislike her own company. Ever since Cutter had disappeared after Virginia's death, Gloria had felt out of sorts. And at the reading of Virginia's will, he had practically ignored her, as if she were a stranger. She just couldn't get over it. They were supposed to be friends. The whole thing was working her nerves. Maybe she should borrow some of Wanda's gum.

She jumped when the phone rang, as though confirming the edginess of her nerves. "Yes!" she answered, her voice sickle-sharp without her wanting it to be. *She had to get a grip.*

"Gloria?"

She recognized the voice. "Harry, sorry about that. I was sitting at my desk totally absorbed. Didn't mean to sound like a shrew."

"What are you working on?"

"A sales flyer for one of the women's clothing stores. Now that the festival's over, a lot of stores are running sales trying to get rid of excess inventory." She heard him sigh.

"Sure miss your work. Can't find anyone with half your imagination."

"Maybe we should team up again. Only this time, you come work for me."

"Huh?"

Gloria told him about the death of Virginia Press and the will and her decision to buy Appleton Printers.

"Well . . . don't that beat all? I guess we'll have to make it a double celebration Saturday."

"What's Saturday?"

"That's what I was calling about. We're all here missing you and wanted a good excuse to make you come. So Dorie and I plan to throw ourselves an engagement celebration. Perth'll be there too. She's doing fine but misses you like crazy. Now we can write something else on the cake besides 'Happy Engagement.' What do you say?"

"I'll be there," Gloria said, feeling her spirits lift. She remembered Harry's ragged oven mitts and thought that a new pair would make a perfect engagement gift, along with two tickets to the Eckerd City Playhouse tucked inside. The mitts she would get from a new kitchen store that had just opened in Shepherd's Field. The tickets she'd get online.

A trip to Eckerd would do her good.

～❦ ❦～

Geri Bickford was still rattled. She couldn't get over Virginia being gone. Gone like a puff of smoke. Twice she had reached for the phone to call her. Once to tell her about something she had seen on TV, and another time to ask about the mail she had gotten regarding her homeowners' insurance.

She stared at the collection of jewelry laid out neatly across the dressing table. Mostly antique pieces that had been in the family for generations. She couldn't believe Virginia had left them to her rather than Cutter. Maybe Virginia figured he'd turn around and sell them. Not that Virginia was terribly sentimental about the jewelry. But it would kill her to think Cutter would sell the jewels for half their value, just for some quick cash.

Kill her. Poor choice of words. A thing like that wouldn't kill her. Not like the cancer that had ravaged her body. *That* had killed her. *And now Virginia Press was dead.* Geri's mind tried to wrap itself around those words, tried to translate them into something tangible. What did that mean—Virginia was dead? It meant Geri didn't have a best friend to call every day. It meant no one to go to the movies with. Or to dinner. Or shopping. No one to tell her to "ignore the old battle-axe" every time Pearl Owens got Geri's goat. It meant loss.

Another loss in her life.

Geri had been sure that Virginia would outlast them all. Virginia was strong, courageous, independent. All traits Geri felt she lacked. It was Virginia who had helped Geri pick up the pieces when she discovered her marriage was a sham. It was Virginia who had helped Geri survive all the vicious gossip when the town learned that too. It was Virginia who'd helped her through those years when Gloria seemed to love only her father. "She'll come around," Virginia would say. It was Virginia who'd stood by Gavin Bickford's grave and stopped Geri from spitting on it in front of the whole town. "No sense giving the old battle-axe ammunition," she'd said. And it was Virginia who'd helped see her through that tough year when Gloria went running off to Eckerd.

And now Virginia Press was dead.

Geri carefully picked up each piece of jewelry and placed it cautiously in her red-velvet-lined box. She would trade all of these and more for another day with Virginia. Now she would have to face Pearl Owens's vicious wagging tongue alone. Already the rumors were circulating like one of those chain letters. She knew what Pearl was saying, and some of the others too. That both she and Gloria had manipulated a dying woman for profit.

Geri snapped the jewelry box shut and returned it to its proper place in the closet. The truth was, this gift was trouble on several fronts. Now she'd have to take out a safety-deposit box at the bank. She'd never worried before about someone coming to her house and stealing the few good pieces of jewelry she actually had scattered among her costume junk. But since the whole town knew about Geri's windfall, and with strangers moving into Appleton every day, she couldn't leave Virginia's expensive stuff around like bait.

Yes, that's what she'd do tomorrow. See Mr. Hotchkins about a safety-deposit box. She'd do that right after she went to see her mother. Everyone knew death came in threes. No telling when her mother would up and follow Virginia. And before that happened, Geri was going to get some things off her chest.

Chapter Eighteen

GERI BICKFORD STEPPED OUT of the car and braced herself against the cold November wind. She shuddered as much from nerves as from the chill and slammed the door of her gold Volvo. The large Tiffany-set opal on her right hand caught the sun, making her finger look like it was on fire. How foolish to wear Virginia's ring, thinking . . . hoping . . . it would give her the courage and grit of her friend, or at least inspire an anemic resemblance.

Absently, she brought her hands to her head, then ran her fingers over her hair, testing to see that all bobby pins were in place and that the French twist was still firmly tucked. Then she adjusted the collar of her brown wool blazer, bringing it up closer around her ears. She needed to get out of the cold. Still, she didn't move but remained on the sidewalk staring up at the house. She hadn't been inside since the fire.

Hannah Quinn's just like everyone else.

How many times had Virginia said that?

She's no plaster saint, and you're not going to burn in hell if you say a few harsh words to her.

Virginia had said that too; had urged Geri for years to have it out with her mother. But Virginia never took Pearl Owens into account, or what Pearl would do if she got wind of a family feud. But then, Virginia never took anyone into account when she wanted to do something.

Geri fingered the opal. Why did everyone love her mother so? It didn't seem fair. Even now, when Hannah seemed to have lost her faculties, they still loved her, while they resented Geri for her own multiple failures. She pushed her collar away from her neck and pulled down hard on the edges of her blazer.

All right, enough of this.

High-heeled boots tapped out Geri's progress up the sidewalk and stopped at the crumbling concrete steps. Her eyes scanned the peeling clapboards, the shutter that hung from a single hinge, windows that looked like they hadn't been washed in a decade. She could almost hear Pearl's whisper of disapproval. She shrugged it off and with a well-manicured finger rang the bell and waited.

A pudgy white-haired woman, wearing a flour-covered, red-checked apron, opened the door. "Oh, my, my, my! Look who's here! Come in, dear! Come in!"

Instead of feeling elated over her mother's reception, Geri felt angry. It irked her that her mother didn't seem that surprised to find her estranged daughter at the door. And the fact that Hannah hadn't even bothered to ask her *why* she was there frosted her cake even more.

Still, she trotted obediently behind her mother, observing the stacks of newspapers on the living room floor, the inch-thick dust on the furniture, the pile of laundry needing folding on the couch. Maybe she had been wrong in agreeing to move Hannah into a condo rather than to Clancy County.

The kitchen was even worse, with dishes piled high in the sink and almost every inch of counter space jammed with baking pans and measuring cups and flour and sugar and all sorts of baking additives. No doubt another batch of cookies for the migrant kids. She wondered if Hannah knew Gloria had been paying her grocery bills. Maybe Geri would add that to the list of things to tell her mother. But when she thought of how angry Gloria would be, Geri thought better of it. Things were just beginning to improve between her and Gloria. It would be unwise, at this point, to test the mettle of their new relationship.

Hannah fussed over one of the kitchen chairs, wiping it down with a dish towel as if someone important was about to sit on it. The action took some air out of Geri's ballooning anger.

"Here, dear, sit down, and I'll make a nice cup of tea." Hannah bustled over to the stove; then the sound of clanking pots and rattling china filled the kitchen. "I've got plenty of Earl Grey. Might even have some English Breakfast, if you prefer."

"Earl Grey is fine, Mom."

"How are you managing? I know Virginia's death was a big loss for you."

Geri pushed away the red-covered One-Year Bible that sat on the table and put her folded hands in its place. "I don't know why you never liked her. Maybe you'd care to explain that now?" She was surprised to hear her mother chuckle.

"She was your friend. It doesn't much matter anymore if I liked her or not, does it? Besides, I try never to speak ill of the dead."

"Well . . . I'm curious. I can't see the harm of you telling me."

Hannah wiped her hands on her apron. "Now, Geri, I know you're grieving over your loss, and I hurt for you too. You had a good friend in Virginia. But I also know you didn't come here to this house, after you haven't stepped foot in it for six months, just to ask me what I thought of Virginia Press." Hannah turned on the stove and placed the kettle on the front burner. "No, dear, you look and sound as if you've come spoiling for a fight."

Geri leaned her elbows on the table and frowned. How had she let her mother steal her thunder? How had she let her reverse the tables, where now Geri was on the defensive?

"I know you have your grievances." Hannah placed two mugs on the table, one in front of Geri, the other in front of a nearby empty chair.

Geri stared at the crude sunflowers painted on each mug and recognized her ceramics project of a zillion summers ago. She marveled that her mother had kept them, then decided it was typical. Hannah Quinn probably had the first crayon drawing Geri had ever made, tucked in the attic somewhere, along with every drawing, sewing project, term paper, and the like that came after.

"I know you've got grievances," Hannah repeated. "And I know you've been holding on to those grievances for years. Guess you've finally come to get them off your chest."

Geri opened her mouth to speak, but nothing came out. She was grateful when the kettle whistled and her mother was forced to return to the stove. She stared down at her opal. *Virginia would be furious if she saw her now.*

"I imagine having Virginia die like that made you think of things like regrets and hurts, maybe resurrected past disappointments. Made you realize you didn't have forever to straighten them out."

Geri's hands came down hard on the table, causing the band

of her ring to scrape against the wood. "That's what makes you so infuriating! You're always right, and you're always so *nice* about it."

Hannah chuckled. "I'm your mother, Geri. I guess I know you better than anyone, except the Lord, of course."

"You told me not to marry Gavin. You warned me. You were right. You told me not to keep such a tight reign on Gloria, that I would lose her if I did. Right again. But why, *why* didn't you help me when I came to you about Gavin? When I told you what he was doing? How he cheated on me every chance he got? Why did you make me go back? Why didn't you let me stay here with you?" Tears oozed from Geri's eyes like caulking from a window.

"Because part of me feared the scandal, the shame. And for that, I ask your forgiveness. But there was another part of me that wanted you to overcome—to face your problems and overcome them. You wanted to divorce Gavin on the grounds of abandonment, not adultery. But you owed it to Gavin—but mostly yourself—to confront him. To lay the charges at his feet. To see if there was any way to salvage your marriage. I knew you still loved him. And even though I didn't think Gavin had the character to make it work, for your sake I wanted you to try. But you didn't."

Geri blotted her eyes with her fingers. "I went back, didn't I? I tried my best to make it work."

"You went back and lived a lie." Hannah picked up the steaming kettle and poured hot water into the sunflower mugs. "You gave up your integrity and Gavin's for the sake of a little peace, for the sake of appearances."

"You know what Pearl Owens is like."

"Yes, I know what Pearl is like. But nothing you did stopped the talk. It was all wasted, your life of appeasement."

"That's really cruel. And so unfair. Gloria thought her father walked on water. What was I supposed to do? Expose him? She would have hated me."

"And she hated you anyway."

Geri winced.

"But only for a season." Hannah pulled the box of Earl Grey from the cabinet and placed it on the kitchen table along with two spoons. "Gloria was angry and hurt. But she loves you, Geri. She's always loved you. She just never felt that you loved her."

"I've tried to do what was best for her—to shield and protect her."

"Be honest now, Geri. It's needed, and a long time in coming. You lived vicariously through your daughter. Transferred your fears onto her. You nearly destroyed the child."

Geri pulled a napkin from the porcelain dispenser and blew her nose. "I didn't want her to be hurt as I was hurt. To suffer—"

"We all suffer. It's part of the human condition." Hannah came up to her daughter and cupped her chin. "Sometimes the suffering is of our own making; sometimes it isn't. And sometimes that's how we learn best. Gloria's got her own path to walk, and when a big-fisted problem comes from out of nowhere to knock her down, you can't take that blow for her. Though you want to . . . oh, yes, though you desperately want to, would give anything, in fact, to take that pain on yourself . . . you can't."

Geri looked into Hannah's loving eyes and knew that her mother had been talking about her own pain, how much she had longed to step in and take some of those blows for Geri. When Hannah smiled knowingly, a wall crumbled between them, just like that, a wall that had been as high and tough and formidable as the Berlin Wall itself. With a twinkle in her eye, Hannah released her daughter and returned to the stove.

"You know the thing that burns me? Really burns me?" Geri said, dropping a tea bag into the now-tepid water in her mug. "It's that Gavin—that womanizing, unfaithful, lousy Gavin—has gotten off scot-free. Gloria still thinks he walked on water, and if I try to tell her he didn't, she'd hate me all over again."

"She knows. I told her."

"What . . . did she say?" Geri's voice trembled.

"Nothing. But it helped her understand some things."

Geri punched the bag of Earl Grey with her spoon, dunking it beneath the water, then letting it bob up again. "I don't know why I didn't come here long ago and have this out. I guess because I was a coward. Or maybe I wasn't ready to hear how right you were and how wrong I was." Geri fished out the bag with her spoon. "It seems all my life I've been heading down one cliff after another, with you trying to stop me. And I resented you for it. I guess I've just been too proud to admit you were right. Sometimes I'm my own worst enemy." She heard her mother chuckle and looked up.

"Sometimes I'm my worst enemy too."

For the first time Geri smiled. "Impossible."

"No, really. For the past two years, I've been struggling to keep up this big old house. Nearly killing myself in the process. Too proud, too stubborn to admit it was just too much for me."

Geri laughed. "And you're admitting it now."

Her mother nodded. "I'm ready to move to Willow Bend."

"For a while I was thinking of putting you into Clancy County."

"I know."

"It was just for spite. Just pure spite. I was mad at you—for turning me away . . . for trying to make me face things I didn't want to . . . for a lot of things. I'm . . . sorry."

"I know, dear."

The next thing Geri knew, she was on her feet by the stove hugging and kissing her mother and feeling her mother's soft, fleshy arms hug her back, then her mother's rosemary-scented mouth kissing her cheeks. And Geri tingled with pure joy.

※ ※

The in-house auditor from the Appleton Savings Bank had been going over Paul and Wanda's books for over two hours. Gloria was getting nervous. "How's it going, Malcolm?" she finally asked.

"It's going."

"Well, does it look good? Will Mr. Hotchkins have any trouble approving the loan?"

"I can't speak for Mr. Hotchkins, Gloria."

"Just take a guess. You've done this before. You know if numbers add up to a good risk or not."

"I never guess about these things. Too many variables: location, credit rating, previous experience, that kind of thing. It's not just about crunching numbers, you know. I do my part, then turn in my findings and let others do theirs. You're going to have to wait like everyone else, till the process runs its course."

"Well, how long is that going to take?"

"Don't know." By the way Malcolm laid out more pencils and repositioned his calculator, it looked as if he was going to be here for the duration.

Gloria threw her hands in the air and caught sight of Wanda leaning against the wall by her desk, smiling. "Welcome to the wonderful world of the small business owner."

"I can't believe all this paperwork," Gloria said, walking over to Wanda. "I filled out forms all night. And the information they want! My goodness, I'm surprised they didn't ask for my dress size." Gloria paused when she realized she was whining. "I guess I thought it was going to be easier."

Wanda chuckled. "Nothing's ever easy. At least, nothing worthwhile. Relax, honey. It's gonna be all right. You'll see. Before you know it, you'll be ordering me and Paul around like a couple of flunkies, and we'll get our revenge by taking two-hour lunches."

"So you think Mr. Hotchkins will give me the loan?"

"It's in the bag. You're gonna be Appleton Printers' new owner. My first suggestion—buy yourself a case of Pepto-Bismol."

Gloria laughed and gave Wanda a hug. "I can't believe how much I want this place."

"Well, God sure made a way, didn't He now?"

Yes, He had, but Gloria didn't like remembering that someone had had to die in order for it to happen. She suddenly thought of the kernel of wheat falling to the ground. *Death before life. Always death before life.* She'd try to see that Virginia's seed money produced a great harvest.

"Hey, kiddo! I heard the good news."

Gloria turned to the familiar voice. She tried not to react when she saw Tracy walk into the print shop in skintight hip-hugger jeans, a belly shirt that fell only inches below her bra line, and above her navel, a tattoo of a long-stem rose that seemed to move when she did.

"Congratulations. Everyone's talking about how you're going to buy this place." Tracy gave the premises a once-over, and the look on her face seemed to say, "Why bother?" Absently, she picked her thumbnail. It was freshly painted in a red that matched her rose tattoo. "Can you step outside so we can talk?"

Gloria hesitated. "Sure you won't be cold?" It had to be fifty degrees outside.

"The cold doesn't bother me," Tracy said, flipping her red hair over her shoulder with a toss of her head and laughing. But she gave her shirt a self-conscious tug.

"I'm leaving for Vegas in the morning," Tracy said, as soon as they got outside. "If you can call it morning—five o'clock. More like the middle of the night, if you ask me. I've pushed up my schedule. Decided not to waste any more time in this two-bit town."

"How can you leave? What about the DWI case? You'll have to go to court soon, won't you?"

Tracy shrugged. "When it's time, I'll come back." But the way she said it made Gloria think it was a lie, that Tracy had no intention of returning. Tracy gave her hair another toss. "Anyway, now that you've come into such good luck—can't believe that old coot left you money—probably a bribe so you'd marry the Monkey—though what I've seen of you and Cutter lately tells me she could have saved herself the trouble. Well . . . *anyway* . . . now that you're in the chips, I was hoping you could lend me a couple of thou." Tracy began to shiver and pulled on her shirt, then wrapped her arms around her bare midriff. "I could really use it. I did manage to scrape some cash together. Even wrangled a little outta my mom. But I'm still short. It's not just the trip. It's setting up the new apartment, the security deposit, the whole bit. Sheesh, it all adds up. My credit cards are maxed—those that aren't cancelled, that is. So I'm really scraping the bottom of the barrel . . ." Tracy's face flushed. "Not that *you're* the bottom of the barrel. I didn't mean it like that. *Anyway* . . . whaddaya say?"

Gloria's eyes wandered to the rose over Tracy's navel, to the tight denim jeans that hugged bony hips, to the metal chain that looked like prison irons around one of Tracy's black leather boots. What was going to become of her friend?

The *tap tap tap* of Tracy's boot telegraphed her impatience.

Still, Gloria remained silent. Tracy had been her friend all her life. There had to be some way to keep her in Appleton. She thought of a half-dozen scenarios—none of them realistic. She felt desperate, panicky, and begged God to give her wisdom.

Maybe it was the tapping boot, or Tracy shivering in that ridiculous outfit, or maybe it was the tattoo undulating every time Tracy shifted her weight, but all of a sudden Gloria realized she couldn't stop Tracy. Tracy was on a train that only Tracy or the Lord could stop. And the only thing Gloria would send with her was her prayers.

"Cutter said he was going to call you and personally ask you to come back to Medical Data," Gloria said, in a final attempt to pull the emergency brakes of that runaway train.

"Yeah, the Monkey called. I was wondering how long it was going to take him to realize he was losing money without me."

Gloria stared, dumbfounded. Tracy's replacement was pulling in as much as Tracy ever had. She cringed when she thought of how she had put Cutter through the humiliation of appearing to grovel, when all along he was performing a kindness for both Gloria and Tracy. "Why didn't you accept?" Gloria asked, trying to keep the anger out of her voice.

"Why should I help that jerk out? Just because he's hurting, I'm supposed to forget all my plans and go back to save his bacon? What do I look like, a blooming charity?"

"You could have a future here in Appleton."

"C'mon, kiddo, get serious. I'm outta here, with or without your money."

"Then it's going to have to be without." Gloria's heart felt as if it were ripping in two as she watched Tracy's face drop.

"I don't understand. You have the money; you can afford it. I helped you when you wanted to leave town. I did everything I could."

"I know you did."

"Then I don't understand why you won't help me now."

"That's exactly what I *am* doing."

Tracy frowned. "Stop the double-talk. Are you loaning me the money or not?"

Gloria shook her head and watched anger gnarl Tracy's face. When Tracy clenched her fist, there was a moment, a single moment as quick as the flick of an eyelid, when Gloria actually believed Tracy was going to strike her. But Tracy just tossed her hair, turned, and walked away. Her boots tapped their farewell on the gray pavement, and Gloria listened while Tracy crossed the street, then turned into Dr. Grant's side parking lot and disappeared. And standing there instead of running after Tracy and telling her she had changed her mind was one of the hardest things Gloria had ever done.

❧ ☙

For the rest of the day, Gloria was sullen and tried to stay out of both Wanda's and Malcolm's way. Physically, she busied herself with emptying supply boxes, tidying shelves, and sweeping corners that hadn't been swept in a long time. Mentally, she alternated between praying for Tracy and justifying the rightness of her decision not to help. It was an awkward seesaw that bumped rather than glided up and down.

She was in the praying position of that seesaw when Wanda's sharp voice reached her in the stock room. "Gloria! Telephone."

Gloria leaned the broom against the wall and wiped her hands on a paper towel. Then she headed for the front office, where she found Wanda hovering over the auditor, almost glaring down at him, and holding the phone in a chubby fist.

Malcolm, it seemed, paid no attention but sat calmly with his calculator, sharpened pencils, and the shop books spread all over Gloria's desk. It was obvious that no amount of pressure was going to force him into rushing the process.

Gloria mouthed a "thank you," took the phone, then turned her back on the pair. She walked as far away as the two-foot cord would allow. The first thing she was going to do when she took over was get handhelds. "Hello?"

"I thought we'd go fishing Saturday."

"Cutter?" Gloria's heart lurched. She turned to the side and saw Wanda and Malcolm staring. She tried to walk farther away but felt the cord yank and stopped. "How are you? I mean . . . how are you doing?" All those dark, murky thoughts she had been trying to sift and organize into their proper boxes suddenly began swirling around as if they had been picked up by the wind and hopelessly scrambled. "I've . . . been worried."

"Then why haven't you called?"

"I did! About twenty-five times, but you were out of town, remember?" She didn't want to think about those nerve-racking days.

"You didn't leave a message."

"What was I supposed to say? I'm sorry about your mother? I hope you're not drinking yourself to death?" Now, why had she said that? Why didn't she just leave it alone? She didn't want to talk to Cutter. Not right now. Not like this.

"You'd do a banner business writing messages for sympathy cards. 'A special message from Gloria Bickford—so sorry about your loss, but do stay away from the Guinness.'"

Gloria closed her eyes and wondered how much of this Wanda and Malcolm were getting and decided everything—at least, Wanda was.

"Gloria?"

"What."

"Thought you hung up for a minute."

"No. I'm here."

"Are you ticked or something?"

"No."

"Sure you are. Why?" Silence. "Come on, now—what's the problem? You're not still ticked about Sadie? Or the fact I gave you back the cuff links?"

Gloria let out an impatient sigh. "I was never *ticked* . . . angry . . . about that." She was startled to feel a check in her spirit and realized the extent of her lie.

"No?"

Gloria turned around and saw the bald patch on the back of Malcolm's head. He may have had his head down, but by the way his left ear tilted toward the ceiling, she knew he was listening. Wanda, on the other hand, was brazenly obvious and stared saucer-eyed while plucking the nest of her bleached-blonde hair. Gloria turned and cupped the phone closer to her chin. This was not the time to discuss anything of importance with Cutter. "Look, I'm not mad, okay? Not now, anyway," she whispered into the phone, but when Cutter asked her to repeat what she had said, she gave up and resumed her normal tone. "I said I'm not mad. So can we leave it alone?"

"Then why do you sound mad?"

"Because you can still rile me faster than anyone I know. You leave town, disappear for days, make people worry, then get uppity because you think they didn't call."

"When you said I made people worry—were you talking about yourself?"

"Well . . . me and . . . others."

"What others? I don't think anyone gave a hoot that I was gone."

"Well, Agnes certainly did, and—"

"Know what I think? I think you're softening, maybe seeing me in a different light. Maybe *liking* me, even, liking me a lot, and not just as a friend, either, and it's scaring you."

Perspiration beaded Gloria's hairline. She closed her eyes, trying to stuff the potpourri of thoughts back into their boxes. How should she answer? What could she say that would make any sense to Cutter? Her commitment to the Lord, to His inerrant Word—was meaningless to him. "Your timing is really lousy. If you wanted to get into this, why didn't you say something at your house after Charlie finished reading the will? You hardly said two words to me."

"As you so rightly surmised, I was hungover. I wasn't in the mood to talk to anyone."

"Well, I can't talk now. I'm at work, in case you've forgotten."

"All right . . . all right. I'll leave it alone, if you say you'll go to the fishing hole with me Saturday. It's the one place I've always been able to relax. And I need that now, a little relaxation."

"I can't."

"Gloria, you've got to help me out here. I'm as jumpy as a flea. Can't sit in one spot for five minutes. Can't relax. And I don't sleep nights. *Can't* sleep. Every time I close my eyes . . . I see Virginia. That woman tormented me all my life. Just never expected her to be able to do it now that she's dead. I'm sure a psychiatrist would have a field day—pin a fancy name on it, tell me it's—"

"Grief. It's called 'grief,' Cutter."

"No, nothing so noble. But whatever it is, it'll go away. Just need some time. But I could sure use a little help now. I figured you're the one person who would understand."

Gloria rubbed her temples. This was the stuff migraines

were made of. "Harry Grizwald invited me to Eckerd for the weekend. Why don't you come along?"

"You've got to be kidding. I'm not up for that kind of thing."

"I'll drive."

"I'd be miserable company. Boorish and sullen. You know how I can get, Gloria. Might even embarrass you in front of your friends. Snap somebody's head off."

"I'll pick you up Saturday, eight sharp—a.m., that is."

"You're twisting my arm."

"It's about time somebody did." She heard him laugh, and that pleased her.

"Okay. You win. But I'd still prefer to go to the hole."

"What about tonight?"

"Say again?"

"We could go fishing tonight."

"Well . . . yeah . . . we could. But it's gonna be cold—low forties, I hear. At least in the daytime you've got the sun, and—"

"Okay. Just thought I'd offer." She was annoyed at how disappointed she felt.

"That was nice of you, Gloria, but I don't want you catching pneumonia on my account—but thanks. It *was* nice, really. Guess I'll see you Saturday, then."

"Yeah . . . okay." Gloria felt her stomach flutter and took a deep breath. "Cutter . . . I might as well come clean—you were right. I was miffed about Sadie and the cuff links." What was with her? Why did she say that, especially now? Before she could get all her thoughts together? And with an audience? She was sure Wanda and Malcolm were getting every word. But now that she had opened her big mouth, it was too late to stop. "I don't know why I was so annoyed. Maybe because of the way you said it, did it—like you were trying to put me on the spot. And I hate that manipulation thing you do. But I honestly did call you . . . more times than I can count. I wouldn't let you go through this . . . your loss . . . on your own." Silence. "Cutter?"

"You're pretty honest, you know? And I admire that. In fact, that's what I like about you and Sadie—your honesty."

The mention of Sadie's name made Gloria's skin prickle. Great—now Cutter was comparing her to Sadie Bellows.

"I know I can be difficult, definitely not a sanguine personality. And I've been an idiot on more than one occasion." Cutter laughed. "Okay, try a lifetime. But I appreciate what you said. It makes me realize that you do like me—*really* like me. And that's a happy surprise, Gloria. You can't imagine how happy."

"Cutter, you're all over the place. First, it's about not calling you, then fishing, then Sadie. Will you stay on topic?"

"You don't want me to stay on topic. But I'll let you figure out why, all by yourself."

After she said good-bye, Gloria turned and saw Wanda with her fleshy arms folded under her large breasts, her face a kaleidoscope of disbelief, dismay, confusion. Malcolm's face, on the other hand, was turned down, obscured; his body hunched over the desk as though deeply engrossed in his work. When Gloria placed the phone on its cradle, she glanced at the papers in front of him and noticed that the one he was so carefully scrutinizing was upside down.

What could she expect? In a town the size of Appleton, everyone knew everyone else's business. She walked to the stockroom and picked up the broom. With repetitious forward movements, she swept the dust and cobwebs and bits of paper into a pile. She bent down to gather it all in the dustpan, then stopped and straightened. She knew what Cutter was implying. Was it true? She had been struggling with her feelings for days. There had been a moment, while Cutter was away on his binge and she was walking the floor with worry, when she'd actually sensed that her feelings had shifted, made a detour somehow onto dangerous ground. But she had attributed that to strain, the culmination of an emotional roller coaster she'd been riding ever since Virginia Press announced she was dying. Now . . . She shook her head. No, it was all nonsense. All misplaced, misdirected, and mislabeled emotions. Because one thing Gloria knew with certainty: She could never be unequally yoked.

She filled the dustpan, then picked it up. As she carried it to the garbage pail in the corner, a slow smile crept over her lips, like an earthworm emerging from its tunnel. "Oh, my." She stopped and stood there for several minutes, holding the dustpan and shaking her head. It wasn't possible. It just wasn't possible. She covered her mouth with her hand to muffle her laughter. The whole thing was just too funny. Hilarious, really. But as she laughed, she couldn't help thinking it was a bad joke, a very bad joke. But God didn't make bad jokes, did He? She had known for some time that God had a sense of humor, but it was never at anyone's expense. He just didn't do black comedy.

"Trust Me," came the familiar still, small voice.

Gloria emptied the dustpan and leaned it against the wall. God was really asking a lot of her this time. "Trust Me" had never been her favorite command, but it seemed that now God was raising the bar. Okay . . . she'd trust Him. What else could she do?

⛥ ⛥

Chapter Nineteen

GLORIA SAW THE LARGE, shiny patch ahead and slowed her Escort. *Black ice.* That's how she had wrecked the Silver Streak, the car Grandma Quinn had given her about two years ago. It was going to be like this all the way to Eckerd. The weatherman had called for a new seventy-two-hour cold front, a record low, and that meant the little two-inch snowfall they'd had two days ago, which was now mostly slush, was going to turn into a patchwork of hazards.

As the car slowed, Cutter opened his eyes. "What's happening?"

"Black ice," Gloria said simply and watched, out of the corner of her eye, as Cutter tilted back on the headrest.

"You want me to drive?"

"No, thanks." Gloria turned down the music—something by Michael Card—so Cutter could go back to sleep. She felt uncomfortably like a schoolgirl—nervous and jittery at being with Cutter, but happy too. There were so many unanswered questions. And several sleepless nights had failed to provide any further answers than the one she already had: *Trust Me.* "You rest," she said, still marveling at the recent turn of events.

"Thank you, ma'am. Mighty thoughtful." Cutter mimicked a Southern drawl. Then, in his normal voice, "Got only about an hour of shut-eye last night."

"What did Virginia say to you . . . the last time you saw her?"

Cutter lifted his head. "This your idea of small talk?"

Gloria shrugged. "Something's bothering you. Maybe if you talk about it, you'll start sleeping again."

The seat made a thumping noise as Cutter brought it to its upright position. Apparently all thoughts of napping had vanished. "What am I supposed to say after a lead-in like that? You know the problems I had with Virginia. I'm not up to rehashing ancient history right now."

"You didn't answer my question. What did your mother say the last time you saw her?"

Cutter stretched his arm backward and grabbed a bag of chips from the seat behind him. Gloria heard a soft *whoosh* as he pulled open the seam, then crunching as his hand rummaged around inside.

"Okay," she said softly, reaching to turn up the radio.

"She told me she . . . loved me." The words came out mangled, like they had gone through a shredder. "A person shouldn't wait until she's dying to tell someone she loves him."

All the longing and anger and regret of a lifetime were in Cutter's words, and Gloria found herself praying, asking Jesus to pour the healing balm of Gilead into him, just as she had poured water into the dry soil of her philodendron this morning, then watched the water stream out the bottom and all over the table. That's what she wanted to see, Cutter with joy overflowing and bubbling from every pore. *The joy of the Lord is my strength.* If only Cutter would come to the Lord.

"You're not saying anything." He closed the bag of chips and tossed it in the back.

"That's because I'm praying."

"For me?"

Gloria nodded and expected to hear some wisecrack. Instead she heard, "I guess I could use a few prayers."

"Virginia really did love you, you know." Even to her ears, the words sounded as fake as Styrofoam. She felt Cutter's piercing eyes probe the side of her face.

"What makes you say such a stupid thing?"

"She told me during one of my visits."

"And that's supposed to do it? A puny secondhand account?" Cutter cranked up the radio, then a second later turned it back down. "Even if it were true, it doesn't matter now. I'm not a kid anymore, and I can't yell, 'Do-over.'"

His hands roamed over the dashboard. He opened the glove compartment, closed it, adjusted the vents directing heat away from him, then opened the window. Cold air rushed past Gloria's face like a blunt object, numbing her nose. Before she could protest, he closed the window, then began drumming on the metal door handle.

"Ever see me play field hockey?"

"Yes, once. Tracy dragged me to a game."

"What did you think?"

"About the game or your playing?" Gloria didn't have to turn her head to know Cutter was giving her a dirty look. "All I remember was going home with a headache from everyone in the bleachers chanting your name. It was almost blasphemous the way they called *Cut-ter—Cut-ter—Cut-ter*—like you were some Greek god they were trying to induce to come down from Mount Olympus."

"What did you expect? I was their star. But I wasn't their

Greek god. I was more like their golden calf, the idol that led the team to the championship. Appleton High hadn't won a state championship in ten years."

"No denying it—you were a good athlete." Gloria knew there had to be some point to all this but didn't want to press.

"You know, I never really liked field hockey. Funny, isn't it? I was good at it, but I never liked it. I was even better at it than I was at football or basketball or baseball. And I was pretty good at those. But field hockey was different. A 'natural,' Coach called me. And I was. So I played, and ran around the dumb field, and made MVP because I figured if Virginia came and saw me . . . well, maybe she'd see how good I was too. And maybe that would finally make her proud . . . make her think I had something . . . was worth something. But Virginia never came. Not once."

Gloria's heart felt like quicksand, and all of Cutter's words were sinking deep. "I guess in some ways we both were short-changed." She reached into her parka and retrieved two gold-plated cuff links from an inside pocket. She cradled the links in her hand as she jogged through the valley of indecision. There were so many reservations, so many questions. *A person shouldn't wait until she's dying to tell someone she loves him.* The words still seared her ears.

She said a quick prayer, hoping against hope that she had not missed the Lord. Then she slowly placed the cuff links in the palm of the open hand Cutter had resting on his lap. She kept her hand there, covering his. "It's unfair of me to say this, and I do so with grave reservations and misgivings because there can never be anything between us as long as we're not like-minded. The Lord means everything to me . . . Someday, hopefully, you'll be able to say the same thing. When that happens, I'd like to explore a deeper relationship. For now, there can't be anything but friendship. You must understand that. But all the same, I want you to know that . . . that I love you." She said it in a near-whisper, inwardly cringing at her timing. At first she didn't think Cutter heard her, or even knew what she had placed in his hand, because he neither spoke nor moved. But then he curled his fingers and entwined them with hers.

"When did you first discover this?" His breath steamed the side window.

"I think it started to dawn on me when you told me about Sadie's visit. Then you clinched it when you disappeared for three days."

"Three and a half days."

"Okay, three and a half days."

"So it was that . . . and Sadie?"

"Yes." Gloria released his hand, then brought hers up to the steering wheel. The next thing she knew, Cutter was scrawling their initials on the misty window. Such a simple, almost juvenile act—and yet it made her feel like weeping. This gift, this love, had swooped down like a hawk, ripped into her heart, and taken her by surprise. It was a joy and a terror both, dangerously embraced the unknown, and could lead nowhere. *Oh, how was she going to manage it all?*

"Remind me to send Sadie a thank-you note," Cutter said, as Gloria skirted past another patch of black ice. And that was how the ice in the car got broken, as the two of them laughed, then spent the next hour talking about Virginia Press.

~֍ ֎~

Confusion reigned as Harry, Dorie, and Perth kissed and hugged first Gloria, then Cutter, and tried talking over one another.

"You look great!"

"How were the roads?"

"How long did it take you to get here?"

"Hope you're hungry."

"You look thinner. Did you lose weight?"

Gloria surrendered her coat and the beautifully wrapped engagement gift to Harry—who then passed them both to Dorie—and tried to answer everyone's questions. Cutter was smiling way too much, and that distressed her, because she thought she had made her concerns clear. Then, just as Cutter got the smile under control, he'd look her way and, pop, there it was, right back on his face, as if she held a connecting wire that she could pull at will and change him into a grinning marionette.

Dorie disappeared with Gloria's coat and gift and came out carrying a small cake that was covered with writing. The word "congratulations" was written twice, and Harry's and Dorie's and Gloria's names were scrawled wherever they would fit. If someone didn't know better, they would have thought Harry and Gloria were celebrating one thing, and Dorie another.

"It's lovely," Gloria said, finally realizing the obvious. Dorie had made the cake.

"Hey, Gloria. Harry tells me you're buying a print shop." It was Perth, her eyes glowing with excitement. "Seems that book I bought you for Christmas will come in handy."

Gloria nodded, remembering the wonderful Christmas they had had together and Perth's gift to her—a book on how to start a business. She took a seat beside Perth on the couch. Cutter chose a chair in the corner, and Gloria assumed it was to allow Perth and the others room to be near her. His thoughtfulness touched her and made her look his way. His elbow rested on the arm of the high-backed Ashington chair, and his entire body listed to the right in order for his palm to cradle his square chin.

But it was the fingers of his right hand, fluttering around his mouth like butterflies, that held her attention. Then she realized that their purpose was to conceal the ridiculous grin that split his face.

"How's school?" Gloria asked, avoiding Cutter's eyes and wishing she could dive without reservations into their new relationship.

"Well . . ." Perth took Gloria's hand and absently played with her fingers. "You wouldn't believe the amount of reading I have to do. And the *papers.* Seems like my professors want a paper every other day. At this rate I'm gonna need glasses before I'm twenty."

In spite of herself, Gloria's eyes wandered back to Cutter just in time to see him stretch out his legs and close his eyes. Maybe tonight he would actually get some sleep.

~❧ ☙~

Cutter pushed his empty plate away. He couldn't remember the last time he had eaten anything this good. "Gloria told me how much you like to cook, Harry. The meal was incredible. As a man more accustomed to cooking like George Foreman than like Emeril Lagasse, I'm grateful." Harry laughed, but Cutter could see he was genuinely pleased. *Since when have you become the model of pleasantries, Press?* When he glanced at Gloria and felt his heart bottom out, he knew the answer.

"I know what you mean. Phil's Diner doesn't have anything like this," Perth said, referring to her part-time job.

"You've *got* to give me that Newburgh recipe." Gloria beamed at her former boss.

"Now you know why I'm marrying him," Dorie said. "He's going to do all the cooking."

Harry laughed. "I think I got the better end of the deal. Dorie's gonna keep the apartment clean and do my paperwork."

"Speaking of which, did you see all that mail that came to the shop this morning?" Dorie asked.

Harry nodded.

Dorie turned to Gloria. "Can't believe the amount of cards and whatnot we've been getting. Last week, Harry announced our engagement in the *Eckerd City Review.* Now all of Harry's friends and business acquaintances are sending their congratulations. Everyone thinks so highly of him, don't you know."

Cutter thought Gloria's confirming head nod was excessive and wondered if Dorie was nearsighted, then decided Gloria obviously thought very highly of Harry too. And for some silly reason, that made Cutter jealous.

"Later, I thought we'd gather around and open them up— all the gifts, I mean. I've been saving them for today. And I . . . we—Harry and I—got something special for you, Gloria, in honor of your new business, so you have something to open too. But what I want to do now is to get organized." Dorie stood and collected the dirty plates near her. "Perth and I will do the dishes." She looked at Perth and jerked her head, bringing the girl to her feet. "That'll give us all some time to digest Harry's delicious meal before we have cake. Just don't expect too much of the cake. After I baked it and saw how pathetic it looked, I wondered if I should have even bothered. But I did want to do my part, don't you know. When it's time, I'll bring the cake and the gifts to the living room."

Gloria piled her empty salad bowl on top of her dinner plate, then the silverware on top of that.

"What are you doing?" Dorie shrieked, as though she had just witnessed an atrocity. "No, no, no." Her head moved from side to side. "What I want you to do is take your young man

318

for a nice long walk. Show him the neighborhood. I'm sure he'll be glad to see some of the places that were a big part of your life when you lived in Eckerd."

"Yeah," Perth chimed. "Take him to West Meadow Market."

Gloria gave Perth a dirty look but didn't offer any resistance when Perth pushed her toward the front door. "Why do I have the feeling you're all trying to get rid of me?"

Perth giggled and put her finger to her lips. "Shhhhhh. Don't let on I said anything, but Dorie's been working on something for you all week. She won't even let me see it or tell me what it is."

Cutter stood nearby, wondering at the silliness of the female animal but thoroughly enjoying it in spite of himself. "I'll get our coats." He disappeared into the bedroom, where three coats lay neatly across the double bed—his, Gloria's, and, he supposed, Dorie's. He slipped on his bombardier-style jacket, then picked up Gloria's gray squall parka and draped it over his arm. When he turned, he saw Harry filling the doorway.

"I didn't like you the first time I met you at The Lakes, son. Don't know if I like you much better now, but for Gloria's sake, I told her you were welcome when she called and asked if you could come." Harry's white hair curled around his ears, and his stomach protruded below folded arms, making him look soft, over-the-hill. But Cutter knew not to let appearances fool him. He was sure Harry Grizwald could be a formidable foe if aroused.

"Is there a point?" Cutter asked, trying to keep his voice pleasant. *For Gloria's sake.* At least that was something they both had in common.

"It's obvious how she feels about you, and I don't mind telling you it's a bit of a shock. You're not a man with much looks or personality, so I'm supposing there's got to be brains somewhere in there, or maybe . . . character not visible."

"Is this the place where I'm supposed to say 'thank you'?"

"Gloria wouldn't fall for just anybody. Still, I'd be tempted to talk her out of it, discourage her, only, problem is, I see that you're smitten too." Harry uncrossed his arms and moved closer to Cutter, making Cutter wonder if he was going to have to defend himself. When Harry put out his hand like he wanted Cutter to shake it, Cutter was dumbfounded. "So I guess the only thing to do is welcome you to the family." With that, Harry grabbed Cutter's hand and pumped it up and down a half-dozen times. Then he let go and left the room.

Cutter stood by the bed, Gloria's parka still dangling from one arm, trying to take it all in. Obviously, these three—Harry, Dorie, and Perth—loved Gloria. That put them all on common ground. He loved her too. But what Harry was saying was that they—these warm, friendly, sometimes silly people—were prepared to love him as well.

And that was saying a lot.

⁖

Cutter couldn't remember his heart ever feeling this buoyant. Between his fingers he held the one treasure that had eluded him for years. He squeezed his hand as though reassuring himself and felt Gloria's small palm tucked inside. He glanced over at her and hoped his joy didn't make him look like a grinning idiot. A guy had to have some dignity.

For the past hour, Gloria had been giving him a tour down Pratt Parkway, pointing out various shops as they went. Finally, they'd reached West Meadow Market, and she told him about the first time she'd met Perth there. He had been touched by her story and made a mental note to be kinder to Perth. After that, they had turned and headed back.

"I'm tired of doing all the talking," Gloria said, her breath forming puffs of steam in the cold air. "It's about time you did some."

"What do you want me to talk about?"

"You can tell me what Harry wanted when he followed you into the bedroom."

Cutter chuckled. "You don't miss a thing, do you?"

"Well?"

Cutter shrugged. "Just guy talk."

"Guy talk?"

A brief hesitation, then he told Gloria what Harry had said. *"Why* do you love me?" he added, because it was something he had been thinking about ever since Harry had cornered him.

Gloria looked puzzled. "That's a strange thing to ask."

"Seriously. I know all the reasons why I love you, but I don't know a single reason why you love me."

"Maybe I shouldn't have said anything. Maybe that was wrong of me. You know my reservations. There are a lot of issues I need—"

"I know . . . I know." Cutter waved his hand in the air. He had waited so long for Gloria to come around . . . had hoped and wished and dreamed too hard to be put off now. "And we'll face them one by one, together. But let's suppose . . . let's suppose for one minute that they're all settled and we're just two lovers walking hand in hand."

"Cutter—"

"Just for one minute, Gloria . . . please."

"Okay . . . shall I list them in order of importance?"

"If you want."

"Well, the first reason would be your money—"

"C'mon. Be serious."

Gloria squeezed Cutter's hand. "Because suddenly God

opened my heart, and there you were inside. I can't explain it any better than that."

Cutter felt disappointed at the vague, almost blasé quality of her statement, but he didn't voice it. Whatever the reason, the fact remained: She *did* love him. And for now, the joy it produced was almost more than he could bear. "You want to know why I love you?"

"It would be nice."

"In order of importance?"

"Sure."

"Okay, let's see now, there's—"

The sound of an explosion ripped into their conversation. Almost immediately, black smoke plumed from a building a few blocks in front of them, and soon after, the shriek of sirens—police and fire engine—filled the air. People ran in all directions. A woman bustled past, carrying a crying child and looking like she was about to burst into tears herself. Suddenly Cutter and Gloria found themselves going against the tide as people swarmed past, fear twisting their faces almost in the same way it had twisted the faces of those fleeing the Twin Towers.

"Maybe we should stay put," Cutter said, worried that someone might knock Gloria over and trample her. But Gloria kept moving. "Gloria! It's not safe." But already she had pulled her hand from his and was running ahead, darting in and out among the throng. "Gloria!" he yelled again, and when she turned he saw the terror in her eyes. But it was different from the terror on the faces of the others. In an instant he understood.

He followed behind her, struggling to keep up, and stopped several yards from E-Z Printing. A ring of police cars had blocked off all traffic, and already a hook and ladder was at the scene. Two firemen in Bullard helmets, tan-and-yellow turnout coats, and bunker pants pulled the live hose closer to the store. Water splashed everywhere. Two other men battered down the front door with axes, then disappeared. All the while, smoke poured from the third-story window.

A second explosion shattered more glass, and Cutter watched in horror as tiny shards fell like confetti onto the pavement. He didn't move, just stood frozen, staring up at the building belching smoke. Gloria stood beside him, covering her mouth with her hand and screaming.

❦

Chapter Twenty

GLORIA FELT THE HEAT of the second explosion on her face and bare hands, felt the shock wave punch her chest as if a doctor were breaking her sternum for surgery. Her heart beat out in rapid, jackhammer-like thuds the names of Harry and Perth and Dorie. *Oh, God, please let them be all right.*

Cutter's sinewy hands grabbed for her and nearly caught her thumb and locked on, but she pulled away in time. Nothing was going to stop her. Not Cutter, not the ring of police, not the swarm of firefighters. Not until she knew her friends were safe.

She pushed through the thin crowd in front of her, barely hearing the horrified cries of bystanders or the loud shouts pressing firefighters into action. She heard Cutter call her name, but his voice was distant, hardly discernable, like the background noise of surround sound. She didn't turn but stumbled forward, choking on air heavy as chalk dust. With one hand she tried shielding her eyes from the stinging smoke that pressed against her pupils and made her eyes tear. She barely saw the blue-clad arm that brought her to a stop.

"Sorry, Miss, you can't come any farther."

"You don't understand." Gloria tried to focus on the patrolman's face. He was young and crisp and clean in spite of the fallout of smoke and particleboard and glass shards and fragments of wood and brick. His appearance made him look strangely out of place in what resembled a war zone. "Those are my friends up there. I was just with them . . . visiting . . . and went for a walk. I have to see if they're all right. I need to make sure—"

"You need to stay right here, out of harm's way." The look on Gloria's face must have been pitiful, because the young officer did a double take, then pulled her through the imaginary line that separated the curious from the essential. He guided her to one of the squad cars and opened the back door. "Why don't you wait inside where it's warm? As soon as we know the status of your friends, we'll let you know."

Gloria wanted to tell him she wasn't cold. Instead, she slipped obediently into the car, grateful she was able to get this close. With a sharp metallic snap, the door closed, leaving her alone, shivering. She hadn't realized she was shivering. How could that be? She *wasn't* cold. She rocked back and forth and clamped one hand around her jaw to keep her teeth from chattering. She felt like throwing up. The heavy, stale air in the car didn't help. It was mingled with smoke and made her want to gag. There had to be someplace she could go to breathe. She reached out, but before she could touch the handle, the door flew open and Cutter slid in beside her. His eyes were red and watery, and Gloria detected a slight wheeze.

"How did you get through?" It was a silly question. Obviously, he had forced his way, like she had.

His head dropped against the seat back, his lips parted as though he had to breathe through both nose and mouth to obtain sufficient oxygen.

"Are you all right?"

He nodded, and gradually his breathing slowed to an easy inhale-exhale rhythm, and then, as though by osmosis, so did hers, though she still felt nauseated. She slipped her hand beneath his, then stared out at the chaos and began praying.

When an ambulance pulled up behind the hook and ladder minutes later, Gloria's teeth began to chatter all over again. Cutter folded his arms around her, holding her close, and eventually his warmth, his even breathing, and his broad shoulder against her cheek calmed her down.

She bit her lip as paramedics pulled gurneys out of the back and disappeared with them into the house. Later, they returned with a body on each stretcher. When Gloria saw that one of the bodies was covered with a sheet, she barely got the door open and her head out before she lost all of Harry's gourmet dinner.

They followed the ambulance in a squad car—Gloria in back with Cutter, clutching his arm for dear life, the young officer in front, driving stone-faced. Ever since the officer had given them the news, a suffocating silence had fallen, as if someone had pulled stockings over their faces and no one could talk. Gloria pressed against Cutter, sinking deep into his side. From time to time, she'd change her position with a jerk as though trying to rouse herself from a nightmare.

Dorie was dead.

Harry and Perth were injured.

What happened, and why?

One minute Dorie was showing off her chocolate cake with funny vanilla writing, and the next minute . . .

Gloria glanced out her window as they turned from Pratt

Parkway onto Sixth Avenue. Pratt Towers was only a few blocks more, and two miles from that, Eckerd City Hospital. At the corner of Pratt and Sixth stood a newsstand, the kind with a slanty wooden roof, and large enough for a person to sit inside. The proprietor was busy stacking bundles of magazines. Off to the side, a man and woman walked a little black terrier, and in front of them two men in suits entered the Blue Dolphin for a late lunch or impromptu business meeting.

How normal it all seemed here, life in the humdrum. It made what had happened at E-Z Printing seem so surreal, so absurd, like Alice's looking glass where nothing made sense. And yet . . . in a place deep inside Gloria, a thought began to form, to take on an ugly shape and torment her. She closed her eyes. Maybe it did make sense. But this was not the time to sort things out. Harry and Perth needed prayer. She had to focus on them. She began mouthing silent prayers and minutes later was surprised to hear Cutter whispering his own.

~❦ ❧~

Gloria felt like she had entered the Twilight Zone instead of the emergency waiting room. Time stood still, or at least it slowed to such a crawl that Gloria was sure she had passed through a time warp into another dimension. She sat upright, back pressed against the curve of the white plastic captain's chair, and watched the hands of the large round wall clock move in agonizing millimeters. She'd done this for hours . . . minutes . . . seconds? She wasn't sure which.

Cutter never left her side. Twice he brought her coffee, but Gloria didn't remember drinking either cup. Finally, a doctor wearing a lab coat and a goatee and looking strangely like Pee-Wee Herman emerged from the corridor. He smiled a lot and didn't wring his hands, so Gloria felt certain the news was good. He told them Harry had sustained minor cuts and bruises and was being released. Perth had a broken right arm and a concussion, and she would have to stay for further observation. Gloria's only reaction was a vigorous nod of the head, like one of those Apple Festival tourists from Japan or India or the Netherlands who didn't understand English very well and just nodded at everything everyone said.

Then the fog lifted, and Gloria found herself back in real time. *Harry and Perth were going to be all right.*

"Glad to hear your two friends got off easy."

Gloria looked up and found the young, clean-cut police officer—the same one who had driven them to the hospital—standing over her with a pad in his hand.

"Now that you've got them off your mind, I need to ask a few questions. Some details need clarifying." He pulled out the ballpoint pen that was clipped to the spiral binder, then flipped open his notebook. Gloria noticed he wore a wedding ring and wondered what it must be like to be married to someone who was far too accustomed to seeing people wheeled from their homes with sheets over their heads. "E-Z Printing belonged to Harry Grizwald? And the building too? And his apartment was on the third floor?"

"Yes."

"Who lived on the second?"

"Perth." Gloria's voice sounded strange in her ears. More like the voice of a little girl than a woman.

"That's Perth McGregor?"

"Right."

"Any relation to Harry Grizwald?" Gloria noticed two large freckles, each the size of a black-eyed pea, on his left cheek.

"They were friends."

"And who was the older woman . . . ?" Pages rustled as the officer flipped through his notes, then stopped when he apparently found what he was after. "Dorie Dobson."

"She is . . . was . . . engaged to Harry."

The officer squinted, and Gloria noticed a skin tag on his eyelid and thought it odd she should notice these trivial details. She wondered if it was to keep her mind off that other shape, the one that had taken over much of her brain.

"What's your relationship with the deceased?"

"She was my friend. So are Harry and Perth."

"And you?" The officer turned to Cutter. "How do you figure in all this?"

"I'm just along for the ride." Cutter drew Gloria closer as though circling the wagons. "This is only the second time I've met Harry. The first time for the others."

The officer tapped the pen against his notebook. "It was sure lucky for both of you that you were out when the bomb went off."

"Bomb?" Gloria and Cutter said at the same time. Gloria felt her mind detonate and that ugly shape explode and splatter into a million accusations.

"Yeah, that's what it looks like. The bomb squad's there now confirming it. Anyway, back to this lucky stroke of yours. What made you leave?"

"Dorie insisted. Perth said she had a surprise for me . . . It was really supposed to be an engagement party for Harry and Dorie, but I just bought a print shop in Appleton, and Dorie had gotten me something or made something for the occasion. I don't know which, but Perth said—"

"Okay, so you left the house. Then what did you do?"

The shape was out now, no place to hide. Fragments flitted through her mind like mimes, vying for attention, then joined to break the silence with a string of words. *A bomb . . . it was deliberate . . . it was hateful . . . it was murder . . . it was the stalker.*

"So what did you do?" the officer repeated.

"I don't know . . . we walked . . . talked . . ."

"Just where are you going with this?" Cutter sounded irritated.

"We're trying to find a motive. Someone didn't like your friend Harry. Somewhere along the line, he must have made enemies."

"Impossible." Even now, Gloria didn't want to accept it. Acceptance meant she'd have to share the blame. "Harry didn't have enemies. He's a sweet, gentle—"

"Last year we got a complaint. Seems he threatened someone at Social Services."

Gloria remembered the trouble Harry had caused when Social Services tried to put Perth into a foster home. "Those charges were dropped," she said, a little too loudly. Hadn't she warned Harry about the stalker? Hadn't she told him to be careful? But even she hadn't believed the stalker would do something like this. It seemed like gross naiveté now. "The charges were dropped," she repeated.

"Aha. But it doesn't sound like something a sweet, gentle man would do, now does it?"

Cutter rose to his feet. "I know you're only doing your job, but Gloria's lost one of her friends, and you're trying to make it seem like—"

"Relax." A strong arm gently pushed Cutter back into his seat. "This is routine. These questions have to be asked. Somewhere out there, Harry Grizwald has an enemy."

Gloria closed her eyes and thought of the last note she had gotten from the stalker. It seemed inconceivable that anyone would go this far to stop the printing of their little flyer. But the vision of Santa Claus lying in the briars with a bullet in the center of his forehead made her realize how stupid she had been. For anyone capable of doing that, killing someone else would hardly be a sticking point. *They were all in danger.*

Her face must have betrayed her thoughts, because the young officer thumped his pad and asked her if something had just come to mind. Then for the next hour, she and Cutter told him about the problems at The Lakes and the flyers and the stalker and the Sam Bryce Detective Agency.

❧ ☙

When Gloria first saw Harry, she had to bite her lip to keep from crying. The whole left side of his face was swollen and already turning various shades of blue and purple. A Band-Aid intersected the peak of his right eyebrow, and at least two more patched his neck. He walked stiffly, testifying to other bruises hidden beneath his clothing. But the worst part was the look in his eyes—a haunted, angry, bewildered look like that of men on the battlefield who've seen their first bloodletting or their first comrade fall.

She fell on his neck, holding him, but not too tightly, lest she jostle one of his injuries. She couldn't stop her tears. For a while, neither of them spoke.

"She was so excited," Harry said when they separated. "You should have seen her, putting out all the gifts . . . She had insisted we not open any of them until the party this weekend." He cleared his throat. "She was a little stubborn, you know. But in a nice way. Not obnoxious or . . ." He looked down at his shoes.

"Do the police know what happened?"

Harry nodded. "I told them all about it when they questioned me. I just hope they get the scum who did it." He wiped his eyes with the back of his hands. "They told me she never felt a thing. Did you know the blast was so strong it ruptured the gas line behind the stove?" Gloria remembered the second explosion. "The whole kitchen's gone . . . gone." Harry rubbed his chin as if it hurt. "Dorie went to the kitchen for a pair of scissors. She was just supposed to cut the tape. She had already removed the brown wrapping paper in the living room—we had watched—but she couldn't get all that duct tape off the box— a shoe box. She thought a wrapped present was inside. She thought the shoe box was just the mailer. I've never seen any- thing like it—duct-taping a present. I guess I should have known something was wrong right then and there, but . . . it just didn't register . . . you know?" He cleared his throat and looked away. "But Dorie was just supposed to cut the tape, then come right back and open it in front of us. Perth and I had been enjoying ourselves watching Dorie fuss with everything. You can't believe how excited she was. She planned on serving her little cake first—then opening the presents. She wanted you to open yours first; then she and I were going to take turns open- ing the others. Anyway . . . when she took so long, Perth headed for the kitchen to see what was wrong. That's when the bomb went off. Perth was closer to the kitchen, so she got it worse than me. But they tell us we're both lucky to be alive." He looked at Gloria with large, sad eyes. "I don't feel very lucky right now. I don't feel lucky at all."

~✺ ✺~

Only ten people showed up for the funeral. The four of them: Gloria, Cutter, Harry, and Perth—who had just gotten out of the hospital that day. The other six were Dorie's hairdresser, her pas- tor, and four ladies from her church—a testimony to Dorie's quiet life. But it suited Harry, who really hadn't wanted anyone but the four of them there. The violent nature of Dorie's death had so shaken him that he had asked those friends inclined to attend, not to. In his mind, a death like Dorie's couldn't be commemorated—not with flowers, or eulogies, or graveside fanfare, or tea sandwiches, or the sound of ice cubes dropping into glasses.

It just had to be endured.

Gloria understood this about Harry and was sure his thoughts now, as he stood by the gravesite, were of his first wife, Lily, as well as Dorie. If Harry's reaction to the loss of his first wife was any indication, Dorie's death would set back his relationship with Jesus another five years.

Oh, Jesus, why did this have to happen? Just when he was beginning to open up to You again?

From a distance, Gloria watched Harry fuss with a bouquet of red and yellow roses—Dorie's favorite flowers—picking at the Baby's Breath and repositioning a fern. He placed the arrangement in a plastic vase staked to the ground by a small metal sling.

She held Cutter's hand and felt comforted by his presence. He had not left her side in three days, except to attend to the funeral arrangements. He had followed Harry's every instruction, attended to the most minor detail, like the anchored plastic vase. He had been an anchor for them all.

Gloria caught Perth's eye and gestured for her to come over. Perth had been standing off to the side, a cast on her right arm, weeping into a hankie. Another funeral. Perth's third in less than two years. Gloria worried that this fresh loss might affect the girl's studies at the community college or alter her plans for applying to Bristol. Perth had been working so hard, had gotten off to such a good start. It would be tragic if she let Dorie's death derail her now.

When Perth reached Gloria and Cutter, the three of them huddled together—Cutter on one side, Perth on the other, and Gloria in the middle. That's how they stayed until all the other mourners had gone.

"It's time we pry Harry away," Cutter said, his voice heavy with resignation, as though this job too must fall on him.

"I'll get him." Gloria put her hand on Cutter's chest before he could take a step. Then she walked toward the gravesite, wondering what she could say to induce Harry to leave. Lost in thought, she almost didn't notice the lone figure standing at a distance among a clump of maples. Her heart caught. She looked again, carefully this time, and saw a man in the familiar black leather, his hair pulled into a ponytail. He stood with one hand tucked, Napoleon-style, inside his jacket, as though implying a threat. And the way he was so brazenly out in the open made Gloria believe he wanted her to recognize him, had even gone out of his way for her to do so.

Her mouth went dry. Was he toying with her? Had he come to see his handiwork? Perhaps boast even? She wanted to cry out but couldn't. She sprinted toward Harry. "Let's go," she said, barely able to get the words out.

"I'd like to stay a few more minutes."

"There's no time." Gloria grabbed his arm and pulled him back toward the spot where Cutter and Perth waited. "If we hurry," Gloria said, breathless from towing the balking man, "we can catch him."

"Catch who?" Cutter said as Gloria and Harry reached him.

"The *stalker*." Gloria turned toward the trees where the stalker had stood only moments ago.

He had disappeared.

"You mean that was the creep that killed Dorie? And you let him *get away!*"

Gloria looked helplessly at Harry. "He caught me by surprise. He carries a weapon, and my only thought was that if we all rushed him, we'd have a chance. I guess I didn't think it through."

"You should have raised the alarm the second you saw him. Then maybe Cutter could have reached him in time." Harry clomped toward Gloria's car—she had driven them all to the cemetery—his heavy feet leaving divots in the grass. Tears welled in Gloria's eyes.

"He's just upset," Perth said, squeezing Gloria's hand. "But I'll talk to him. Try to calm him down." She kissed Gloria's cheek, then trotted after Harry.

"You handled it the way you thought best." Cutter put his arm around Gloria's shoulder. "Don't start beating yourself up. Harry's all emotion right now. Besides, it's a male thing. He's envisioning how he would have made the guy pay. He's probably been feeling helpless. Probably played the bomb scene over and over in his mind a thousand times, and thought maybe things would have turned out differently if only he'd done this or that." He tightened his hold on Gloria. "Anyway, that's how I'd feel."

"Thanks," she said, thinking how kind he was but knowing that Harry was right. She should have sounded the alarm.

❧ ❧

When Gloria and Cutter reached the car, Perth gave them a thumbs-up from behind Harry's back, apparently indicating that all was well. Except Gloria noticed that Harry's face was flushed and that he kept his head down, avoiding her eyes. She inserted the key into the car door and unlocked it. Harry was the first to open his door.

"It's all right," she said in a near-whisper, and she watched his eyes soften with gratitude just as he disappeared into the back. Perth followed. Then Cutter slid into the front passenger side. Gloria was ready to get in when she heard a shout.

"Miss! Excuse me, Miss." A man in gray overalls charged toward her.

Gloria eyed the shovel in his hands and stepped back. She had seen him tending one of the new graves and assumed he was the caretaker, but now . . . she wasn't too sure. He stopped in front of her, big drops of sweat running down the sides of his nose. His chest heaved as he gulped air. This close, he looked sixty, maybe more, and obviously out of shape. If he tried anything, she was reasonably sure she could handle it.

Both of his hands were caked with dirt; so were his shoes and overalls. He wiped his empty hand on his pant leg, then dug into his front pocket and pulled out a sealed envelope. "A man asked me to give you this." He handed it to Gloria.

"What man?" Gloria asked, already knowing the answer.

"Don't know. He was dressed in black. Had a ponytail and nose ring."

Gloria ripped open the envelope, pulled out a folded paper, and read the words, *"YOU'RE NEXT."* She crumpled the paper into a ball. "What do you know about this?"

Either her expression or her voice or the way she moved into his comfort zone must have frightened the caretaker, because his face turned the color of his overalls, and he backed away. "I don't know anything, except that this guy gave me ten bucks to give you the note."

"Which way did he go?"

The caretaker shrugged. "I . . . don't know, lady. He just got on his motorcycle and left . . . that way." The man's hand waved in no particular direction, so when he turned and scurried away, Gloria let him go.

~◠ ◠~

Cutter watched Officer Wingate of the EPD, the same sometimes-smiling, sometimes-stone-faced kid that had driven them to the hospital—write down every word Gloria was saying in his notebook.

For all the good it would do.

Cutter was under no illusion. If J.P. Gordon and Charlie Watts couldn't spot and stop the stalker in little Appleton, how were Wingate and the rest of the EPD going to do it here in big, sprawling Eckerd City? Still, Cutter had insisted that Gloria report her encounter and turn in the note. Maybe forensics could do something with it. And maybe the police artist could sketch a decent picture from Gloria's description. Wingate seemed eager enough, like any new kid on the block looking to elevate his status.

Still . . . Cutter wasn't going to hold his breath.

He listened to Gloria answer Wingate's questions. It sounded like they were on their third rep. He wondered if Wingate was being extra thorough, or if it was just police procedure to ask the same question this many times.

He watched Gloria's forehead fold into creases and wondered how he was going to tell her she couldn't stay a few more days with Harry and Perth like she planned. They were all bunking out at the Comfort Inn about five miles from The Lakes. Harry's building was still sealed off with yellow police tape, and no one could tell them when that would change. But things were progressing in the right direction. The gas company had already fixed the main. And this afternoon a structural engineer was scheduled to check out the integrity of the building to see if the damage was repairable or if the building would have to be condemned.

They had all been living from hand to mouth, buying underwear and clean clothes and toiletries as needed. No one had been allowed to go to Harry's apartment to retrieve anything, or even to see if there was anything left to retrieve. And understandably, Gloria didn't want to leave Harry or Perth in this state.

But if Cutter had anything to say about it, she was going to. Not that he was in a position to really tell her anything. Or *demand* that she listen to him. Especially now that he was trying to correct his former overbearing ways, since Gloria didn't seem to care for them. But in his mind, her safety superseded all other concerns, even if pushing the issue meant making Gloria angry. He had decided, right after Gloria got the note, to take her back to Appleton. For one thing, the town was smaller and easier to patrol. For another, it was familiar territory. The home advantage.

Now to sell her on the idea.

He was prepared to resort to any means. There was no way he wanted to end up like Harry Grizwald, who was probably even now raking himself over the coals of *"If only I . . ."*

∼❧ ❦∼

Cutter didn't know how he'd managed it, but he had. And with very little persuasion or pressure, either. He suspected it was because Gloria understood about the home advantage too. He'd always known she was much smarter than anyone else gave her credit for.

Gloria was going home. With him.

It had been a teary good-bye for everyone except Cutter. He had stood quietly on the sidelines, just like he had been doing for the last several days, and felt the palpable sadness in the air. Even when the hugs and kisses were passed around like sweets, he had remained untouched. But when Harry shook his hand and whispered that he didn't think Gloria could go wrong with the likes of him, Cutter had to swallow hard in order to keep a lump from forming in his throat. He knew Harry didn't give his approval readily.

Now, whizzing along I-80 with Gloria at his side, he allowed the memory of Harry's words to warm him and was surprised to feel his eyes moisten. He glanced over at Gloria. Her head was tilted back, her face toward the side window. He was relieved. It wouldn't do to have the woman he loved see him blubbering like a girl. He had never subscribed to the thinking that men should get in touch with their feminine side. As far as he was concerned, a man didn't have a feminine side—unless, of course, the guy was a wimp. It was natural for a man to want to be in charge, to take control. It had always puzzled him that Gloria had never appreciated his efforts in that area when they were growing up. Now he understood that what she hadn't appreciated was the *way* he'd done it.

Well . . . he would change. He already had. At least, in some ways. For one, he didn't think about Sadie or any of the others. He didn't picture their bodies or feel their imaginary hands running through his hair or down his back.

He only pictured Gloria. He knew she probably wouldn't like that, but he couldn't help it. He couldn't help wondering what she looked like under her layers of clothes, or how she would react when he touched her in those secret places. And he wasn't likely to find out, either, anytime soon. But there was a passion about her—all wrapped up and safely hidden beneath her soft, quiet exterior—that stirred him. He had seen it in her eyes, felt it in the touch of her hand, heard it in her voice when she had told him she loved him. It boiled his blood. And that made his new watchword, *discipline*, all the more important. He slid his hand across the space between them and touched her fingers.

"You want me to drive now?" came a sleepy voice from the side.

"Nope. You just relax."

"Thanks for driving. 'Course, it's not just anyone I'd let drive Bluebird."

"Don't mention it. And I appreciate the vote of confidence."

"How far away are we?"

"Another hour. Then we'll go straight to J.P. and tell him what happened. After that, you're under house arrest until we can figure out how to keep you safe." He glanced at her and saw she was still looking out the side window. No use procrastinating. This was as good a time as any to bring it up. Perspiration pooled around his collar. He cleared his throat. Several times. "'Course, you could always move in with me so I could keep an eye on you." Gloria's laughter made his heart sink. "Why not?"

"Can you just hear what the church ladies would say? Can you imagine what my *mother* would say? And forget Pearl Owens. My goodness, she'd have a field day."

Now it was Cutter's turn to laugh. "I'm not suggesting we live together. I'm suggesting we *marry*."

"Cutter, you know that's impossible. We have issues, remember? I told you I couldn't let our relationship progress any further until certain things were resolved. It would never work. It can't work when we're so far apart spiritually."

"I was listening. To every word. Only, you're in danger, and that's all I can think of now. How can I let you out of my sight? It would drive me crazy. I'd be wondering and worrying every minute. The only way I can protect you is to be with you twenty-four hours a day. And I know the only way you'll let that happen is if . . . we get married."

Gloria gave him one of the sweetest smiles he'd ever seen, then turned back to the side window.

"Well? What do you think?"

"I think we're being followed. At first I wasn't sure. A lot of bikers wear black leather and have ponytails, but now I'm certain."

Cutter checked his rearview mirror and saw a black-clad figure on a motorcycle. Cutter was driving in the left lane. So was the biker. Though there were scores of cars in the right lane and a trail of cars behind the Harley, only two cars separated Cutter from the stalker. A vision of the biker riding up to his window and whipping out a shotgun, then blasting away, filled Cutter's mind.

Too much NYPD Blue.

There were far too many witnesses for the biker to make that kind of move. But up ahead, when Cutter turned onto RR40, it would be a different story. There, you could go for miles and not see another car. If he were the stalker, that's where he'd strike, presuming the stalker knew the area. *And what was Cutter going to do about it?*

His mind buzzed like a Milwaukee chainsaw, chopping apart several alternatives: One—he could get off now and try to find a police station. But that was a pretty lame idea. The roads off I-80 around here were mostly rural, and he wasn't that familiar with the area. There was a good chance he'd end up in some deserted place, cornered by the stalker. Two—he could continue driving along I-80 until the stalker got tired and just stopped following him. Another bad idea. Bluebird had only a quarter of a tank of gas left. Three—he could call the police on his cell. Sounded good. But was it? Chances were the stalker would take off as soon as he saw a squad car and disappear along the zillions of miles of roadway veining the countryside.

No, not one of the ideas had merit. *Think, Press, think.* He couldn't let anything happen to Gloria. It was up to him to get them both out of this safely. *God, we're in trouble here. I know I have no right to ask, but I really need Your help.* The prayer whirled around and around in his head, while Gloria stared silently at the side mirror. They went on this way for a good five miles. Then the thought hit him. The Four-Towns junction was the perfect place for a showdown—four wide roads forming an intersection, room enough for an army of squad cars to set up a blockade, deep gullies along the sides of the roadway, and enough rough vegetation to keep anyone from making a premature exit off the pavement.

He'd call J.P. and tell him to go there and set a trap. Then he'd lead the stalker right into it.

He pulled the cell from his shirt pocket and dialed the number he'd learned when he was eight years old and found his father dead on the living-room sofa from a heart attack. When J.P. answered, Cutter offered no pleasantries, only a terse summary beginning with the explosion in the Eckerd apartment and ending with their current situation.

"What did he say?" Gloria asked after Cutter hung up and slipped the phone back into his pocket.

"He said he and Charlie Watts and Jack Springer and some backup from the other towns would be waiting." Gloria frowned. "And he said not to worry. They'll get us through this." A glance at the rearview mirror told Cutter the stalker was now only one

343

car behind them. "He also said to use the cell to keep him posted. You have your cell, just in case?"

Gloria nodded, then reached into her purse—the purse she had been able to retrieve from Harry's apartment only late yesterday, after the engineer said the building was structurally sound enough for her and Perth and Harry to go there and collect a few belongings. She pulled out her phone and groaned after she powered it on.

"What's wrong?"

"Battery's low."

"All right, keep it off in case we need it for backup. Mine's fine, so there shouldn't be a problem." Cutter gnawed the inside of his mouth. Another thirty miles and they'd be getting off I-80. That's when it was going to be tough—those seven miles on RR40 before they reached the junction.

⚬⚬

The sound of Gloria's heartbeat whooshed in her ears as Bluebird sped down the highway. She closed her eyes. Outside, the landscape was a blur, and that, plus the motion of the car, made her nauseated. When she felt her nails dig into her palms, she opened her eyes and was surprised to see her hands balled into tight fists. She inhaled deeply, trying to calm down. They had to keep their wits. Not panic. She was glad Cutter was driving. He was a lot more aggressive behind the wheel than she was, and they'd need that now. It would take all of Cutter's skill, plus God's grace, to get them out of this safely.

Up ahead, she spotted the large green sign for RR40 and was about to mention it to Cutter when she felt Bluebird swerve. She grabbed the armrest just as Cutter sliced through a small opening between two cars and moved from the left into the far right lane, crossing two lanes of traffic. She glanced at the side mirror and saw the stalker's motorcycle also cut right. *Oh, faithful Jesus, protect us.* Gone were the illusions that this issue would go away or end in some benign fashion. The stalker had killed Dorie, maybe Benny Holt—Santa Claus—and who knew how many others. What were two more lives to him?

Trust Me.

Gloria curled her fingers around the strap of her seat belt and bit back tears. *Oh, Jesus, why can't You show me angels positioned on Bluebird's hood and trunk, or the stalker's tires going flat, or the asphalt splitting open and swallowing him up, or . . .* With a deep sigh, she sank into her seat, still clutching her belt. *I do trust You, Jesus—I do. I know Your ways are perfect. Let Your will be done.*

~❧ ☙~

By the time Cutter saw the RR40 sign and moved toward the exit, the Escort and Harley were no longer separated by another car. The stalker's motorcycle roared only inches away from Cutter's bumper, its chrome-plated T-handlebars glinting in the sun. They were both going much too fast. Cutter hit the brakes and took the winding ramp on two wheels. The tires squealed as they left rubber and a burning smell. The motorcycle kept pace.

"Let me have your phone," Gloria said, sounding shaken.

"Why?"

"I'm calling J.P. to tell him where we are."

Cutter pulled the phone from his pocket and handed it to Gloria. Her fingers were white from grasping her seat belt. She dialed; then Cutter listened as she updated J.P.

While Gloria talked, Cutter watched the stalker move closer, then begin to pass. The next thing Cutter knew, the motorcycle was parallel to his door. *What was the guy up to?* The road was deserted, but it was treacherous here with its hairpin turns. Not a good place to make a move.

Cutter clutched the steering wheel, then floored the gas pedal, taking another turn on two wheels. For a minute, the car threatened to overturn, but it landed back on all fours with a bounce, then a skid. It took all of Cutter's skill to keep the car from spinning out. When he did, he didn't even slow down but pushed the pedal even harder. They had gained some ground, but only a little. The Harley roared near Cutter's left bumper. *What did he have to do to shake this guy?*

Trees and telephone poles whizzed by in a blur as Cutter tried to calculate how far they still had to go. When he saw the blue-and-white billboard announcing the Dutch Inn's homestyle cooking, he knew they were only four miles from J.P. *Thank You, God.*

Barely a half mile later, Cutter saw the yellow zigzag sign. "Brace yourself," he said, as his hands tensed around the wheel. If he judged the turn just right, and if there were no oncoming cars, he could make it. But he'd have to concentrate. Keep focused.

As he entered the bend, Gloria screamed. The Harley had gained and was once again parallel with Cutter's side. "He's got a gun!" she shouted.

Cutter glanced left. The next thing he heard was the crack of breaking timber as his car grazed two saplings on the side near the shoulder.

It was too late. He couldn't get the car back on the pavement. Two tires were already on the soft dirt shoulder, and his speed propelled him farther in that direction. For a second, the car took flight, actually hovered in midair as the dirt shoulder gave way to nothingness, then a steep slope. Then came a grinding metallic sound as the car came down hard on the incline and toppled to the left. The chassis scraped against rocks and under-brush as it slid all the way down the embankment on its side. Cutter had a vague sensation of Gloria's limp body listing toward him, held only by her seat belt. Objects ricocheted around his head: his cell phone, Gloria's purse, two empty Styrofoam cof-fee cups, some papers, a pen. Blood trickled from his mouth and from Gloria's forehead. When the car finally shuddered to a stop, he reached over with a trembling hand and shook Gloria, who hung in the air like a rag doll. The left side of the car had become the floor. The right side, Gloria's side, was now the ceiling.

Please, God, let her be all right.

She opened her eyes. "What . . . happened?"

The motor was still running, and Cutter smelled oil. Some-thing must have ruptured. Even if he and Gloria could put the car back on its wheels, he'd never be able to drive it up that embankment. He studied the terrain in front of him and sud-denly knew where they were—in the forest on the other side of the fishing hole.

"You all right?" He shook Gloria again. She nodded with a moan. "Okay. Try to open your door. Use your legs." They would both have to climb out her side, using the door like an overhead hatch.

It took a while for Gloria to twist around so she could face her door. When she did, she slipped the toe of her shoe under the handle and pulled. When it clicked open, she pushed against the door, hard, with both feet, making it snap out. For a minute, Cutter was afraid it would slam back shut. When it didn't, he helped Gloria with her seat belt.

"Get your cell," Gloria said when she'd finally worked her legs through the door. She hung upside down like a daredevil on a trapeze. "But first give me a push."

He did, then searched for the phone but couldn't find it. When he saw Gloria's purse dangling from the steering wheel, he grabbed that. Her cell would have to do. He pulled the purse strap over his shoulder and across his chest, then released his seat belt and felt his body drop against the door beneath him. It took a while for him to curl his legs under him, but finally he got his feet to touch the door. Using the door as a springboard, he pushed up, grabbed the edge of the open portal and pulled himself out. Gloria was crouched nearby, waiting, the right passenger tire still spinning over her head.

In the distance, Cutter heard the loud muffler of the Harley, as if the stalker were pacing his bike, thinking of what he should do next. Any minute now, he might decide to head down the ravine. Cutter crouched next to Gloria and took a quick inventory. She looked all right, except for that cut on her forehead and the fact she kept rubbing her right leg. Behind them was the stalker; ahead was rough terrain. They couldn't stay here. They had to go forward. But would she be able to make it?

When Cutter heard the sound of twigs breaking and loud pipes getting louder, the whole issue became academic.

"Let's go," he said, grabbing Gloria's arm.

Chapter Twenty-One

CUTTER HAD BEEN in these woods a thousand times. That would be his advantage. He knew just where the vegetation grew thickest, the location of the bog, the granite sill, all those areas where a motorcycle couldn't go.

But their escape would be hard on Gloria. Already she favored her right leg. She'd need his help. He put one arm around her waist and propelled her forward. Behind him he heard the motorcycle sputter, then crash. He squandered precious seconds looking backward to see what had happened. The motorcycle and rider were sliding down the embankment, but not together. The motorcycle skidded on its side, ripping the undergrowth as it went, until it hit what looked like a stump, then flipped end over end. To the right, about two yards away, the stalker was making his own descent on his back, his hands grabbing frantically at saplings and underbrush in an attempt to stop. Even from this distance, Cutter heard groans as the stalker's back scraped across rocks and sticks that protruded from the slope.

Finally, the motorcycle ended its riderless ride with a crunch as it became entangled in the dead branches of a felled tree. Cutter noticed that the front wheel was bent. The stalker would have to continue on foot. The advantage was now theirs.

Cutter didn't bother waiting to see the stalker come to his own abrupt stop beneath some thornbushes. Instead, he turned, handed Gloria her purse, wrapped his arm tighter around her waist, and pulled her forward.

"I couldn't find my phone. Use yours. Call J.P. Tell him what's happening."

As he half lifted, half dragged her, Gloria managed to open her purse, fumble inside, and pull out the cell. When Cutter saw she had trouble balancing the purse and phone in one hand and punching in J.P.'s number with the other, he pulled the purse away and let it drop onto the carpet of pine needles beneath their feet. "Leave it," he said, as Gloria tried to slow down and retrieve it. "There's no time." The crunch of cold, dry vegetation told Cutter the stalker was no more than eighty yards behind.

Now with both hands free, Gloria quickly raised J.P., then spoke in short, rapid sentences. They had run off the highway. About three miles from the junction. The stalker had run off too. But was pursuing. On foot. They were one mile south of the fishing hole. And heading . . .

"To the old smokehouse," Cutter said, loud enough for J.P. to hear. Since they had gotten out of the car, Cutter had been trying to formulate a plan. A few yards ahead, the vegetation got so thick it would be impossible for the stalker to find them, unless he was like those Native American trackers from the movies, who could tell if a person spit on the side of the road and how long ago. But Cutter doubted that were the case. Once inside the thicket, he and Gloria would head for the collapsed smokehouse. Unless you knew it was there, you'd never find it, not the way it was covered with all that overgrowth.

"We're heading for the smokehouse," he heard Gloria repeat, obviously to insure that J.P. got the message. There was fear in her voice. Then she added, "Okay, J.P. I'll keep the phone on, but I don't know how long the battery will hold."

And then Cutter heard a shot.

Then another.

An unmistakable whizzing sound near Cutter's shoulder made him turn to the left just in time to see the bark of the tree in front of him splinter.

He quickened his pace, hardly letting Gloria's feet touch the ground. A few yards more and they would disappear into the thicket. Another shot rang out, and pulpy bark coming from somewhere directly over his head rained down on him like snowflakes. "J.P., you better get here, pronto!" he yelled, hoping his voice would reach the receiver Gloria still held in her right hand. But the hand dangled limply at her side, and when Cutter looked, he saw blood dripping down her wrist.

"What . . . ?" The phone slid from Gloria's hand, made a small hop on the ground, then disappeared into the carpet of pine needles. He barely caught her as she stumbled.

"I think . . . I'm shot." Surprise laced Gloria's voice, but she was still on her feet, still moving forward. It was obvious she had taken the stalker's first bullet.

"Where are you hit?" Cutter didn't slow down. Even now, the *crunch crunch* of vegetation underfoot warned them that the stalker was close behind.

"I don't know . . . my right shoulder, I think . . . that's where I see the blood . . . but I don't feel anything." Another bullet exploded in the tree beside her just as Cutter dragged her into the thicket.

"Hang in there," he said, lifting her as much as he could with his right arm. His muscles burned. Willpower alone enabled him to hold and drag her like he did. With each step, she leaned more and more heavily against him.

Oh, God, please don't let her die.

The quarter of a mile to the smokehouse was gained in inches. Branches, briars, and hanging vegetation tangled with their hair and ankles and clawed their exposed flesh. From time to time, Cutter would stop, hold Gloria like a limp doll against his side, and listen. Once he thought he heard the rustle of footsteps, but they sounded far away. Even so, he found himself praying, asking the God of his youth, the God he had barely spoken to in years, to protect them, to keep Gloria alive, and to send J.P. in time—though he thought prayer a useless gesture. Why should God listen? Cutter was a stranger by choice, a stranger who had kept his distance for most of his life. He had even been proud of that fact, as though it were proof he could handle things on his own. But now, something deep within him welled up—something he thought he had smothered to extinction—making him cling to a wild hope that God really was listening.

Because this was one thing he couldn't handle alone.

~◈ ◈~

Gloria felt Cutter's strong arm clutching her waist and propelling her forward. She felt dizzy . . . light-headed . . . and found it hard to concentrate. She was sure she had blacked out at least once, maybe twice, because one minute she was near some trees, and the next minute she was being clawed by brambles and bushes. It had to be because she was losing so much blood. The entire right side of her shirt and jacket was wet. She thought it strange that she felt no pain, only fatigue. She was so very, very tired. How long could she go on losing blood? Now that they were off the road, it would take J.P. a lot longer to find them, to get them help. Would he be in time? A sudden thought bolted through her brain like lightning: Or . . . was this the day she was going to die? She was only mildly surprised to realize that the prospect of her own death didn't frighten her. It's not that she wanted to die, or that she wasn't saddened by the possibility of her life being cut short. It was just that she knew with certainty where she would end up. If she died, she'd wake up in Jesus' arms. And that would really be something.

Cutter's arm jerked around her waist—apparently trying to get a better hold—and when it did, Gloria remembered. *What was to become of Cutter? Would he die today too?* At least she had told him she loved him. At least she had been able to give him that. Her head lolled forward, and it took all her willpower to snap it upright. She couldn't black out again. She had to help Cutter as much as she could to get to safety. Because nothing could happen to him. If he died . . . Pain stabbed her chest as she thought about what that would mean. With her last ounce of strength, her spirit cried out to God. *Please, God, don't let Cutter die in his sin. Don't let anything happen to him until You've given him a chance to know Jesus.*

She heard a still, small voice say, "Trust Me"; then everything went blank.

～❦ ❦～

By the time Cutter got them to the smokehouse, he was covered in blood. Mostly Gloria's, but some of his own where briars and other prickly vegetation had connected with flesh. His one prayer, the prayer he repeated over and over, was "Please, God, let Gloria live." She seemed barely conscious and no longer walked at all. The last several yards, Cutter had carried them both, his muscles quivering and screaming with pain.

With his foot, he flattened a spot where he could lay Gloria. She moaned as he put her down on the matted underbrush, then leaned her against the trunk of a large birch. Her eyes rolled, showing the whites and making them look like hard-boiled eggs. Cutter hesitated, fearful that if he left she might die, then realized he was squandering precious seconds.

He flew at the partially collapsed smokehouse like a madman, clawing frantically at the vines and bushes covering the door. The small, half-buried house creaked and groaned as if it were about to finish its collapse. *Was it safe?* Cutter pictured the roof caving in on him and Gloria and burying them alive. He pushed the thought from his mind. They had to go in. There was no choice. Out here, their every movement was an invitation for another bullet. It was still possible that the stalker could stumble upon them.

He finally uncovered the door, then gave it a fierce jerk, but it wouldn't budge. He clawed at it with his fingers, digging his nails into the rotting wood, feeling splinters pierce deep beneath his nails. When the pain became too great, he picked up a rock and tried wedging it between the door and the frame. He was rewarded, after several seconds, when the door gave way enough for him to curl his fingers around the edge and pry it open.

Inside, it was dark as pitch. He tried not to think of what might be crawling around in there and entered, feeling for obstacles with his hands.

In its prime, the smokehouse had been large, with two pits —one on either side—for charcoal and hickory wood and grating overhead for hanging meat on rib hooks and gambrels. Now the pits were nothing more than piles of rubble. With his foot, he cleared the center. Then he felt his way back outside. Quickly, carefully, he picked Gloria up and carried her inside.

This was not the carrying-over-the-threshold he had once dreamed about. The thought that he might be carrying Gloria into her tomb made him shudder. He hovered by the opening, straining to adjust to the darkness. Finally, he moved into the interior, feeling more than seeing his way around. When he reached what he believed to be the middle, he bent down and carefully laid Gloria on the ground. She made no sound, and his heart thumped with dread.

Get on with it, Press. Cover your tracks.

He forced himself to leave her and hurried outside. Quickly, he fluffed the matted area where Gloria had sat, covered the blood spot on the birch bark—where she had leaned—with piles of pine needles and leaves, then gathered any blood-covered vegetation and tossed it through the open door of the smoke-house. Finally, he repositioned most of the vines he had just torn from the wall and door, then slipped inside, closing the door behind him.

The darkness of the closed smokehouse was almost pal-pable. Cutter stretched out his hand as though trying to part a weighty curtain. When that failed, he lowered himself to the floor and crawled toward where he thought Gloria lay. His heart raced. *Was she still alive?*

He felt her leg first, then worked his way up, probing, grop-ing for her neck and, after finding it, placing two fingers in the hollow of her throat. He wanted to shout for joy when he felt a feeble pulse. She was alive. But if he had any chance of keep-ing her that way, he'd have to find out where she was hurt and stop the bleeding. He slid his hand carefully across her chest and felt her wet shirt. The right side of her jacket was wet too. She had lost a lot of blood. Just how much blood could a person lose and still live? He didn't want to think about it. Instead, he probed for a wound and found one beneath her shoulder blade—obviously the site of entry—then another one under her arm. He didn't think any organs were hit, but the blood loss was enormous. Just touching the area had soaked his hands. He wondered if the bullet had hit an artery.

Moving as quickly as he could in the cramped quarters, he pulled off his jacket, then his shirt. With difficulty, he removed Gloria's jacket, then wrapped his shirt tightly under her armpit and around her shoulder. He didn't want to jostle her again, so he just draped her jacket around her, then slipped on his own.

He sat near her head, resisting the urge to cradle it on his lap. Keeping her flat seemed best—maybe the wound wouldn't bleed so much, though he didn't know why he thought that. He bent low, as close to her ear as possible. "Hang in there," he whispered. "Just stay with me. We're going to get out of this." One hand pressed the wound in her back; the other pressed the wound under her arm. "I love you, Gloria. I've always loved you, and I'm not going to let you go now."

Dirt matted his hair. It coated his mouth. It lay in the corners of his eyes as if he were a corpse who had tried to dig out of his own grave. Between his dirt-caked hands, he held back the life's blood of the only woman he had ever loved. The woman who had finally—*finally*—told him she loved him too. If Gloria didn't walk away from this grave, then he didn't want to come out either.

❧ ❧

The blackness blotted out all sense of time. Had they been there five minutes? Twenty? An hour? Cutter could only guess. He thought he had dozed, yet when he became aware of the utter darkness again, his hands were still clamped fiercely on Gloria's wounds. He noticed he was breathing shallow, almost indiscernible breaths that seemed to match Gloria's. His head had found a rock to rest against, and he thought it odd that the hard, cold surface seemed almost comfortable. For a second he wondered if he was dead. Then he wondered if he was alive but dreaming. The utter silence, the utter blackness, made him believe either of these possibilities. So when the shot rang out and made him jerk and knock Gloria's head to the side, he was more pleased than frightened because he heard her moan.

Gloria was still alive.

But when he heard more gunshots, and the scraping and creaking of the door as it began to open, then saw the blade of light slice through the darkness like a scalpel, his pleasure gave way to fear.

"Did you think we forgot you?" came J.P.'s deep, booming voice just as the beam of his flashlight reached Gloria's sprawled body.

Cutter just sat there, pressing on Gloria's wounds, and watched J.P. turn back toward the doorway and yell to someone outside to call an ambulance. Then once again, Cutter bent his head close to Gloria's ear and told her how much he loved her. From the beam of J.P.'s flashlight he saw her eyelids flicker once, then again, then again and again, as if she was telling him that everything was going to be all right.

Epilogue

GLORIA WALKED UP the steps of the Appleton Full Gospel Tabernacle with Cutter Press at her side. Three months had passed since J.P. had rescued her from the smokehouse. The doctors told her later there was no way she should have come out alive—she had lost that much blood. The stalker's bullet had nicked her axillary artery. The doctors at Four-Towns Hospital were calling it a miracle.

Those around Appleton who didn't believe in such things were divided into two camps. The first believed Clive's chilly old smokehouse had acted like a refrigerator and slowed Gloria's blood flow, thus saving her. They didn't understand that with every contraction of Gloria's heart, blood was forced into the axillary artery and was literally spurting from her side. The other camp believed that Cutter's tourniquet, plus the pressure he had applied with his hands on the wounds, had saved her life. Both camps, along with the believers in miracles, had spent hours in debate. Gloria suspected the debate would continue for years to come.

For her, there was no debate—no doubt that it was her faithful Jesus who had saved her life. She *was* a walking miracle, and walking next to another miracle. She smiled at Cutter as he held the heavy church door open for her. He'd said he wanted to know more about this God of miracles. That was two months ago. Last week he had came to know God personally. In another two, he would be baptized.

And those weren't the only things bordering on the miraculous. Their own US senator, Pierce Haskell, had opened an investigation into the practice of big foundations manipulating the environmental movement for profit, starting with the Slone Foundation. Even though one of J.P.'s men had killed the stalker in the shootout, eliminating a perfect witness, Senator Haskell claimed he still had ample evidence to "blow the lid off."

Perth was back in school, and Gloria had bought out the Luggets and was still getting used to being a business owner. And she had another cat, a little orange kitten she'd named Sandy.

"Morning, Gloria. Morning, Cutter."

Gloria smiled sweetly at Pearl Owens, who stood in the narthex greeting all the arrivals. "Morning, Pearl." She noticed that Pearl lingered over Cutter, her hand tightly pressing his before letting go.

"My, my, my. I just can't get over you being here at church. Wouldn't Virginia just split a stitch if she could see you now?" Pearl's face glowed with pride, as if it were all her doing that Cutter Press had made his peace with God. She leaned her large body forward, bringing her mouth close to Cutter's face, looking almost like she was about to nibble his earlobe. "Now all you have to do is marry this little lady here, and that would clinch it for Virginia."

Cutter looked Pearl in the eye and said in a calm voice,

fraught with merriment, "And when I do, I'd like you to be standing at this very door, greeting our guests."

Pearl turned as crimson as one of Grandma Quinn's Olympiad roses. "Why . . . why, I'd be *honored.*"

Gloria avoided Pearl's eyes and bit her lip to keep from laughing. Cutter's remark in no way came as a surprise. He had been talking about marriage a lot lately. Gloria had grown to love him more than she'd thought it was possible to love anyone, though she still had her reservations. First, there was still that womanizing issue—though Cutter had removed the picture of the Playboy Bunny from his car mirror, and she supposed that was a good sign—and secondly . . .

Gloria slipped her arm through Cutter's and felt soreness in her right shoulder. Rehab twice a week was working that problem out. And Jesus was more than up to working out the rest. For her part, she was going to take it slow. Let Jesus do His thing.

Oh, yes, indeed, she believed in miracles. So did Cutter. And when you believed in miracles and knew the miracle worker Himself, anything could happen.

Author's Note

Dear readers:

 There's always immense joy and relief, and some sadness too, when completing the writing of a novel. Return to Appleton, the sequel to Waters of Marah, was a labor of love but was difficult too, since I had to squeeze in two moves—one out of state—during its crafting. But God's grace is always sufficient, and so it was in my situation as I packed and unpacked, and packed and unpacked yet again. I actually managed to meet the deadline with two weeks to spare!

 The thing I think I liked most about Return to Appleton was the issue of Gloria falling in love with the very person she had despised all her life. The idea of pairing up Gloria and Cutter didn't come until I was almost finished writing Waters of Marah. But when it did come, I must confess it was a bit of a surprise. The two characters seemed too incompatible, with too much water under their bridges, too many grievances. But after I got used to the idea, it struck me not only as a little humorous, but so natural too, so something God could and does do in real life—making enemies capable of loving each other.

Oh, how great is the love of God! And how deep. It can overcome any-thing. And when His love operates in us, so can we. The very ones we thought we could never love, suddenly become lovable.

If you liked the book, drop me a line. I'd love hearing from you!

Blessings and love,

Sylvia Bambola

Website: http://www.sylviabambola.com

E-mail: sbambola@stimanatee.net

DISCUSSION QUESTIONS FOR READERS' GROUPS

1. When Gloria discusses the advisability of Cutter paying five thousand dollars to an informant, she cringes because she thinks she's starting to sound like her mother. Why is it almost impossible not to emulate the negatives of our parents? And can this tendency be overcome by emulating our heavenly Father? If so, how?

2. In chapter four, one minute Gloria is looking up at the sky feeling close to Jesus, and the next minute she's losing her temper with her mother. What happened? Why is it so easy for us to lose our peace?

3. In chapter four, Geri Bickford is like a Pharisee, concerned with outward appearances, like Gloria wearing jeans to church instead of slacks or a dress. And while she thinks going to church is a good thing, she's very uncomfortable with all the Bible study and praying Gloria is doing. How easy is it for you to focus on appearances rather than inward realities, whether in yourself or in others? Have you ever come across someone who is fine with your church attendance, but the minute your faith starts getting more intense, they get nervous? Why do you think that is?

4. Geri and her mother don't get along, and Gloria and her mother don't get along. Is this a trend you see in families? If there is a history of broken relationships or sinful behavior in your family, what can you do to change the pattern?

5. Gloria ran out of Grandma Quinn's house rather than hear the truth about her parents. Besides physically running away, what are some other ways we run from truth? Does the truth always set us free? (Read and discuss John 8:31–36.)

6. Geri Bickford wanted to get even with her mother, Hannah, for denying Geri a roof over her head when she wanted to leave her husband. She did this by trying to put her mother into a nursing home, literally taking away the roof over Hannah's head. What are some ways families punish each other for past transgressions? Why is forgiveness the only solution?

7. When Gloria apologizes to her mother for not telling her she was paying Grandma Quinn's grocery bill, her action breaks down a barrier that had existed between them for years. The next scene shows Gloria's mother reaching out too—she's now willing to consider putting Grandma Quinn into a condo instead of a nursing home. How has love and forgiveness broken down barriers in your life, and maybe even taken one of your relationships on a new course?

8. Geri Bickford was compulsive about her home and her appearance, wanting everything to be perfect. She believed that if she was perfect, then people would like her and not talk about her—that she'd gain their respect. When we don't know or when we forget that we are all sinners saved by grace, the search for approval is an easy pit to fall into. What are some other ways people try to prove their self-worth?

9. It was obvious that God was the One responsible for opening Gloria's heart toward Cutter and filling it with love. Yet when that love turned from filial love into romantic love, was Gloria correct in not committing to the relationship? What were her reasons? Did she decide based on how she felt, or on what she believed to be right? Why is it important to be equally yoked? What are some of the tragic consequences if you're not? What does Scripture say?

10. Many of Gloria's and Cutter's problems stemmed from misunderstandings: He'd always liked her but didn't know how to show it, and she felt humiliated by his attentions. How many of our hurts and conflicts with other people come from a failure to understand each other? What happened when Gloria and Cutter finally talked honestly with each other? How have some of your problems with others stemmed from misunderstandings?

11. Why was Gloria not afraid of dying but was afraid that Cutter might die? Also, why did Cutter start praying to God when he and Gloria were in danger? How does faith affect our view of death, and how does a life-threatening situation make people start reevaluating their faith, or lack thereof? September 11, 2001 for example.

12. Gloria's decision to speak up publicly about the whole environmentalist issue took courage and meant she had to make sacrifices, even put herself in danger. Maybe you've never been harassed by a stalker, but what kinds of stands have you made that have taken courage? How many of Gloria's actions were courageous, and how many were naïve? How would you weigh the costs of taking a stand versus the need to protect yourself and the people you love? In such a situation, where would your source of strength and courage come from?

13. Gloria desperately wanted to help Tracy, but in the end she realized that "helping" her friend with money would only be hurting her. How far do you go to help someone who is making bad choices? What is the line between being a friend to that person and letting yourself be used? Or worse yet, enabling his or her bad behavior?

Gloria Bickford may be named after the legendary actress Gloria Swanson, but she has none of the grace, beauty, or backbone of her mother's favorite film star. In fact, everything Gloria does is a disappointment to her beauty-queen mother. Especially rejecting the marriage proposal of Cutter Press. So, at the insistence of her pushy best friend, Gloria abruptly leaves behind all the smallness of life in her hometown. Her new job in Eckerd City will make it possible to see her secretly beloved Tucker.

Waters of Marah
ISBN: 0-8024-7905-7
ISBN-13: 978-0-8024-7905-1

RETURN TO APPLETON TEAM

ACQUIRING EDITOR
Andy McGuire

BACK COVER COPY
Michele Straubel

COPY EDITOR
Michele Straubel

COVER DESIGN
UDG DesignWorks
www.thedesignworksgroup.com

COVER PHOTO
Steve Gardner and Photos.com
www.pixelworksstudio.net

INTERIOR DESIGN
Ragont Design

PRINTING AND BINDING
Dickinson Press Inc.

The typeface for the text of this book is
Centaur MT